# Calliope Day Falls... in Love?

Other books by Charles Haddad

*Meet Calliope Day*
*Captain Tweakerbeak's Revenge*

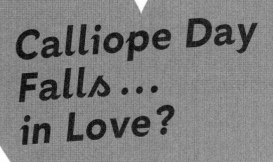

# Calliope Day
# Falls...
# in Love?

DISCARD

## by Charles Haddad
## illustrated by Margeaux Lucas

DELACORTE PRESS

Published by
Delacorte Press
an imprint of
Random House Children's Books
a division of Random House, Inc.
New York

Visit us on the Web! www.randomhouse.com/kids
Educators and librarians, for a variety of teaching tools, visit us at
www.randomhouse.com/teachers

Library of Congress Cataloging-in-Publication Data
Haddad, Charles (Charles Harold)
   Calliope day falls . . . in love? / Charles Haddad.
      p. cm.
Summary: While trying to discover who left a love poem in Noreen's
ice cream during a blackout at the roller rink, fourth-grader Calliope
Day learns some very interesting facts about boys.
   ISBN 0-385-73070-5 (trade) — ISBN 0-385-90100-3 (GLB)
   [1. Interpersonal relations—Fiction. 2. Poetry—Fiction. 3. Love-
letters—Fiction. 4. Letters—Fiction. 5. Humorous stories.]   I. Title.
   PZ7 .H1163 Cal 2003
   [Fic]—dc21
                                                          2002013058

The text of this book is set in 12-point Figural.
Book design by Melissa J Knight

Printed in the United States of America
May 2003
10   9   8   7   6   5   4   3   2   1
BVG

# Calliope Day Falls ... in Love?

# *No Gentleman*

Calliope Day wasn't fooled by Rodney's greasy tweed jacket and lopsided bow tie. She knew he was no gentleman. That's why she eyed him as he kept glancing over his shoulder at her.

It was a wintry Sunday afternoon in late March and Spackle's indoor roller rink throbbed with shouting, skating, shoving kids. Calliope glided hand in hand with her best friend, Noreen Catherwood.

Ahead of Calliope and Noreen skated Rodney. Again he glanced back at his fourth-grade classmates.

What is he up to? Calliope wondered as she wobbled along in white skates scuffed nearly black from a winter of hard use.

Noreen's black skates, on the other hand, still shone as if brand-new. Calliope suspected that Noreen let her maid, Louisa, polish them every Saturday night. It looked like Louisa had also ironed Noreen's white blouse, which stood erect, as if at attention. And, while she was at it, maybe Louisa had ironed Noreen's ponytail as well. Not a hair strayed from the black ribbon that pulled back Noreen's brown hair. In its rigid perfection, the ponytail was a tempting target. What boy wouldn't want to give it a good yank? Was that what Rodney had in mind?

Rodney had given up any pretense of stealth and now stared directly at Calliope and Noreen. Calliope squeezed her friend's hand to reassure her. But, truth be told, Calliope needed reassuring as much as Noreen needed Calliope. After a winter of Sundays at the skating rink, Calliope had learned she was better at falling down than circling around and around. There wasn't a tree in South Orange or Maplewood she couldn't monkey up in her bright red Keds. Yet in skates she careened into the rink's low wall and toppled over when trying to stop. Yes, it was better to skate clutching Noreen's hand.

That seemed especially true now, given that Rodney was chuckling to himself as if enjoying a private joke, probably at Calliope's expense. He had been tormenting her since kindergarten.

Calliope couldn't understand why Rodney hated her so much. They had so much in common! They both lived in the same neighborhood of simple houses in the shadowed valley of South Mountain. *And,* as the youngest in their families, they were both tormented by older brothers.

Rodney peeled away from the line of skaters circling the rink, and looped into the empty space in the middle.

Calliope wondered if Noreen noticed Rodney's troubling shift in behavior. She glanced at her friend. Sharp nose raised ever so slightly, Noreen gazed ahead and smiled faintly as if bemused by the picture of herself mingling with kids whose parents had to drive their own cars.

Noreen, of course, traveled to and from the roller rink and Indian Trail Elementary School in a red chauffeured Mercedes the size of a small school bus. Did Rodney know this? Calliope doubted it, given the blackened windows of the Mercedes. You could see just fine out of those windows, but no one could see in. Calliope knew. Not only had she ridden in the Mercedes, but she had been to Noreen's castle of a house perched high atop South Mountain.

Out of all the kids at school, rich and poor, brainy and boneheaded, Noreen had anointed Calliope as her best—and as far as Calliope could tell, only— friend. It was a friendship that left kids and teachers chewing the eraser ends of their No. 2 pencils in befuddlement. Even Calliope didn't quite get it.

# *Here We Go Again*

Rodney was eyeing them with a devilish smile. He'd now looped around to face Calliope and Noreen and then dropped to a crouch. The better, apparently, to gather the speed to knock them over like a couple of bowling pins.

Calliope couldn't skate well enough, especially with Noreen in hand, to weave out of the circling line and make a clean escape.

That left only one defense: shrieking. And any girl who heard another one shrieking felt obliged to join in. So if Calliope could shriek loud enough to attract the attention of the other girls in the rink, she just might repel the oncoming Rodney.

Calliope gulped a chestful of air, threw back her head and let loose. Her throat vibrated like the strings of a guitar. Calliope imagined that her shriek was rattling the crystal ball dangling over the rink.

But that was just in Calliope's imagination. In fact, the din of creaking wheels and giggling kids swallowed up her call for help. No girls rallied to her defense, save one. Noreen turned, forehead wrinkled with irritation, to glare at Calliope. Then she saw Rodney and began to shriek, too.

Their shrieking made Calliope's ears ring but it didn't seem to faze Rodney. On he raced, head down and grinning.

Calliope couldn't bear to watch another moment. She threw up her hands, never letting go of Noreen. A veil of fingers hid Rodney from view but Calliope could still smell him. Her nostrils twitched from a whiff of his sweaty tweed. And then his elbow clipped her on the hip. Calliope spun around, spinning Noreen with her. Thankfully neither of them fell—this time.

"Watch it, Rodney!" Calliope yelled. She watched as Rodney gracefully skated away without bumping a single skater. On the other side of the rink Rodney stopped, grinning.

If Rodney had meant to impress Calliope or Noreen, he'd failed. Noreen narrowed her eyes in a withering look that could have silenced a laughing hyena.

But Noreen's disapproval did not deter Rodney. In fact, it seemed to egg him on. Again and again he whizzed through the other skaters to hit Calliope just enough to spin her. It was as if he was trying to knock Calliope free of Noreen. But Calliope held Noreen's hand even tighter, as the two of them spun around and around. Noreen's face had turned a sickly green and Calliope was so dizzy now that one more bump would surely topple her.

Calliope seriously considered just throwing herself down on the rink floor and getting it over with. What stopped her from such a humiliating surrender was a most unusual sight. Careening in front of her was Kevin Jefferson, boy brainiac of the fourth grade. Calliope had never seen him at the rink before. And it didn't look like Kevin had skated much. In fact it looked like he had never skated at all. His arms windmilled as if trying to reverse direction, and his mouth was shaped in the O of a silent cry.

Kevin might have been the worst skater Calliope had ever seen, but she was still glad to see him. That was because Kevin veered into Rodney's path.

Rodney and Kevin went down in a tangle of arms and skates.

Calliope and Noreen didn't linger to savor Rodney's takedown. Hand in hand, the two of them stumbled out of the line of skaters. Walking, however awkward, seemed safer than trying to skate away. In the rink's adjoining cafeteria, the girls stopped and hugged. "Boys!" wheezed Noreen.

Calliope couldn't agree more. She'd come to regard boys as you would stray dogs. Some boys looked friendly enough from afar but you'd learned that, not only might they bite, you never knew when that bite would come. And you rarely knew why they bit.

Calliope eyed the bustling cafeteria, crowded with rolling boys with wandering eyes and idle hands. Who among them would lunge for Noreen's ponytail next?

# Not the Proudest Moment

As moments go it wasn't Calliope's proudest. She was still shuddering at the memory of herself shrieking, eyes covered, at Rodney's approach.

To console herself Calliope had ordered a heaping bowl of her favorite ice cream, tutti-frutti surprise, vanilla ice cream dyed red, white and blue. It was pricey but Calliope bought two scoops. Its brilliant multicolored swirl made other kids stop and gawk at your bowl—and that alone was worth the money to Calliope.

She and Noreen had secured a low table at the back of the rink's cafeteria. From there they had a sweeping view of the swirl of kids on the rink in front of them. No boy could swoop in without the girls seeing him first.

Calliope doubted anyone could see them now, anyway. The lights had been dimmed for the big dance number. Overhead the crystal ball flashed, turning the bodies of skaters into flickering silhouettes moving in time to the thumping beat of the loud music. Calliope swayed her head to the beat.

"You'd better eat your ice cream," chided Noreen.

Calliope squinted at her bowl of tutti-frutti. Her scoops had melted into a rusty-colored soup. She must have been silently stewing over her brush with Rodney for some time. "Look who's talking," said Calliope, pointing at Noreen's melting green ice cream.

Noreen didn't answer. She sat upright, with pinky raised, hovering over her bowl. Every now and then she plucked out a green sliver and laid it on a napkin alongside her bowl, where nuts lay in neat rows.

Noreen could have saved herself the trouble of de-nutting her pistachio ice cream by ordering strawberry or chocolate. But no, that would have been too easy. Noreen wanted the taste of pistachio minus the lumpy imperfection of the nuts. That was Noreen, thought Calliope with a sigh. Always trying to re-make the world to her liking.

For a moment Calliope considered lifting Noreen by the frilly white collar of her blouse, guiding her back to the counter and making her trade in the melting bowl of pistachio for French vanilla. Now, that was the flavor for Noreen. Rich and creamy, it tasted like a million bucks.

Calliope slurped a spoonful of soupy tutti-frutti. The creamy ice cream was working to salve her wounded pride. At least Rodney had given her a new adventure to regale kids with at lunch on Monday. Of course she would have to fiddle with the facts some. There was no way Calliope wanted anyone to think a boy had rescued her, especially a runt like Kevin. In her new and improved version, Calliope would stick out her skated foot, tripping Rodney. He'd go sailing.

Only one thing troubled her. What would make the best clincher, sending Rodney into the rink's low wall or over it?

Calliope's dad would have known how to end her tall tale. Dad's stubbly face, with his yellowing teeth and oniony breath, shimmered in the back of her imagination. What a storyteller he had been! Again she heard him tell the story of Iggy McNewton, the boy who could shrink himself down inside an atom. There Iggy befriended all the protons, neutrons and electrons. It was an unforgettable story and Calliope had amazed her first-grade teacher with her mastery of basic physics. Dad was always doing stuff like that, spooning her wise tidbits with his big yarns and practical jokes.

Now Dad was gone. He'd died three years ago of cancer. But his love of storytelling lived on in Calliope. How could it not, seeing as he'd named her after the Greek muse of epic poetry? Muses, Dad had explained, were these nine sister spirits who worked for the big boss of all Greek gods, Zeus. He commanded them to inspire the humans to greatness. If by greatness Zeus meant getting people to stand up and take notice of you, Calliope was doing her best.

Calliope couldn't wait to tell her story of besting Rodney at the rink. She was sure everyone would laugh. Everyone except Noreen, that is. Calliope could see her now, looking down that sharp nose, insisting that that was not the way it happened at all. "Hey," Calliope would counter, "it's my story. I can remember it any way I want to."

This would surely set them squabbling and the thought of it made Calliope smile. Fighting with Noreen was such fun. It was like squaring off in a game of foursquare with your toughest opponent. Except Noreen preferred words to rubber balls.

You couldn't find two more different opponents than Calliope and Noreen. They were like rubber band and ruler, Calliope thought with a smile. Noreen was always measuring to see how far Calliope had crossed the line of what Noreen deemed proper behavior for a young lady. And Calliope was forever stretching to see how far she could reach beyond the last notch on Noreen's ruler.

It didn't sound like they'd get along at all. But, in fact, Noreen loved it when Calliope made up whoppers, snuck pink plastic fangs into class or waggled Barbie heads on the tip of her pinky. Why, Calliope wasn't sure. The best she could figure was this: It was no fun being a ruler without something to measure. And, thanks to Noreen, Calliope had learned it was a lot more fun stretching the rules if someone protested.

Truth was, Noreen paid a lot more attention to Calliope than her own family. It wasn't that her mother and two teenage brothers didn't love Calliope. They just didn't have the time to show it. Mom worked. Calliope's brother Jonah was busy going to Seton Hall University and her brother Frederick—well, who knows what he did. He surely didn't spend a lot of time at home, except for eating and sleeping. Which meant that Calliope got stuck with most of the housecleaning and laundry.

Harrumph. This was not what she wanted to be thinking about on a Sunday afternoon. What she wanted to do was make Noreen laugh.

# Noreen Honks

You'd never guess from her twig of a body that Noreen could honk like a goose. But when Calliope made her laugh, she could. Making Noreen laugh wasn't easy. Luckily, Calliope was good at it.

She scanned the rink now for inspiration. There weren't any piles of toppled skaters, but she did see something that caught her eye. It was Kevin, who sat alone atop a carpeted bench. Strewn across the bench were the parts of his disassembled skate. He'd apparently figured out not only how to unscrew the blade but also how to detach the sole of the skate and its eyelets. Twisting a curl of his hair, Kevin squatted hunched over his knees, studying the parts laid out before him. The poor skate reminded Calliope of the scarecrow in *The Wizard of Oz* after the flying monkey demons have knocked the stuffing out of him.

Calliope chuckled and stabbed a finger toward the hunched figure on the carpeted bench. "Oh, look, Boy Brainiac is reassembling his skate into a death laser."

"Get out," scoffed Noreen. But she did look up from her ice cream. Her eyes narrowed sharply, cutting through the rink's gloom. At the sight of Kevin, Noreen smiled, if only slightly.

Well, that's a start, thought Calliope. But now she needed a little more help. She got it when a boy skater collided with Kevin's bench and toppled face first into his disassembled skate.

Calliope glanced at Noreen. Her left cheek dimpled but she didn't start honking.

Kevin wasn't helping much. Why didn't he yelp in protest or roll off the bench in a tangle of arms and legs with the colliding skater? Instead he ignored the boy crumpled at his feet and his eyes remained glued to the skate. Who did he think he was, a real-life Dexter, boy scientist?

Calliope moved on. Aha! Now, here was something sure to make Noreen at least smirk, if not honk with laughter.

Rodney was perched on the corner of a table full of girls, yakking away while trying to straighten his bow tie, which kept flopping to one side and then the other. All the while he kept an eye on a heaping bowl of ice cream in front of a girl named Carol Anne. She was the one girl in school who was richer than Noreen. At least that was what Carol Anne said. Noreen despised her the way you did a fly that wouldn't buzz off.

"What are they talking about?" wondered Calliope aloud.

"Who?" asked Noreen, looking up.

Calliope pointed toward Carol Anne.

"Oh, that's easy to guess," said Noreen. "Rodney's trying to sweet-talk Carol Anne out of her ice cream."

"She'll never buy it."

"Oh no?" Noreen nodded toward Carol Anne as she spooned ice cream into Rodney's mouth.

"Oooh," Calliope and Noreen groaned in unison.

"I thought Carol Anne had more sense," said Calliope.

Noreen smiled. "She reminds me of Ashley."

Ashley was Noreen's older sister. Calliope had never met her. She'd left for college before Calliope and Noreen had become friends. "What do you mean?"

"Boys were always trying to get Ashley to look at them."

"How?"

"They'd throw paper airplanes at her, bump into her, send her notes. Ashley liked it."

Calliope nodded. She'd seen the kids at the back of the school cafeteria who were always trading scraps of notebook paper. In fact, she'd once intercepted one of those scraps. Scrawled in boy handwriting was "I see London, I see France. I see Sheryl's underpants." Calliope grimaced at the memory.

"Even if boys made fun of her underpants?"

"Didn't seem to faze her."

"Well, no boy is ever going to make fun of my underpants—and live!"

Noreen shrugged.

"What, you'd let them?"

"No ..."

"No, but . . ."

"Love does funny things to a girl," Noreen said with a sigh.

"Not this girl," said Calliope, glaring at Rodney as he prepared to accept another spoonful of ice cream with a big smile.

Thank goodness at that moment a skater bumped straight into Carol Anne, who lurched forward, smooshing her ice cream into Rodney's eye.

Calliope heard a strange if familiar sound. It came from her right, where Noreen was doubled over, her nostrils flared in honking laughter.

# *The Red Note*

Noreen suddenly stopped honking. She shot up out of her seat, legs crossed. Clearly she had to use the restroom—and pronto.

Poor Noreen, thought Calliope. She couldn't so much as giggle without suddenly having to pee. Calliope suspected that Noreen's mother, Mrs. Catherwood, had somehow wired Noreen's bladder to her funny bone. Mrs. Catherwood didn't approve of her daughter having too much fun. That wasn't very ladylike. Well, Noreen didn't look very ladylike right now, hobbling with her legs crossed toward the bathroom at the back of the rink.

As Noreen entered the girls' room there was a loud *pzzt*. Then the rink went dark. Calliope heard the thuds of skaters slamming into one another and the wall. Girls shrieked, although more in fun than in fright. Spackle's roller rink lost its lights at least once every Sunday. Calliope wondered if the teenagers manning the rink didn't blow the fuse on purpose just to juice up the day.

Any minute now, Calliope said to herself as she sat alone in the dark waiting for the lights to flicker back on. She began to fidget. Not in fear, of course, but in boredom. What she needed was a distraction.

Calliope's eyes, now used to the dark, wandered to the bowl of soupy green ice cream beside her. She'd always wondered if Noreen's favorite flavor of ice cream really tasted like pistachios. Why not give it a try? Noreen wouldn't return until the lights came back on.

Calliope spooned up a mouthful of the pistachio ice cream. Not bad. Not bad at all. She began shoveling it in.

Suddenly there was another loud *pzzt* and the lights flickered and then came back on.

Uh-oh, thought Calliope. Caught red-handed! She was hunched over Noreen's bowl, soupy green ice cream dribbling down her chin. Calliope dropped her spoon into the bowl and looked around quickly.

There was no sign of Noreen, thank goodness. But what was this? A red paper square no bigger than a bite-sized Nestlé's Crunch bar was balanced on the lip of Noreen's bowl.

At first Calliope figured the paper must have been a wayward missile thrown by one boy at another. Or *she* could have been the target. A lone girl such as herself was a tempting mark for a table of boys. Calliope scowled at the tables around her, but she didn't see any snickering boys.

Now that she thought about it, the paper couldn't have been thrown. It wasn't crumpled into a ball or folded into the shape of an airplane. And, if thrown, the paper surely would have landed in Noreen's bowl, splattering Calliope with ice cream.

But then, if not a missile, what was it? Calliope glanced around quickly. There was still no sign of Noreen. Calliope picked up the red square of paper. Her fingers felt lines of indentations. Could it be a note? Her fingers, fumbling in haste, struggled to unfold the paper.

Inside she found twelve lines. The first was perfectly centered, but each following line drifted a little farther to the right. The type looked like it was sliding off the page.

And another odd thing. The lines looked stamped, not printed out as from a computer. How strange, thought Calliope at first, but then she figured it out. The author had used a typewriter. Her college brother, Jonah, had one in his room at home. You didn't even have to plug it in. As a small girl she had loved to sit in bed with the small typewriter in her lap, banging on the keys. It stamped out letters just like the ones in this note.

By now Calliope had forgotten all about Noreen. Her eyes began to devour the first lines on the paper.

```
Your knees are knobby,
  and your skating I fear
  a bit wobbly . . .
```

Calliope cupped a hand to her mouth, stifling a laugh, and read on.

```
You fell once or twice
  mumbled something un-nice . . .
```

Wasn't that just like Noreen? She had a way of putting you in your place without ever uttering a nasty word. Calliope read on.

> Let them laugh, let them stare,
>     now why would you care?
>         When you're Noreen, my Noreen,
>         you skate as you please.
>         Noreen, my Noreen,
>             would you please skate with me?

Calliope's face flushed the color of the note in her hand. This was not some throwaway insult. It was a real love poem! Like the ones her dad used to make up about her. Again she saw Dad's round face bristling with gray stubble. Mouth cocked back in a half grin, he teased Calliope with his latest rhyme about her. She was his exotic butterfly Leopia Calloria, his playground Tarzan, his poet monkey. Her heart skipped like a flat stone across still water as she realized that some faceless boy among the mob of Sunday skaters had noticed Noreen and Calliope wobbling side by side. And he'd chosen to fall in love with Noreen. Calliope felt the passing rush of Cupid's arrow brush her cheek.

You should be grateful, Calliope told herself. Who wanted some boy tagging around after her? Yet Calliope felt anything but grateful. Instead she found herself comparing her knees to those of Noreen's. Weren't Calliope's just as knobby? And surely she fell as often as Noreen. *More* on a bad day!

Calliope's grip tightened on the note until it began to crumple. She considered shredding it and scattering the note's words to the swirl of the rink. But she couldn't bring herself to destroy it. She kept reading the verse over and over.

"What's that?"

The voice came from behind Calliope and she immediately recognized it as Noreen's.

"Ah ... ah ... ," Calliope stammered as she stuffed the red note into her pocket. Recovering her composure, she seized the offensive and questioned Noreen back. "Where have you been?"

"Huh?" said Noreen, caught off guard. Then she brightened. "You won't believe what happened to me."

"Tell me, tell me," said Calliope, propping her elbows up on the table. She rested her head in her upturned hands, gazing up at Noreen, all ears.

# Calliope-rella

The rink's blackout had stranded Noreen with a bunch of other girls in the bathroom. When the lights flickered back on they'd found a girl passed out on the floor. The other girls had screamed at the sight of the little body sprawled at their feet, but not Noreen. She had taken control.

Noreen dispatched a girl to fetch water, which Noreen splashed in the fainted girl's face. The poor thing woke up sobbing and Noreen directed another two girls to hug and comfort her. In no time at all the fainted girl was ready to walk out of the bathroom by herself. Noreen had saved her the embarrassment of having to be carried out in front of the whole rink.

All in all, pretty impressive, thought Calliope. You could tell Noreen thought so, too. She was so wrapped up in telling her story that she'd forgotten about the red note.

Not so Calliope. A sharp corner of the note dug into her thigh, as if urging her to surrender it to its rightful owner. But she couldn't bring herself to do it.

Was she jealous? Well, maybe a tad. Her real concern was this: What if Noreen went gaga over the note, hunted down its author and forgot all about Calliope? It sounded far-fetched, but Calliope wasn't taking any chances.

At least that was what Calliope told herself as she walked home, skates strung across her neck. It was late afternoon. She hopped from slab to slab of the sidewalk and glanced up at the tall trees that lined her route. Their leafless limbs looked like long-nailed fingers clawing at the gloomy sky.

Calliope shuddered and began to regret having turned down a ride home in Noreen's chauffeured car. Yet how could she have accepted? It would have been just like Noreen to remember halfway home her glimpse of the red note in Calliope's hand. Then Calliope would have had to give it back.

Ahead Calliope saw the Musclemobile. That was what her mother called her brother Frederick's 1967 orange Camaro. He only used it to take girls out on dates. But without fail the Camaro would break down and Frederick and his date would have to push it home.

Maybe that was why Frederick was always dating a new girl. Of every new girl who walked in the door Calliope would innocently ask, "Where's What's-her-name?" The question never failed to make both Frederick and the girl scowl—the girl at Frederick and Frederick at Calliope. Frederick might scowl and clench his fist but he never retaliated. Not with the girl, and often Mom, standing there. But he would strike back later, by spiking Calliope's orange juice with a dollop of ketchup or hiding a rotten banana in her room.

Calliope walked past the Camaro and turned down the warped concrete walkway that led to her purple house with turquoise shutters. As she clattered onto the small porch the front door opened, revealing a woman holding a carpet sweeper. It wasn't a maid, like at Noreen's house, it was just Calliope's mom.

Mom peered over Calliope's shoulder and into the street as if expecting to find something.

Calliope knew her mom was looking for Noreen's car. "I decided to walk home," explained Calliope.

Mom studied Calliope a moment longer and then handed her daughter the carpet sweeper as if passing the baton in a relay race.

Calliope accepted it dutifully. She felt proud that Mom had come to count on her to help clean the house. But then again, who else was there? Neither of her brothers had so much as looked at a carpet sweeper since age sixteen. And they were too big now to boss around.

"I finished the downstairs," said Mom as she threw on a long cloth coat. She usually left to go grocery shopping when Calliope returned home on Sundays.

Calliope nodded, heading toward the stairs.

"And, of course, there's the laundry," said Mom as she went out the front door.

Oh, joy.

# Poetry by Flashlight

"Your knees are knobby," Calliope recited to herself, fingering the red note that was now in the pocket of her pajamas. "And your skating, I fear, a bit wobbly." She tittered in the dark, lying faceup in her bed. Who in the world could have written such words? No boy she knew came to mind.

As far as she knew, boys didn't write. They drew jet fighters and snarling space monsters. And their pictures never included girls—unless as evil princesses who ended up blasted to bits.

Not all boys wanted to blast girls. Her brother Frederick, for one, enjoyed taking them out on dates in his Camaro.

For her brother Jonah, girls were curiosities, like a cat clock with rolling eyes. They were fun to wonder about but he never took them seriously.

Neither her brothers nor the boys at school who only saw girls as evil princesses seemed like the type to write love poetry. Calliope sighed. It was such a mystery.

It wasn't every day she was stumped. She considered herself a regular Nate the Great. Why, just last week, she had correctly fingered Thomas as the culprit who'd pasted Noreen's spelling homework upside down under her desk.

But fingering the mystery poet of this note would require a detective mind greater than her own. Luckily she knew just where to find it. First, though, she'd have to wait for her family to fall asleep.

Struggling to stay awake, Calliope listened as her family nodded off one by one. The first to go was Mom. She popped in to kiss Calliope good-night en route to her own bedroom next door. Next Calliope heard Jonah flop on the living room couch beneath her. Jonah always said he was going to study but Calliope knew better. After a while she heard his heavy book clunk to the floor, signaling he had fallen asleep. Now, what would Frederick do?

He answered by clumping down the attic stairs. Minutes later Calliope heard the Camaro on the street outside her bedroom window rattle to life. Ah, Frederick must have a date. Which means he'd be out for the evening. Ever since he'd received his driver's license, Frederick had turned into a bat on the weekends, sleeping during the day and staying out much of the night. Calliope knew, because she was a bit of a night prowler herself.

As the rattle of the Camaro faded into the night, Calliope slipped out of bed. She scampered down the stairs, halting at the bottom to peer into the living room. There Jonah indeed slumbered on the couch.

Calliope breezed past him, ruffling his dirty

brown hair, then flew through the kitchen and into a small dinette, where a cage sat atop several crates pushed against some back windows. Unlatching the cage, Calliope reached inside and retrieved a large fluffy white bunny with one black eye. She stuffed him under one arm and then scurried back upstairs into her bed.

"What do you think, Mortimer?" asked Calliope, pushing the red note under the bunny's twitching nose. She lay cheek to cheek with Mortimer, scrunched at the bottom of her bed under the covers. One hand flattened the note on the sheets while the other trained a flashlight on the poem.

Mortimer pressed his wet nose against the note.

"Here's my theory," said Calliope. "I don't think the author is a boy at all. I think it's Carol Anne."

Not only did Carol Anne think she was richer than Noreen, she thought she was more proper, too. She and Noreen were always trying to outlady each other, vying, for example, to see who could shine her shoes brighter. It would be just like Carol Anne to make fun of Noreen's skating.

"Well?" said Calliope, looking triumphantly at Mortimer.

Mortimer sat impassively, obviously unimpressed by Calliope's theory. You know what? Mortimer was right, Calliope decided. Carol Anne had no sense of humor. And her rhyming? Calliope winced, remembering Carol Anne reading one of her poems in class. Besides, if Carol Anne were teasing Noreen, she

wouldn't have stopped at the knees. No girl would have. She would have poked fun at Noreen from head to toe.

But if not Carol Anne, who? Who?

Calliope rolled over onto her back and closed her eyes. She pulled Mortimer onto her chest and tried to picture a boy who'd write poetry. An image flickered across the back of her eyelids but it wasn't of any boy.

Again she saw the bristling round face of her father. Calliope's dad was as alive as ever in her imagination. More so in some ways. Dad had become an outlined figure in a coloring book where her imagination could paint him in any way she chose. She wondered now, for instance, who Dad had been as a boy. Had he written poems to girls? She bet he had.

Calliope pictured him now as a fourth grader at the roller rink. He sat at a center table, flocked by girls. Each begged him to write a poem about her, but Dad politely declined. He'd only write for the special girl with the frizzy blond hair and red Keds.

Calliope felt her face flush in the darkness under the covers. Had her father come back to life in the body of some little boy? But why, then, was he writing to Noreen and not to her?

# The Beauty Costume

The morning light splashed into Calliope's face like a bucket of cold water.

"There you are!" Calliope heard her mother exclaim.

"Geez, Mom," croaked Calliope. She wrinkled her eyes shut against the light, and her hands groped for blankets that no longer covered her.

"And I thought you'd escaped and run away," continued Mom.

"Huh?" Calliope turned to squint up at her mother, who stood above her, holding back the blankets and pointing at Mortimer, still nestled on Calliope's chest.

Calliope bolted upright, hugging Mortimer. "Don't be mad," she sputtered, knowing full well Mortimer wasn't allowed in her room after bedtime. "I couldn't have fallen asleep without him. He was my blankie." By blankie, Calliope meant the threadbare baby blanket she'd slept with until a year ago, when it had unraveled in her fingers and her mom had made her throw the pieces away.

Mom eyed Mortimer and sighed. "What's that in your blankie's mouth?"

Calliope glanced down to see the red note protruding from Mortimer's whiskers. He'd already gnawed off a corner and his wriggling nose inched toward the poem. "Oh, that," said Calliope, yanking the note out of Mortimer's mouth. She heard it tear but didn't look, instead crumpling the note and tossing it behind her. "It's nothing."

"Nothing?"

Calliope ignored the question.

Mom glanced down at her watch and frowned. She had already lost interest in the note. Without looking up, she turned toward the door. As she exited Calliope's room, she called out, "You'd better put your blankie back in his cage or you're going to be late for school."

Calliope set Mortimer down on the bed and rolled onto the floor. Lying on her belly, she reached under her bed and retrieved the note. "Oh, Mortimer," she groaned as she sat up. The note was torn nearly in half.

Lovingly Calliope carried the note over to a card table opposite her bed. Strewn across the top were paper, crayons, pencils and—bingo—tape. She taped the note back together the best she could. The words didn't quite match up, but no matter. She now knew the poem by heart.

Calliope closed her eyes and tried again to conjure up the mystery poet but the only face that drifted across the back of her eyelids was a boyish-looking Dad. Could there really be a boy out there like him? The thought gave Calliope goose bumps. This was a boy she had to find.

Calliope slumped in the metal chair. On the card table in front of her was a flyer for the French Canadian circus troupe Cirque du Soleil. It featured a girl acrobat in a red-and-white-checkered leotard and tutu. Her blond hair was a forest of little upright ponytails tied off in red ribbons. She gazed ahead, sphinxlike in whiteface and big ruby red lips.

That stony unreadable face gave Calliope a wonderful idea. She trembled with excitement. There was no need to hunt down the mystery poet. She'd draw him to her. Like this acrobat! Calliope would make herself up to look so interesting that the mystery poet would forget all about Noreen. Ha! Knobby knees were nothing compared to what Calliope would offer him to write about.

# *Brothers!*

Only something truly special could distract Frederick from a sizzling pan of steak and eggs. That was how Calliope knew her outfit was a stroke of genius. Frederick looked up from his frying pan as she paraded into the kitchen with Mortimer under an arm. He stood silent at the stove in his standard uniform of black boots, untucked T-shirt and army jacket. A spatula dangled from his hand. An egg popped.

"What?" said Calliope, stopping. Slowly she turned, modeling her outfit for Frederick. She wore baggy red pants festooned with colored balloons, and a pink sweatshirt that said "Whatever" in black ink. On one foot was a blue sock in a red Ked, while the other sported a red sock in a blue Ked.

But the clothes weren't the best part of her outfit. That dangled like a tail from a rear belt loop on her pants. It was a charm Calliope had whipped up in a flash of inspiration. She'd woven the hair of three Barbie heads—a blonde, a brunette and a redhead—into a heart-shaped knot. Threaded through the knot were little silver bells.

Calliope shook her bottom and the bells tinkled.

Resist that, Mr. Mystery Poet. This charm was Calliope's poet bait and she planned to tinkle her way across the neighborhood on the way to school.

Already the three-headed charm was working its magic. At the sound of the bells Jonah emerged in the doorway of the pantry behind Calliope. He held a brimming jar of homemade granola and stuffed handfuls of it into his mouth.

Calliope shook her head as she watched Jonah rain bits of oatmeal and nuts onto the floor around his feet. Of course she would be the one who'd have to clean up his mess later. Brothers!

Jonah studied Calliope for a long, munching moment. Then he lowered his hand and spoke. "Running away to the circus, are we?"

Was that a compliment or a put-down? It was hard to tell with Jonah. His words sounded sweet, yet they often made Calliope wince, like he was offering her a crowbar dipped in chocolate.

"Maybe, what's it to you?" said Calliope, trying to tease a compliment out of him.

Jonah frowned. "But who will do my laundry if you run away?"

"Ha, ha, very funny," said an exasperated Calliope. So much for weaseling a compliment. She stomped a foot. "Now, move over. I'm hungry."

She brushed past Jonah into the pantry. She grabbed a box of Cheerios and sulked off to the windowed alcove off the kitchen that served as the dinette. After returning Mortimer to his cage, she sat on the narrow table wedged into the tight space.

Outside the window she heard the singsong chirping of a chickadee perched on Mom's bird feeder. Strange, but this morning the chickadee seemed to be singing for Calliope. "Your knees are knobby," she sang to herself in time to the chirping, "and your skating a bit wobbly."

If only it were true that someone was outside her window singing out her name in rhyme. She sighed and pitched one Cheerio at a time into her mouth. They tasted as stale as cardboard, but she kept tossing them down her gullet.

"What," said Jonah, standing at the opposite end of the dinette table, "no orange juice?"

Calliope looked down at her bowl of dry cereal. Oops, she'd indeed forgotten the signature ingredient, which made her Cheerios different from and better than anyone else's.

"Our baby sister is acting awfully strange this morning," mused Jonah.

"And I bet I know why," said Frederick. He clomped into the dinette, carrying the frying pan by its handle, which was draped in a towel. He sat down in front of the standing Jonah. From the head of the narrow table he grinned wolfishly down at Calliope.

Calliope figured he was up to something but she ignored him. She'd had her fill of teenage brothers this morning.

Jonah, however, took Frederick's bait. "What do you mean?"

"I mean," said Frederick between heaping forkfuls of egg, "she's fallen in love."

"Get out," said Jonah.

"I have proof."

Calliope turned sharply to face Frederick. She watched as his greasy fingers pulled a red piece of paper out of a top pocket of his army jacket. The poem—Calliope gasped. It must have fallen out of her pocket in the pantry. Now he'd taken it.

"Thief!" she screeched, jumping to her feet.

Smiling, Frederick waved the poem like a red flag.

It was impossible to move quickly on foot in the narrow dinette—and Frederick knew that. But Calliope bet he never figured she'd belly flop onto the table and slide across it into his face, which was what she did.

A surprised Frederick fell back against Jonah. But he didn't lose his grip on the poem. Instead his arm shot up, raising the poem out of Calliope's reach.

But Jonah succeeded where Calliope had failed. He plucked the note out of Frederick's fingertips and stepped back. Without Jonah to lean on, Frederick fell to the floor. For once he looked stunned.

"Thanks," Calliope wheezed to Jonah, but then realized she'd spoken too soon.

Jonah had no intention of returning the poem. He unfolded the red paper and began to read. "Not bad, not bad at all," he pronounced. "This boy is quite the poet."

"Who's a poet?" said Mom. She breezed into the dinette, her cell phone pressed against an ear and a breakfast bar sticking out of her mouth.

"Calliope's lover," said Jonah.

Mom spit out the breakfast bar. "What!"

"Here, see for yourself," said Jonah, turning to hand the poem to Mom.

At the sight of the red paper, Mom's eyes flashed as if she recognized it from upstairs.

Would she put two and two together? Calliope wasn't waiting to find out. She jumped up off the table and landed feet first on Frederick's stomach. He had been trying to sit up but her feet slammed him back down on the floor with a loud *oof.*

Using Frederick's muscular stomach as a springboard, Calliope bounced up, arm outstretched, and seized the paper from Jonah.

"Goodness," said Mom, recoiling in surprise.

Poem in hand, Calliope dashed through the kitchen and into the living room.

"Calliope!" she heard her mom call out from behind, but she didn't stop. "Sorry," she called back, "gotta go or I'll be late for school." And with that, Calliope ran out the door, three-headed charm tinkling in her wake.

# *Trolling for Poets*

Calliope knew her neighborhood the way you knew your favorite song—by heart. Ear cocked, she awaited the opening refrain. There it was, the *swoosh, swoosh, swoosh* of a broom. It was wielded by Mrs. Blatherhorn, who was sweeping her already spotless front steps.

Friend and next-door neighbor Mrs. Blatherhorn—or Mrs. B., as Calliope loved to call her—watched Calliope after school until her mom returned home from work. Mrs. B.'s stern face brightened as she noticed Calliope, and she waved good morning.

Mrs. B.'s smile fell at the sound of a loud bang. She turned sharply to frown at a long wing-tipped car rumbling down the driveway next door. It was Mr. Oglemeyer off to work in his rusting Ford Fairlane. The Fairlane's tailpipe belched black smoke and again exploded. Its bang echoed off the small houses that sat shoulder to shoulder across the narrow street.

Calliope laughed and waved good-bye to the frowning Mrs. B. Soon Calliope came to Pizza Park, so named by her for its wedge shape, like a slice of pizza.

It was black-dirt pizza topped with matted brown grass and stones.

On the other side of the park the houses tripled in size. Most were made of wood, with high steps and banistered verandas. Many of the houses gleamed with purple, red and yellow gingerbread trimming.

Did Calliope's mystery poet live in one of these beautiful houses? It was fun to think he might. She'd never been inside one.

Calliope bounced her backpack so that her charm jingled loudly. She thought of Frederick trolling his plastic worm along the cattails of Sumner's Pond. Would her bait lure the mystery poet? At the moment all she was snaring were some cats, which prowled atop the banisters and meowed.

In the middle of the neighborhood of big wooden houses sat Calliope's school. A low building of sooty brick, it was fenced off from the surrounding homes. The school looked like a hobo who'd wandered into the wrong neighborhood and fallen asleep in a back-yard.

Calliope's route led her to the rear of the school, where she was pretty much alone. Most kids either rode buses, which emptied out at the front of the school, or walked up the front sidewalk into the main lobby.

Not Calliope. She liked sneaking up on school. There was no entrance here on the rear of the school. You had to hop a low fence to enter the schoolyard.

One reason Calliope liked this route was that she'd found a secret clubhouse of sorts. Beneath a lone sycamore tree stood a rickety old picnic table. In the spring you could sit half-hidden behind the sycamore's low branches. Calliope loved to sit there and watch kids stream into school from behind the leafy veil.

In winter, of course, there was no veil to hide the table. Anyone could see it, if they paid attention. But luckily nobody but Calliope ever did. That is, until today. Now someone *else* had discovered her secret hiding place.

# Nice Pair of Heads

What was Kevin doing crouched face first in the dirt under Calliope's table?

"Hey!" barked Calliope, sounding as miffed as she felt.

Kevin jumped, banging his head on the table's underside.

"Ouch." Calliope winced. Kevin said nothing, although he looked like he sorely wanted to rub his bruised head. Instead he crawled out from under the table, careful to keep his hands cupped together. He stood up in front of Calliope but stared down at his frayed brown low-top sneakers.

At first neither Calliope nor Kevin said a word. They didn't have to. Their clothing spoke for them. Calliope's pink sweatshirt answered "Whatever" to the "Proud to be a Nerd" written across Kevin's chest.

After a long moment, Kevin extended his cupped hands toward Calliope and unfolded them like a butterfly's wings.

Calliope couldn't believe what lay in Kevin's palms. It was the biggest, orangest beetle she had ever seen. The thing had jaws like the teeth of a staple remover. Could such a monstrously glorious bug really live in New Jersey? Calliope hoped not—especially if it hung out around her picnic table, of all places.

"It's quite rare, you know," said Kevin.

Thank goodness, thought Calliope.

"Would you like to hold it?" Kevin asked as if offering her a kitten.

"Ah . . . no thanks."

Still, she couldn't take her eyes off the thing. There was something fishy about it, if you could say that about a beetle. It rested in Kevin's hand like a rock. You'd think it would want to fly away but not a leg twitched. "Is it alive?"

"Sure. It's just . . . just resting."

"Resting? Like a stone, you mean."

"No, really. Look." Kevin tapped the beetle's rear and it inched across his hand without twitching a leg.

Calliope raised an eyebrow.

"So you don't want to touch it?" said Kevin, sounding disappointed.

Calliope crossed her arms, securing a hand under each armpit.

With a sigh Kevin slipped the beetle into a pocket. But there was no hiding those fierce jaws, which pressed out menacingly from his pants. Either Kevin had tamed that beetle like a dog or it was stone dead, thought Calliope.

But if the beetle were stone dead, why would Kevin carry it around? What a strange boy, thought

Calliope, turning to head toward the school. As she turned, her charm tinkled.

"What's that?" said Kevin.

Calliope stopped. "You mean this?" Again she wiggled the charm.

"Wow, did you make that?" said Kevin, pointing at the dangling heads.

"Uh-huh," said Calliope, shaking the heads.

"I didn't know girls liked to pinch off Barbie heads," Kevin said.

"Well, I'm not just any girl."

Kevin slipped a finger into a coil of his hair and began twisting it hard, as if trying to figure out what kind of girl *would* pinch off Barbie heads.

"Want to touch it?" said Calliope, unclipping the charm and holding it out toward Kevin. He hung back.

"Go on," said Calliope, "they won't bite."

Slowly Kevin reached for the charm. When his fingers touched the braid, Calliope loudly chomped her teeth.

Kevin recoiled.

"Sorry," giggled Calliope. Again she offered the charm to Kevin, but he kept his distance this time. "Oh, come on," she said. She really wanted a boy's opinion of her handiwork, and timid little Kevin was the only one handy.

She tossed the charm to him. He stepped back and the heads landed at his feet. In the dirt the charm must have looked less threatening. He squatted,

studying it now. Running an index finger along the heart-shaped knot, he murmured, "It's so . . . so . . ."

"Beautiful?" offered Calliope.

"Intricate—like a helix."

"A heal-what?"

"A helix," repeated Kevin, drawing a spiral in the air with his finger. "You know, a coil."

Kevin sure was smart. Was he sneaky, too? He *had* managed to creep unnoticed into Calliope's hiding place. She pictured him soundlessly slipping a red note onto the lip of Noreen's ice cream bowl and then fading back unnoticed into the dark rink.

"Ke-vin?" Calliope called playfully.

"Huh?" Kevin answered without looking up. He'd begun unraveling the knot as if to understand how it had been tied.

"Have you been following me?"

Kevin looked up sharply. "What?"

"You heard me."

Kevin's eyes shifted back to studying his frayed sneakers. Rising, he mumbled, "I told you. I was chasing that beetle."

"Uh-huh," said Calliope, sounding unconvinced.

Just then the first school bell rang. "Oh, gosh," said Kevin, "I forgot all about Mrs. Perkins. I promised to help her start up the class computers this morning." He dashed off toward the school, the beetle jouncing in his pocket.

Calliope scooped up her dusty charm and studied the half-tied knot of hair. Had she unraveled the mystery of the ice cream poet?

# "Rod" Is Not a Car Part

As she dangled upside down from a high bar, Calliope's head buzzed as if hornets had nested between her ears. But questions tormented her, not hornets. Should she surrender the red note to Noreen, even though she hadn't yet found the mystery author? Or *had* she found him? And if she had, should she tell Noreen that Kevin liked her?

"You're awful quiet down there," said Noreen.

Calliope looked up at Noreen. It was recess and the two girls occupied a lone high bar at the back of the school playground. Ankles crossed, Noreen sat upright with her back against a wooden supporting beam.

"Noreen, do you like Kevin?"

"You mean the brain wonder?"

"Yeah."

Noreen raised her nose ever so slightly and considered Calliope's question. "He's kind of quiet, but I guess he's all right."

"But you don't *like* him, like him?"

Noreen's face pinched in concentration. Then she blushed and pointed a finger down at Calliope.

"You like him, don't you!"

"What?"

"I knew it! *That* explains the nutty outfit."

Calliope crossed her arms and pouted.

"Don't look so mad," said Noreen. "It happens to most girls eventually."

"What happens?" Calliope asked suspiciously.

"Falling in love."

"I'm not falling in love!"

Calliope began swaying back and forth, gathering momentum to swing back on top of the bar. She needed to straighten out Noreen right this minute. But she stopped in midswing. Something had slipped out of her pocket. She looked down to see her heads staring up at her from the worn grass below.

"Ooh, what's that?" Noreen called from above.

"That," said Calliope, unhooking her legs and falling into the dirt, "is my charm." She was happy to change the subject. "What do you think?" Calliope handed the dusty heads up to Noreen.

"It's different, I'll give you that," said Noreen, dangling the charm in front of her. "Is this why Kevin likes you?"

"Noreen, I told you . . ." Calliope stopped as she saw Noreen's gaze shift to something over her shoulder. Calliope turned to see a boy standing behind her in a grease-spotted tweed jacket and a frayed, lopsided bow tie.

"Oh, hello . . . Rod," she said, pronouncing the short name as hard as the metal cylinder inside any car. Calliope knew he hated to be called that. He preferred the grander Rodney.

Rodney ignored Calliope. "Did you make that?" he asked Noreen, pointing up at the heads dangling from her fingertips. He sounded impressed. Was he trying to make up for tormenting them at the rink?

Noreen acted miffed, as if she hadn't forgotten. Calliope knew better. Rodney's attack at Spackle's was long since forgotten. What, then, was Noreen up to, ignoring Rodney for a long moment? When she finally spoke, it wasn't to answer no. But neither did she say yes. What she said was "Do you like them?" Then she tinkled the heads for Rodney.

"Hmm," said Rodney, offering up an open palm. "May I?"

Noreen shrugged and dropped the heads into Rodney's hand.

Rodney nodded approvingly as he examined the heart-shaped knot of the charm.

"Pretty neat, huh?" said Noreen.

"You bet," said Rodney, beaming up at her.

"Oh, I didn't make it," said Noreen.

"No?"

"It belongs to Calliope."

"Really?" said Rodney.

"Yeah," said Calliope, crossing her arms and glaring at Rodney. Ha! Now he'd have to compliment her, something he'd never done before.

Nor would he do it now. His fingers curled around the charm. Then he cocked back his arm and hurled the charm over Calliope's head.

"Hey!" cried Calliope as she watched her charm

sail high and far, finally plummeting into a thicket of rhododendrons bordering the playground.

Calliope shoved the smirking Rodney aside and sprinted off to retrieve her charm. When she was halfway down the playground the school bell rang, signaling the end of recess.

No sooner had the bell rung than a towering woman with a pencil-thin smile stepped in front of Calliope, stopping her cold. It was Mrs. Sterne, the principal. "B-b-but," sputtered Calliope, pointing toward the thicket.

"No buts," said Mrs. Sterne. "Recess is over." She spun Calliope around and shooed her toward the line of kids entering the school. Calliope glanced over her shoulder. She'd get her charm back—no matter what.

# Cat and Mouse

"Really, your charm wasn't *that* great," said Noreen.

"It was to me," grumped a pouting Calliope.

The girls sat side by side in a classroom where desks were clustered in groups of four.

"Why did you have to tease Rodney?" nagged Calliope.

Noreen smiled faintly.

"You're not turning into Ashley, are you?"

Noreen ignored the question and instead began chanting, "Calliope and Kevin, sitting in a tree . . ."

"Don't start that again!" Calliope turned away sharply, giving Noreen the back of her head. Noreen's ponytail whipped the back of Calliope's head as she too turned away.

Fine, be that way, thought Calliope. She looked up front, waiting for Mrs. Perkins to resume class. The teacher sat atop a high stool in front of the chalkboard, surveying the kids drifting back into her classroom. Most milled about their desks until Mrs. Perkins suddenly clapped three times. The sharp sound broke like thunder over the students and they scrambled to their seats.

Mrs. Perkins clearly wanted to begin, sitting with an open history book in her lap. But someone wouldn't let her.

Rodney stood, bow tie askew, holding a pink flower with big petals that flopped like a beagle's ears. He offered the showy flower to Mrs. Perkins.

At first Mrs. Perkins tried to ignore Rodney by looking hard at the book in her lap and loudly flipping the pages. If that was a signal for Rodney to take his seat, he didn't get it. He just stood there, inching his flower closer and closer to Mrs. Perkins's nose.

With a sigh of resignation, Mrs. Perkins finally looked up at the flower. She looked weary. Calliope didn't blame her. Mrs. Perkins had a drawerful of gifts from Rodney.

Calliope watched as a curious standoff began. Mrs. Perkins wouldn't take the flower but Rodney still held it out to her. He stood, beaming, like a dog awaiting a pat on the head for bringing in the newspaper.

Mrs. Perkins finally caved in. "Why, thank you," she said, snatching the flower out of Rodney's hand, and nodded toward his chair.

Rodney meandered, savoring his triumph, through the desks to his seat. He sat next to Kevin in the cluster of desks just in front of Calliope and Noreen.

Kevin already had his notebook open. He was famous for his dog-eared and ever-present notebooks. Kevin took down Mrs. Perkins's every word. No wonder he was the best student in the class. Maybe even in the whole fourth grade.

Kevin sat now, hand poised with pen above the page. When Mrs. Perkins began to speak, his hand hit the paper with a furious scrawl.

Rodney, on the other hand, had no notebook. Nor did he seem to be listening to Mrs. Perkins. Instead he was poking his head over Kevin's shoulder to see what Kevin was writing.

Without looking up, Kevin raised his shoulder to block Rodney's view. Undeterred, Rodney leaned forward to see around the raised shoulder. Kevin hunched forward and Rodney leaned sideways. Rodney kept shifting. Poor Kevin was twisting himself into knots trying to shield his notebook from Rodney's prying eyes.

Calliope tried hard to follow Mrs. Perkins's story about how Columbus thought he'd discovered a new continent, when it was really only the island of Hispaniola. Really she did. But her attention kept drifting back to the seesawing boys in front of her.

How different yet alike they were, thought Calliope. Each wanted Mrs. Perkins's approval. But Rodney tried to win it with gifts and flattery, while Kevin used good grades and a helping hand.

Was one of them the mystery poet? Calliope considered the evidence. Did Rodney like Noreen? He had been hanging around her lately but Calliope had never seen him with either pen or book in hand outside class.

Kevin, on the other hand, could be found most summer afternoons in the town library, nestled in a beanbag chair with a book.

Calliope watched Kevin now, hand racing across his notebook as Mrs. Perkins talked. He seemed more secretary than poet.

Neither Rodney nor Kevin seemed much like Calliope's dad. Her dad had read a lot but mostly in the bathroom, where he kept a stack of half-finished books. He'd use bits of what he'd read—a funny name or line—to make you laugh. No, Dad didn't need wilting pink flowers to make you like him. Humor was his gift.

Calliope sighed. Her search must go on. And for that she'd need her three-headed charm. Just wait till she got her hands on it again. With wagging finger she'd scold, "This time you'd better scare up the right boy."

# Missing Heads

Where were the heads?

Calliope lay belly down, again pawing the dirt under the thicket of rhododendrons at the back of the schoolyard. Nothing. She rolled over onto her back and peered up through the leathery evergreen leaves. No sign of her Barbie heads there, either.

It made no sense. She and Noreen had been alone when Rodney had tossed Calliope's heads into the shrubs. Puzzled, Calliope wiggled out from under the bushes. It was then that she saw the showy pink flowers budding on the back of the bush. It was unusual to see bushes bloom in late March but the weather had been awfully warm the past few days.

Calliope hadn't been the only one to notice the blooming rhododendrons. "Rodney," she muttered. He must have found the heads while picking a flower for Mrs. Perkins. But how had he gotten around Mrs. Sterne in the first place? Easy, Calliope now realized. The principal had been preoccupied with shooing Calliope back to class.

"Oh no you don't!" sputtered Calliope, jumping to her feet. She set off to pay Rodney a visit.

Rodney never talked about home but Calliope knew where he lived. She'd once seen him peering out of a large window on the second floor of a brick building. The building served as the office of Spanoli & Sons Auto Fix-it Shop. Rodney's last name was Spanoli. It was no more than three blocks from her house.

Calliope stood now in front of the little brick building. She looked up at the second-story window, but the curtains were drawn. She didn't see anyone inside the office. No matter. Calliope let herself inside. Bells jingled overhead as she entered, but no one appeared at the worn front counter.

"Hello?" When no one answered, Calliope walked around the counter and through a swinging door that opened into the garage itself.

The cavernous garage was empty except for an aging red convertible. Two pairs of denim-clad legs in black boots protruded from under the car.

Calliope walked up to the longer pair of blue legs and squatted, craning her neck sideways to peer under the convertible. Underneath was a figure lying faceup on a small cart. "Hello?"

This time her call was heeded. The sound of squeaking wheels echoed in the garage as a man rolled out from under the convertible. He stared at Calliope a moment, knitting up his grease-stained eyebrows. Then he beamed at her with a mouthful of yellow teeth. "You're Frederick's little sister?"

"Yes, sir," answered Calliope. "Are you Mr. Spanoli, Rodney's dad?"

Mr. Spanoli nodded and then called out, "Hey, Duane, it's Frederick Day's little sister."

The other set of blue legs rolled out from under the car, revealing a boy who looked strikingly like Rodney, except he was tall, bearded and wore a grease-stained T-shirt. Duane also flashed a mouthful of yellow teeth at Calliope.

"Well, how's that car doing?" said Mr. Spanoli.

"My mom's Saturn?"

Mr. Spanoli laughed. "Not that boring old thing. The Camaro!"

Calliope remembered now that Frederick had won the car in a poker game. He and some friends had rolled it down the street to this garage, where Mr. Spanoli had resurrected it in a day. In a hushed voice Frederick had pronounced Mr. Spanoli's hands gifted, as if he were a famous surgeon.

"The Musclemobile is fine, I guess," said Calliope, picturing Frederick's car sagging against the curb outside her house.

"Don't tell me you have a car that I need to look at," said Mr. Spanoli, chuckling at his own joke.

"Me? No, sir. I've come to see Rodney."

"Who?"

"Rod."

"Oh, him I know." Mr. Spanoli also preferred the shorter, metallic-sounding Rod—but not as an insult. He studied Calliope's "Whatever" sweatshirt and baggy balloon pants.

"Is he home?" Calliope asked.

"He's upstairs," said Mr. Spanoli, nodding toward the ceiling, "hiding."

"From me?"

"I don't think so," said Mr. Spanoli with a laugh, "although he's never had a girl visitor before. Especially one so, ah, dressed up."

Calliope blushed as Rodney's father beamed at her.

"May I see him?" Calliope asked.

"I don't see why not. Take the stairs behind the front desk."

# Dust Balls and Dirty Dishes

Calliope found a small apartment at the top of the stairs. She stood in a room that was both the kitchen and the living room, with windows looking out onto the street. A pile of unwashed dishes towered high in the sink. If those dishes had been in her sink, Mom would have blown a gasket, as Frederick would say. Nor would her mom have cared for the dust balls swirling across the wooden floors like tumbleweeds. And Mom would have paled at the sight of the grimy green couch and matching chair under the window. Calliope's furniture was frayed too, but it was clean.

Ugly furniture. Dust balls. Unwashed dishes in the sink. All this grime seemed to be telling her something, like a message scrawled on a dirty windshield. As Calliope's eyes swept the apartment she realized the message lay in what was missing. There wasn't a single picture of Rodney's mother—either with him or his father. There were lots of pictures of Calliope's father at her house. If Rodney's mother had died she imagined they would have pictures of her, too.

Rodney's parents must be divorced. And it must have been a bad one. It was as if she'd never existed.

Any trace of her had been erased. Air whistled through Calliope's teeth like a cooling radiator venting steam. It was going to be darn hard to hate Rodney now.

Calliope remembered that first year after her father's death. Woe to anyone who mentioned his name or reminded Calliope of Dad. Such a person was sure to receive a kick in the shin, courtesy of Calliope. That went double for boys. And it took a while before she could look at his picture.

Did Calliope somehow remind Rodney of his mother? Maybe she had blond hair, was adventurous or collected Barbie heads. Was that why he had always been so mean to Calliope?

Well, if so, Calliope knew how to take care of that! She'd draw out Rodney's meanness like pus from an infected cut. That was what Mom had done to her. She'd made Calliope talk and talk about Dad. How much she missed him; how unfair it was that he'd had to die. And it *was* unfair, darn unfair.

Talking didn't end the pain. But it did turn the pain into something she could handle, sort of like a difficult brother you could learn to live with. She'd been through it. Now she could show Rodney how to live with his loss.

But first she had to find him. She called out his name, but he didn't answer. Still, she didn't give up. She walked down a hallway leading off the main room. There were two doors opposite each other at the end of the hall. One door had a knob blackened with grease; the other shone grease-free. That was the door Calliope knocked on. "Rodney?"

No one answered, but Calliope heard what sounded like a mouse scrambling for the safety of its hole. She turned the knob and the unlocked door opened. She stepped inside to find a room that looked like it belonged in another house.

*Clean* would be too dirty a word for this room. There were no swirling dust balls or grimy slippers. The room's sole decoration was a cloth replica of a dollar bill. It hung flaglike above a tall metallic bookshelf. Beneath the flag sat a transparent plastic piggy bank bursting with coins.

Calliope inched toward the shelf, eyes peeled for a leaping Rodney. He could be like a panther, hidden and watching, ready to pounce at the most embarrassing moment.

At the bookless shelf she picked up a magazine from one of the many stacks of them. "*Young Entrepreneur.*" She read the magazine title aloud softly. The word *entrepreneur* buzzed in her nose, so she figured it must be French.

But she didn't need the French-speaking Noreen to figure out what the word meant. The magazine's cover with a boy in sport coat and bow tie brandishing a fistful of dollar bills gave it away.

Boy, Rodney sure had money on the brain. So did Calliope's mom, but this was different. Mom worried about having enough money to pay the bills. Rodney seemed interested in having more than enough.

In that way Rodney was sort of like Noreen, with her red Mercedes and towering house. Except Noreen never thought about money. Not even when she forgot to bring some to school to buy an ice cream at lunch. She assumed someone would buy it for her and Calliope always did.

Rodney was turning out to be more fascinating than she'd ever imagined. Motherless, obsessed with money and a suck-up. What would Calliope discover next about him? He'd always been like a book she'd never bothered to read beyond the first couple of pages. Now she wanted to devour his whole story.

Calliope put *Young Entrepreneur* back and picked up a magazine from another stack. This one she recognized immediately. It was *House Magnificent,* which Mom leafed through while waiting in line at the supermarket.

What would a boy be doing with *House Magnificent?* She began to flip through it and stopped at a glossy photograph spread across two pages. In the picture a willowy woman and her daughter sat in high-backed wooden chairs in a cavernous room with a marble floor. Each sipped from a flowered teacup, pinkies raised.

Calliope would recognize those raised pinkies anywhere. They belonged to Noreen and her mother, Mrs. Catherwood.

Oh ho ho. Wait till she told Noreen that Rodney kept a magazine photo of her by his nightstand. What would Noreen say—would she even believe Calliope?

As Calliope pondered these questions, she heard a creaking sound and froze.

# The Boy in the Basket

Calliope cringed in anticipation. But there was no pounce, no shout of "Aha!" just the creaking. Her eye fell on a waist-high wicker basket at the foot of Rodney's bed. She hadn't paid much attention to the basket before, but she studied it now. The foot of the basket bulged like a python that had just swallowed a pony—or maybe a nine-year-old boy.

Calliope set down *House Magnificent* and tiptoed over to the basket. Silently she raised the lid.

At first nothing looked out of the ordinary. Then she noticed that the dirty socks and underwear piled high in the basket inched up and down like a pair of breathing lungs. And wasn't that a tweedy elbow poking through a pair of boxer shorts?

Suddenly the laundry spoke. "Dad, please. I don't want to learn how to clean the carburetor."

So that was what Rodney's father had meant. His son was hiding from him! He didn't want to help out in the garage.

Oh, dear. Calliope felt her resolve to be good to Rodney wilt like the talking underwear she eyed. It wasn't every day you got a chance to embarrass Rodney and she couldn't bring herself to fritter it away.

"I don't know," she said from deep in her throat, trying to imitate the voice of Mr. Spanoli.

The laundry didn't respond for a moment. Then it asked weakly, "Dad?"

"Guess again," said Calliope.

She watched as Rodney's head rose slowly out of the laundry. His normally ruddy face blanched as white as the underwear hanging off his ear. He sputtered, but no recognizable words came out.

Rodney looked thoroughly flummoxed and Calliope felt his embarrassment. She'd gone too far and her conscience let her know it, throbbing like a stubbed toe. She scrambled to apologize, if only indirectly.

"I—I—I just came over to say that if you really want to keep my Barbie heads, they're yours. Honest."

That said, she just wanted to go home. She scurried toward the bedroom door but stopped in the doorway at the sound of a loud *splat* against the hardwood floor. She glanced over her shoulder. Rodney was lying with cheek smooshed against the floor amid a pile of dirty clothes. He must have toppled the wicker basket trying to climb out.

"No . . . wait," he mumbled through a scrunched mouth.

He sounded neither angry nor embarrassed, which struck Calliope as odd. If she'd been sprawled facedown on the floor her tongue would have been

knotted with embarrassment. Against her better judgment, she stopped.

Rodney slithered out of the basket and rose to his feet. Righting the basket, he stuffed the clothes back inside. Then he straightened his lopsided bow tie. All in all, he acted as if tumbling out of a laundry hamper were a perfectly normal thing to do.

It was an amazing performance, thought Calliope.

"These heads," Rodney said to Calliope, "are they the ones I threw into the bushes at school?"

"Yes," said Calliope, "but—"

He raised the palm of his hand to stop her from speaking further.

"I'm sorry," he said.

"You're what?" Calliope wasn't sure she'd heard right.

"I said I'm sorry. I shouldn't have thrown your Barbie heads into the bushes."

Had Rodney knocked himself silly tumbling out of the basket? He'd never apologized to Calliope before. Not even when he had wiped his hands, sticky with fresh blue finger paint, on her new white T-shirt in second grade.

"Soda?" asked Rodney.

"Sure," croaked Calliope. Her throat had gone dry. Was it from shock?

Rodney guided Calliope to the edge of his bed to sit. "I'll be back in a jiffy," he said, then left the bedroom.

Calliope sat obediently, dazed by Rodney's unexpected friendliness. Still, a faint voice in the back of her head wondered, What is he up to?

# The Luckiest Girl

True to his word, Rodney returned in a jiffy, a can of 7UP in each hand. It was Noreen's favorite soda, not Calliope's, but she accepted it from him all the same.

Rodney pulled up a footstool and sat at Calliope's feet. Was he trying to make her feel important? If so, he was doing a good job.

Calliope popped open her 7UP and raised the can up to her nose. The spritzing soda tickled her nostrils, working like smelling salts to revive her from her daze. This soda, she now wondered, was it not like the flower Rodney had given Mrs. Perkins? Was Rodney trying to flatter her?

Calliope couldn't think of anything she had that Rodney might want. There were only a few coins in her piggy bank.

But there was something she wanted from Rodney. She was dying to find out the truth about his mother. And, if he'd let her, to comfort him, just a little.

She sipped the 7UP. The icy soda watered her dry throat and she regained her voice. "So," she ventured cautiously, "do you live alone with your dad?"

Rodney's head twitched as if shaking off the question. Calliope tried again: "I used to stay home alone after school."

Rodney finally spoke, although not about his family. "I'm so sorry but I don't have your heads."

If Rodney was trying to stop Calliope from asking about his mother, he succeeded. "What do you mean?"

"I mean, somebody else must have taken your heads."

Calliope studied Rodney's face, deciding whether to believe him. Normally she wouldn't have but he was being so nice. If he hadn't taken her charm, then who had? It was all very puzzling.

Rodney seemed bent on confusing her even more. "You know," he said, looking adoringly up at her, "you're the luckiest kid in school."

"How's that?" she asked. She had tried to feign indifference but her voice betrayed her keen interest.

"You're best friends with the richest girl in school," Rodney answered.

Aha, thought Calliope, now Rodney's showing his hand. The apology. The soda. The politeness. It was all about "Noreen, my Noreen." He sure had a thing for her. But could Rodney really be the mystery poet? Calliope surveyed his room again. Not only weren't there any books, there wasn't any paper or a typewriter in sight.

Calliope's eyes drifted back down to the boy sitting at her feet.

"I bet you know more about Noreen than anyone else." Rodney looked up at Calliope with pleading puppy-dog eyes.

Calliope couldn't resist. "Did you know that Noreen rides home every day in a big red Mercedes?"

"No!"

Calliope nodded. "And her house is like... like..."

"Buckingham Palace?"

That's how the magazine had described Noreen's house but Calliope knew better. "Well, not exactly."

"What do you mean?" said Rodney, sounding a shade less friendly than before.

"It's hard to explain unless you've seen Noreen's house for yourself."

"Are you saying you've been inside?" scoffed Rodney.

"Are you kidding? Lots of times."

Rodney leaned back, folding his arms with a look that said, Yeah, right.

"Well, I have."

"Uh-huh."

So much for playing Mr. Oh-I'm-so-sorry. Rodney had reverted to his old maddening self. Well, Calliope would show him. "I've had tea and cookies with Noreen *and* her mom."

"You just read that in the magazine."

"That's not true," Calliope shot back.

Rodney looked unimpressed.

Calliope glared down at him and considered

kicking over his little stool. Then she had a better idea. "How would you like to see Noreen's house for yourself?"

"Who's going to take me—you?" Rodney asked with a small laugh.

"Exactly."

"Yeah, right."

"You'll see. I'll get Noreen to invite you home and then won't you feel stupid."

No sooner had Calliope challenged Rodney than *she* began to feel like the stupid one. Why, she wasn't exactly sure. But she suspected it had something to do with Rodney grinning as if he'd just won the lottery.

# How Could You?

"How could you?" Noreen whispered harshly to Calliope, who sat alongside her in the back of the red Mercedes.

Calliope shrugged. What could she say? She'd rather eat brussels sprouts for a month than admit the truth, which was that Rodney had tricked her. Now she'd entrapped Noreen into inviting Rodney home.

The trap had been surprisingly easy to set. Noreen and Calliope were short one member of the team required for their science project. So Calliope had suggested to Mrs. Perkins that she add Rodney to their team. Noreen had stomped her shiny black leather shoe in protest but Mrs. Perkins loved the idea. "Maybe you girls can get Rodney to take his homework seriously," Mrs. Perkins had challenged.

Noreen could never say no to a teacher.

It had been a victory, all right, but a costly one for Calliope. The harshly whispered question was the only thing Noreen had said to Calliope since her chauffeur, Charles, had picked them up after school. As the Mercedes purred toward her house, Noreen stared straight ahead, arms crossed. She didn't even offer Calliope an icy soda out of the little fridge hidden under the backseat's armrest.

Calliope sighed, fingering the white plastic garbage bag nestled between her legs. It bulged with empty cans, milk cartons, newspapers and cardboard tubes—all of which they had to fashion somehow into a working invention for Mrs. Perkins. This junk was Calliope's contribution to the science project. Noreen was providing her house as their laboratory. What would Rodney add—other than serving as a wedge between Calliope and Noreen?

Calliope glanced up front at Rodney, who was busy buttering up Charles.

"You handle this Mercedes like a fighter pilot dodging a barrage of enemy fire," oozed Rodney.

Calliope thought she might be sick—and it wasn't from the motion of the car. Luckily she wasn't alone.

"Hey," Noreen barked at Rodney, "don't bother Charles while he's driving."

"It's quite all right, miss," Charles assured her.

Noreen glowered at Calliope.

Geez, thought Calliope with a cringe, she couldn't wait for this afternoon to end. Then she'd be free of Rodney and the horrible boast she'd made to him. Never again would she let someone goad her into bragging. For now, though, she was just as trapped as Noreen. They would both have to endure an afternoon of Rodney.

Thank goodness the Mercedes was soon pulling

in to the circular brick driveway of Noreen's house. The car had barely stopped before Rodney popped out.

That was a big no-no. You were supposed to wait until Charles unlocked the doors and let everyone out, one by one.

Though first out of the car Rodney hadn't gone anywhere. He stood with his head tilted back and a hand cupped to his brow, staring up at the soaring front wall of Noreen's house. "Wow," he whispered, "it *is* Buckingham Palace."

"No," corrected Calliope, slipping up behind Rodney, "this palace belongs to the Queen of Hearts."

"Huh?"

"You'll see," said Calliope. She slapped her lumpy garbage bag into his behind, trying to nudge him toward the house.

Noreen strode past Calliope and Rodney and disappeared through the arching doorway.

Someone was still peeved. No matter, thought Calliope. She'd make it up to Noreen later. Right now she had to keep a sharp eye on Rodney. Who knew what he'd do next? She lingered behind him, not letting him out of her sight.

He poked along, savoring every detail of the driveway, towering front bushes and heavy wooden front door. The eight-sided foyer stopped him cold. His eyes bulged at the sight of the white marble floor, each tile featuring a little red heart.

"See? I told you," said Calliope. "Now off with

those shoes." She pointed at Rodney's scuffed loafers. The only one allowed to wear shoes in Noreen's house was Mrs. Catherwood.

As they slid in their socks across the great foyer, Calliope enjoyed Rodney's awed silence. She knew it wouldn't last. Before long he'd open his big mouth again, this time to try to charm Mrs. Catherwood. Calliope wondered if he'd tucked away a showy pink flower for the occasion.

A lot of good it would do him. Mrs. Catherwood was no Mrs. Perkins. Imagine a spelling-bee judge who not only asked you to spell the hardest word in the dictionary but spell it backward as well. That was Mrs. Catherwood.

Mrs. Catherwood liked Calliope but in the way a queen enjoyed her court jester. What would she make of Rodney in his greasy tweed jacket and lopsided bow tie? Calliope savored the thought.

# Queen of Hearts

Calliope found Noreen with her mother in what Calliope called the throne room. It was cavernous and empty, except for a centered oasis of ancient furniture. At the heart of this oasis sat a coffee table on an Oriental rug. On one side of the table were two wooden chairs and on the other a high-backed chair with crushed-velvet cushions.

In the high-backed chair sat Mrs. Catherwood, holding a flowered teacup in one hand with her pinky raised. The slender fingers of her other hand toyed with a pearl necklace as she inspected her daughter. Noreen sat across from her mother sipping tea, also with her pinky raised.

Calliope knew to stand under the high arch of the doorway, waiting to be recognized.

Not Rodney. He rushed into the room, planting himself between Noreen and her mother. "I want to thank you," he gushed, "for inviting me to your beautiful house."

Oh, boy, thought Calliope, Rodney had done it now. Nobody addressed Mrs. Catherwood until she addressed you first.

Mrs. Catherwood didn't reply, looking through Rodney to her daughter.

"Mother," said Noreen, lowering her teacup, "this is Rodney. He's come to help us with our science project."

Mrs. Catherwood's gaze drifted to Rodney. A faint smile crossed her lips as she eyed his jacket and bow tie.

"Mrs. Catherwood, may I ask you a question?" said Rodney.

Mrs. Catherwood signaled her consent with a slight nod.

"Is it true," Rodney began grandly, "that the rug I'm standing on once belonged to Suleiman the Magnificent?"

Oh, please. Calliope snorted. Rodney didn't know who was president of the United States, let alone anything about Suleiman the Whoever. He was either making this up ... or had read it in *House Magnificent.* No matter. His little performance sounded phony.

Not so, apparently, to Mrs. Catherwood. She drew back, studying Rodney with a raised eyebrow. "Don't tell me you're familiar with the history of the great tapestry of the Ottoman Empire?"

Rodney smiled as if he knew all about it.

"Why, Noreen, what an impressive young man."

Geez, thought Calliope, Rodney could wring a smile out of a granite slab. Even hard-to-impress Noreen looked awed at how quickly Rodney had charmed her mother.

This had to stop—and now. Calliope rattled her bag of junk from the doorway. "Aren't we forgetting something?"

Mrs. Catherwood glanced toward Calliope. "All right, you three," she said, dismissing them with a wave of her hand. "Run along to your project. Don't hesitate to call Louisa if you need anything."

"Who's Louisa?" Rodney whispered to Noreen as the three of them left the throne room.

"Our servant, of course."

Rodney beamed.

Oh, brother, Calliope thought. She trailed behind Noreen and Rodney as they climbed the great winding staircase that led upstairs to Noreen's bedroom.

Noreen's bedroom was big and airy with lots of windows. Blond-wood bookshelves spanned the walls, brimming with the most fascinating knick-knacks. There were earthen tea sets, lacquered boxes of all colors and dancing Buddhas carved out of stone and wood. Her father collected this stuff on his world travels and sold it to expensive stores in New York.

Noreen's knickknacks drew Rodney like a pirate to buried treasure, but Calliope had seen it all many times before. She just wanted to get cracking on their project. She plopped down in the middle of Noreen's carpeted floor and emptied her bag. Out poured soda cans, Popsicle sticks, fuzzy wires, coat hangers and milk cartons.

"Now," she said, rubbing her hands together, "what should we make? A Ferris wheel? A space station? How about a left-handed smoke shifter?"

Calliope chuckled, thinking she'd made a pretty good joke. She looked up to see if Rodney or Noreen had thought so too.

Neither of them paid any attention to Calliope. They were too busy playing some kind of compliment game. Rodney circled the room, praising everything from Noreen's Buddhas to her high canopy bed.

Enough already, thought Calliope, eagerly waiting for Noreen to tell Rodney to knock it off. But she didn't.

Noreen stood erect at an end bookshelf, hand on hip and nose raised ever so slightly, issuing thank-you after thank-you.

At this rate, worried Calliope, they'd never get started on the science project. Which would mean Rodney would have to come back. Ha! Calliope bet that had been his plan all along.

Well, it wouldn't work. Calliope knew how to make Noreen forget all about Rodney and his sickening deluge of compliments.

# A Poet Unmasked

Captain Tweakerbeak was the most interesting of all Noreen's exotic knickknacks. In a head no bigger than a jumbo gum ball, Captain Tweakerbeak had stuffed a vast library of human sound. Yet you couldn't play back any of it on command. The captain was like a CD player that had developed a mind of its own. One minute he'd coo "Darling, just darling" like Mrs. Catherwood, and the next moment he turned into Bugs Bunny asking Elmer Fudd "What's up, Doc?" You never knew what the captain would say next. Which made him more fun than Saturday-morning cartoons.

The captain was an African gray parrot who lived in a tall cage in a back corner of Noreen's room. There he sat perched on a swing, head cocked to focus one eye on a small television sitting atop a stool just outside his cage. The captain eyed Pepé Le Pew as he tried in vain to persuade Penelope the cat to love him.

Poor Pepé. He was a skunk who couldn't help raising a stink. Just like Noreen couldn't help that she was rich, nor could Calliope help that she liked to collect Barbie heads. That was just who they were. Could the mystery poet help wooing girls with rhyme, Calliope wondered?

Captain Tweakerbeak cocked his head to eye Calliope. "Ooh, *ma chérie*," he cooed just like Pepé.

"Oh, stop," said Calliope, blushing. She opened the door to his cage and extended an arm toward the parrot. Up the captain climbed along Calliope's arm until he reached her shoulder. Then he nestled into the curve of her neck as if it were his favorite place. Calliope certainly hoped it was.

With the captain aboard, Calliope crept up behind Rodney.

"*Awk*," said the captain, eyeing Rodney, "are you a good witch or a bad witch?" Glinda of *The Wizard of Oz* couldn't have said it better herself.

The sound of the captain's voice drew Noreen like a doting mother to her small child. She elbowed Rodney aside and began to scratch Captain Tweakerbeak under the neck. The captain threw back his head and gurgled loudly. "Captain, really," fussed Noreen, but she kept scratching despite her professed disapproval.

Calliope happily noted that Rodney now stood behind Noreen like yesterday's favored toy.

But unlike a toy, Rodney could speak. He renewed his flattery with a vengeance. "So many books," he gushed. "I bet you've read every one of them."

If Noreen had she wasn't saying.

Most boys would have sulked off under Noreen's

lack of interest. But not Rodney, observed Calliope. He just switched tactics. With a loud crunch he slid on his knees into the junk strewn across the floor. "Come on, guys," he said, picking up a milk carton, "we haven't got all afternoon."

Still Noreen ignored him. "Watch this," she said to Calliope, and began to rub her knuckles slowly and deeply into the captain's little gray skull.

"Ooh la la," cooed the captain.

Noreen cooed back, *"Je t'aime beaucoup,"* and nuzzled the captain's chest.

Calliope didn't need to speak a word of French to understand what was going on here. The captain had won the heart of his Penelope—and Rodney was none too happy about it. His face reddened with jealousy. Rodney glared at the captain for a long moment and then did a very odd thing, especially for a boy. Especially for a boy who didn't have a book in his room.

He began to recite poetry.

The poetry did the trick. Noreen turned to look down at Rodney.

He winked at Noreen as if confessing to some unsolved mystery between the two of them.

Noreen's brow wrinkled with confusion.

Of course Noreen had no idea what Rodney was referring to. How could she? Calliope had never shown Noreen the red note. But Calliope knew every word of it by heart. That was why she could do what she did next.

"When you're Noreen, my Noreen, you skate as

you please," interjected Calliope, finishing the poem for Rodney. "Noreen, my Noreen, would you skate with me, please?"

"Noreen, my Noreen?" muttered a befuddled Noreen. She turned to look at Calliope.

Calliope shrugged as if she'd done nothing more than recite any old nursery rhyme.

Noreen wasn't buying it. Her eyes narrowed like a tough cop preparing to grill a suspect.

# Apology Not Accepted

Way to go, Mom!

Not only had Calliope's mother shown up on time, a first in and of itself, but she was even early. Her arrival at Noreen's had spared Calliope from a grueling cross-examination. When Louisa announced Mom, Calliope grabbed Rodney by the arm and dragged him sputtering out of the bedroom.

Now Calliope sat in the cramped backseat of Mom's car. She strained not to slide down the sagging seat into Rodney. Calliope had tried to climb up front but Mom had stopped her, insisting she ride in back to keep her guest company.

Some company. Rodney sat with his arms crossed, glaring out the window. Calliope crossed her arms too and tried to concentrate on the passing scenery. Her gaze, though, kept drifting back to the boy smoldering next to her. Could Rodney really have written the poem on the red note? It seemed so unlikely, yet how else would he know the words?

The mystery of it gnawed at Calliope. The more she thought about Rodney, the more he blossomed in her imagination. She pictured him hunkered over an old typewriter, typing poem after poem by candle-light in the middle of the night.

Calliope's tongue burned with questions and it would burst into flames if she stayed silent another moment. "Did you really write that poem about Noreen?" she asked Rodney.

Rodney didn't respond.

Undeterred, she tried harder. "It was really good, you know."

The compliment drew Rodney's head from the window but he still wouldn't look at Calliope, preferring instead to stare straight ahead.

"I mean it," pressed Calliope.

Rodney uncrossed his arms and looked down at the hands in his lap. "Do you really think so?"

She nodded.

"Can I ask you a question?" Rodney said, still studying his hands.

"Sure," she said brightly, thinking she'd finally won him over.

"How come you know the words of my poem and Noreen doesn't?" Rodney looked up at Calliope for the first time.

"Oh, that . . ."

Rodney's look hardened.

"Don't blame me," said Calliope. "You stuck your love note in the wrong ice cream."

"No I didn't."

"Well, you stuck the note in Noreen's ice cream while I was eating it."

"So you stole my poem?"

"Not exactly!"

"Then how come you never gave it to Noreen?"

He had her there. When Calliope didn't answer, Rodney recrossed his arms and again stared out the window.

Calliope glanced up to see Mom frowning at her in the rearview mirror, wondering, no doubt, why Rodney wasn't smiling. Which meant soon she'd be butting in, asking questions of her own, questions Calliope didn't want to answer.

But the truth was, Calliope didn't want Rodney angry at her, either. She wanted him to confide all about his secret life as a poet.

Why did Rodney write—and why to Noreen? Was it that she—not Calliope—somehow reminded him of his mom? Or did he really love her? Calliope wanted answers but she knew there was only one way now to win over Rodney, and it wasn't pleasant. "I'm sorry, okay?"

Without turning from the window, Rodney said, "Apology not accepted."

"What?" cried Calliope.

"You heard me."

"Oh, come on."

"All right," said Rodney, turning again to face her, "but only on one condition."

"What's that?" she asked warily.

"You give my poem to Noreen."

"Fair enough," said Calliope, relieved.

"And tell her what a great guy I am."

"Now, wait a minute," protested Calliope. "That's two conditions."

"Math was never my best subject."

"What is?" sneered Calliope.

"Is everything all right back there?" Mom called out.

"Yes, Mom," Calliope chirped. Then she leaned toward Rodney and said through her teeth, "Oh, all right."

Rodney relaxed against the seat for the first time.

What a maddening boy, thought Calliope. But she had to give him credit. Rodney was a clever rascal. Her brother Frederick would have just pounded her into submission. Not Rodney. He never clenched a fist. All the same she felt as if he'd twisted her up like a stick of licorice.

All right. Calliope would do Rodney's bidding. But she wanted something in return, like answers to some of her questions. "How come you like Noreen so much?"

Without answering, Rodney returned to staring out the window.

Oh, no, Calliope thought, he wasn't getting off the hook this time. She jabbed him with a sharp question. "Is it because Noreen reminds you of your mother?"

Rodney turned sharply to Calliope, glaring at her with watery red eyes. He probably didn't know it but he had answered at least one of her questions. She'd seen that look lots of other times. It was the look of a kid whose parents had just divorced.

"Stop talking about my mother," Rodney growled.

"I can talk about your mother if I want to," Calliope shot back.

"Oh no you can't—she's too good for you."

"Is that so?" snorted Calliope. "Maybe you hadn't noticed but we do live in the *same* neighborhood."

"Not my mother," Rodney crowed. "She lives in a big house now, just like Noreen."

So Calliope was right. Noreen did remind Rodney of his mother. Calliope studied Rodney, who had returned to looking out the window. He spoke again but this time as if making a promise to himself. "Someday I'm going to live in a grand house that has flowered wallpaper instead of grease on the walls."

"And that's why you like Noreen?" Calliope offered.

"Don't forget the Mercedes," Rodney added.

Oh, brother, thought Calliope with a sigh. How was she going to tell all this to Noreen?

# Calliope 'Fesses Up

"Well?" Noreen sat cross-legged on her high bed, the captain perched on her shoulder. He cocked an eye down at Calliope, who squirmed at Noreen's feet.

Calliope knew that the captain and Noreen were awaiting an explanation. Why was it that Calliope and Rodney could both recite a poem about Noreen? But Calliope said not a word, just handed the torn and nibbled square of red construction paper to her friend.

Noreen took Calliope's offering between her index finger and thumb, holding the square out as if it were a snotty tissue. "What's this?" she asked suspiciously.

"It's the answer to your question," replied Calliope.

Noreen raised an eyebrow. "Must you always be so dramatic?"

Calliope shrugged. Asking her to forgo drama was like asking the sun not to shine.

With a sigh Noreen carefully unfolded the ragged scrap of paper and smoothed it out on the bed in front of her. The captain tilted his head until it aligned with the note's slanted type. After a moment he whistled like a sailor.

"Are you saying Rodney wrote this?" asked Noreen.

"He confessed on the ride home the other day." Then Calliope confessed herself, explaining how she'd plucked the note from Noreen's ice cream at the rink.

Calliope bowed her head, expecting a scolding. When none came she glanced up at her friend, who looked befuddled. "But why?" Noreen mumbled.

"I think," Calliope said, remembering the ride home with Rodney, "you remind him of his mom."

"Oh," murmured Noreen. She drew the note to her heart.

Head cocked like the captain's, Calliope eyed her friend. Noreen's left cheek wrinkled up as if trying to ride out the jab of a passing stomach cramp.

Calliope suspected she knew more about Rodney than she had let on. "What's the story with his mother, anyway?"

At first Noreen didn't answer. Then she whispered, "His mom ran off with another man."

"No kidding! Are you sure?"

Noreen nodded. "He was a friend of my dad's."

"Does this mother-stealer live in a mansion like yours?"

"Bigger."

Calliope's eyes grew wide as she tried to imagine a house bigger than Noreen's. She couldn't quite see the entire picture, but she was starting to get a clearer read on Rodney. Did he think that by living in a big house too he could win back his mother? Maybe that was why he was saving up all that change.

" 'Somewhere, over the rainbow,' " Captain Tweakerbeak crooned, " 'bluebirds fly.' "

Calliope smiled sadly at the captain. "He's right, you know."

"What do you mean?"

"Rodney is like Dorothy, dreaming of a better life in a faraway land."

"Hmm," said Noreen.

Had Noreen heard Calliope? She doubted it, given the faraway look in Noreen's eyes. Calliope poked her foot. "Earth to Noreen, over."

Noreen turned slowly to face Calliope, a corner of her mouth twisted up in a wicked half smile. "Do you want to do something really naughty?"

Oh, no. Calliope preferred to sit upright in a hard wooden chair and smile sweetly.

# Beauty Hurts

With the captain as her helmsman, Noreen led Calliope on a winding journey through the bowels of her house, eluding both Louisa and Mrs. Catherwood. They ended up in front of a door on the opposite end of the long hallway from Noreen's room.

Calliope followed her friend into a room that was most unlike Noreen's. It had pink walls adorned with the gleaming white-toothed faces of television, movie and pop-music stars. But what really caught Calliope's eye was a vanity. It had a big mirror that reflected a desktop cluttered with crusty-lipped makeup bottles. "Whose room is this?" Calliope asked in amazement.

"Ashley's."

Of course! Noreen's college-age sister, remembered Calliope. Ashley was a girl who let boys write poems about her underwear.

Noreen kneeled in front of the vanity and the captain hopped off her shoulder. He strutted in front of the mirror, cackling, "Pretty boy, pretty boy."

Noreen rifled through a deep drawer. "I know it's here somewhere. Aha!" she exclaimed, withdrawing a silky pink box studded with little plastic hearts from the drawer. Still kneeling, she caressed the box. Gingerly she lifted the wobbly lid. Inside was a stack of letters, cards and scraps of paper not unlike the red note. She withdrew a card in the shape of a flashy automobile.

"What's that?" said Calliope.

"Guess."

"A love poem to Ashley?"

Noreen nodded. "Do you want to hear what it says?"

"Should we?"

"Just this one."

"All right," said Calliope, plopping down cross-legged next to Noreen.

"You are the waxy shine on my car," read Noreen. "The silvery gleam of its hubcaps after I wash them."

"Not bad," said Calliope, stroking her chin. "Still ..."

"Not half as good as Rodney?" offered Noreen.

Exactly, thought Calliope. She wondered if Noreen was thinking what she was, that there was something irresistible about a boy who longed for his mother and wrote poetry—even if he was mean to Calliope. Could such a boy ever like a girl who played with Barbie heads and talking parrots? Calliope said nothing of this to Noreen but instead asked, "Why do you think boys like Ashley so much?"

Noreen pointed her sharp nose up at the ceiling, lost in thought. "Perhaps," she said finally, "it was her smell."

"Her smell?"

"Yes," said Noreen, definitively this time. Her nose sniffed and then she motioned for Calliope to do the same.

Calliope closed her eyes, tilted back her head and breathed deeply. Her nostrils twitched with a faint smell that was a mixture of baby powder and lilacs. "Hmm," murmured Calliope, smiling. She wouldn't mind hanging around Ashley one bit.

"Okay," said Calliope, opening her eyes, "what else?"

"Well," mused Noreen, "Ashley wore pretty flowered dresses, dusted her eyelids light blue and painted her lips red."

Picturing Ashley all dolled up gave Calliope a wonderful idea. "Let's dress up—"

"Like Ashley," added Noreen excitedly.

"And pretend we're going on a date!"

# Why, You Little Devil

Noreen sashayed in front of the vanity mirror in a blue-flowered pink dress that hung down to her ankles. Batting her blue-painted eyelids at Calliope, she cooed, "Well?"

"Oh, Ashley," sighed Captain Tweakerbeak, sounding not unlike Scarlett in the movie *Gone with the Wind.*

"My turn," said Calliope, jumping up and edging Noreen away from the vanity. Calliope studied her creamy round face in the mirror. How did she want to make herself up? Not like a clone of Ashley, that was for sure.

Her fingers wandered through the junkyard of crusty makeup bottles. They finally stopped on a bottle of purple eye shadow. Perfect, she thought, opening the bottle and painting her eyelids.

"Oh, that's lovely," said Noreen in a tone suggesting she meant the opposite. She stood looking down her sharp nose at Calliope.

What did Noreen, who wore a white blouse and black skirt every day, know about makeup? Calliope ignored her friend and rouged both cheeks with red blush. Purple and red—now, that was a combo, thought Calliope, admiring herself in the mirror. Still, something was missing.

Again her fingers traipsed along the bottles, stopping this time at a jar of styling gel. She unscrewed the top and dabbed a finger in the goo. Yes, she thought, and scooped up a wad of gel on the tips of two fingers. Then she gathered up a handful of hair and slathered it with goo. In no time at all she'd fashioned the hair into a curved horn. She made a matching horn on the other side of her head.

"Why, you little devil," squawked the captain.

Calliope smiled, admiring herself in the mirror. She could also see the reflection of Noreen behind her, gazing in disbelief.

Now Calliope needed a matching outfit. She bounced into Ashley's deep closet. Minutes later she emerged, blue jeans draped across one arm, wearing a glittering purple leotard. "Look," she said, twirling in front of Noreen, "it fits perfectly."

"Ah, yes," Noreen said haughtily.

"And what's that supposed to mean?" Calliope said, stopping in midtwirl.

"Do you really think anyone would be caught dead with you looking like that?" Noreen pointed down at Calliope's leotard.

"What's wrong with the way I look?"

"Oh, nothing—except that you look like you're dressed up for Halloween as the dance instructor from Hades."

Calliope beamed at that.

"It wasn't a compliment," said Noreen.

"No? Well, at least I don't look like I'm wearing a flowered sack."

Calliope and Noreen glared at each other for a long moment. Then Noreen made a T with her hands. "Look, I know how we can settle this."

"Settle what?" said Calliope, playing dumb.

"Settle who gets to be Rodney's girlfriend."

"Who said anything about that?" said Calliope, sneering.

Noreen eyed Calliope with a faint smile and continued. "We'll bake cookies."

"Cookies?"

"Yes," explained Noreen. "We'll each bake Rodney a plate of cookies and whichever cookies he likes best will determine who gets to be his girlfriend."

This had to be a trick, thought Calliope. Noreen couldn't find the oven in her own kitchen, let alone bake. "No fair if Louisa helps."

"You think I can't make cookies?"

Calliope didn't answer.

"Well, I'll show you," sniffed Noreen. "Rodney's going to just love my cookies."

"Uh-huh," Calliope said skeptically. Calliope's marshmallow-chocolate-chunk cookies, made from scratch, were famous in her neighborhood.

"So is it a deal?" said Noreen, extending a hand.

Calliope spit into her palm and took Noreen's hand. "Deal."

# Who's That Girl?

Calliope knew what Noreen was thinking. Go ahead, keep Ashley's purple leotard for the weekend if you want to. All the better to scare Rodney with.

But Noreen had it all wrong. Calliope was no devil. She was a glittering horned fairy. What lovesick poet wouldn't swap his typewriter for a chance to meet such an enchantress?

Noreen, of course, didn't understand poets. How could she, the poor thing? She was only slightly more imaginative than the white blouse she wore to school every day.

Calliope kept these thoughts to herself, instead indulging Noreen's fantasy of her as Devil Girl.

Devil Girl easily slipped her blue jeans over the glittering leotard. But there was no way to hide purple eye shadow and horns. She'd have to be snuck past Louisa and the Queen of Hearts, who would never approve of a girl leaving her castle looking like that.

Not to worry, Noreen assured her as she led Calliope through a warren of stairs and dark hallways. In no time they popped out a rear entrance. On the wall was an intercom and Noreen pushed a button. Charles appeared outside the door in the red Mercedes.

Calliope thought Noreen smiled a bit too sweetly as she waved good-bye to the Mercedes rumbling down the red-brick driveway.

No matter. She was free to test her costume on the outside world. Could she turn heads? She imagined glittering past a group of people, who all muttered among themselves, "Who's *that* girl?"

Sure enough, Calliope caught Charles peeking at her in the rearview mirror. She sat on the edge of her seat, turning her head so that Charles could get a good look at her. "Well, what do you think?"

"Having fun?" offered Charles.

True enough, but that wasn't what Calliope wanted to hear. She wanted Charles to gush and fawn and exalt her beauty.

Calliope slumped back into the seat, feeling a bit like Cinderella. The clock was ticking, she knew. Soon her eye shadow would start to smear and her horns to wilt. She was in a race against the fading magic of her costume.

In that race, going home would be a serious detour. Mom would greet her with a hurried hello as she rushed about with her Dustbuster. If Frederick was home he'd only try to crush her horns. And Jonah would study Calliope as if she were some witch doctor visiting from the Amazon jungle.

That was why Calliope didn't go inside when Charles dropped her off at home. She dallied on the front porch until the Mercedes disappeared around the corner. Then she dashed off toward Herschel's Deli, a couple of blocks away. Surely there'd be some boy inside buying a comic book or a bag of snacks on an early Saturday evening.

Inside she found a boy, all right. Only he had a grizzled face and wore a bloody apron. It was Herschel. He looked plenty scary but Calliope knew the truth. His trembling hand couldn't squeeze the juice out of a kosher pickle.

From behind his counter, Herschel eyed Calliope with a bushy eyebrow raised. Was he interested in her outfit? Calliope decided to find out. She raised her arms ballerina-style overhead and twirled. Her leotard glittered like a sparkler.

Herschel winced as if blinded. "Whatever happened to girls wearing pretty flowered dresses and pink bows?"

"Oh, Herschel, don't be so old-fashioned," chided Calliope.

Herschel shrugged. "I'm an old-fashioned kind of a guy. So sue me." With that, Herschel turned to cut open a box of snacks.

So much for coaxing Herschel into saying Calliope was pretty. She turned to scan the cramped deli for another potential admirer. Who she found instead was Kevin. He stood half-hidden among the racks of comics. In one hand dangled an opened bag of potato chips. The other held a rolled-up comic book. His greasy lips, flecked with bits of potato chips, formed a questioning O. He stared at Calliope as if she were some exotic beetle, exciting in its strangeness.

"What?" snapped Calliope. She couldn't stand Kevin's silent gawking another moment.

"Are you trying out for the Easter play at school?"

"No."

Kevin looked confused. "Then how come your eyes are purple and you're dressed funny?"

"Can't a girl dress up once in a while?"

"You mean," Kevin said, as if struggling with a new math concept, "for no other reason than to just do it?"

Well, when you put it like that, dressing up did sound dumb. Still, Calliope liked it. But she'd like it even more if someone other than herself thought she looked pretty. Her dad would have understood.

# Make-believe Boyfriend

You'd have thought it was Easter Sunday. Noreen gleamed in her shiny black shoes and crisp white blouse. As for Calliope, she'd again donned her balloon pants and pink "Whatever" sweatshirt. Pretty festive, considering it was just a plain old Saturday.

The girls faced each other across the small table in Calliope's dinette. A heaping plate of cookies sat in front of each.

Calliope smirked at Noreen's cookies. Clearly Louisa had not helped her one bit. Dry and lumpy, Noreen's cookies could pass for wood chips.

As for Calliope's cookies, they were perfect disks, filled with hunks of gooey chocolate and marshmallows. She could barely resist eating one herself.

Noreen was beat before they'd even started, thought Calliope. But did she cry uncle? Anything but. She gazed at Calliope's plate as if it were empty.

From beyond the dinette Calliope heard a familiar *rizz,* which rose and fell, rose and fell. The sound signaled the approach of Calliope's mom. Sure enough, she appeared in the dinette's archway. In one hand she brandished a Dustbuster and in the other a palm-sized telephone.

"Mom, please," said Calliope, "can't you see we're busy?"

"Busy?" said Mom. She eyed the girls and the plates of cookies and frowned. "Tell me again why you baked the cookies?"

"We're expecting company, Mrs. Day," answered Noreen.

Calliope glared at Noreen but she knew it was hopeless. Noreen couldn't tell a half-truth if you wrote it out for her in large black letters and taped it to her forehead.

"Whoever it is must be pretty special," said Noreen's mom.

"Oh, he is," gushed Noreen.

"He?" said Mom. Her Dustbuster began to growl.

Calliope groaned to herself, eyes cast up at the ceiling. Why couldn't Noreen just say they were waiting for a friend, not a he?

"You mean," said Mom, waving the Dustbuster at the cookies, "all this is for a boy?"

"Not just any boy," Noreen politely corrected.

"No?" said Mom, looking anything but relieved by Noreen's assurance.

Noreen wagged her ponytail. "He writes poetry."

Mom's Dustbuster stopped growling and she smiled as if finally grasping the punch line of an inside joke. "That's sweet, but why today? Jonah's birthday isn't until next month."

"Eww," Noreen and Calliope whined in unison at the mention of Jonah's name.

"Who then?" said Mom, befuddled.

"Rodney," Noreen said dreamily.

"Rodney?" said Mom. "Auto garage Rodney?"

"Sure. I bet he's an artist just like his father." The voice belonged to Frederick, whose head suddenly appeared in the dinette's archway. "What Rodney's dad can do with a '67 Camaro is a work of art."

Frederick's nostrils twitched. He eyed Calliope's cookies with a wolfish grin.

Oh, great, thought Calliope, covering her cookies with both arms.

Eyes wide, Noreen stared up at Frederick as if he were indeed a giant wolf. She wasn't used to teenage brothers.

"Shoo," said Mom, revving her Dustbuster in Frederick's face. "Can't you see we're having girl talk?"

But Frederick didn't budge. His eyes locked on the cookies peeking out from under Calliope's protective embrace.

Calliope sighed. She knew there was only one way to get rid of Frederick. She picked one of the bigger cookies up off her plate and tossed it to her brother. There was a flash of teeth as Frederick snatched the cookie in midair. Cookie in mouth, he clomped out of the dinette. With relief Calliope heard him ascending to his attic lair.

Mom flashed Calliope a quick thank-you smile and then resumed grilling Noreen. "Now tell me, what do these cookies have to do with Rodney? It doesn't have anything to do with that red note from the other day, does it?"

Calliope and Noreen glanced furtively at each other.

"It's simple, Mrs. Day," Noreen assured her.

Calliope imagined Noreen as a cheery animated character who doesn't see the anvil dangling over her head. With bated breath she waited for Noreen to say something that would bring that anvil down on both of them.

"You see," Noreen explained, "Rodney will try both our cookies and pick the ones he likes best."

"And?" prompted Calliope's mom.

"If he likes my cookies, then I get to be his girlfriend. If he picks Calliope's, *she* gets to be his girlfriend."

"Girlfriend?" sputtered Calliope's mom. Her Dustbuster renewed its growling. "Aren't you girls a little young for dating?"

"Mom, please," erupted Calliope, cutting Noreen off before she could do any more damage. "It's just make-believe."

"It is?" said Noreen.

"Yea-ess," insisted Calliope, giving Noreen a hard look that silenced her. While still glaring at Noreen, Calliope addressed her mother. "It works like this, Mom. We send Rodney home and then go upstairs and dress up again—"

"Ah," cut in Mom, "just like last Saturday with the purple eye shadow."

"Exactly," said Calliope. "The winner pretends she's on a date with Rodney. The loser, of course, has to play Rodney."

"She does?" Noreen said, grimacing.

Thankfully Calliope's mom ignored Noreen for once. She eyed her daughter for a long moment and then asked, "Have you clued Rodney in on this game?"

"Eww, Mom, that's gross."

Calliope's mom revved her Dustbuster, which sounded as if it were muttering "Yes ... no, yes ... no."

She bit her lower lip as if struggling to accept the truth of her daughter's explanation. "Sometimes I swear you're nine going on forty," she said. With a wave of her Dustbuster, she turned to go. "All right. Rodney can come. But I'm going to be listening from the other room."

"Fine," said Calliope with a sigh. She watched her mother meander toward the living room, running her Dustbuster along anything within reach.

"Do you really think he'll come?" Noreen whispered across the table.

Calliope didn't answer, her eyes trailing her mother, who stopped in front of the couch that sat between the two front windows.

Gazing out the window, Mom vacuumed the sill again and again.

"Yeah," Calliope finally answered Noreen, "if my mom doesn't scare him away."

Noreen turned to watch Calliope's mom too. "Calliope?"

"Huh?"

"Were you serious?" asked Noreen, turning back to eye Calliope.

"About what?"

"About just pretending the winner is going out on a date with Rodney?"

Calliope faced Noreen, smiling wickedly. "What do you think?"

# No Contest

Sure enough, Rodney showed up, although he took his sweet time in arriving, if you asked Calliope. She'd given up all pretense of patience and had taken to pacing back and forth behind her seat at the dinette table.

In contrast, Noreen sat calmly, hands folded on the table in front of her, and gazed out the dinette's windows at Calliope's mom's thicket of a garden.

At the sound of the doorbell, Calliope rushed to the dinette's archway and peered out toward the front door. She couldn't quite see the door around her mother. But she heard her mom greet Rodney.

"I hear you're quite the poet."

"What?" replied Rodney.

Rodney's modesty surprised Calliope. Was it to impress her mother? That sounded like something he might do.

"Oh . . . right," said Rodney, recovering, after an awkward silence. "Thank you, Mrs. Day."

Calliope raced back to her seat as she heard her mom lead Rodney into the dinette.

When he entered, the first thing Calliope noticed was his bow tie. She'd never seen it so ungreasy. And it was almost straight. Did Rodney suspect something other than a cookie tasting?

In one hand Rodney held an invitation. Calliope had given it to him in school, explaining it was her way of making up for stealing his poem. And yes, she'd done as he'd asked, giving Noreen the poem and saying what a swell guy he was.

Rodney had accepted the invitation, beaming.

Calliope had made it herself, fashioning a replica of a giant chocolate chip cookie out of brown construction paper. Inside the paper cookie Noreen had written in precise small letters that they needed him to help choose what recipe to enter into a contest at the YWCA.

Rodney laid the invitation down on the table and hungrily eyed the plates of cookies. "Where do I begin?"

"Just a moment," said Calliope. She looked up at her mother, who stood behind Rodney, and wriggled her fingers in a gesture of good-bye.

"All right, I'm going," said her mom, "but I'll be within earshot."

The moment her mother disappeared into the living room, Calliope pushed her plate of cookies at Rodney. "Why don't you start with these?"

Rodney glanced at Noreen, who gracefully nodded her consent. He picked up one of Calliope's cookies as if against his better judgment. He turned the cookie over and over. What did he expect to find? Dead flies instead of chocolate chips? He raised the cookie to his nose and sniffed.

"That's it," erupted Calliope. "Just taste it, will ya?"

Again Rodney glanced at Noreen, who nodded. He nibbled a corner of the cookie. His eyes twinkled and the cookie disappeared into his mouth like a branch into a wood chipper. He grabbed another cookie and then another and another. Soon crumbs encrusted his lips and Calliope's plate was half empty.

Calliope smiled triumphantly.

"Oh, Rodney," Noreen purred. "Aren't you forgetting something?"

"Sorry," said Rodney, and grabbed a lump off Noreen's plate. Without inspection he tossed it into his mouth.

At first Rodney tried to smile as he chewed. But it took every muscle in his mouth to grind up Noreen's lump masquerading as a cookie. Around and around and around went his jaw. Finally he gave up trying to grind the cookie into submission and just swallowed. His eyes bulged as the cookie went down.

"Well?" said Noreen.

"Is there any milk?" Rodney croaked, his face reddening.

"Sure," said Calliope, popping up out of her seat. She returned moments later with a big glass of milk.

Rodney snatched it out of her hand, slopping milk

onto his sleeve. He drained the glass, head thrown back, gulping like a tree toad.

"Well?" Noreen asked again, this time more insistently.

Rodney put down his empty glass. Without hesitation he declared, "I pick Noreen's cookies."

"What?" blurted out Calliope.

"Now, Rodney," Noreen said, glancing at Calliope, "are you absolutely sure?"

"Oh, yeah," said Rodney, "no contest."

"No contest?" Calliope jumped up out of her seat. "You nearly choked to death."

"Now, now," tutted Rodney, "don't be a sore loser."

"Sore loser my—"

"Calliope," Noreen cut in with a harsh whisper, nodding toward the living room, where Calliope's mom was surely eavesdropping.

Calliope bit her tongue until it hurt. Calming, she grumbled, "Let me see one of those cookies," and then swiped one off Noreen's plate. She popped the cookie into her mouth as Noreen looked on, smiling.

Geez, thought Calliope as she chewed. Noreen's cookies could choke a beaver. What had she used for batter, Silly Putty?

Her tired jaws slowed and she had a depressing thought: Rodney must really like Noreen. Why else would he say her cookies tasted good? In defeat Calliope spit the mauled cookie out onto her plate. "All right, you win."

"You mean it?" said Noreen, apparently not expecting Calliope to cave without a scene.

Calliope plopped back into her seat, letting her head droop onto an upraised palm.

Smiling faintly, Noreen looked up again into Rodney's face. "Rodney," she cooed.

"Uh-huh?" Rodney said dreamily.

"Would you recite another poem . . . about me?"

"You mean right now?" said Rodney.

Noreen signaled yes through a slight widening of her smile.

"Uh . . . I don't have any more. I'll have to make up a new one."

"Well, go ahead."

"I can't do it right here. I need . . . a typewriter." Rodney pronounced the word triumphantly.

The corners of Noreen's lips turned down in the slightest of pouts.

"No problem," said Calliope, standing.

"Huh?" said Rodney.

Calliope didn't explain but dashed upstairs. She returned moments later with Jonah's little type-writer, clanging it down on the table in front of Rodney.

Calliope sat back down and she and Noreen looked up at Rodney.

"I can't just write a poem here and now," he sputtered.

"Why not?" asked Noreen, raising her sharp nose.

"I'm an artist," huffed Rodney. "I have to wait for my muse to strike."

Consider it done, thought Calliope. She picked up

one of Noreen's cookies and bounced it off Rodney's head.

"Hey!"

"There," said Calliope, "the muse has struck. Now write."

# The Poet's Lair

Would Calliope have won Rodney's heart if she'd baked silver dollars inside every one of her cookies? She considered the question as she sat alone atop the highest bar of a jungle gym in Pizza Park. Beneath her swarmed a playground of jubilant kids celebrating an unseasonably warm Saturday afternoon.

One girl in particular caught Calliope's eye. Feet braced against a bottom bar, she leaned out, letting the breeze flap her ponytail. A silvery clasp in her hair glittered like a fishing lure among the sea of kids.

Sure enough, Calliope saw a boy weaving his way toward the shiny clasp. He circled the jungle gym twice and then dove at the girl, giving her ponytail a good yank before speeding off across the playground.

The girl squealed but more in delight than in protest. Her smile welcomed the boy to try again. But, having had his fun, he rejoined his friends clustered around a seesaw.

And so it would have been with Rodney, Calliope decided. He would have gladly pocketed her silver dollars, only to choose Noreen's cookies just the same. Noreen could have served him chocolate-covered grasshoppers and he would have munched them down as if they were the finest peanut brittle. It wasn't Calliope's cookies Rodney disliked, it was the chef.

Well, ditto for her. Rodney was smart, all right. But Calliope didn't care for the way he used his smarts. He tricked people. People like her.

Rodney, Rodney, Rodney. Surely he wasn't the only boy who wrote poetry, Calliope told herself. Lots of kids had divorced parents. Had it brought out the poet in other boys?

Calliope looked hopefully across the playground. She saw boys battling each other with stick swords. Others wrestled in the dusty grass. And still others ran alone in circles. Not a one struck her as poet material.

She cast her eye farther afield. Her gaze came to rest on a lone turtle the size of a picnic bench at the back of the playground. This turtle, a weave of metal bars topped with a flattened shell as a seat, had been Calliope's first jungle gym. Apart from the main playground, it sat rusting and forgotten. So why, then, could she make out a hunched figure through the side bars of the turtle? She craned her neck for a closer look and noticed that the figure wore a tweed jacket.

Rodney, playing in the dirt? Not likely, given that his room didn't have a speck of dust. He must be hiding, concluded Calliope. But from what? That was for Rodney to know and Calliope to find out.

She monkeyed down off the jungle gym and circled toward Rodney. Hidden behind a screen of bushes, she imagined herself a tiger creeping up on an antelope grazing with its head down. Indeed Rodney didn't look up once as she neared.

At a thick tree trunk Calliope stopped. She studied Rodney's back. Could she get atop the turtle without him noticing her? It couldn't hurt to try.

She slunk up and on top of the turtle. Slowly she flattened herself belly first against the rusting metal and pressed an eye against a slit in the shell.

Rodney was sitting cross-legged, chewing on the eraser of a yellow pencil. A notepad rested on his right knee.

So it was true, thought Calliope, rolling over onto her back and looking up at the wide blue sky. Rodney was indeed the author of that wonderful poem. She'd had her doubts when he couldn't write anything on Jonah's typewriter last Saturday. Now she'd caught him, evidence in hand, in his poet's lair.

Who would have thought? Calliope chuckled. Mr. Clean found his muse in the dirt under a rusting metal turtle in Pizza Park. Wait till she told Noreen. But first things first. She wanted to watch an artist at work. She rolled over, again pressing her eye on the slit.

Rodney's notepad was blank. Pelting him with a cookie hadn't reawakened the sleeping muse inside his head. She must have flown south for the winter, Calliope thought, and giggled to herself.

Rodney sighed and raised his head a half inch, revealing a dog-eared notebook teetering on his left knee. "Come on, come on," he grumbled, flipping

117

through the pages. Suddenly he stopped, smiling at the page between his fingers. Then he began writing on the pad on his right knee, keeping one eye on the page in the notebook.

There was no mistaking that dog-eared notebook. Calliope had seen Kevin scribbling in it a thousand times in class. Again she pictured him trying to shield it from Rodney's prying eyes. Had Rodney finally persuaded Kevin to lend him his notebook? It seemed unlikely, given how Kevin clutched it to his side at all times. But why, then, would Rodney steal Kevin's notebook? There wasn't any big test coming up and surely Rodney wouldn't find Kevin's endless class notes interesting.

The mystery vexed Calliope but she didn't intend to stay vexed for long.

# The Stolen Notebook

Calliope dropped her head over the side of the turtle and boomed, "Hello!"

Her move surprised Rodney as planned. He bounced up, banging his head on the top of the turtle. The notebook slid off his knee and Calliope reached out to grab it. Notebook in hand, she jumped to her feet.

"Hey!" cried Rodney, scrambling out from under the turtle. He lunged at Calliope but she dodged his hands.

Winded, Rodney retreated a step and then growled, "Give me back my notebook."

"*Your* notebook?" challenged Calliope.

"Yeah," said Rodney without conviction.

She raised an eyebrow.

"Well . . . Kevin lent it to me."

"Oh, really?" scoffed Calliope.

"Yes, really."

"Why?"

"I don't have to tell you," said Rodney.

"Fine," said Calliope, turning to jump off the turtle. "I'll just ask Kevin myself."

"No—wait."

"Yes?" said Calliope, turning back to face Rodney.

"You know how I stink at social studies. Well, Kevin was kind enough to lend me his notes to study for Monday's test."

"Yes, you do stink at social studies but there isn't any test Monday."

Calliope watched the muscles of Rodney's jaws move as if he was grinding his teeth. She wagged the notebook at him. "If you want this back, you'd better tell me the truth."

Rodney raised his arms as if preparing to lunge at Calliope again but he didn't. Instead he flicked a hand at her. "All right, I'll tell you the truth—but you're not going to like it."

"Oh? And why's that?"

"Because I think Kevin has been stealing my poems."

The notebook nearly slipped out of Calliope's grasp.

"At first I didn't believe it myself," said Rodney.

"You're full of it," said Calliope, regaining her grip on the notebook.

Rodney nodded at the notebook. "Go ahead, see for yourself."

"I'll do just that," said Calliope, opening the notebook while keeping an eye on Rodney. But she forgot all about him as she flipped through the pages.

What she found inside the notebook stunned her. There were no math problems or notes on the American colonists. Instead Kevin's notebook was filled with page after page of doodling, passages copied from books and snippets of funny conversations overheard in class.

Calliope stopped at a drawing that filled a page. It was of Mrs. Perkins, her stick-thin arms and legs flailing, falling backward as she missed her stool. Geez, thought Calliope, maybe Kevin wasn't such a goody two-shoes after all.

"Keep going," nudged Rodney.

Calliope didn't need any encouragement. Her fingers raced through the pages while she wondered what would turn up next. Then she stopped again, this time to study a full-page poem. "Your knees are wobbly," Calliope read softly, and the notebook sank in her hands.

"I told you," crowed Rodney. He extended a hand to Calliope, his fingers beckoning for the return of Kevin's notebook.

But Calliope didn't surrender it. She couldn't bring herself to concede that Rodney was right. Yet Calliope had to admit it didn't look good for Kevin. He'd copied down all this other stuff. Why not Rodney's poem? There was only one way to find out for sure.

She jumped down off the turtle.

"Hey!" protested Rodney.

But Calliope didn't heed his call to stop. She ran toward Kevin's house on the other side of Pizza Park.

# Spy Family Romanoff

Kevin's house looked like a slumbering brontosaurus. Its long wooden frame sprawled across an entire corner of the block.

Notebook clutched to her chest, Calliope huffed up the tall steps to a simple glass door. She peered through the glass and rang the doorbell. She half-expected a maid to answer, as at Noreen's.

It wasn't a maid who answered. A scraggly old cat meandered to the door, sat back on its haunches and stared up silently at Calliope.

The kitty looked friendly enough, so Calliope opened the unlocked door and stepped inside. "Here, kitty, kitty," said Calliope, stooping to pick up the cat. But it jumped through her free arm and headed farther into the house.

Calliope followed. She began to feel a bit like Alice following the White Rabbit down the hole. The scraggly old cat led her through a maze of narrow passages and small rooms. There weren't any talking doorknobs but Kevin had other stuff equally strange. Red, white and orange cables sprouted from holes in the wall and ran stapled along the baseboards. She passed a room filled with computers blinking red, white and yellow numbers. Over the computers hung a bank of small televisions mounted on the wall, each tuned to a different channel.

This wasn't the White Rabbit's burrow but James Bond's hideout. What if Kevin and his family were a nest of spies—like in that movie, *Spy Family Romanoff*? That would explain all Kevin's note taking.

Boy, wouldn't it be exciting if Calliope was right?

Heart pounding, Calliope followed the kitty into one room and out of another. Finally they reached a wide archway that opened onto what looked like a living room. There, sitting on a long puffy couch, was Kevin, wedged between a man and a woman. Had he been captured by enemy agents?

Calliope silently hung back in the archway, listening. The kitty sat at her feet, listening too.

The woman held last week's math test in her hand. A red A– glowed atop the paper. "I'm a little disappointed," she said. Her tone was more sad than harsh.

Kevin listened, chin buried in his chest, studying his frayed sneakers.

"We know you can do better," said the man, draping an arm across Kevin's shoulders.

Do better? It had been a very hard test, remembered Calliope. Her mom had been jubilant about Calliope's B+.

Kevin was trapped, all right, but not by enemy

agents. These were his parents. Calliope decided to come to Kevin's rescue—if only accidentally, so to speak.

The kitty must have been thinking the same thing, for it suddenly meowed.

All heads on the couch turned to face the kitty and then Calliope.

"My notebook!" Kevin jumped up and rushed over to her. She handed him the notebook and he received it as if she had returned a long-lost favorite stuffed animal. "Where'd you find it?"

"In the park."

"Pizza Park?" Kevin sounded mystified. He caressed the frayed edges of his notebook, lost in thought.

"Kevin?" It was Mrs. Jefferson.

"Hmm?" Kevin replied absentmindedly.

"Won't you introduce us to your friend?"

"It's Calliope," said Calliope, stepping out from behind Kevin. "Calliope Day."

"Calliope?" said Mrs. Jefferson, "as in the Greek Muse?"

"Exactly!" It wasn't every day Calliope met someone who understood the meaning of her name. She remembered the bundled cables, televisions and Kevin's notebook. Had he been spying on her, reporting back to his spy parents? "How'd you know that?" she asked suspiciously.

Mr. Jefferson beamed. "Kevin's mother did her Ph.D. work in Greek mythology at Harvard."

"You mean Harvard as in University?" said Calliope.

With a laugh, Mrs. Jefferson said, "Now it's my turn to be impressed. How would you know about Harvard at your age?"

"My brother Jonah wanted to go there," said Calliope, "but Mom said we couldn't afford it."

"I'm sorry to hear that," said Mrs. Jefferson, sounding truly sorry. She addressed Kevin. "Why don't you invite Calliope to lunch? That's the least we can do to thank her for finding your notebook."

"Can I?" Kevin exploded, and then, seeing his parents' look of surprise, turned to stare down at his sneakers.

You bet Calliope wanted to stay for lunch. How else would she learn whether Kevin had written the poem to Noreen and whether his family were really Russian spies? Raising her nose ever so slightly, she said in her best imitation of Noreen, "You're too kind. If it's not an inconvenience, I'd love to stay for lunch."

Kevin looked up from his sneakers, head cocked back to study Calliope. She imagined him puffing out "Who...are...you?" like the big caterpillar in *Alice's Adventures in Wonderland.*

Calliope could have asked the same of him.

# Death by Butter Knife

"Well," said Mr. Jefferson, rising with a slap of his khaki-clad thigh. "I'd better be getting back to work."

On a Saturday? Very suspicious, thought Calliope, her eyes tailing Mr. Jefferson as he disappeared through the dark maze of hallways.

Calliope turned back to see Kevin anxiously eyeing his mother.

Mrs. Jefferson rose but she didn't leave. "I know," she said brightly, "I'll make you tuna salad with carrots, celery and sprouts on nine-grain bread."

Mmm, sprouts. Calliope had tried those once. They had a taste that reminded her of the time she'd fallen face first out of a tree and gotten a mouthful of grass.

Luckily Kevin wasn't partial to sprouts, either. "Mom, if you don't mind, I think we'll just make ourselves a couple of PB and J sandwiches."

Calliope endorsed Kevin's proposal by nodding enthusiastically.

Although she looked disappointed, Mrs. Jefferson didn't persist. But neither did she go away. She followed them down another dark passage. The passage emptied into a cavernous room with a brick floor.

They could have been standing in the kitchen at Grunting's, a restaurant where Calliope and her mom often stopped for lunch while running errands. Like Grunting's, this room had a great steel grill with a dozen burners. Long, unpainted wooden planks formed the counter. Looming against one wall stood a tall icebox with sliding glass doors. The other walls were paneled with cabinets.

Calliope must have been gawking, for Kevin proudly explained his restaurant of a kitchen. "My dad bought all this stuff from a place that was going out of business."

"So your dad is a chef?" Calliope sounded a bit disappointed.

Kevin and his mother smiled in unison.

"What's so funny?" grumped Calliope, wondering if she'd somehow said something stupid.

"My dad could burn water," explained Kevin. "He just thought it would be fun to have a kitchen that looks like a restaurant."

Kevin's restaurant kitchen turned out to be not as fun as it looked. Its vast cabinets held not a single chip or cookie. The peanut butter Mrs. Jefferson set out was as thick as school paste.

There was plenty of bread but it was either brown or lumpy with nuts. Finally Kevin found four slices of white bread crystallized with freezer burn. They were buried at the bottom of the fridge as if banished to Siberia. "I've been saving these for a special occasion," he confided.

Mrs. Jefferson dogged her son's every step as he assembled bread, peanut butter and jelly. Her eyes bulged as she watched Kevin stab a dull knife into the jar of peanut butter. The knife stuck like the Sword in the Stone and Kevin struggled to pull it out. Mrs. Jefferson leaned forward, hands outstretched. She looked ready to throw herself in front of the knife should Kevin slip and plunge the dull blade toward his heart.

Not even Kevin could be that big a klutz. Calliope recalled the last time she'd made herself a PB and J sandwich. She chuckled at the memory of herself twirling the butter knife on the tip of her index finger. Mrs. Jefferson would never let Kevin do something like that, and Calliope's heart sank a little bit for him.

"Mom," Kevin asked, having survived the sandwich making, "would it be all right if we ate in my room?"

"Well . . ." Mrs. Jefferson hesitated.

"I promise we'll leave the door open so you can check on us if you want," Kevin added quickly.

"All right, then."

That's it, thought Calliope, no warning against smearing jelly on the carpet or bedsheets? That was what Calliope's mother would have pestered them about. She wouldn't have cared less whether the door of Calliope's room was open or shut.

Following Kevin out of the kitchen, Calliope glanced back at Mrs. Jefferson. By the sad look on her face you'd have thought Kevin was leaving her and going away on an African safari. And, in a way, it turned out they were.

# The Electronic Graveyard

Ha! And her mother thought Calliope's room was messy. Compared to Kevin she was the Queen of Clean. Kevin's room looked like the elephants' dying ground in old Tarzan movies. But instead of elephant bones, the skeletal remains of televisions, computers and VCRs lay strewn across the floor. Scattered among the hunks of electronic parts were books, comics and papers.

Calliope surveyed this graveyard from the doorway. Kevin stood next to her, using his notebook as a tray for their sandwiches. "I like to see how things work," he said, shrugging at his messy floor.

"I guess." Calliope's eyes searched for a clear spot to sit and eat. Her gaze stopped on the oddest picture she'd ever seen. Well, not a picture, actually, although it was framed and hung from the wall. It was a glass-paneled box filled with neat rows of giant multi-colored beetles, butterflies and who knows what else pinned to Styrofoam. In the top row was an orange beetle with giant pincers.

"Now I know what part of New Jersey your beetle

came from," said Calliope, pointing at the pinned orange monster.

Kevin gazed down sheepishly at his sneakers. "I was taking my African rhinoceros beetle to school for show-and-tell," he whispered.

"Sure you were," said Calliope, poking him in the ribs.

He smiled but didn't look up from his sneakers.

Calliope's stomach growled at her to find somewhere to sit and eat. The most promising place looked like a high bed set between two windows. Its smooth quilt rose like a high plain above the jungle floor.

Atop the bed sat the only whole computer in the room. It had a little blinking green light that beckoned Calliope to come sit. But Calliope doubted a rat skilled at running mazes could find a route through this mess.

Kevin must have heard Calliope's growling stomach. "Come on," he said, raising his notebook above his head as if preparing to ford a stream. He began high-stepping through the wrecked computers and TVs. Calliope pranced behind him.

Three feet from the bed Kevin stopped, steadied himself and then lunged toward it. He landed on top, spilling the sandwiches onto the quilt. Calliope leaped after him, belly flopping onto one of the sandwiches.

"I'll eat that one," offered Kevin, picking up the squashed sandwich. He set both sandwiches on his notebook and then laid the notebook on top of the computer, setting it between them. "Lunch is served."

Such a gentleman, thought Calliope, although she didn't say so.

They sat cross-legged across from each other and bit into their sandwiches. Thank goodness for the jelly. Otherwise Calliope doubted she would have been able to swallow a bite. The sandwich reminded her of Noreen's cookies.

"Sorry," mumbled Kevin. "I guess we should have stuck with the tuna salad." He gobbled down his sandwich so fast that his tongue probably didn't have time to taste it.

It looked like a good strategy to Calliope and she followed suit. After all, it wasn't Kevin's cooking that interested her but his family. She had a million questions to ask him. "How come your parents have all those wires, computers and televisions?"

"That's their office."

"You mean they work out of the house?"

"Uh-huh."

"So no one will see them?"

"Well, I don't know about that."

"I do," said Calliope, winking at Kevin.

Kevin's eyebrows knitted but his confusion looked a little too contrived to Calliope.

"I knew it," she pronounced. "You *are* the spy family Romanoff."

"We're the what?"

Calliope leaned forward, whispering conspiratorially. "What side are you on—ours or the Russians'?"

For a moment Kevin stared in disbelief. Then he began to giggle.

"What?" said Calliope, sitting up straight.

"My parents aren't spies."

"No?"

"They're money managers."

"Is that like spying?" asked Calliope hopefully.

"I wish," said Kevin.

"Then what is it?" said Calliope. Although disappointed, she was still intrigued.

"It's when you buy and sell stocks and bonds for other people."

Hmmm, thought Calliope, stocks and bonds. Still sounded pretty mysterious—and that was good enough for her. She pronounced Kevin and his family most intriguing, her highest compliment.

But Kevin didn't say thank you. He didn't even appear to be listening to Calliope anymore. He stroked his notebook and murmured, "I must have dropped it in the schoolyard on the way home."

"I don't think so," said Calliope.

Kevin looked up at her. "What do you mean?"

# Confession Time

"Stolen?" Kevin's brow wrinkled as if resisting the idea. But in a moment he gave in, his forehead uncreasing. "Rodney?"

Calliope nodded.

"Man," said Kevin, pounding his notebook. "I don't get him. Why is he so interested in my stuff?"

"It's not to cheat on any test," quipped Calliope. She immediately regretted her wisecrack.

Kevin's chin sank like a lead sinker to his chest. Twisting a lock of hair, he stared down at the notebook. "You didn't read it, did you?"

Calliope's face flushed with embarrassment. "Well, I couldn't help it," she whined in defense.

"Oh no?" Kevin grabbed the upper corners of his notebook, sealing it tight against the computer.

"Kevin?"

He didn't answer but stared down at the notebook as if it were the only thing in the room.

"I have to ask you a really important question," pressed Calliope.

"What?" Kevin said grumpily without looking up.

"Did you write a poem about Noreen?"

"No."

"Are you absolutely sure?"

"Of course I'm sure," rasped Kevin.

"Oh, man," sighed Calliope, "so it *is* true."

"What's true?"

"You stole that poem from Rodney."

"What!" Kevin looked up sharply from his notebook.

"Stop," protested Calliope, embarrassed by Kevin's feeble pretense of ignorance.

"I have no idea what you're talking about," insisted Kevin.

"Oh yeah?" Calliope swept Kevin's hands from the notebook and threw it open. She flipped to the page with the poem about Noreen. "Okay, then what's this?"

Kevin's eyes bulged at the sight of the poem.

"You *did* copy this poem from Rodney."

"I did not!"

"Kevin, please," said Calliope, rising to go in disgust.

"*I* wrote this poem and it isn't about Noreen," bellowed Kevin, thrusting a pointed finger down at the open notebook.

Calliope had rarely heard the soft-spoken Kevin speak so loudly. His words now hit her like a gust of hot air, knocking her back on her haunches. Her eyes obeyed his pointing finger and looked at the page opened between them. This time she read the whole poem, right down to the last line, which read: "When you're Calliope, my Calliope, you skate as you please.

Calliope, my Calliope, would you please skate with me?"

Calliope swallowed hard. So she'd had it all backward. It was Rodney who'd copied the poem from Kevin, inserting Noreen's name for her own. That was why he couldn't write a poem at Calliope's house the other day. He wasn't awaiting inspiration. Just an opportunity to swipe another poem from Kevin.

She glanced sheepishly up at Kevin. If he never spoke to her again she wouldn't blame him.

But Kevin looked anything but angry. He'd lost steam like a cooling radiator and had returned to staring at the notebook. Meekly he asked, "You're not mad, are you?"

"Me, mad? About what?"

"You know . . . me writing a poem about you."

Calliope waved off the question as if Kevin were crazy. But what did she feel? Embarrassed, that was for sure. But she also felt the relief that came with fitting the last piece of a challenging jigsaw puzzle.

And a new feeling crept up behind her, whispering in an ear: Kevin liked *her*—her!—not Noreen. The idea of it hit Calliope like a swinging door that catches you off guard, whacking you on the back of the head.

Finally! A boy had noticed her. But now what? Did she feed Kevin carpet fuzz and Cheerios and put him back in his cage if he got out of hand? That was what she did with Mortimer, the only other boy she knew who liked her. Somehow Calliope didn't think carpet fuzz would satisfy Kevin.

Heck, she didn't even know if she liked Kevin. He certainly wasn't anything like her father. Dad could charm the broom away from the Wicked Witch of the West. Kevin, on the other hand, could barely get up the nerve to say hello to Calliope, let alone say he liked her. Yet he'd written this wonderful poem.

Kevin really was the *mystery* poet.

"Nobody gets you, do they?" said Calliope, speaking for herself as well.

Kevin looked up from his notebook. "What do you mean?"

"I mean, all the kids think you suck up to the teacher, and Mrs. Perkins thinks you love to take down everything she says. But none of that's true, is it?"

Kevin shrugged, his eyes again drifting back down to the notebook. "I have a confession to make."

"Oh?" said Calliope.

"I did take something—but not from Rodney."

# A Regular Pippi Longstocking

Kevin leaped off the bed, landing with a crunch among the electronic debris.

What now? wondered Calliope as she watched him root through his disemboweled computers, televisions and VCRs. Suddenly she heard a familiar sound among the clattering of metal and plastic. It was the jingling of small bells.

"My charm!"

Sure enough, there dangling from Kevin's fingertips were three bedraggled heads.

Kevin kneeled now, head bowed, as if awaiting a scolding.

But a scolding wasn't what Calliope had in mind. Her lost heads had helped her figure out what to do with this closet poet who fancied a girl who smelled faintly of rabbit and dill pickles.

"I know why you *borrowed* my charm," she teased.

Kevin glanced up.

"You wanted to write a poem about it, didn't you?"

"I did?"

She nodded, smiling down expectantly at him.

"You mean right now?"

Without answering, she curled into the bedspread like a cat getting ready to have its head scratched.

"All right," said Kevin, stroking the snarled braid of the charm as if it were a rabbit's foot. "I'll try." His gaze drifted up and for a long moment he studied the ceiling. Then he began to recite.

"No brothers Mario, nor Pikachu. No Sonic, no Zelda will do."

Kevin stopped, glancing over at Calliope curled atop his bed.

"Go on," she purred.

"When Calliope Day has something to say, Calliope Day says it her way."

Kevin's voice crescendoed, his eyes fixed on Calliope.

"She'll bind up three heads, add some bells, and then off she tingles, to raise a little . . . hell!"

"Kevin," Calliope pretended to scold, "such language!"

"Sorry," said Kevin, but he didn't look sorry at all. His gaze lingered on Calliope.

"What?"

"Well?" said Kevin.

"Well, what?"

"You know."

Calliope knew, all right. Kevin wanted to know if she liked his poem. No, scratch that. He wanted to know if she liked him.

Did she?

She certainly liked the picture he'd drawn of her with his words. Smart, free-spirited and brave. You'd have thought she was the Pippi Longstocking of Indian Trail Elementary.

Did that make Kevin her Mr. Nilsson, Pippi's faithful monkey companion who did everything with her? "How would you like to learn how to skate?"

Kevin frowned. "I know how to skate."

Calliope folded her arms in skepticism.

"I was that bad?"

Calliope nodded.

"Well, it was my first time."

"Do you think your mother would let you go again?"

"Maybe," said Kevin, smiling sheepishly up at Calliope, "if someone invited me."

Boy, poets didn't give up, did they?

# Skate-Marching

Skating it was not. Maybe skate-marching. Kevin raised each skate high and then clunked it back on the scuffed wooden floor of Spackle's rink. Not once did Calliope see him actually roll.

She trailed behind him like a watchful mother following a toddler on a bike with training wheels. Will you please pay attention? Calliope muttered to herself as she watched Kevin. He clomped head down, writing in his notebook, paying little attention to the kids whizzing past him. He was an easy mark.

Sure enough, Bobby Applegate sailed out of nowhere and clipped Kevin on the shoulder. Kevin spun like a top, arms outstretched, his fingers clinging to his notebook. On the third spin he lost his balance and toppled down on his rear.

If the fall hurt either Kevin's bottom or his pride, he didn't show it. "Wow," he slurred, his eyes a bit crossed. "I've never done *that* before!" He slapped open his notebook on the floor and began writing again.

Calliope rolled up to him, the toes of her skates squeaking as they dug into the floor, trying to stop.

She stopped, all right—after slamming into Kevin and then toppling down beside him.

"Sorry," wheezed Kevin, winded more from writing than skating.

"It's not your fault. I still don't know how to stop," she scolded herself aloud. She rolled over to rest faceup on her raised elbows. Catching her breath, she studied the boy beside her. He was hunched face first into his notebook. "You don't get out much, do you?"

"Huh?" said Kevin without looking up.

"Never mind," said Calliope. Wearily she considered lifting him up for the fifth time and her arms quivered at the thought. "What do you say we get some ice cream?"

Kevin looked up with a pout. "No more skating?"

"Maybe later," said Calliope. She wobbled to a stand, then reached down and grabbed him by the elbow, guiding him to his feet. Together they clomped off the rink and collapsed onto the first carpeted bench outside the low wall.

"Hey, look," said Kevin, pointing to the cafeteria tables behind them.

Calliope turned to see Noreen sitting primly at a table. Beside her stood Rodney. He set a bowl of pistachio ice cream in front of Noreen and then tucked a napkin neatly under her chin.

Amazing, thought Calliope. Noreen hadn't raised her sharp nose in disapproval when Calliope had unmasked Rodney as thief rather than poet. But then again, Noreen had always liked her pancakes drenched in syrup and Rodney knew how to pour it on thick.

Noreen had turned him into a valet of sorts. She ordered him around as if training for the day she'd ascend to her mother's velvet throne. Rodney obeyed without complaint.

Watching Rodney fawn over Noreen made Calliope's skin crawl.

"Ice cream?" asked Kevin.

Well, maybe it wasn't fawning she objected to but the particular fawner. "Please," she said, smiling sweetly at Kevin.

# Betty and Veronica

Noreen had a tree house that could turn Tarzan green with envy. It sat in a young oak in her backyard, equipped with TV, DVD player and popcorn popper. But what Calliope liked best was its big leather couch.

She draped herself now upside down on the couch, hair brushing the carpeted floor. In her hands she held a comic book Kevin had said she just had to read. It starred RoboBeetle, a mechanical bug that squashed a race of giant mutant houseflies.

Mutant houseflies, mechanical beetles? Kevin, Kevin, Kevin. A comic book connoisseur you are not. Calliope reminded herself to take Kevin to Herschel's and help him pick out a decent comic book. Say, something starring Wonder Woman. Now *she* was a superhero, outfoxing evildoers as much as giving them a good thrashing.

Calliope glanced up at Noreen. Her friend sat erect on the couch, face buried in a Betty and Veronica comic book. On the cover Archie, arms loaded with shopping bags, grunted as he trailed behind Veronica. In Calliope's eyes his face morphed into Rodney's. She almost felt sorry for the bow-tied Romeo.

"Noreen, are we through hating boys?" asked Calliope, sounding a bit disappointed.

"Don't be silly," said Noreen from behind her comic.

"Even Kevin and Rodney?"

Noreen lowered her comic, revealing a sly smile. "Kevin and Rodney are different."

"How so?" Calliope sounded skeptical.

"They're not boys."

Not boys? Now, that would be news to Rodney and Kevin, Calliope suspected. "Noreen, what are you talking about?"

"Look," said Noreen, sounding gently superior like Mrs. Perkins. "Boys are scabby, smelly things, right?"

"Duh."

"And they live to torment girls."

No argument there. "So what's your point, Noreen?"

"Well, does Kevin torment you?"

"No."

"Does he smell?"

"Not particularly."

"See?" said Noreen, smiling at Calliope. "He's not a boy."

Calliope swung herself right side up on the couch. "Okay, Miss Smarty-pants," she challenged. "If Kevin is not a boy, then what is he?"

"A friend."

Noreen had a point. There were boys who didn't necessarily want to pull your hair or knock you down. There was Calliope's dad, for one. Was Kevin another? He certainly wasn't anything like her dad. But so what?

It was dawning on Calliope that boys, like girls, were as varied as seashells on a beach. For sure, some boys were like those shells that bristled with spikes. Step on one and you'd be sorry. Some girls were like that too. But other boys were like conches, harboring mysteries inside like the roar of the ocean. Those were the boys she wanted as friends.

No, from here on out, it was going to be hard, darn hard, to hate every boy who buzzed her at Spackle's. She might miss a friend well worth treasuring.

A friend, say, like Noreen. The two of them were like Betty and Veronica, as different as French vanilla and tutti-frutti ice cream, yet still the best of friends. Calliope's face twisted up in a funny smile as an idea popped into her head.

"What?" asked Noreen, noticing Calliope's smile.

"Let's make up our own comic book!"

"Really? About what?"

"Us, of course."

Noreen jumped up excitedly and ransacked the well-stocked tree house until she found a drawing pad and a purple crayon. "What should we call it?" She gnawed on the end of the crayon, lost in thought.

Calliope's eyes lit up. "How about . . . *Watch Out, World! Here Come Calliope and Noreen!*"

Noreen clapped her hands together. "I love it!" In bold purple letters, she wrote the title across the top of the page, extending the *e* of Calliope's name until it entwined the leg of the *N* in *Noreen.*

Whatever came next, they were in it together.

## About the Author

Charles Haddad is a journalist for *Business Week*. This story, like *Meet Calliope Day* and *Captain Tweakerbeak's Revenge,* is set in his hometown, South Orange, New Jersey. Charles Haddad attended Sarah Lawrence College and Harvard University. He lives in Atlanta.

# A Matter of Circumstance

*Also by Heather Graham Pozzessere
in Large Print:*

An Angel's Touch
Forever My Love
A Perilous Eden
The diMedici Bride

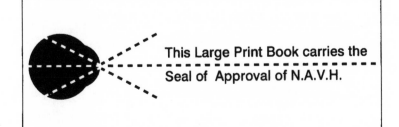

# A Matter of Circumstance

# Heather Graham Pozzessere

**Thorndike Press • Waterville, Maine**

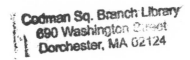
Published in 2001 by arrangement with Harlequin Books S.A.

Thorndike Press Large Print Romance Series.

The tree indicium is a trademark of Thorndike Press.

The text of this Large Print edition is unabridged.
Other aspects of the book may vary from the original edition.

Set in 16 pt. Plantin by Myrna S. Raven.

Printed in the United States on permanent paper.

**Library of Congress Cataloging-in-Publication Data**

Graham, Heather.
     A matter of circumstance  / Heather Graham Pozzessere.
          p.  cm.
      ISBN 0-7862-2623-4 (lg. print : hc : alk. paper)
      1. Americans — Bahamas — Fiction.   2. Undercover operations — Fiction.   3. Kidnapping — Fiction.
      4. Bahamas — Fiction.   5. Large type books.   I. Title.
      PS3557.R198 M38 2001
      813'.54—dc21                                              00-030293

# A Matter of
# Circumstance

# 1

From one of the assorted ketches, catamarans, speedboats and yachts, a Jimmy Buffet tune was rising high on the air, tarnished by only a shade of static. The late afternoon was tempering the heat, and a breeze was flowing in from the water, cooling Sean Ramiro's sun-sizzled arms and chest. To all outward appearances he was as negligent and lackadaisical as the carefree Sunday loafers who laughed, teased, flirted and played around the docks. But when he raised his head for a moment, tilting back the brim of his Panama hat, a careful observer might have noted that he surveyed the scene with startlingly intense green eyes.

All seemed peaceful and pleasant. A lazy afternoon by the water. Girls in bikinis, guys in cutoffs, tourists with white cream on their noses, and old geezers in bright flowered shirts. Kids threw fish tails to the gulls that hovered nearby. Sean arched his shoulders back, grimacing at the feel of the wooden dock piling that grated through the thin material of his cotton shirt. He'd been sitting

there a long time now.

Farther down the dock Sunday fishermen were cleaning their catches. A young sailor in tie-dyed cutoffs was hosing down his small Cigarette boat. A group of beer drinkers passed him, heading for the refreshment stand that was located where the rustic-looking wooden docks gave way to the cold reality of the concrete parking lot.

Sean heard a little titter of laughter and gazed sideways, annoyed to realize that he had become an object of fascination for two well-endowed teenagers in string bikinis. He tensed, swearing to himself. If something was going to happen after this long and futile day, it would surely happen now, while the kiddies were in the way.

He lowered his head, feigning a nap, hoping they would go away.

At his side, what looked like a credit-card-sized AM/FM receiver suddenly made a little buzzing sound. Sean picked it up and brought it to his car.

"Hey, Latin lover!" Anderson teased. Sean looked up; he could see Harvey Anderson in the refreshment stand, chatting while he turned hot dogs on a grill. "You got a fan club going there, you know? I think you should be on grill duty. You're too pretty to blend into the woodwork."

Sean idly moved the radio in front of his mouth. "Anderson, it's not that I'm too pretty — you're just too damned ugly. You'd scare away the devil himself."

Todd Bridges, unseen, but not far away in the parking lot, broke in on the conversation. "Must be those Irish eyes, Sean. Keep 'em lowered, eh?"

"Todd . . ."

"Hey, who said duty was a chore?" Harvey interrupted. "Will you look at that? I am in love! Thunderstruck and all that junk. Now I really think you should be grilling the hot dogs, Ramiro! Ah, I'd like just a whiff of the air she breathes!"

Harvey was always falling in love with anything in a bikini. But Sean idly turned his head, tilting the brim of his hat just a shade. He arched a dark brow and was surprised to discover that his breath had caught in his chest.

This time Harvey was right on the mark.

She was coming in from the end of the dock. She walked slowly and casually, and with the most sensual grace Sean had ever witnessed. She wasn't wearing a bikini, but a one-piece thing cut high on the thighs, and man-oh-man, did those slim sexy thighs go on forever.

If someone were to have asked Sean

Ramiro what he first noticed about a woman, he would have given it a little thought, then answered with honesty, "Her eyes." Eyes were the mirror of the soul, as the saying went. And so he looked first at her eyes.

He couldn't see their color, not from his position, not with the way he was forced to squint into the sun. He did see that they were sparkling like the sun, that they were large and exquisite, that they were framed with thick lashes . . . that they enchanted.

He didn't know why, but his eyes fell then to take in the whole of her. Her easy, idle movement. Her walk . . .

He was — even on duty — spellbound by that walk. The never-ending length of her golden tanned legs, the curve of her hips. He liked her waistline, too, smooth and sleek. Just like Harvey, he was instantly in love. Spaghetti straps held the yellow swimsuit in place. The top was straight cut, but she needed no help to display her cleavage. Her still-damp skintight bathing suit couldn't hide the fact that her breasts were firm, round, perfect. Sean realized that he felt a bit like a kid in a candy store, almost overwhelmed by the desire to reach out and touch.

"Will you look at those . . . eyes," Harvey breathed in awe.

"What is it?" Todd demanded from the parking lot.

"Boy, did you draw the wrong straw!" Harvey told him.

Sean looked back to her face.

It was a perfect oval. High boned. Classical. She could have posed for history's most famous artists, and not one of them could have found a flaw. Her mouth was generous, but elegantly defined. Sean could imagine her laughing; the sound would be as provocative as the curve of those lips. Her nose was long and straight, and her eyes — those wondrous eyes! — were framed by high brows that added to their captivating size and beauty. And her hair . . .

Her hair matched the coming of the sunset in glorious color. It wasn't blond, neither was it dark. It was a tawny color, like a lion's mane, with deeper highlights of shimmering red to match the streak of the sun against the sky.

"I am in love!" Harvey repeated.

"Oh, watch your hot dogs!" Todd grumbled from the parking lot.

Sean grimaced, jerking involuntarily as the radio suddenly gave out a burst of static. Then Todd's voice came back on the air.

"I just got a buzz from Captain Mallory. Someone pulled in faulty information.

11

Blayne isn't here, and he isn't coming. He's got a reservation on a flight north at six."

For a moment Sean completely forgot the woman, as he closed his eyes in disgust. Damn that Blayne! The senator had received threats against his life, but he had lifted his naive nose to the police, who had bent over backward to protect him. Still, as public servants, it was their job to protect him.

They'd been tipped off today that Blayne, who had mysteriously disappeared, had ordered a catered lunch delivered to the docks this morning for a sailboat registered as the *Flash Point*. Meanwhile, another threat had been phoned in to the police. Of all the lousy details to draw, Sean had drawn this one. He'd had to spend the whole stinking day on the dock, waiting for Peter Blayne to make an appearance and to see that he got off the docks without mishap.

Now it seemed the fool had never been anywhere near the docks to begin with, nor intended to be. The boat had gone out earlier, but without the senator aboard.

Sean opened his eyes again. Not even his disgust at the wasted day could really have any effect on him — not when he was staring at *her*, and she was coming closer. A scuba mask and a pair of flippers dangled from

12

one hand as she moved along, still at that lazy, no-hurry pace. Her face was tilted upward, and the smallest signs of a smile curved her lip, as if she was savoring that soft kiss of sun and breeze against her cheeks.

Just like some ancient goddess, Sean thought, and he could almost see her walking along at that slow confident pace, naked and assured, in some flower-strewn field, while a primitive drumbeat pulsed out the rhythm of her fluid motion and an ancient man bowed down before her.

"Hey!" Harvey's voice, quiet and tense, suddenly jolted Sean from his daydream.

"What?"

"It's back. The *Flash Point*. Way down the dock — she didn't berth where she should have!"

Sean stared down the dock. It was true. The *Flash Point* was in, and two kids — or young men — were securing her lines.

He stood, slowly, carefully, unaware that he grimaced as all the muscles in his six-foot-two frame complained. Absently he rubbed a shoulder and stared down at the ketch. Nice. It had three masts and probably slept a dozen in privacy and comfort.

It was Blayne's boat, and someone had gone out on it. But if Peter Blayne was really

catching a six o'clock flight, they couldn't possibly have picked him up and brought him back on the ketch. It was six now.

Someone behind him began an excited conversation, half in Spanish, half in English. Two men cleaning fish were talking about a woman, trying to decide if it was "her" or not. Without thinking, Sean tuned in the words, then tuned them out, more concerned with the arrival of the *Flash Point* than he was with "that rat's old lady."

He supposed he should saunter down and ask a few questions. Pulling his open shirt across his chest to conceal the holster strapped underneath, he stared at his quarry, then started toward it. He rubbed his jaw and the dark stubble there, wondering if he didn't look more than a little like a bum. Good for sitting around on a dock idly, but a little scary, maybe, to the elite teenagers battening down the *Flash Point.*

He didn't realize how quickly he was moving until he suddenly plowed into somebody — and knocked them down. He started to bend down and offer a hand, then he noticed that he wasn't the only person racing toward the *Flash Point.*

From the end of the pier a slim, handsome young Latin with a grim look of purpose

14

and something bunched in his arms was hurrying toward the ketch — or toward the end of the dock. Sean wasn't sure.

What he *was* sure about was the man's identity.

It was Garcia. Definitely. Julio Garcia, old Jorge's son. He had his father's flashing dark eyes and arresting, near-gaunt face.

Sean immediately felt tension riddle him. The police might have been wrong about Blayne's whereabouts, but if so, it seemed a strange coincidence that the people threatening him had received the same faulty information.

"You stupid ox!"

Momentarily startled, Sean stared in the direction of the feminine voice that had spat out the epithet. It was her. The sensually swaying woman with the never-ending legs and great eyes.

Eyes . . .

They were topaz. Not brown. Not green. Not hazel. They were the color of light, shimmering honey, sparkling now like liquid sunlight, like precious gems reflecting the last dying rays of the sun in a burst of rebellious glory.

And he'd just knocked her down flat, without a word of apology. He could reach out and touch her. He could . . .

15

He offered her a hand. She took it with delicate fingers, watching him warily.

If only Garcia wasn't just yards away . . .

"Hey!" The voice came from down the dock. Garcia was gripping the arm of one of the kids who had been working on the *Flash Point*. "I don't know what you're talking about!"

Even from this distance Sean could hear the kid's angry retort to whatever Garcia had said. Then the kid's voice lowered, and Garcia said something with a frightening vehemence.

Sean didn't know that he had dropped the woman's hand when she was halfway up until she thudded back to the wood with a furious oath. "You are the rudest person I have ever met!"

He barely heard her; he was too tense, watching Garcia.

"Don't you speak English? *Estúpido!*" the woman snapped.

Absently he offered a hand to her again.

"Don't touch me! Just move, please. Honest to God, I don't know what's wrong with people these days!"

Sean ignored her, anxious to reach Garcia. But even as he stepped past her, the kid with Garcia looked up and started yelling. "Hey, Mrs. Blayne! Can you do

16

something with this guy? He insists that the senator is aboard and I keep telling him that he isn't!"

Blayne!

Sean swung around and stared at the beauty he'd just knocked over, then ignored. Mrs. Blayne? His wife? She couldn't be! Blayne was in his mid-forties or early fifties if he was a day; this woman was twenty-five, twenty-eight, tops!

She was impatiently dusting herself off after her fall on the sandy dock, but she smiled at the kid with a rueful shake of her head. "Tell him Peter had to be in Washington tonight. He isn't on the *Flash Point* — he probably isn't even in the state anymore."

The kid started speaking earnestly to Garcia. Sean was momentarily frozen, with two thoughts registering in his mind.

Blayne wasn't here; they had all been wrong, and it was probably for the best. Garcia hadn't identified himself during any of the threatening calls, but who else could be so violently angry with the senator except for some crackpot? And Garcia was definitely a crackpot.

The other thought, which interrupted his professional logic in a way that annoyed him, was about her. She was married to the

man. And quite obviously for his money, since the age difference was definitely vast!

It was irritating, and somehow it hurt — for all that any feelings on his part were ridiculous. She was just a dream. The absolute, perfect dream you might see on the page of some magazine, then forget just as soon as the page was turned. Yet he wanted to shake her. To demand where her morals were — and her dignity and pride! — that she would marry an old guy like Blayne just for the sake of material possessions.

But even as he thought that, he smiled a little ruefully. Because the question that was really bothering him was, why him and not me? I'm thirty-three and as healthy as the "ox" you just called me. I'm the one who could show you what life was meant to be, just what you were built for, lady!

He reminded himself that he didn't like blondes. But any man, face-to-face with this particular blonde, would want her.

"Roberto, man, it is her! Julio, the old lady!"

Sean frowned, realizing then that the two fishermen were yelling to Garcia. He was halfway to the man himself, but paused.

The two fishermen jumped into a speedboat.

"Hey, wait —" he called to them. Where

the hell was Harvey? Couldn't he tell something was happening? But how would he? Nothing illegal was going on. Two men had jumped into a speedboat, and Julio Garcia was talking to a kid. Nothing to get arrested for, but . . .

"Get out of the way! Get down!"

The heavily accented command came from Julio Garcia. Sean ducked, then fell flat as a whole barrage of bullets was suddenly spewed haphazardly in his direction. He tasted sand as he fell hard against the wood, reaching for his .38 caliber Smith & Wesson as a second barrage began.

Julio was fast; he kept firing as he raced down the dock. The shots rang out discordantly against the absolute and lazy peace of the afternoon, shocking everyone, causing chaos and so many screams that Sean didn't know where to look.

The woman!

He rolled just in time to see that the thing under Julio's arm had been potato sacking, and that Julio had looped it over her head, thrown her struggling but constrained figure over his shoulder and made a wild leap for the speedboat.

Sean didn't dare shoot; he would hit the woman.

He didn't think; he just reacted. He dove

into the water, determined to reach the boat before it could jet out into open water and head for the endless nooks and crannies that the mangrove islands could provide.

## 2

He wasn't accustomed to making mistakes. A homicide detective simply couldn't make mistakes and expect to live.

But as he dove into the murky water his gun was swept from his hand by a stinging collision with the wood and instantly disappeared into a growth of seaweed. Still submerged, Sean could hear the motor of the speedboat revving up, and he knew he didn't have a spare second left. It seemed necessary at any cost to reach that boat and then come up with a plan of action, minus his gun.

His fingers grasped the edge of the boat while it was already in motion. Water splashed into his face, blinding him, gagging him. He held on, feeling the tremendous force of the pressure against him.

Ass! he accused himself, but too late. To give up now would be to risk the murderous blades of the propeller, so, thinking himself the greatest idiot ever to draw breath, he grated his teeth against the agony of his hold and tried to bring his body as close as pos-

sible to the side of the boat.

The motor was suddenly cut, and Sean remembered just in time to ditch his ID card and gun clip.

"*¿Qué pasa? ¿Qué pasa?*"

He heard the furious query, then a colorful spate of oaths in Spanish. Someone reached over the side of the boat to pull his half-drowned body over the edge.

He was dizzy; his head reeled as he lay soaked between two side-to-side seats. He gasped in a breath even as he heard the motor rev into motion again and felt the vibrations with his entire body.

The three men — Garcia and the two fishermen — were fighting away, screaming and gesticulating over the terrible hum of the motor, an occasional word of English slipping into the Spanish tirades.

"What happened? Who the hell is he?"

"I don't know. Why didn't you kill him?"

"We're not murderers!"

"We agreed if we had to —"

Something pounded viciously against his head, and Sean groaned despite himself. Twisting, he saw that the burlap sack containing the girl was stretched out over the seat so that her feet dangled right over his head, only the toes bared.

Of all things he noticed that her toenails

were filed and manicured and glazed in a deep wine red. For some reason that irritated him. Maybe he realized he'd half killed himself over some mercenary socialite.

"Why did we take her?" one of the fishermen whined.

"She's twice as good as the old man! Hey, if he wants her back, he'll see that my father is set free!" Garcia proclaimed.

"So who the hell is this guy?" the second fisherman asked.

Sean, blinking furiously, more to clear his head than his eyes, pushed himself up to his elbows. If the stinking motor would just stop! He would need his wits to get out of this one. In the last few minutes the sun had decided to make a sharp fall. The boat was carrying no lights. Everything seemed to be a haze of darkness: the sea joining the sky, the men seated in the motorboat nothing more than macabre silhouettes. There weren't even any stars out. He was grateful that there didn't seem to be any other boats out, either.

He felt, though, that all the men were staring at him. Especially Garcia, who was seated next to the bundled, struggling figure in burlap.

Her toes crashed into his nose when he

tried to elbow himself into a better position.

"*Me llamo* Miguel Ramiro," he began, yelling above the motor, but just as he started screeching, the motor was cut.

"*Cállate!*" Garcia snapped. Shut up.

Sean heard the water lapping against the side of the boat, then a woman's shout from nearby, and Garcia's quick answer. They came alongside a much bigger vessel, some kind of motorized, two-masted sailboat. A ladder was dropped down; Garcia motioned the two fishermen up first, then turned to stare down at Sean. Despite the poor light Sean could see the dark, wary glitter in his eyes.

"Who are you?"

"Miguel Ramiro."

"And who is Miguel Ramiro?"

The woman — Mrs. Blayne — could blow the whole thing in a matter of seconds, but he had to come up with something. He damn well couldn't introduce himself as a cop. He inclined his head toward the burlap. "She is mine," he replied in Spanish.

Garcia arched a dark brow, then leveled the gun at Sean. "Then you take her up the ladder — and then explain yourself."

Sean struggled to his feet between the wooden seats. He bent over the burlap, trying to figure out just where to grab her.

He obviously made a mistake, because his hand encountered something nicely rounded, and the bundle let out an outraged shriek and began twisting and squirming all over again.

"Stop it!" he snapped in English. A recognizable piece of anatomy swung toward him, and in sudden exasperation he gave it a firm swat. Her outraged cry reached him again, and he tried to murmur convincingly, "It is Miguel. I am with you, my darling."

Garcia's brow arched higher; Sean figured he couldn't press his luck too far and decided it didn't matter in the least right now which part of her anatomy he came in contact with. He reached down, gripped her body and tossed her over his shoulder, wincing as she came in contact with a sore spot, right where he had hit the deck to avoid the gunfire.

"Up the ladder," Garcia said.

Sean nodded and started up. His squirming burden almost sent him catapulting back down.

For Garcia's benefit he swore heatedly in Spanish, then added contritely in English, "My love, please! It is me, Miguel!"

Her reply was inarticulate, but Sean knew what she was saying: who the hell was Miguel?

Maybe he would be better off if she remained wrapped in burlap for a while. He probably wouldn't have to carry this thing off for too long. Harry and Todd had been on the docks. Search boats and helicopters would be out soon.

Yeah, but the coastline was a maze of islands and shoals and shallows and roots. . . . The mangroves, the islets, the Everglades. . . . They had sheltered many a criminal throughout the years.

He couldn't think about it that way. He just had to play the whole thing moment by moment.

Starting now.

He crawled over the starboard side of the sailboat to find four people already studying him in the light of a single bulb projecting from the enclosure over the hull. There was a short, graying woman, plump and showing traces of past beauty, and a younger woman, somewhere in her early twenties, with huge almond eyes and a wealth of ink-dark hair. Then the two fishermen. They must have seen him on the dock all day, just as he had seen them. Well, he would just have to make that work to his advantage. They were both in their late twenties or early thirties, jeaned and sneakered, and dark. One wore a mustache;

the other was slimmer and as wary as Garcia himself.

Garcia came up the ladder right behind Sean. They all stared at one another for a moment, then the older woman burst into a torrent of questions. What was going on here? Who was this man? Who was struggling in the sack? Where was Peter Blayne? Had they all gone loco?

Then she burst into tears.

Garcia took both her shoulders and held her against his chest. "Mama, Mama! It will be all right! We were wrong, you see. The senator was not on his boat. But his wife was — we've got his wife! And if he wants her back, we must get Papa back first. It's better than the senator."

The woman looked dubiously at the sack that twisted over Sean's shoulder, then pointed a finger in his direction. "Who is he?"

"That," Garcia said, rubbing his chin and looking keenly at Sean, "is something we're still trying to figure out."

Sean sighed deeply and spoke in heavily accented English. "I told you, *amigo* — I am Miguel Ramiro. And I am in love with her."

Garcia started to laugh, and the fishermen laughed with him.

"And she is in love with you, too, *amigo?*"

27

Garcia asked skeptically.

Sean gave them a sheepish look, then gritted his teeth, because the girl in the burlap was screeching something and twisting with greater fury. He smiled grimly and gave her a firm swat once again, which shut her up for several well-needed moments.

"*Sí sí!*" Sean cried passionately. He irritably muttered a few epithets in Spanish, then added, "But you know these *Americanas!* She's fond of the hot Latin blood in private, but when we are in public I am not good enough to clean her shoes!"

"She's a senator's wife and she's having an affair with you?" Garcia said.

"I told you —"

"I believe it, Julio," the younger woman suddenly interrupted him. Sean paused, gazing her way. She was looking him up and down with an obvious appreciation that was quite gratifying — he needed someone to believe him!

"Maria, I did not ask you."

But Maria put her hand on Julio Garcia's arm and gave him a sexy little smile, her almond eyes wide. "But I tell you, because I am a woman, too, yes?"

"Yes, you are all woman, little one," Julio said pleasantly to her, and she laughed delightedly.

"Latin men make the best lovers, yes, Julio?" She giggled. "I see it all well! She is married to some dull old man, but who can live like that? So she finds Miguel —"

"*Sí!* I was the gardener!" Sean said quickly.

"And he is *muy hombre!*" Maria laughed. "So she calls him in on the side, but pretends, Oh, no! Never!"

The fishermen started to laugh again, too. They were all grinning like the most amiable friends.

Except that Garcia was leveling his gun at Sean's chest.

"Juan!" Garcia said. "Start her up. We leave the motorboat right where it is. We go to the cove where we intended. Mama, Maria, you go below. Now!"

"But —" Maria began.

"Now!" Garcia snapped, and Maria, with one last sultry grin for Sean, obeyed.

Sean and Garcia stared at each other, both ignoring the grunts and oaths that came from the burlap bag.

Sean heard the crank as the anchor was pulled in and felt the motion as the sailboat began to move.

"Amigo," Garcia said softly, "do you know what is going on here?"

Sean shook his head vehemently and lied.

"I only know that she is mine. You took her, and I followed."

Garcia shrugged and stared at him a while longer.

"I mean you no harm. I mean no man any harm. All I seek is freedom for my father."

Sean remained mute, thinking that this wasn't the time to explain to an impassioned man that spraying a populated dock with bullets and kidnapping a young woman were not sound means to reach the end he sought.

"I know nothing of your father. I am here for her."

"So stay with her. But if her husband does not produce my father . . ."

"Then what?"

"Then we shall see. Justice should be equal." He waved the gun.

"Your father is not dead," Sean said.

Garcia shrugged again, then smiled. "But you will be, and the woman, if you cause trouble."

Sean lowered his head. Where the hell was everyone? There didn't seem to be another boat in the water; he hadn't heard a single damned helicopter out searching. . . .

Night had fallen. And the Atlantic was one hell of a big ocean!

"Put her down."

Sean braced himself, then lowered her to the deck.

"Get the hood off her," Garcia continued.

His captors had spoken Spanish to one another, and Sean had spoken Spanish to them, but he was certain that Julio Garcia's English was completely fluent. Once she started to talk he could well be in serious trouble, despite his story.

"The hood!" Garcia snapped.

Sean hunched down and moved to take the burlap from her — a difficult procedure, because she was struggling so wildly. At last it came free, and she stared at him — glared at him — with eyes so wild they might have been those of a lioness, and her hair in such a tangle it could have been a massive tawny mane. She was pale, and those fascinating tawny eyes of hers were as wide as saucers, but she'd lost absolutely none of her fight. She stared at him and recognized him as the longhaired, unshaven, rude Cubano who had knocked her down just before this mess had begun.

"You!" She hauled back and struck him hard on the chin.

His eyes narrowed, and he thought quickly. No self-respecting man in his invented position would accept such behavior.

He hauled off and slapped her back, bringing a startled gasp from her — and further fury. She tore at him, nails raking, fists flying. Grunting as her elbow caught his ribs and her nails his cheek, he managed to wrap his arms around her, bringing them both crashing down on the deck. Scrambling hastily, he straddled her, caught her wrists and pinned them.

That didn't calm her at all. She called him every name he'd ever heard and writhed beneath him.

Garcia, still holding his gun, suddenly caused her to go quiet with his laughter. "Miguel," he told Sean in Spanish. "You have yourself a tigress here. Maybe it is good you are along."

Sean saw that she was struggling to understand the words, but her knowledge of Spanish just wasn't good enough. Then she started to scream again. "What the hell is going on here? I warn you, I will prosecute you to the full degree of the law! You'll go to prison! Let me go this instant! What in God's —"

"Shut up!" Sean hissed at her. "I'm on your side!"

Garcia crouched down beside them. She surely realized that she was in trouble, but if she hadn't before, she must now, because

Garcia leveled the gun at her temple.

"Mother of God, but you've got a mouth!" he said in English. "Don't threaten me. Think of your sins. If your husband doesn't get my father out of that prison, you will die." He grinned. "You and your lover will die together."

Her eyes reverted to Sean's again, registering shock. "He's not —"

Sean didn't really have any choice in the matter. His hands were occupied securing hers. He had to shut her up

He leaned down and kissed her.

Her mouth had been open, and he came in contact with all the liquid warmth of her lips, exerting a certain pressure that he hoped would be a warning.

She struggled anyway.

He held his fingers so tightly around her wrists that she didn't dare cry out. Garcia, chuckling again, rose.

Sean tried to take that opportunity to warn her. He moved his lips just above hers and whispered, "Behave! Shut up and follow my lead. For God's sake, the man has a gun and is upset enough to use the damn thing! I'm —"

"Get off me!" she whispered vehemently in turn. "You . . . kidnapper!"

"I'm not with them! I'm —"

"Get off me!"

"Shut up, then!"

She clamped her lips together, staring at him with utter loathing. He sighed inwardly, wishing that he hadn't bothered to stick with her. The hell with her. Let them shoot her!

Then she was talking again, this time to Garcia. "Look, I still don't get this. If you'll just let me go now we'll forget all about it. I promise. You can't get any money through me. I just don't have any. And as for him —"

"Shush!" Sean interrupted, glaring at her. He wasn't about to be shot and thrown to the sharks for his above-and-beyond-the-call-of-duty attempt to save her.

She was going to try to interrupt him again. He tightened his hold on her, his eyes daring her to denounce him to Garcia. He tried to come up with his best and most abusive Spanish to keep Garcia entertained and drown her words.

She must have put on suntan oil sometime during the day, because one of her hands slipped from his grasp, and she used it to lash out at him. His patience was growing thin. He was even beginning to wish that he had decided to practice law, as his mother had suggested. So far he'd been half drowned, thoroughly abused and was

surely bloody and bruised from her flying fists and nails. This couldn't go on much longer.

What had happened to terrified victims?

"Don't touch me! Let me go! Get your filthy paws off me! You son of a bitch! Who the hell —"

He had to do something before they both wound up shot and thrown back into the sea.

She just wasn't going to see reason. Sighing inwardly, Sean twisted her quickly to the side and brought the side of his hand down hard just at the base of her skull. With a little whimper she fell peacefully silent at last.

Mandy hadn't panicked at the sound of gunfire; it had come too suddenly. Nor had she really panicked when the burlap had been thrown over her. That, also, had been too sudden. She hadn't even really panicked when she found herself absurdly cast into battle with the rude, green-eyed, unshaven Latin hulk on deck.

But when she returned to awareness in a narrow bunk below deck she *did* panic, because what brought her to awareness was the terrible feel of rope chafing against her wrists.

She was tied to the headboard of the small bunk, tied so tightly that she couldn't begin to move her arms.

She almost screamed — almost — as a feeling of absolute helplessness overwhelmed her. Not only were her wrists tied, but her ankles, too. Someone had tossed a worn army blanket over her poorly clad figure, but it didn't cover her feet, and adding insult to injury, she could see the cheap, filthy rope that was attached to the same type of panel posts framing the foot of the bunk. Someone knew how to tie knots — good knots.

Oh, hell! Just like a Boy Scout! Did they have Boy Scouts in Cuba?

She closed her eyes and tried to swallow the awful scream that hovered in her throat; she tried to reason, but reasoning seemed to give her little help.

What the hell was going on?

Facts, facts . . . Peter always warned her to look to the facts. Okay, fact: she had gone out this morning with a few students to study coral markings. Pleasant day, easy day. Peter had seen that a lunch had been catered. They'd done some work; they'd partied and picnicked, and absolutely nothing had been wrong in the least. Mark Griffen had given an excellent dissertation on the

shark's incredible survival from prehistory to the present, and Katie Langtree had found some exceptional examples of fossilized coral. Easy, fun, educational, pleasant . . .

Her only responsibility — her one big worry for the day! — had been to see that the *Flash Point* was returned in good shape: galley clean, equipment hosed. And even that had seemed like a breeze, because the kids had vowed to do all the work, and they were a dependable group. They also knew they would never use the yacht again if she wasn't returned shipshape.

So . . . facts! They'd come in, they'd docked. Mark had started rinsing the deck; Katie and Sue had been at work in the galley; Henry Fisher had been covering the furled sails. Everything in A-B-C order. She had stepped off the *Flash Point*, seen that the kids were hard at work at their tasks, then started lazily down the dock, looking forward to a cold canned soda from the refreshment stand.

Facts. . . .

Next thing she knew, she was out of breath and flat on her back, with a tall dark man standing over her and not paying the least attention to her — even though he had just knocked her down in the rudest fashion.

37

She briefly pictured his face; unshaven; his hair a little long and near ebony in color; his nose as straight as a hawk's; his skin sun-darkened to a glistening bronze. And against all that darkness his eyes had been the brightest, most shocking green. If she lived to be a hundred she would never forget the impact of those kelly green eyes against the bronze of his skin.

Facts!

She had said something to him, something about his rudeness. He had barely paid attention. She'd realized then that he must be Latin—Cuban, Colombian, Nicarauguan. Spanish speaking, as were so many of the area's residents.

English or Spanish speaking, no one had the right to be so rude!

Rude! How the hell could she be worrying about rudeness right now! Fact: she was tied hand and foot to a bunk, and some wacko was running around with a gun. He'd already shot up half the docks; she could only pray he hadn't killed someone.

And she had been the target! Why? Why on earth would anyone kidnap her? She didn't have any money to speak of. She did okay, but paying one's electricity bill on time was tremendously different from coming up with hundreds of thousands of

dollars to meet a ransom demand!

No, no . . . kidnappers demanded ransom from others, not the victim. Peter had money. Not tons of it, but he was certainly one of the affluent. Because of their deep friendship, Peter would surely pay to keep her from being — Don't think of it!

Murdered . . .

"Oh, God!"

The little breath of a prayer escaped and she fell into sheer panic once again, whimpering and tugging furiously at the ropes. All she managed to do was tighten the knots and chafe her flesh until it was raw.

"Oh, God!" she repeated, panting and lying still. Her wriggling had brought the blanket up to her nose; she was going to sneeze.

Why?

The question came back to haunt her again. There was a lot of money in south Florida. Tons of really rich people lived here. Why not abduct a banker's daughter, or a plastic surgeon's wife? Why her? Peter would pay for her, yes, but Peter just wasn't worth that much!

And who the hell was the green-eyed Cuban? Or Colombian, or whatever he was?

Involuntarily she moistened her lips with the tip of her tongue and squirmed uncom-

fortably. Panic was zooming in again. The young, intense, dark-haired man had been the one to shoot up the dock and throw the burlap over her. Then everything had been a blur; her strongest memory was of a motor screeching through the night, stopping long enough for her to hear a furious volley of Spanish, then starting up again. And then someone had touched her, and naturally she had tried to escape. The dark-eyed man had first imprisoned her. But once she had been freed from the burlap it had been that same rude, green-eyed man who had imprisoned her a second time. Rude! He was much more than rude! He was brutal. He'd slapped her, subdued her, kissed her — and knocked her out. And the other man had been saying something about Peter being her husband and the scruffy Latin being her lover!

"Oh, God!"

It seemed to be absolutely all she could think of to whisper, but then, the Almighty was surely the only one who could banish her absolute confusion and growing terror.

Once again panic, a sizzling sensation inside of her that grew and swelled and overwhelmed, seemed to be taking charge. She struggled some more and realized sickly that, once again, all she achieved was a

greater misery. The knots grew tighter, and the coarse hem of the blanket tickled her nose.

She blew at it, trying to force it beneath her chin. Tears welled in her eyes, and she decided firmly that she wasn't going to cry.

And then she wondered why not. There was a group of crazy Latins outside who were intending to murder her — or worse. She'd already been mauled and bruised, and she didn't understand any of it, and she just very well might wind up shot, so why the hell shouldn't she cry?

For one minute she suddenly lay very, very still, her memory going back . . . back.

If it had been three years ago she wouldn't have cared in the least. They could have done anything, and she simply wouldn't have cared. She could remember standing over the coffins, Paul's and the baby's, and hurting so badly that she yearned to be dead, too, to be going with them, wherever that might be. She could even remember the thought; take me, God. Take me, too. There is nothing left for me, nothing at all. . . .

She'd cried then. Cried until there were no more tears, cried until she'd been numb, the only thought in her mind that it was so unfair. But of course, no one on earth could explain why life could be so horribly unfair,

41

and in time, still baffled, she'd had to learn acceptance, because the only alternative was insanity.

Peter had been there for her.

Crushed and nearly broken himself, he had still been there for her. Peter, her parents, her brother. But despite her love for her own family, Peter had been the one who somehow gave her the greatest comfort. Perhaps because his loss had been as keen: his only son, his only grandchild.

Huge burning tears were forming behind her eyes. She blinked furiously, trying to think of Peter. He was so strong, so moral. He'd never wavered under fire; he always did what he thought was right. He always went by principle. She wasn't going to cry, and she wasn't going to break. Somehow, no matter what happened to her, she would rise above these people.

She tensed, aware that someone had come below. Twisting, she could see that she was in the stern of the old sailboat. Another bunk, identical to the one she lay on, was straight across from her, and two small closets at the end of the bunks stood at the stern. There was a slatted wooden door just past her head; her entire space of confinement couldn't have been much more than fifty square feet.

Two people were somewhere beyond that door. At least two people, laughing and talking in Spanish. She strained to make out the words, but they spoke too quickly.

Why the hell hadn't she paid more attention to Spanish in school? Why? Because the teacher had been a horrible nasty woman whom everyone in the entire school had thought was creepy. She'd had the most awful way of pointing her finger and saying, *"¡Repitan, por favor!"* in a sickeningly sweet voice, and no one had paid her the least attention.

Irrelevant! Totally irrelevant right now! She'd been hearing Spanish all her life; surely she could comprehend something of what was being said, she insisted to herself.

She did. At long last she did.

*Cerveza.*

Someone was asking someone else if he wanted a beer. Great! That bit of genius would surely help her vastly!

But then she stopped worrying about her comprehension or lack thereof. Footsteps were approaching the door. Her muscles cramped with tension from head to toe, and panic sizzled through her once again.

She was helpless, absolutely helpless. Trussed like a pig on its way to the slaughterhouse. Totally, horribly vulnerable.

The door opened; she thought about closing her eyes, but too late.

One of the men ducked as he stepped through the door. He straightened too soon, cracked his head and swore beneath his breath. He turned to her and she found herself staring into his eyes.

Green eyes. Bright, startlingly . . . tense as they stared into hers.

He glanced over his shoulder quickly, then moved to kneel down beside her.

"Mrs. Blayne."

He said it in English, and she couldn't detect any hint of an accent.

"Mrs. Blayne, are you all right? Juan was assigned to watch me all night. I couldn't get back to you. Maybe he trusts me now. I'm not sure. This is important, please listen."

He was reaching toward her.

She couldn't help herself; she let out a small scream. Oh, God, what was going on? Who was he? How on earth could he be on her side when he seemed to be just like them?

The young man with the dark eyes suddenly appeared in the doorway, laughing, saying something about *amor.*

"*Amor?*" Mandy shook her head. Lover!
"N—"

A hand clamped down over her mouth,

stifling her words, stealing her breath. He twisted his head toward the man at the door and laughed, too, and when he spoke next there was an accent in his words.

"Amigo, you got a gag anywhere?"

The dark-eyed man chuckled and responded in Spanish, then turned away. Then the green-eyed stranger leaned his furious face so close to hers that she felt the whisper of his breath and the blaze of his body heat.

"Damn it! The next time I try to say something, you shut up and listen!"

There was no accent at all this time . . .

He straightened and slowly drew his hand away. Still terrified, and completely baffled, Mandy stared up at him in silence.

"Good," he murmured grimly. "Now —"

"Who the hell —" she began, then froze. He was leaning toward her again, tangling his fingers in the hair at her nape, bringing his mouth to hers. . . .

The dark-eyed man was at the door again, she realized, staring at her. And at him. At the green-eyed stranger.

Who was kissing her again. Pressing his mouth to hers urgently, feverishly, heatedly. Stealing away any words she might have spoken.

# 3

*Cerveza* . . .

He tasted of beer, and though she stiffened and tried to twist away, she was in that horrible position of helplessness, chin caught by his powerful hand, mouth overpowered by his.

But beyond the terror, beyond the fury, beyond that awful helplessness, the kiss wasn't that bad.

Wasn't that bad!

Oh, Lord, she was getting hysterical. This was insane; she was going insane already. So much for inner strength. Not that bad! It was wretched; it was humiliating!

And it could get much, much worse, she reminded herself, and that was her last thought, because suddenly all the little sensations seemed to overwhelm her, and she felt as if she was nothing but burning kinetic energy. She felt the rasp of his bearded cheek and the warm texture of his lips, the moistness that seemed like lava, and the taut muscles of his chest, crushed hard against her breast. She felt the whisper of his breath

and thought ridiculously that he smelled rather nice, and that the slight taste of beer wasn't so awful, either, and really, she could live through this, because what other choice did she have?

The man in the doorway chuckled again, saying something and addressing the green-eyed man as Miguel.

At last "Miguel" drew away from her, but those green eyes remained on hers, as bright as gems, sparkling out a warning so potent that it might have been written on the air.

He kept staring at her as he answered the other man. What he said she didn't know, she just kept staring back into those green eyes, wishing with all her heart that she was free, not trussed and tied here so ignominiously. Wishing that she could reach up, wrench out a thatch of that ebony hair and punch him through a wall!

And then she was afraid all over again. Deeply afraid. Because every man on the sailboat could come in at any time and do anything to her, and all she would be able to do in turn was fight until her wrists bled from the cruel chafing of the rope.

She averted her eyes from his at last and suddenly realized that it was day. Ugly old curtains were pulled over the tiny portholes, but light was filtering in nevertheless.

She'd slept here the night through, and of all the ridiculous things, while her life hung in the balance, she was suddenly and desperately the recipient of nature's call. They were still prattling away, so she burst out in interruption, "I have to go to the bathroom."

They both stopped speaking and stared at her.

"*¡Baño!*" she snapped. "I have to . . . go!"

Then they both stared at each other and started laughing again. Miguel said something; the other man, addressed as Julio, shrugged, then turned away.

She cringed as Miguel pushed aside her hips with his own so he could sit and lean over her. He gave a disgusted oath, granted her another sizzling glance and moved on to his objective: freeing one of her wrists.

She breathed a little more easily, closed her eyes and prayed for strength, and said carefully, "Who are you?"

He glanced back toward the door quickly, then whispered, "For God's sake, trust me! Go along with me!"

Julio was back; she couldn't say anything more. Actually, she could have, because she didn't trust Miguel in the least, but somehow she chose not to.

He kept working on her wrist. She gazed

past his broad bare shoulder to Julio. "Señora Blayne," he told her, "we really do not wish to hurt you. If you can behave, you will be well. Miguel says he can handle you —"

She couldn't help but interrupt. "Oh, he does, does he?" she asked, flashing Miguel a glance of pure loathing.

"And for your sake, señora, I hope he speaks the truth."

Her right hand fell free. Miguel clutched it, inhaling with concern at the rope burns there. She tried to snatch it from him, but he held tight, warning her with his eyes once again.

She clenched her teeth against the tears that threatened. He started to free her other hand. When her left wrist was released he moved to her feet. Rubbing her wrists, she turned her head defiantly to stare at Julio.

"Why are you doing this? You're mistaken if you think that Peter Blayne is a wealthy man. He isn't. If you're asking a huge ransom for my return you won't get it."

"*Señora,* we do not want money. Money, bah, what is that? A man wants money, it is easy. He works for it."

A new fear settled over her; they didn't want money! Then . . .

Julio suddenly pounded his heart. "Freedom! You will be our ticket to freedom!"

"But . . ."

Her feet were free. Miguel was standing above her again, taking her hands.

"Let me go! I can stand by myself."

He looked as if he were going to argue with her, but he didn't. He released her, and she swung her long bare legs over the bunk and attempted to stand in a huff.

She keeled over instantly, right into his arms. And she felt those hated hands encircle her waist, holding her steady.

"Damn you." She tried to slap him, but he ducked, and she cried out when he caught her wrists. They were so sore!

Julio laughed. "You and Miguel had better make up, *señora*. Oh, you needn't worry — or pretend. We will say nothing to the senator about your affair. He might not think an unfaithful wife worth much."

"I'm not —"

"You said you had to go to the head!" Miguel snapped, his English heavily accented again.

She was certain that this ordeal had cost her her mind.

He muttered something to Julio in Spanish, then reached for her arm and

wrenched her to her feet. Julio moved out of the way, and Miguel led her roughly through the little door and three feet down a narrow hallway to another door.

"The head!" he snapped, shoving her in.

Face flaming, she slammed the door.

And then she didn't even have to go anymore. She pressed her palms to her temples, dizzy, nauseated — and scared. He'd said she should trust him. How the hell could she, and who was he, anyway?

She tried to take deep breaths, and at last she felt that at least she wasn't going to be sick. She noticed then that the facilities were quite clean, and managed to use them. The water that ran into the sink was sporadic, but clear and clean, and she splashed a lot of it over her face, thinking how good it was to rinse the salty stickiness away. She stared into the mirror over the sink and saw that her eyes were as wide as gold doubloons; her cheeks appeared far too pale beneath her tan.

Feeling dizzy again, she gripped the small sink. At last she opened her eyes and stared longingly out the circular porthole. The sailboat's outer rail hid any view of the water, but she could see the sky, and it was a beautiful blue, with just a few puffs of cottonlike clouds.

51

What a glorious day! Monday. She should have been at work by now, joining her colleagues at the site. White-smocked and gloved, she should have been up to her wrists in dirt, seeking the treasures beneath it.

Where was help? The whole dock had been chaos. Surely the police had been called. Surely someone — everyone! — knew that she was missing by now. They would have known it as soon as she had been taken; there had been witnesses all over the place!

*"Señora Blayne!"*

Her name, snapped out in a feminine voice, was followed by a rough pounding at the door.

"What?" she yelled back.

"Open the door! I will give you a robe, and you can take a shower."

Mandy gazed instantly at the tiny shower cubicle; the longing to feel clean was a strong one. She didn't know how many hours they had been at sea. She had no idea of where she was, or what the chances were that she would ever get back to civilization alive. It just didn't make any sense to turn down a shower.

Mandy threw open the door to find a young woman standing before her, a very

young woman, somewhere between eighteen and twenty-one.

What she lacked in age, though, she made up for in manner. She was beautiful in an exotic way, with flashing dark eyes and a voluptuous figure, well defined in tight jeans and a red sweater, and with a head of richly curling, near-black hair.

She was shorter than Mandy's five-feet-eight inches, which for some odd reason — she was clutching at straws! — made Mandy feel just a little bit better.

The Latin girl lifted her chin, eyeing Mandy regally, then stuffed something made of dull gray terry into Mandy's hands.

"I am Maria. Here, take this. The bathing suit is not much covering, eh?" the girl said, and once again swept Mandy with a disdainful glare. She chuckled, displaying a fine set of small white teeth beneath her generous rose-tinted lips. "Not that you have much to cover!" She shook her head. "What Miguel sees in you . . . but then, maybe he has not had enough to distract him!"

Mandy was about to tell her that she really didn't give a damn what Miguel saw in anyone. All she wanted to do was get away from the whole stinking lot of them. She decided to keep silent, though she wasn't sure

why, because she certainly didn't trust Miguel.

"Thanks for the robe," she said flatly, and closed the door, smiling bitterly as she heard the girl burst into an outraged spate of Spanish. Maria was no part of the power here, that much was obvious. She was nothing more than a young girl — uncertain, insecure, and perhaps idolizing the handsome well-built Miguel.

Mandy turned on the water; it came out cold, but she hadn't been expecting anything better. Stepping beneath the weak spray even as she peeled away her bathing suit, she started shivering vehemently — and not from the cold. Fear swept through her again as she wondered just what was going on. Who was Miguel? Who was Julio? And, for that matter, just who the hell was Maria? And if they were after "freedom" instead of money, just how did they think she could supply it?

She swallowed convulsively and found a fairly new bar of soap. She let the water run over it as she stood there behind the strangely new pink plastic curtain in a state of something akin to numbness. She didn't want to use anything of theirs, but she decided that the soap would be okay if she let the water rinse away layer after

layer in a pool of suds.

And then suddenly she began to feel better — angrier, but better. She really did have to fight them; she couldn't allow herself to be so victimized. Fight them . . . and use any means that she had. Maria's very childlike insecurity was a weapon she must remember and use.

She would get to the bottom of this! She would find out exactly what they wanted — and see that they never got it! There would be a chance for escape somewhere along the line. There would have to be!

She closed her eyes and ducked her head beneath the trickling water to rinse her hair, shaking and shivering still, but now just a bit calmer, a bit more in control. It was amazing what a cold shower could do.

But just then — just when she had convinced herself that she could survive! — she heard her name spoken again, and spoken much too close!

"Mrs. Blayne . . ."

She let out a shriek of horror, aware that the husky, low-timbred, unaccented tone belonged to green-eyed Miguel.

"Damn you!" he swore next, and she shrieked again, because his arms were suddenly around her, wrapping her in the pink plastic curtain. She dragged in a breath to

scream again, but that massive tanned hand of his was suddenly over her mouth, and to her absolute horror he was standing behind her, touching her, in the tiny confines of the shower stall.

He pulled her hard against him. All the naked length of her back was against his chest and hips; he wore only a pair of cut-offs, and she could feel with painful clarity all the rippling muscle that composed his shoulders and arms, all the short dark hair that ran riot over his chest. She squirmed, near hysteria, but she managed only to wedge her bare buttocks more intimately against him.

"Stop it, please, will you?" he begged her in a whisper, dipping his mouth near her ear. "I'll explain if you'll just —"

His hold had loosened. With a burst of strength she wriggled away from him and opened her mouth to inhale again for a frenzied scream, too frightened to realize that her scream could do nothing but bring her other captors running.

"Damn it, you're worse than a greased pig!" he rasped out, and then his hands were on her again, but far worse. Because this time, in his attempt to restrain her, his fingers closed over her breast before finding a hold against her ribs again, and he'd already

regained a smothering hold over her mouth.

Still swearing beneath his breath, he manipulated her around to face him, and that, too, was far worse, because then her breasts were pressed against his chest and her hips were horribly level with his, and she had never been forced to realize so staggeringly that a man was a man, and this one was made of iron. She almost passed out, but the water, cold and beating against her back, revived her, and she found herself tilting her head to stare into those incredibly green eyes. She realized a little belatedly that he was angry and aggravated, but intense and serious and not — apparently — about to molest her. Not any more than he already had, that was!

"Listen! I'm not going to hurt you! I had to come in here because I had to talk to you without the others hearing. Mrs. Blayne, please, promise me that you won't scream again and I'll move my hand."

Promise that she wouldn't scream. . . .

She wasn't sure that she could. The screams just kept building inside of her. She was standing naked in a two-by-two cubicle, crushed against a near-naked stranger with the muscled build of a prizefighter. Screaming was instinctive!

"Please!" he urged her again.

She didn't know why she nodded at last. Perhaps because she didn't have any choice. And perhaps because she wanted to believe him, because she wanted to trust someone. Perhaps it was something in his eyes that promised pride and integrity and sincerity. Perhaps it was because she would pass out and pitch helplessly against him, if she didn't breathe soon. . . .

Slowly he eased his hand from her mouth. His eyes slipped from hers for just a moment, traveling downward, then upward once again, locking with hers.

"Mrs. Blayne," he whispered, "I'm a cop. If you want to come out of this, play along with me. I'm all that can stand between you and —"

"A cop!" she gasped incredulously. A cop? The hell he was! Where was his badge? Where was his gun? Cops didn't help kidnappers. They didn't assault the victims!

"Mrs. Blayne, I'm with —"

"If you're a cop," she demanded, shaking, realizing all over again that she was naked with him in a tiny space, "where's your badge?"

"I dumped it. I lost my gun coming after —"

"Get out of here!" she snapped suddenly, aware that hysteria was rising in her again.

"Cops don't crawl into the shower with kidnap victims! They don't —"

She hadn't realized how her voice was rising until his hand fell over her face again, shutting her up.

"*Shh!* Are you trying to get us both killed? If they even get a whiff of who I am, I'll become shark bait, lady. And I'll be damned if I think you're worth it!"

Her eyes widened. Could it possibly be true? His Spanish had been perfect; his English, when he spoke to her alone, had no accent whatsoever. Yet when he spoke to Julio, he sounded as if he was barely comfortable with the language. Like a chameleon, he could change in the wink of an eye. . . .

"Eh? Miguel?"

They both froze as someone rapped on the door again and called out to Miguel. A barrage of Spanish followed. Miguel held still for a moment, then called something back, something that she didn't understand a single word of.

Footsteps moved away from the door. Mandy was crushed so tightly to his chest that she felt the expulsion of his breath and the rapid beating of his heart.

He stared down at her then with absolute dislike and fury. Still holding her to him, he reached around and turned off the water; it

seemed that his striking eyes became razors that sliced right through her.

"Listen to me, lady. Listen good. I'm a cop — whether you believe it or not. Go along with me. I'm only going to warn you once, because, honey, I can bail out of this thing real easy by myself. I spent all night talking my heart out to convince them that I'm a refugee, too, that I was your gardener, that you're married to a man twice your age, and therefore became involved with me hot and heavy. They didn't take you to kill you or rape you. Julio Garcia is a desperate man, but fairly ethical, for a kidnapper. I don't trust his companions all that far, however. Julio decided to keep me around because he thinks I can keep you under control. Blow that, and we could both be dead. Pull one more stunt against me and I swear I'll jump overboard and swim out of this thing. I don't mind sticking around to fulfill my job, but I'll be damned if I'll keep worrying about getting killed *because of* you instead of *for* you!"

She stared at him, shaken by his anger, shaken by the intensity of his words. Was he really a cop? Or was he one of *them*, just a little more educated, a far better actor? What a way to control a captive, to convince her that a cop was with her and on her side!

He shook her suddenly. "Do you understand?"

She lowered her eyes, then closed them quickly. All she saw when she looked down was his muscled and hairy male chest, slick and hard against her breasts. And of all things, she felt her nipples harden against him.

"Yes!" She gasped, trying to escape him, but he held her against him, and she shook in sudden horror and confusion. "Yes! No! I don't understand any of this. I —"

"Just go along with me now! Julio just said to get the hell out, lunch is ready. I don't have time to try to convince you any further."

He released her completely and stepped out of the shower stall, finding a towel to dry his slick shoulders and chest. He didn't look back at Mandy but stuffed the towel toward her, then found the gray terry robe and shoved that to her over his shoulder.

Quivering and confused, Mandy hurriedly accepted the towel, though she didn't bother to dry herself thoroughly, and fumbled into the robe. It was worn and fell to her feet, but it didn't make her feel especially secure. She wrapped it around herself as tightly as she could, then knotted the belt.

His back was still to her, but just inches

away. Beneath his tan she noted a smattering of freckles across his shoulder and thought them curious, considering his coloring.

Oh, God! Who the hell was he really?

"Are you decent?" he asked her.

She started to laugh, but caught herself quickly, afraid that if she got started, she would never quit. "You didn't worry whether I was 'decent' or not when you charged into the shower!" she accused him.

"Shh! Damn you!" he said in a vehement whisper, whirling around, hands on hips, to face her.

Her lip started to tremble, but she didn't intend to let it. She tossed back her head and stared at him dubiously. "Do cops always run around in the pursuit of duty with no weapons, no ID and no shoes?"

He groaned impatiently. "I told you —"

"Oh, I know what you told me," she said. "I'm just not sure I believe a word of it."

He closed his eyes and sighed, then stared at her in exasperation. "Gamble, then. You're with me, or you're not. But if you're against me, remember, I'm gone."

"Gone? From where?" she demanded.

"From wherever we are. Near Cat Cay, I think. I'm a hell of a good swimmer. A dive overboard, that's all it would take. They

don't watch me like they're going to watch you."

"And why the hell should they trust you?"

"Because I know how to play this game, lady," he said grimly.

"Either that, or you're one of them."

He smiled with a certain malicious humor and advanced those few inches to her, rounding his fingers over her shoulders so that she almost screamed again from the pure electricity of that touch.

Never had she seen anything as intense, as compelling, as frightening — as dangerous! — as the kelly green blaze of his eyes. She couldn't speak; she couldn't have screamed even if it had been her most ardent desire. She could only stare at him in silence.

"Lady, place your bet quickly. We've got to go now, unless you want Julio in this head along with the two of us! If I were you, though, I'd change my tune — quickly. I'd admit to this ignoble affair and cling to me as if we'd been passionately involved for ages! Hey —" he cocked his head, daring her "— you might not like your other options. Julio is fairly ethical, but those other two have been talking about your *senos* all day."

"My — my what?" Mandy swallowed.

"Breasts, Mrs. Blayne. They're quite entranced with . . . them."

She started to jerk away, and he laughed without a trace of amusement. "Like I said, there's only so far I'll go for you if you won't cooperate. So have it your way. I'm a fugitive like the others, probably a murdering rapist. Take me — or leave me."

She swallowed again, lowering her eyes, desperately trying to decide whether to trust him or not. She didn't. . . . But what were her options?

He'd kissed her, struck her, abused her! But not done half of what he might have, she reminded herself.

He was already reaching for the door. She clutched his arm, and he turned back to her, arching a dark brow.

"If you're really a cop, why can't you overpower them? Why can't you arrest them?"

"Oh, God help me!" he breathed, looking heavenward. "Mrs. Blayne, should I really introduce myself as a police officer? And arrest them? Now that's a laugh. I'll say, 'Hey, let's go to jail.' I haven't got a weapon on me, but they'll just say, 'Sure, let's go, you want to put us in jail, fine.' "

Mandy flushed. "But you should be trying. . . ."

"I *am* trying!" He swore heatedly. "I'm trying to keep you alive — and I'm trying to stay on top of you myself to keep these guys

from deciding that, hey, they have you, so what the hell . . . if you catch my meaning, Mrs. Blayne. Although God knows you seem to be strange enough! Maybe you'd enjoy their attentions. Did you marry Peter Blayne for his money? Yeah, I could be way off. Maybe you'd enjoy the excitement."

"What?" Stunned, outraged, she shrieked the word.

She should have learned not to shriek by now. He slapped a hand over her mouth before she could blink and drew her against his hard length in a frightening manner, staring down at her with danger sparking from his eyes.

"Shut up!"

Shut up? She had no choice. So she blinked, realizing that this man — this cop? — thought she was the senator's wife, just as the others had assumed. He actually assumed that she'd married an older man for money. Oh, how dare he!

His hand moved from her mouth. She smiled very sweetly, narrowing her eyes. "No, Miguel. I married Peter Blayne because he's fabulous in bed, and I don't need any excitement! So lead on. Just keep your hands off me and I'll be as quiet as a mouse."

He grinned crookedly, and she was star-

tled at the effect of his expression on her. He was a handsome man, really handsome. Dark, tall, broad, muscled, sexy and very physical. And fascinating, with those strange bright eyes. And when he looked at her in that dry, insinuating fashion she felt an involuntary sizzle sweep through her. One she instantly denied, vehemently denied. She was still in love with a memory, still convinced that only a deep and rich emotion could ever create such steaming awareness. . . .

She closed her eyes, dizzy. What if he wasn't a cop? And what if he was?

It was insane. Was she cracking already? So weak that she was willing to cling to anyone — especially anyone male and muscled — because she was scared? She wasn't. She wasn't!

His scent was all around her, the roughness of his touch, that feel of steel in his arms. She wanted to trust him.

"Mrs. Blayne," he said softly, with a touch of amusement, "I won't touch you, but I suggest that you *do* touch me now and then. You were having a passionate affair with me, remember?"

"Why . . . why," she whispered, head lowered, "would they believe that? Why would they believe that you would risk

your life to be with me?"

He chuckled dryly. "Because Latins are a passionate people, Mrs. Blayne. They usually love deeply, hate deeply — and possess their women as loyally and heatedly as they do their pride."

She stared at him, searching his features, seeking an answer, and she prayed that she wasn't a victim more of his arresting features and eyes than she was of the circumstances.

"Are you Latin?" she asked him.

"Half," he answered curtly.

"Miguel!"

The call came from very near the door. Had they been overheard? Mandy started to shiver all over again. If he *was* here to help her and she caused him to be murdered, she would never forgive herself in a thousand years — even if he was an SOB.

Damn him! She wouldn't tell him that she wasn't Peter's wife, either!

"Let's go!" he hissed.

She nodded. He took her hand, and she didn't resist him, but just before he opened the door he twisted his handsome head ruefully toward her and mouthed out a quick query.

"I almost forgot. What's your name?"

"Blayne! You know —"

"Your first name, stupid!"

"Amanda!"

"Mandy?"

"Only to friends," she said pointedly.

He smiled. "And lovers, Mrs. Blayne? Mandy, let's go!"

## 4

Lunch consisted of a salad and *arroz con pollo*, chicken and rice, served belligerently to Mandy and charmingly to Miguel by Maria and another woman, up on deck.

Mandy had tried her hardest to assimilate the layout of the craft during her quick walk through the hall to the steps leading topside. There hadn't been much to assimilate. The vessel was old, at least forty years, worn, but well-kept. There were another two sets of sleeping quarters past the head, then a shabby salon and a galley, and to the extreme aft, the captain's cabin.

The older woman had stared at Mandy with extreme disapproval as they moved through the galley. Mandy had ignored her, but she hadn't been able to ignore the smell of the food; the aroma was captivating, and she was forced to realize that she was starving.

The deck of the motorized two-masted sailboat was lined with old wooden seats, and that was where Miguel led her. Mandy kept her mouth shut for several minutes

while she perused her surroundings and her curious party of abductors.

There was Julio, called Garcia by the others; the young woman, Maria; the older woman; and two more men, one a heavyset fellow with a swirling mustache, the other gaunt and hungry-looking. Mean, Mandy thought, and far different from Julio Garcia, who, strangely, had the look of a poet.

They all laughed and chatted in rapid Spanish, drinking Michelob out of bottles and eating off paper plates as if they were simply out for a picnic at sea.

Including Miguel. He laughed and chatted along with the others, tensing only slightly beside her when some apparently ribald comment was made about her by either the man with the mustache — Juan, she thought his name was — or Roberto, the gaunt man with the lascivious eyes.

If Miguel was on her side, he certainly knew how to enjoy himself in the interim. He ate with a hearty appetite, complimenting the two women on their cooking. So far Mandy hadn't been able to pick up more than a word or two of the conversation, but mannerisms were universal, and it was easy to tell that Miguel was managing to fit right in. There was only one difference between him and the other men: they were

carrying large guns in shoulder holsters.

Miguel had none. He was still barefoot, bare chested, clad in his wet cutoffs, assuring her that he could not be hiding a weapon anywhere on his person.

She turned her gaze to the ocean surrounding them, wondering how far they had come, and in what direction. Miguel had told her that he thought they were near Cat Cay, which meant the Bahamas. She saw nothing around them right now but the sea and sky, and her heart sank in desolation. She might never be found, never be rescued! There might well be hundreds of uninhabited islands in this stretch of the ocean. She'd been taken away in a little speedboat, and now she was on an old sailboat. The police — if they could even look for her now that they were out of American waters! — wouldn't even know what they were looking for.

The police!

She twisted her head slightly and stared at Miguel, seated so casually beside her, idly holding his beer and laughing at one of Roberto's jokes. Was he really a cop? It was hard to believe at the moment! He was taller, stronger, tougher than the other men, muscled but trim, lean and mean-looking. If he was a cop, why the hell hadn't he done something?

She told herself that no amount of muscle could combat a bullet, that maybe he was doing his best just to keep them both alive. It was hard, though, even if she realized that half her problem was that she resented him heartily for assuming that she was Peter's wife and that, being younger, she had latched on to him for material reasons.

And maybe she also resented him out of sheer frustration. By God, he was physically beautiful. His stomach was taut, his legs long and hard, his shoulders those of an Atlas.

That dark hair; those flashing eyes, emerald in the sun; that handsome face, high boned with arching dark brows, teeth pearly white against the full sensual curve of his mouth. . . . Not even the thick shadow of beard detracted from his looks. He seemed like a bulwark of character and strength — and he wasn't doing a damn thing for her! Just chatting away in Spanish and drinking his *cerveza!*

Maria collected his empty plate, and he stretched his free arm around Mandy. She tried not to stiffen; it was a casual gesture, and she decided she would rather trust him than be left vulnerable to Roberto's naked ogling.

Maria took Mandy's plate less than gra-

ciously, eyeing her maliciously, and to Mandy's own surprise she returned that nasty glare and inched closer to Miguel.

"Mandy." He spoke softly and she jumped, turning to look up at him. "You want something to drink?"

The accent was back in his words.

"Ah, yes. A diet Pepsi, please."

He started to laugh. "What do you think this is? They've got beer, water, guava juice and Coca-Cola. 'Classic', I believe."

She recognized his dry humor and just barely held her temper in check. "A Coke!" she snapped.

He started to translate her request to Maria, but Maria snapped, "I heard her," then disappeared below.

Maria returned with the soda and sat staring pointedly at Mandy. The older woman said something to her, which she ignored; then Julio grated out something impatiently and the two women — along with Roberto, Mandy noticed gratefully — went below deck. Mandy sipped her Coke, thinking that a soda had never tasted so delicious before. She stared around again, tensing as she realized that there was a small island on the horizon, and that a pleasure boat was anchored just beyond its beach.

How far away was it? she wondered yearn-

ingly. Three miles — or five? And did it really matter? If she had to, she could manage a five-mile swim. . . .

"So, Señora Blayne, you are resigned to our company, sí?"

She started, forced into an awareness that the oddly genteel Julio Garcia was watching her.

"Resigned?" she queried regally, ignoring the pinch of Miguel's fingers suddenly tightening around her shoulders. "Not in the least. Perhaps," she added sarcastically, "you'd be so kind as to explain to me just what you're after so that I may become . . . resigned!"

Julio gazed curiously at Miguel then returned his dark soulful eyes to hers. "Miguel has not explained it to you?"

"She gave me no chance, this one!" Miguel pulled her closer against him, irritating her beyond belief by playfully fluffing her hair. She stiffened against him, but his hold was a powerful one for all its casual appearance, and she had no recourse except to smile grimly at Julio Garcia.

"I haven't the faintest idea of what is going on."

Julio shrugged and grimaced. "Your husband betrayed me, Mrs. Blayne. He swore to have my father freed. Empty promises."

74

My husband is dead, she thought with fleeting pain, and he never betrayed anyone in his life.

"My fath— my husband," she amended quickly, "is a senator, not a warden! What are you talking about?"

"He is still in prison! Jorge Garcia — statesman, poet, one of the finest, most courageous freedom fighters ever to live! — still rots in prison! Peter Blayne promised to have something done. He said to trust in the law! Well, I have tried his laws for years! Ever since the Mariel boatlift —"

"Wait a minute!" Mandy interrupted in a burst of passion. "Are you trying to tell me that your father was a prisoner — a criminal — in Cuba, but that we should let him roam free in the United States?"

"*Idiota!*" Julio shouted, then went on in an irate shouting spree.

"Julio, Julio! She does not understand!" Miguel said, trying to soothe him.

Mandy was more furious than ever. She couldn't believe that this whole thing was over another criminal! "Don't swear at me in Spanish! Say it in English. *No hablo español!* This is the United States of America —"

Suddenly that long-fingered sun-bronzed hand was over her mouth again, and bril-

liant green eyes were boring into hers. "*Quieta! Cerra la boca,* Amanda!" Miguel snapped. "You want English? Shut your mouth. You don't understand! Julio, I will take her forward and explain, eh?"

Julio exploded into rapid speech again, pulling his gun from his holster and waving it around. Mandy inhaled deeply in shock as Miguel dragged her to her feet, his hand still over her mouth, and half led, half dragged her to the few clear feet of space that surrounded the main mast.

"Damn you!" he grated out tensely, releasing her mouth at last, but only to grip her shoulders and stare down at her like the wrath of God while he spoke. "Are you trying to get us both killed?"

She tossed her hair back. "He's crazy! I won't —"

"Yes, he's crazy! And that's exactly why you'd better start paying a little heed. Don't you know this story? Doesn't your husband ever talk to you about his work?"

Her husband? Oh, Peter . . .

Yes, Peter talked to her. But she'd been so involved with her own work lately that she hadn't really seen him in a while. She shook her head stiffly. "I don't know anything about any of this! Except that if Peter has refused to let some murderer roam the streets, then —"

He took a deep breath, a bitter breath. "For your information, Mrs. Blayne — Mrs. Bigot! — not everyone who came in on the Mariel boatlift was a murderer!"

"I am not a bigot! But don't you dare try to tell me that Castro didn't empty his prisons on the U.S.!"

"Oh, great! So everyone who is Cuban —"

"I didn't say that!"

"But you meant it!"

"The hell I did!"

"What are you, the head of the DAR, Mrs. Blayne? Your impeccable bloodlines go back to the *Mayflower*, I take it!"

"As a matter of fact," Mandy lied coolly, "they do!" She suddenly felt as if she was going to burst into tears. She hadn't meant to offend him, but she'd be damned if she would be responsible for putting a criminal — be he Irish, German, Spanish or all-American — back on the streets.

Her lashes fell over her eyes; she didn't understand why this terrible antagonism had suddenly erupted between them. He was her lifeline, however tenuous. She was simply terrified, and trying not to be.

Frightened, but determined to be strong. And there were so many chinks in her armor!

He was still angry, but was holding his

temper in check. He spoke flatly to her, still holding her shoulders, his voice very distant.

"Jorge Garcia was not a murderer, a rapist, or even a thief. He was a political prisoner, but the charges trumped up against him could have sent him before a firing squad. He was, once upon a time, a brilliant man. Rich and a philanthropist, a lawyer, a scientist. He still had a few friends in the Castro regime, but even so his enemies managed to have him labeled as dangerously insane. He was sent out on the Mariel boatlift and consequently wound up with dozens of other cases, waiting to be reviewed by the immigration board."

"You're trying to tell me that Julio's father is not just a good man but a great one?"

"From all I've heard, yes."

She shook her head, her temper growing. "So we're at fault! The Americans are at fault, and it's okay for Julio to attempt to assassinate Peter and kidnap me."

"I didn't say it was all right! Julio has obviously snapped. Yes, gone mad, in a way. Apparently he's been frustrated half to death. It doesn't make him right. It just explains his behavior. You can't do anything — your husband probably couldn't even have done anything, no matter how hard he tried, ex-

cept speed up some paperwork."

"Then why are you yelling at me?"

"I'm not yelling!"

"You sure as hell are!"

He released her shoulders abruptly. "Excuse me, Madame DAR. It's my Latin temper, you know."

"You're stereotyping yourself — not me!" Mandy snapped.

"I'm not trying to do anything except get us both out of this. I'm a cop, not a lawmaker, and not a politician. I don't even know what I'm doing here myself! But, Mrs. Blayne, please, if you're at all interested in living, please don't get into moral fights with Julio Garcia!"

She stared at him, then tossed her head. From the corner of her eye she glimpsed the island she had seen before — and the massive pleasure craft anchored right before it.

"I, uh, won't argue with Garcia anymore," Mandy said absently.

"Good. I don't think he wants to harm anyone. I —"

He broke off, frowning, as excited shouts suddenly came from the aft deck.

"Let's see what's up," Miguel murmured, and he started back. Mandy didn't follow him. She stood dead still where she was, feeling the ocean breeze,

feeling the sun on her face.

The boat wasn't far away. No more than three miles, she was certain. And she really was a good swimmer. Her captors were so excited about whatever was happening off their own craft that she could probably be halfway to that other vessel before anyone even noticed that she was gone.

She hesitated just a second longer, thinking of Miguel. She didn't want to worry about him, yet she did. She had the sneaking suspicion that his presence had saved her from sexual abuse by the leering Roberto, and she didn't want him harmed on her behalf.

But he had managed to make himself one of them. They wouldn't kill him. At least, she convinced herself in those moments that they wouldn't. And if he was a cop, he would know how to take care of himself. She had a chance to escape, she didn't dare risk losing it.

She moved at last, staring forward. They were all there now: the two women, Roberto, Juan, Julio — and Miguel.

"A bloodbath!" she thought she heard someone say. But she wasn't really listening — or thinking.

Quietly she moved portside, stepped to the rail and dove into the water.

It was a good clean dive. The gray robe bulked around her somewhat, but to obtain her water safety certification every three years she'd had to swim a mile in her clothes — shoes, too — so the robe shouldn't be that bad. And of course she could always ditch it. And arrive at a strange boat stark naked. What a thing to think of at a time like this! Swim . . .

She broke the surface and took a breath, stroking smoothly, aware that she would have to pace herself to make the distance. Stroke, breathe, stroke, breathe. The sun was high in the sky, warm; the water was almost as warm as that sun, and very blue here, where it was deep. It felt good to swim, to feel the salt against her face, to feel the promise of freedom. . . .

She cocked her head, inhaling, stroking, and heard shouts distantly from behind her. She clenched her teeth in dismay, having hoped to gain more distance before they discovered her absence.

She paused for a second, treading the water, to see what was happening. She was shocked to see that they were all watching her — not angry, but pale as a troop of ghosts.

"Stop, Amanda! Stop!"

It was Miguel shouting, and as she turned

to begin swimming again with stronger strokes, she swore inwardly. Damn him! He'd said he was on her side, but he was the one standing on the rail, ready to dive after her and recapture her.

The salt stung her eyes; she felt like crying as she heard the splash of his body entering the water. He was coming after her. She renewed her strokes, still hoping she could outdistance him. She was good, she reminded herself. She really was a good swimmer. . . .

But so was he. And he was stronger. In a matter of seconds he was almost at her feet.

"Amanda! Get back!"

His hand slid around her ankle, a vise that jerked her under water, then into his arms. She choked and gagged and came up against his chest, gasping.

"Damn you! Damn you!" she shrieked, furious and ready to cry. She could have done it except for him. "I hope you rot in hell for all eternity. Liar! You son of a bitch. You —"

He still looked white and grim. He shook her. "Get back. *Now!*"

He gave her a strong shove back toward the boat. The terry robe seemed to be locked all around her now, hampering her movements. She couldn't seem to swim at

all anymore; she couldn't untangle her arms.

And Juan and Julio had already climbed into a little dinghy with no motor. They reached furiously, desperately, for the oars, then began coming toward her.

Miguel gave her another shove.

"I can't!"

He jerked at her robe; she tried to hold the sodden material while struggling to stay afloat.

"Take it off!"

She'd never heard such a fervent command. The robe was suddenly gone. "Swim!" he bellowed, shoving her.

She didn't have to swim; the dinghy was right behind her, and Julio and Juan were bending over, grasping her arms. Naked and humiliated she was lifted from the water and cast to the rotting floorboards of the tiny dinghy.

Instinctively she brought her knees to her chest and locked her arms around them, and only then did she realize that they weren't paying her the least attention — they were pulling Miguel into the dinghy after her. He landed half on top of her, dripping wet. There was nowhere to move, and when she tried to shrink closer within herself, he opened his eyes and stared at her

with such grim fury that it was as if his eyes had become a glittering inferno that meant to consume her.

He was still gasping for breath, but he threw the robe over her as he shook his head in disgust. "Stupid woman!" he muttered.

Julio muttered a few words to Juan, gesticulating with a sharp intake of breath, and it was then that she realized the awful danger she had almost encountered. Surrounding the little dinghy was an assortment of at least five fins. Shark fins . . .

And the creatures were still swimming about, thrashing, nearly upsetting the tiny dinghy.

"Sit!" Miguel snapped, and the other two men instantly obeyed.

Mandy shivered miserably beside him as he fumbled for the oars and slowly, carefully, rowed the dinghy toward the sailboat.

Oh, God! She'd nearly swum into the middle of a school of sharks! She would rather be shot ten times over than die such a gruesome death. This man had actually dived after her, pitting himself against the same danger. . . .

"Up, and carefully!" he told her tensely when they reached the boat. Julio and Juan went up the rope ladder first. Julio looked very gray, and she thought that he might be

a kidnapper, but he hadn't wanted to see her die — not that way! "Up!"

Somehow she was touching the wet rope ladder. Clinging to it. She didn't feel as if she had any strength at all.

He was behind her, using the force of his body to protect hers against its own weakness. She closed her eyes, fighting dizziness.

She could still hear the sharks thrashing in the water. She turned back and froze in renewed fear. The water was red now. Blood red. The others had turned on one of their own kind and were ripping it apart with their huge jaws and razor teeth. . . .

"Amanda, go."

One foot after the other. Again and again. Julio was there to drag her over the rail. She pulled the robe about her shivering body and lay on the deck, spent, exhausted, and still in shock.

She saw the sun above her, slowly sinking into the west. She felt the chill of a night breeze coming on. The sky was becoming pink and crimson and beautifully gold, and the moon, pale but full, had risen even before the sun could set.

Twenty-four hours . . . it had been a full day, she thought numbly. A full day since she had been taken, and suddenly none of it mattered except for those last few minutes.

She had always thought that she would never really be afraid to die, but she was. And she would have died. In her furious quest for escape she would have stirred up the water to such an extent that the mindless beasts would have found her — except for him.

She was dimly aware that he had come aboard the boat, dimly aware that tense Spanish was being spoken in bursts all around her.

She opened her eyes. Maria, her huge almond eyes ablaze, was staring down at her. She spat on the deck, then began speaking again.

*Puta.* That was one word Mandy recognized. Maria was screaming because Miguel had almost died to save his Anglo whore. She was trash; she was not worth it.

Julio said something curtly; Maria started to speak again, but he slapped her.

Mandy knew she had acquired a serious enemy. She couldn't even care about that. She felt totally exhausted and numb, and she shivered with spasms she could not halt.

She opened her eyes once again in startled surprise when someone leaned down to her, wrapping strong arms around her.

She met glowing orbs of green: Miguel's eyes. She was too entangled in the robe to

fight him, nor did she even think that she should. She stared at him, unable to find the words for an apology, unable even to form a "thank you" on her trembling lips.

Spanish broke out all around her again, but she didn't worry about it. In absolute exhaustion she laid her head against his chest and closed her eyes again.

"I am taking her below," Miguel said determinedly, breaking into English.

"*Sí*. Do it then, *amigo*," Julio agreed.

"*Madre de Dios!*" Juan swore, but Julio interrupted him.

"She will do us no good dying of pneumonia!"

Miguel walked past them with Mandy in his arms. She opened her eyes just before they came to the steps.

Night had almost fallen. It seemed to come so quickly out here on the water. Only a few stretches of gold and crimson lay against the eternal sea and sky. And then, as if they had been a delusion, those colors faded to black.

They moved through the galley, through the salon, down the hall. He used his foot to kick open the door, then laid her on the narrow bunk, swathing her in the blanket, holding her, his eyes enigmatic, only the pulse in his throat displaying any emotion.

"I — I'm sorry —" Mandy began.

"I swear to you," he interrupted her, "I *am* a cop! If you trust me, I'll get you out of this!"

He had every right to be furious, she knew. He'd put his own life on the line — for her. She shivered all over again, knowing she would never have had the nerve to dive into the water if she had known about all those sharks.

Suddenly there was a rapping at the door. Miguel stood quickly and opened it.

The older, gray-haired woman was there, a wooden tray in her hand. She spoke Spanish softly and gazed down at Mandy with the closest thing to sympathy that she had yet seen.

The woman lifted the tray, offering it to Miguel.

*"Gracias, gracias,"* he told her, then she asked him something, and he answered her, stepping aside to allow her to enter the room. She sat down by Mandy's side, touched her forehead and cheeks, offered a weak smile, then wagged a finger beneath Mandy's nose, giving her a motherly scolding. She touched Mandy's cheek once again, shivered and then left.

"What . . . ?" Mandy began, struggling to sit.

Miguel stuffed a shot glass of amber liquid into her fingers. "Drink it — it's rum. It will stop the chill."

She couldn't drink it. "Miguel . . ."

"Señora Garcia," he told her, wrapping his fingers around a second shot glass and setting the tray on the opposite bunk, "is not at all happy that her son took you. They meant to take your husband. Drink that!"

"Miguel . . ."

"Mrs. Blayne, by tomorrow they plan to reach some remote and private island where they have a little cottage. Juan will then return to Miami with the ransom note. Obviously your husband won't have any real power to give the Garcias what they want, but negotiations will start. At that time they will also be one man short. They don't want to hurt you. If you would have just one bit of faith in me and give me a little time, I could manage to settle this thing without risking your life."

"Miguel . . ."

"Drink that!"

She brought the shot glass to her lips with still-trembling hands, then gasped at the potency of the liquor, choked and coughed. He sat beside her and patted her back, but with little mercy. He tilted the glass toward her lips again.

"All of it!"

On her next try she drained the glass. He took it from her hands as she wheezed for breath once again. He swallowed his own without a grimace, haphazardly returned both glasses to the tray, then turned back to her.

He touched her lip, her cheek. "Good," he said. "You've got a little color back."

She lowered her head, her fingers plucking at the blanket. "I'm sorry. I had to do it." She moistened her lips and stared at him again. "Thank you," she whispered stiffly. "You saved my life."

"Line of duty," he told her, his eyes narrowing peculiarly on her hand. He clutched it, looking at the raw marks that still surrounded her wrists. "Do they hurt?" he asked, staring into her eyes again.

She shook her head. It was only a little lie.

The door suddenly burst open to reveal Julio Garcia. He gave a curt order to Miguel. Miguel shook his head vehemently. Chills of fear crept over Mandy again; she knew that they were arguing about her. Her wrist was suddenly shoved up toward Julio's face. He hesitated, then said something back to Miguel. Miguel glanced her way curiously then nodded to Julio. Then Julio, too, was gone, snapping out the cabin light as he went.

Darkness fell all around them. Mandy knew that she was still shivering, that he was still staring at her in the darkness.

"What . . . what was that all about?" she asked faintly.

"He wanted me to tie you up again."

"You tied those knots?"

"Yes. I had to make them good."

She sniffed in the darkness. "They *were*."

He didn't reply at first. Then he merely said, "Move over."

"What?"

"Move over. I can tie you up, or sleep next to you."

Something rebelled inside her. She wanted to tell him to tie her up, that she would rather suffer through that again than have him sleep beside her.

But she didn't. She didn't ever want to experience that panicky feeling of being so helplessly bound again. She didn't want the rope chafing her flesh until it was raw. And she felt so horribly tired and exhausted.

She moved as close as she could to the paneling that rimmed the bunk, painfully aware of his length and heat as he crawled in beside her. He didn't say a word. In time her eyes adjusted to the darkness and she realized that he was lying there very stiffly, hair still damp from his dive into the water, his

profile clean and fascinating as he stared upward into the night.

"Miguel?" she whispered softly.

"What?"

"I really am sorry. I felt that I had to try. . . .
It isn't that I distrust you so much, it's just
that the opportunity was there. Thank you. I
mean it. And I'm terribly sorry about
putting you in danger."

She felt him shrug. The narrow bunk was
barely wide enough for one person; two
would necessarily feel each other's slightest
movement.

"It's okay," he returned in the darkness.
And then he was silent again.

"I know you're angry —"

"I'm not angry." He rolled toward her and
touched her cheek in the darkness, lightly,
for the briefest moment. Then he jerked his
hand away from her, as if remembering
something.

"I know what it's like to run for freedom,
Mrs. Blayne. To seek escape at any cost. Go
to sleep. You'll need rest and awareness,
should another opportunity come along."

She swallowed and nodded, but knew she
would never sleep. Escape . . . freedom.
They seemed like hollow empty echoes now.
He knew what it was like. That was what he
had said.

She wished fervently that he was not beside her. And yet she was fervently glad of him, too. Of the feel of heat and strength.

She might detest him for some of the things he had said and done, but he was on her side; she had to believe that. And even if she feared him just a little in the deepest recesses of her heart, she could not help but admire him and believe in him.

Only a fool — or a very brave man — would dive into water teeming with sharks to save a woman who had done nothing to deserve it of him.

Sleep was impossible. She lay there miserably for hours and hours, not daring to move, not daring to get any closer to him.

Memories drifted in and out of her mind, good ones, bad ones, some from the distant past, some more recent. She couldn't tell if the man beside her slept, or if he continued to stare into the darkness, lost in the recesses of his own mind.

Somewhere in the night exhaustion and nerves overwhelmed her and she fell into a restless sleep. But even there the memories plagued her. Her son's tiny coffin seemed to float in space, and then the larger one, Paul's. Then the coffins began to change. Darkness and shadow became red, dripping red, blood red, and she could hear and see

the terrible gnashing teeth of the sharks. . . .

"Shh, shh! It's over! I'm beside you . . . you're all right!"

She stiffened, unaware that she had cried out, biting her lip.

"Mandy, go back to sleep. Easy . . ."

His hand was on her hair; his body was like a heat lamp next to hers. His voice was like the soothing whisper of an ocean breeze.

And maybe because she was still half-lost in a shadow land herself, she allowed herself to listen to that whisper, to be soothed by that strong masculine touch.

She sighed softly.

"You're all right," he whispered again. "It was just a dream."

The tension fell away from her body, and she slept. And this time no dreams came to plague her, just the pleasant sensation of being held safely in strong arms.

## 5

In the morning she came awake with a curious sense of peace, followed by a haunting disillusionment.

The senses could play such tricks upon the mind! She'd awakened to so many brilliant mornings feeling the lapping of waves, the movement of the ocean beneath her, the coolness of the dawn, and salt-flavored air all around her. Awakened smiling, warm, secure, content, her husband's arm wrapped around her, the lazy tempo of a night's anchorage away from the bustle of the city like a blissful balm.

All the things that went with it came back to her: laughter from above; calls that the "sleepyheads" should awaken; the smell of sizzling bacon — and then whispers. Whispers because Peter would be telling Miranda that the kids should be up, and Miranda would be hushing him, lowering her voice still further, and reminding him that the "kids" were still newlyweds, and newlyweds didn't spring right up from bed; they liked to stay there a while.

And of course by then Mandy and Paul would both be awake, staring at each other, giggling and trying very hard to shush each other so that his concerned parents wouldn't hear them. Then they would shoot out of bed anyway, because Jonathan would have awakened by then, and they were both still so overawed at being parents that they sprang to attention the second he opened his tiny mouth and let out his earsplitting cry.

Then they would be grabbing for robes, because the older Blaynes would come bursting in, so overawed at being grandparents that they too sprang to instant attention.

And then the bacon would burn, and it would have to be started all over. But it wouldn't matter, because they would have all weekend to dive and snorkel and swim and fish and play, and the real world would be miles away. The *Flash Point* would be their fantasyland until they all returned to their responsibilities.

Mandy opened her eyes and felt a nearly overwhelming hopelessness sweep through her. Those times were gone, Miranda was gone, Jonathan was gone and Paul was gone. She blinked against the sudden agony of reality. She hadn't felt this way in ages; she'd

learned to insulate herself, to remember the good times, to find other things in life. She could even laugh aboard the *Flash Point*, bring flowers to the cemetery and smile as she remembered her infant son's beautiful smile.

It was this boat; it was this stinking boat. It was so much the opposite of all that had been beautiful. She was a prisoner, not a beloved wife, not an adored daughter-in-law, doted upon by her husband's happy parents. This was a rotting hulk, not the graceful *Flash Point*. It was all a mockery. There wasn't a grain of truth in any of the sensations.

Except that, rotting hulk or not, this vessel rolled on the sea just like any ship. The sea, the sky, the salt air — they were never ending. No matter what came and went in life, they would remain the same. But the warmth . . .

Mandy rolled over quickly. Miguel had taken the sodden robe off her when he put her on the bunk. Now she was barely covered by the worn blanket he had bundled around her. She was still warm, still warm from his body heat, gone now, but haunting her as thoroughly as the dream.

Mandy pulled the blanket back to her chin, wondering at the anguished stream of

emotions he could elicit from her. She felt drawn like the proverbial moth to the candle, but she felt a little ashamed, too. He'd dragged her around half-naked — completely naked actually — bound her, knocked her out, reviled her — and saved her life. She knew exactly what he thought of her; he had said it in so many words. He'd prejudged her as a mercenary bigot, and he deserved to pay for that. Yet in his absurd way he was going above and beyond the call of duty, and he was certainly the most extraordinary man she had ever met.

And that was the main reason she resented him, Mandy thought. In the past three years she had become very independent. She'd been friends with Peter; she hadn't leaned on him. They both had their own work, and work had kept them sane.

But last night . . . last night had taught her something that she hadn't wanted to learn. Paul was gone; love was gone. Oh, every minute hadn't been perfect. They'd fought; they'd yelled. Any two people did that. Neither one of them had been able to cook worth a whit; she'd wanted a puppy; he'd thought one child was enough. Little things, big things. That was life. You just couldn't zoom through agreeing on everything. But through all those things there had been love.

She'd barely known two years of it, but it had been good and solid and real. She had known when she buried her heart and very nearly her existence with her husband and son that she could never settle for anything less — and also that she didn't ever want to know that kind of love again. The pain of loss was so unbearable, so like a set of knives that whittled and whittled away at the insides. . . .

She closed her eyes, inhaling and exhaling.

No, she didn't want to love again. And she certainly wasn't in danger of falling in love with this stranger. But it was dismaying to learn that sensation remained; just like the endless sea and sky, the basic need remained. A need to be held, to feel strength when one was failing, security when all was darkness. To admire, to respect a man, to like the feel of rippling muscle beneath her fingers, the tangy scent of sea and man, the gentle touch of fingers against her cheek.

She gave herself a furious shake, hoping to clear her mind of fantasy. She had to learn to get through these days one by one. She needed some good common sense. If only she had paid attention yesterday she would have known that the sharks were in the water and she would have never made

that ridiculous attempt to escape. She had to learn to be wary and alert — and to try to remember that this was a team effort.

She started suddenly, aware not of sound but of a presence at the door. It was open, and Miguel was standing there, watching her with a strange dark expression. She frowned, and the expression faded. He was once again the same enigmatic man she was coming to know.

"I was trying to let you sleep," he said, sauntering in. His hair was damp, and he smelled like soap, and though he was still clad in cutoffs, they were different ones, undoubtedly borrowed from one of the other men. He carried a towel-wrapped bundle, which he gave her, tossing it over the blanket to land in the vicinity of her middle.

"Clothes. They're Maria's. She wasn't very happy about lending them, but Señora Garcia told her that you couldn't run around naked."

Mandy couldn't keep a rueful smile from creeping across her lips as her lashes fell over her cheeks. "Thanks," she said softly. "And thank Señora Garcia. Is there any chance of coming up with a toothbrush?"

"Yes, as a matter of fact, there is. Check below the sink in the head, there's a nice supply. Seems Julio is a tooth fanatic. He

told me his teeth were riddled with cavities when he first came to the States. He's been trying to preserve the rest ever since."

"What about you?" she murmured.

"What?"

She kept her lashes downcast, wondering why she was so curious about him. "When you left Cuba . . ."

"I wasn't born in Cuba."

"But you said —"

"Oh, I am Cuban. Half. I just wasn't born there."

"Here?" She gazed up at him.

He grinned at her, sudden amusement in his eyes. "Here? Was I born in a boat? No. I wasn't born in the water, or in the Bahamas, which is where I'm pretty sure we are."

"I meant —"

"I was born in Dublin, Mrs. Blayne."

"Dublin! Ireland?"

He quickly brought his finger to his lips. "Would you please shush! Are you that determined to hang me?"

"No! Really, I'm sorry!"

She sat up as she spoke, and the blanket dropped to her waist.

She reached for it again quickly, embarrassed, and dragged it back around her before looking at Miguel again.

That strange expression was back . . .

dark, tense. And hungry. Suddenly she was aware of exactly what it meant. He might be a cop, but he was a man, too, a man who found her appealing. He might think very little of her as a human being, but as a woman he found her appealing. Sexually appealing.

And that fact was not something he realized with any great fondness.

She tossed her hair back, a little bit indignant, and a little bit shaken.

She suddenly felt like teasing him! It would provide revenge that seemed very sweet. After all, he thought she was a mercenary woman who had married an old man for his wealth and position. And he was thoroughly convinced that she was a complete bigot. He deserved any torture she could dish out, even if he had dived into the sharks.

"Oh!" she murmured, sweetly distressed, holding the blanket to her breasts but allowing it to fall from her back. Then she had to lower her head and smile discreetly, because she had drawn exactly the response she wanted from him. He had stiffened like a poker. His jaw had squared, and she had heard the grating of his teeth.

She cleared her throat. "Really!" she whispered softly. "I wouldn't want to hang

you at all. I appreciate everything that you've done for me!"

"For you and your husband, right?" he asked her softly.

"Peter? Ah . . . yes, of course."

She lowered her eyes again, very aware that he was doing his best to keep his distance from her because she was — in his mind — a married woman. His own assumption! Poor baby! Compelled by a sense of duty to dive into sharks after her. Compelled to sleep beside her to keep her from being bound and tied.

A part of her appreciated that sense of duty. But she didn't at all appreciate his continual jumping to conclusions about her, nor any number of his macho techniques. She'd suffered at his hands; he could damn well suffer at hers. He had taken his own sweet time to inform her that he was a cop, and he'd grabbed her in the shower to do it.

She gave him another wide-eyed innocent stare. "Do you know what the island will be like? I mean, what will the, uh, sleeping arrangements be?"

"You're stuck with me again, Mrs. Blayne. They'd set up a room for your husband. It will be yours — and mine — now."

"Oh."

"Don't worry, Mandy, love. I'll be as safe to be with as a teddy bear. Married women aren't my style. Especially —"

"Bigots?" she inquired sweetly. "A young bigot married to an old man for his money?"

"Your words."

"Ah, but Miguel! Doesn't that scare you to pieces? What if the story were close to the truth? Poor young me, married to poor old Peter! I mean, after all, think about the situation! You half attacked me at first, but then I discovered that you're my savior." Dragging the blanket with her, she came up to him, still smiling sweetly. "And here you are . . . young . . . muscled like a panther. I could just lose my mind!" she told him, lightly stroking his cheek with the tips of her nails.

He didn't move. Not a muscle. Not until he grinned slowly and snaked an arm around her so swiftly that she wasn't even aware of his intent until it was complete. She was pulled against him, while his fingers brushed tantalizingly over the small of her back and her buttocks.

"Mrs. Blayne — Mandy, darling!" he drawled in a soft and perfect parody. "Aren't you forgetting that your husband is a wonderful, wonderful lover?"

"Let me go!" she snapped. He'd meant to

call her bluff! He did, pushing her from him. "Like I said, *Mrs.* Blayne, I'll be as safe as a teddy bear."

She recovered somewhat and smiled coolly again. "Good." But she was bluffing again. Touching him had been dangerous. Coming too near him would always be like tempting fire. She had realized it too late.

"Dublin!" she muttered beneath her breath. "Like hell! Cop — I wonder."

"I am a cop."

"*Miami Vice,* I take it." She sighed elaborately. "Humph. Where is Sonny Crockett when you need him?"

"Metro Miami. Investigator, homicide. Homicide gets kidnappings and death threats. And I'm sorry about not being Sonny Crockett. Luck of the draw, what can I tell you?"

"The truth is always nice."

"That is the truth."

"You're a half-Cuban detective who was born in Dublin?"

He laughed. "I think I fascinate you, Mrs. Blayne."

"Egos like yours always fascinate." The words were out quickly; she suddenly regretted them, along with her foolish actions. "I'm sorry," she said for what felt like the thousandth time. "Really, I am. I'm alive.

I'm grateful." She couldn't help looking back up at him and shrugging. "And you're a teddy bear, if you say so."

"I am."

He was still grinning, aware that he intrigued her. And if he was bitter about what he considered her bigotry, he was also amused. It was a mixture of feelings she didn't particularly appreciate, but what did it matter? They had been cast into this situation together, she by no choice at all, and he simply because he had become a little overinvolved in his job. Besides, he could laugh at her all he wanted. She had one on him, too. She wasn't Senator Peter Blayne's wife.

His smile faded suddenly as he watched her, and he sounded tense when he spoke next. "You can, uh, take a shower and get dressed now if you want. Breakfast is on, and then we're going on to the island."

Mandy nodded wearily, reminded that she was still a captive. She whispered her next words. "Do you really know where we are?"

"Yes, I think I do."

He stiffened suddenly, and she realized that someone had come up behind him in the hall. His next words carried the heavy Spanish accent again. "Now, my love! In the

106

shower. We eat, we go!"

The door closed. She wrapped herself in the still-damp robe, collected the clothing he had given her and slipped from the cabin to the head.

She was delighted to find a stack of new toothbrushes beneath the sink, so pleased that she issued a little cry of sublime happiness. Then she paused, shivering to discover that joy could be found in such a little thing under these strange circumstances. But, she told herself wryly, it seemed that as long as she was breathing and alive there could be elation in little things, and she might do well to seek it out.

She was uninterrupted in the shower this time, though she didn't close the curtain completely but kept a wary eye on the door, determined to be prepared if someone did burst in on her. That thought made her shiver and burn all over again, and she wondered once more at the contradictory range of emotions Miguel could elicit from her. She clenched her teeth as she rinsed her face, reminding herself again that he was just a cop doing his duty as he saw it and that his opinion of her was a harsh one.

This wouldn't last long! It couldn't! If they'd met at a cocktail party she would have coolly accepted his hostile notions,

shrugged, then forgotten him. It was nothing more than the situation and her fear that were creating this horrible tendency to lean on him, to care what he thought. She didn't know anything about him. Not even his whole name. Not whether he was married or not, maybe a father of four or five. Maybe . . .

She turned the water off and dried herself quickly, then dug into the clothing that Maria had so grudgingly lent to her. Well, pooh to Maria — Mandy didn't like the clothes. The shirt was some kind of a ridiculous halter top in bright red that should have been worn in the early seventies. The cutoff jeans had been tie-dyed with a total lack of artistry and were too big, but at least they came with a ribbon belt. The whole effect was ridiculous, and Mandy thought wryly that Maria had planned it that way. For God's sake, what was the girl jealous of? Mandy wondered irritably. Then she decided she was glad she wasn't eighteen anymore; it was a hard age, when it seemed that women, especially, struggled to find security.

And then she wondered why she cared what she wore as long as she was wearing something, and why she cared one way or another about Maria's psyche, when the girl

was doing everything in her limited power to be miserable.

Chin up, kiddo, she told herself. This whole thing boiled down to attitude. The sharks had stripped away her courage yesterday; she was going to dredge it back up for today. She was caught in a nightmare vortex, but even nightmares came to an end. This, like all things, would pass.

Thus determined, she swung open the door — only to have her head-high attitude quickly lowered a peg in confusion, because it wasn't Miguel waiting for her when she emerged, but Roberto. She didn't like the way he looked at her, and she didn't like the way he reached for her arm, sliding his hand along her ribs. She jerked away from him, saying that she was quite able to walk by herself, and hurried topside with him at her heels.

The first thing Mandy saw was the island — if one could call it that. It was really nothing more than a large growth of mangroves with a few handfuls of sand creating a spit of beach. Straining her eyes against the sun and the foliage, she could see some sort of ramshackle structure.

Roberto shoved her in the back. "Move."

She did so, quickly taking a place beside Miguel, who was already eating. The food

smelled wonderful. It appeared that they were eating omelets. Even the coffee smelled rich and strong.

Maria, pouring more coffee for Julio, lowered her rich dark lashes and gave Mandy a narrow glance, sniffing delicately at her appearance. Julio barked out something to her, which brought on an immediate argument, with Maria stamping her foot and sullenly shouting and gesticulating. Julio gestured back, totally infuriated, and to her own irritation Mandy found herself inching closer to Miguel, barely aware of the arm that came around her shoulders, except that it gave her a sense of safety and security.

She didn't have the faintest idea what the argument was about, except that she was involved, and if Maria had been in control of the weapons Mandy would surely have been shot on the spot.

Señora Garcia stood up suddenly, clapping her hands over her ears and snapped out a single word. Julio and Maria both ceased their fighting instantly; Maria tossed her head in silence and stalked off below deck, while Julio slipped an arm around his mother's shoulder and spoke to her softly, apologetically.

Miguel took that opportunity to whisper to her, "Maria resents waiting on you. She

thinks that you should be made to work. Julio says that you cannot be blamed for your husband's incompetence."

"Peter is not incompetent!" Mandy snapped indignantly.

He gave her a strange gaze, then looked away. "That's rather beside the point right now, isn't it? Here comes Maria. Take your food."

Maria, still sullen, was approaching Mandy, balancing a mug of coffee and a plate at the same time. Mandy accepted the coffee and set it down with a stiff, *"Gracias,"* then held up her hands to accept the plate.

Maria — purposely, Mandy was certain — let go of the plate just short of Mandy's hands.

The hot eggs spilled over her bare legs, burning. Mandy jumped to her feet to get the scorching food off her, while Maria jumped back, ostensibly in a startled fit of apology.

It was suddenly too much for Mandy to handle; she took two furious steps forward and caught the startled Maria by the shoulders and shook her.

"You little brat! Grow up! I didn't ask to be here, you idiot! You hurt me again and I'll find a way to hurt you back!"

Maria instantly started screaming as if

Mandy had been trying to throttle her. Miguel leaped between the two, wrenching Mandy hard against his chest. Julio was shouting again in disgust, and Mandy suddenly realized with a little swallow that he was the only one who hadn't pulled out his gun. Both Roberto and a nervous Juan had their weapons aimed right at her.

She was wide-eyed with fright for a second, then she tossed her arms into the air. "You want me to behave? I'll behave! But keep that spoiled brat away from me!"

She spun around with such vengeance that she took even Miguel by surprise, returned to her seat and sipped her coffee while she wiped off her legs, looking for damage.

There was absolute silence for a moment. Then Mandy heard Julio say in English, "Clean it up, Maria."

"Me! The American whore dropped it. Julio, she half strangled me. *Me* — your cousin! — and you take her side!"

Mandy glanced up just in time to see Maria's huge almond eyes filling with tears. "Oh, for God's sake!" she snapped, and stood, doing her best to scoop up the eggs that lay on the deck onto the fallen plate. She shoved them at Miguel with a viciousness that caused him to raise one brow, but

he gave her an amused grin and a little thumbs-up sign, then turned to give the plate to Maria.

Maria looked as if she would not accept it. She opened her mouth and closed it again, then finally snatched the debris and flounced away to discard it below.

Mandy hadn't seen Señora Garcia moving, but suddenly the dignified lady was standing before her, holding another plate. Mandy hesitated; Miguel sat down beside her. "Take it," he advised softly.

She did, thanking Julio's mother with another *"Gracias."* Señora Garcia smiled grimly in return and started into a soft monologue that left Mandy staring at her, quite lost.

"The *señora* apologizes to you for Maria's behavior," Miguel told her. "The girl is her niece, and not her daughter. If she had raised her, she would not be so rude. She would be much more a lady."

Mandy didn't know what to say; she merely nodded. She liked Mrs. Garcia, but she didn't know what she thought of her as a mother. After all, she had raised Julio, and Julio was definitely a kidnapper.

"Eat," Miguel warned her. "We are going to the island."

Mandy was startled to discover that she

could eat with such an appetite; she was hungry, and the food was excellent. She finished one cup of coffee, then Señora Garcia came back over and offered her more. She asked Miguel something, and Miguel laughed.

"What?" Mandy asked.

"She asked if you wouldn't prefer Cuban coffee. I told her no."

"Did you?" Mandy asked him a little coolly. "As a matter of fact, I like Cuban coffee."

"Now and then, eh? Patronizing the locals?"

"Oh, God!" she muttered. "You're as bad as the rest of them! *You're* the damn bigot!"

"Shut up!" he told her suddenly.

"I will not —"

His fingers closed around her arm and he bent down to whisper to her tensely. "Mandy darling, we do not sound like a sweet pair of illicit lovers sitting here arguing about coffee!"

She glanced at Julio quickly and saw that he was gazing at the two of them suspiciously. She lowered her head quickly, then made a point of arguing back in a whisper that could be overheard.

"I'm sorry, Miguel, really!" She ran a finger delicately down his chest. "I'm just so

afraid of everything! And Peter will certainly find out about the two of us now. . . ." She let her voice trail away.

Miguel's eyes were on her in amazement — an amazement he quickly hid as he slipped an arm around her shoulders again. "You could always tell him the truth. You could get a divorce."

"Oh, but Miguel! I just love the money! Think what it does for us! I love making love in the Jacuzzi. I love the silk sheets, the champagne we sip — just touching one another — in the sunken garden. . . ."

She heard him swallow sharply and, despite everything, she had to lower her head with a little shiver. What was wrong with her? She should be ashamed, but all she could think was that there were certain triumphs to be gleaned in any situation!

When she raised her head again she discovered that all the men were staring at her, and that she didn't like the look in their eyes at all.

She inched closer to Miguel again and heard him swallow sharply. This time she didn't take any great pleasure in the effect she had caused.

"Well," Julio said stiffly, rising. "Juan — supplies. Roberto — get the dinghy ready. Juan — you and I will take Señora Blayne

first. You will come back for the others. Move quickly now. You'll need the day to get back." Juan rose, following orders like a trained puppy.

Mandy discovered then that she didn't want to leave Miguel's side; she was nervous, but also grateful that she would be with Juan and Julio, not Roberto. Small comfort, but all she had.

"Señora Blayne — come!" Julio had a hand extended to her; she hesitated, so Miguel prodded her slightly. She stood, but didn't take Julio's hand. He shrugged. "Starboard, Mrs. Blayne. The dinghy is ready. Mama, you come, too."

Mandy preceded him to the rope ladder and climbed over without looking back. Juan was there, ready to help her into the dinghy. She cringed at the feel of his hands on her waist, but he released her quickly, and once again she was grateful that he was not Roberto.

Señora Garcia followed her down; Juan helped her, too, with the greatest respect. Julio came next, then the dinghy moved away from the ship.

Mandy stared straight ahead, toward the island.

Sean couldn't believe his good fortune —

just Roberto and Maria left aboard with him. If he could only assure himself that the two of them were occupied he could take a chance at the ship's old radio. He'd found it easily that first night, when he sat around with the three men drinking beer and telling them his woeful tale of being madly, passionately in love with a married woman, a rich American bitch, but oh, so sweet!

"Hey, Miguel, help me!" Roberto told him. He was pulling boxes of food from the galley cabinets to the deck.

"*Sí, sí,*" Sean said agreeably and ambled down to the galley.

Maria was there. She turned and leaned against the counter, giving him a broad, welcoming grin.

"Hello," she said in a soft, sultry voice.

He smiled, because she was such a pretty kid — with such a lot of growing up to do. Circumstances, though, hadn't been in her favor. Maria had grown up in a household of political protesters. Her father and mother had died; her uncle had been jailed in the old country and then the new.

Sean felt that he could understand her, and even Julio Garcia, in a way that Mrs. Peter Blayne never would. Julio didn't know that he was wrong; in his own way he had been at war all his life. Involved in a dying

protest that knew no rules, all was fair. He was too young to remember the revolution when Castro had overthrown Batista. He only knew that suppression had given way to new suppression.

He wanted to be an American. He just didn't know how. Just like Maria. She wanted to be a woman. She wanted to be free and liberated. She didn't know how to go about fulfilling her wishes, either.

"Hi," he answered casually.

Julio had given her a little pistol, too. She had it tucked into the waistband of her very American designer blue jeans.

He was very tempted to reach for it. Maria would be incredibly easy to seduce and overpower.

But the timing was wrong. Julio and Juan had Amanda Blayne on the shore, and though Sean instinctively believed that Julio would never kill her on purpose, he just might panic and become dangerous because of his very nervousness. He hadn't quailed at all when he had riddled the dock with bullets.

Maria sauntered up to Sean and drew a bloodred nail over his naked chest. "You are stupid!" she told him huskily. "She is not for you. You will grow tired of her, yet you risk so much for her!"

He had to think about that one. She is not for you. . . .

No, she wasn't. She was a married woman. And though he had acquired a reputation for his nightlife and the chain of broken hearts in his wake, he'd always stopped short when it came to married women.

He was supposed to be distant, professional. Yet she — far beyond the situation — was making him crazy. At the moment he wished with all his heart that he'd never lost his mind and gone diving after the speedboat. He wished he'd never thought of his story. . . .

He wished that he'd never seen her face. Her perfect, beautiful, delicate Anglo face. Tawny eyes, tawny hair, tawny . . . flesh. Sun golden, sleek, curved, sensual. He wished he'd never seen her, touched her, known her, watched her, listened to her. . . .

It made professionalism damn near impossible. He even hated the fact that he liked her. Liked her brand of determination, so wholehearted that she'd been ready to swim miles in the dusk for freedom. So heated that she refused to bow to anyone — not even with a trio of guns aimed at her.

He gave himself a shake, took both Maria's hands, smiled and placed them

119

back by her sides. "*Chica,* I walk here by a slender thread already. You want your cousin to kill me for your honor?"

"Julio?" She sniffed indelicately. "If Julio were a real man we would not be in this fix. He would have taken the right man, not some *puta.*"

"Maria! Bring the food!" Roberto ordered from above.

She grimaced, but decided not to disobey the order. It seemed that everyone knew Roberto had a streak of meanness in him.

Maria disappeared above deck. Sean reached beneath the cabinet and started gathering up supplies with one hand while he reached across to the radio with the other, keeping his eyes trained on the ladder and the hatch above it.

At first he could get nothing. He had to forget the supplies and give his entire attention to the ancient radio. Finally a voice came in — and to Sean's vast relief and amazement he realized that he'd reached the Coast Guard.

Quietly he tried to give his location and discovered with little surprise that search parties had been out since they disappeared. He warned the voice over the radio that he might have to cut out quickly. He advised the man as to the number of kidnappers and

said that Juan would be coming back in to make their demands, then assured the man that the senator's wife was fine.

He was surprised by the silence that followed.

"Lieutenant Ramiro, the senator's wife has been dead over a year."

"What?" Sean shouted, then realized what he had done. He lowered his voice quickly. "She's here, with me. They nabbed her, and I came after her!"

"Oh, you've got a Mrs. Blayne all right, but she's not his wife. She's his son's widow. But he's tearing his heart out over her just the same. Just keep calm, lieutenant. It may take us some time to find you."

"I am calm," Sean retorted dryly. "I'm a ten-year vet with the force. Don't you come barging in. Garcia is as nervous as a cat."

"We'll tell the FBI. You keep a lookout. You're out of the U.S., but I'm sure they'll get complete cooperation from the Bahamian authorities. We'll advise the senator that his daughter-in-law is doing —"

Sean heard Roberto yelling at Maria as he approached the ladder. He flicked the radio off and turned back to stacking cans.

"That's enough!" Roberto snapped, holding his gun on Sean. Sean knew that Roberto didn't trust him. The man just

wasn't the trusting sort. They were a strange alliance, Roberto and Julio. Julio the idealist; Roberto the thug.

Sean stood up, shrugging. Roberto waved the gun at him. "Go up. The boat is back."

Sean obediently went up to the deck. Juan was back with the dinghy, and Maria was handing the supplies over the rail to him.

"I'll help," Sean told her.

"*Gracias,* Miguel," she purred softly.

He took over her work, moving mechanically and grinning despite himself.

So she wasn't the senator's wife. He'd been torturing himself for nothing. She'd been intentionally driving him up a wall, but now . . . now it was his turn.

"Miguel! Come aboard!" Roberto ordered.

Juan was staying on the sailboat so he could return to Miami. He waved to Sean, who crawled down to the dinghy.

Sean looked at the island before him. It would still be dangerous getting out of this mess; Roberto was a danger all by himself.

And he was still a cop, and she was still one of the citizens he was sworn to protect. He just couldn't stop that damn grin.

Because she was going to pay.

## 6

It might have been a paradise, one of those quaint little outer islands where only those with their own boats might venture, a little piece of heavenly unaltered nature.

The island was beautiful, Mandy thought wryly, feeling the pressure of Julio's hand on her back as he urged her along. There was a stretch of beach so miraculously white it might have been snow rather than sand; to the left of the beach was an outcrop of coral and rock, fantastically entwined with the mangrove roots. To the right a stretch of rock and mangroves jutted out into the sea, creating a natural harbor. It was too small a spit of land to hold a hotel, just a dot on the ocean, but it was one of the loveliest little islands Mandy had ever seen.

"Señora Blayne, *por favor!*"

Julio prodded her once again, and she realized that she was stopping every few feet to look around. He was ushering her toward the structure she had seen between the trees, and she wondered why he should be so insistent. There was nowhere for her to

go, and he certainly couldn't think that she intended to overpower him — especially since he was carrying a gun.

She shrugged wearily and continued walking. Señora Garcia had already entered the ramshackle place through a screen door; Mandy followed her, curiously surveying her surroundings.

It was an old frame house, with a kitchen being the first room, and something like a parlor behind it, and two doors at the rear of that parlor. Someone had cleaned the place, and Mandy could only assume that that someone had been Señora Garcia. Even clean, though, it was dismal. There was a double-sided fireplace between the kitchen and the parlor, a rickety old table in the kitchen, and an even more rickety sofa in the parlor. There were two mattresses on the floor lined up against the wall by the left rear door. And there were three pickle-barrel end tables, one by the sofa, one between the mattresses and one near the fireplace. There were no electrical wires — what had she been expecting? — and the only concession to contemporary standards seemed to be a battery-powered icebox next to the counter in the kitchen.

"Go through," Julio told her. His mother glanced at her unhappily and started to say

something, but Julio interrupted her.

"She can be trouble! You have seen so!"

Mandy kept walking. Julio indicated the left door, and she opened it.

It was a bedroom, or at least it resembled a bedroom. There was a mattress on the floor. And there was another door at the rear.

"Is that a bathroom? Or am I allowed to ask?" Mandy asked bitterly.

Julio compressed his lips and nodded. Mandy found herself studying him curiously. He was a young man, handsome, with curling dark hair and a slim, sinewy build. But his dark eyes were full of such a feverish tension! She couldn't believe that he would really harm her; he seemed such a different type from Roberto.

A trickling of unease sped along her spine, and for all that she was usually ready to strangle Miguel, she suddenly wished desperately that he was with her.

"Yes, it is a bathroom. Old and faulty — and the water is brackish. Do not drink it. You understand?"

She nodded.

He smiled peculiarly, a little sadly. "This is it, Mrs. Blayne. Make yourself at home. I'm afraid it will take some time to reach your husband and have my demands met."

He turned to leave her.

"Wait a minute!" Mandy cried, not at all sure what she meant to do, but suddenly determined to make the young man with the nice mother go straight.

"Julio! Señor Garcia! Listen to me. You haven't harmed me. Not really. I feel that this is all a great misunderstanding. If you were to bring me back now — well, I wouldn't press charges. I guess you wouldn't get off scot-free, because you did fire bullets all over the docks. But I don't think you hit anyone, did you? Really, Julio, you don't want to be a criminal! You could go for an insanity plea — temporary insanity. Mental duress. Julio, they will straighten your father's situation out. It just takes time. You don't want him to be free while you're forced to be in jail, do you? You can't get away with this. Think about it. What good is it going to do when you do get hold of Peter? Julio, if we stop this whole thing right now, I'll do my best to help you. Peter will —"

"Mrs. Blayne," Julio interrupted laconically.

"Yes, Julio?"

"Shut up."

From sheer surprise, she did so. He gave her a rueful smile, turned and left her. When

he closed the door she heard the sharp final sound of a bolt sliding home.

"Damn you!" Mandy muttered, threading her fingers through her hair in frustration. "Damn you, you idiot!"

Exasperated and desolate, she sank onto the mattress. For several moments she just sat there, pressing her temples between her palms. Then she lay back on the bed and stared around. There was nothing to see. Nothing but four walls and the door to her primitive bathroom. There was only one window in the room, and that had been boarded over. There was nothing but gloom.

She wished she could sleep. She wished that they had left her just a square inch of window to look through. Time hung so heavily! Each second seemed like an hour, and her imprisonment had only begun. All she could do was lie there in the gloom with her own thoughts — which were not particularly good company.

Every once in a while she heard voices from beyond the door. They were faint, and she couldn't make out a thing, because they were speaking in Spanish.

Where the hell was Miguel?

To her irritation, she was longing to see him. Longing desperately to see him, just because she couldn't stand the shadowed

gloom and her own company anymore.

She tried to think about her work; she tried to think of all the little tedious things she had to do when she got back. She tried to think about the sea, serene and calm. She even tried to imagine sheep jumping over a fence so she could sleep and keep her mind from going a million frustrated miles an hour. Nothing worked. She had never imagined that simple confinement could be so frightening, so wearing. She thought that soon she would go mad; she would race for that bolted door and scream and cry and beat her head against it.

Just when she felt that she had reached that point, the door suddenly swung open. Mandy blinked against the sudden light, shielding her eyes.

For a moment she froze; it was Roberto. Roberto, giving her his lascivious white-toothed smile. She shivered inside, going as cold as ice. She was alone in this room with nothing but a white-sheeted mattress, no avenue of escape. No strength, no hope — and fully aware of the man's feelings regarding her.

No, no, Julio wouldn't allow it. Miguel wouldn't allow it. But where the hell *was* Miguel?

"Amanda?"

She took a deep breath and felt the blood move through her veins once again.

Miguel stepped past Roberto and stared at her, offering her his hand.

She didn't think anything then. She bolted from the mattress, straight toward him, grasping that hand and pressing herself against the strength of his naked chest, her head lowered.

She felt his free hand on her hair, hesitant, then soothing. He wrapped an arm around her and led her through the tacky parlor, Roberto at their heels.

Julio sat at the kitchen table, playing cards with Maria. Señora Garcia was standing over a frying pan set on a Sterno stove on the counter. She was cooking hamburgers; it might have been the great American barbecue.

Miguel started to move away from Mandy; she inched toward him with a little gasp, drawing a snicker from Maria. Mandy stiffened, while Miguel accepted two plates of food from Señora Garcia. He shoved them at Mandy with a curious expression, then turned back to accept two cans of Old Milwaukee.

"Two hours, no more," Julio warned Miguel without looking up from his game.

*"Dos horas,"* Miguel agreed, *and Julio did*

*look up then, but not at them. He stared at Roberto, who insisted on keeping his gun out and trained on Miguel.*

"I'll spell you soon, amigo," he said.

Roberto leered at Mandy and shrugged to Julio. Mandy thought she saw Julio shudder slightly, and she wondered again how these two had come together, an idealist and a . . . vulture.

"Come on," Miguel urged her with his Spanish accent. *"Dos horas!"*

She had no idea what he was talking about, but she eagerly followed him outdoors.

It was late afternoon again. The sea stretched out eternally before them, touched by the reflection of the dying sun, sparkling and rippling like something magical. Even the white beach seemed to shimmer with the colors of the coming evening, gold and pink, delicate mauve and diamond glitter.

Miguel walked beside her; Roberto followed at a distance. "This way," Miguel advised, walking toward the part of the beach where the rock and mangroves formed a secretive little haven, shadowed now in dusk.

She looked back. Roberto had paused. He was sitting on the beach, watching them, but giving them a certain distance. Mandy ex-

pelled a long sigh, which drew a sharp gaze from Miguel.

"He makes me nervous," she muttered.

If she'd expected reassurance, she didn't get it. "He doesn't thrill me, either," Miguel agreed. "But forget him for now. I spent hours arguing to get Julio to agree that you would go mad and be far more difficult to handle if you didn't get out a little."

He led her as far away from Roberto as possible, to the place where the roots met the rocks.

"Have a seat, Mrs. Blayne," he told her with a grin.

She sat on a stump, balancing both plates of hamburgers until he settled himself on the sand beside her. He opened both cans of beer, then handed her one as he took his own plate.

"Thanks," Mandy muttered, then lowered her head, because she was thinking about him, and she didn't want him to guess. She was on the stump; he was at her side, the breadth of his bare shoulders and back at her knee, his dark head angled toward her, his rich green eyes looking out to the sea.

She found herself liking everything about him; his height, his build, those eyes — even his scruffy jaw, strong beneath the beard. He

was attractive — and she was attracted. She despised herself for it, because she considered herself sane and mature, and thought she knew enough about the human psyche to keep herself under control. She'd barely known him for forty-eight hours, yet she was desperately glad of his presence, ready to race to the sound of his voice, more than willing to trust herself to him.

Naturally. She sensed that he was all that stood between her and Roberto. But he was a cop — that was his job. There was no reason she should feel so . . . quiveringly grateful. Especially when she knew what he really thought of her!

"Eat," he told her, and she saw that he was looking at her then, rather than the sea. And that there was a peculiar glint of amusement in his eyes.

Mechanically and a little warily, she brought her hamburger to her mouth. It seemed to stick against the dryness of her throat, and she sipped the beer to force it down.

Miguel seemed to have no such problems. He ate his hamburger with a hearty appetite, then leaned back against her legs, very relaxed — like an idle beach bum — while he sipped his beer.

She stiffened, ready to jerk her legs away.

She stopped herself only because she knew that Roberto watched them, not fifty feet away.

The water, stretching out before them, was magically beautiful, as were the white purity of the sand, the wild and primitive tangle of mangrove and coral, the eternal sky, the twilight. . . .

And the two of them. He was touching her, relaxed and lazy, as if they were the only two people on earth, a man and a woman.

She set her half-eaten hamburger down and sipped the beer. She was so glad to be out of that room, away from her own thoughts.

Yet she was so nervous, so horribly aware of him: of his tanned flesh, so sleek over the rippling muscles of his back and shoulders; his hair, ebony with the coming of the night; his scent, as fresh and salty as the night air, and here, in this wild splendor, so masculine that she felt nearly consumed just by his presence. . . .

It was all because she had to rely on him, she told herself furiously. Circumstance! At a cocktail party she would have walked away from him.

But here she couldn't walk away. Being with him was playing dangerous havoc with her emotions and her senses, and she knew it.

But what was she afraid of? He assumed that she was married to Peter, and he steered clear of married women; he had told her so with indisputable passion.

Maybe she should be glad, grateful to learn that her instincts and emotions still functioned. She worked, she laughed, she enjoyed people, but she hadn't really felt anything in so long. Maybe even the fear and the fury were good; she was reacting, and there had been times when she had felt that anything would be better than the horrible numbness. But this . . .

Even Peter had tried to introduce her to a string of young men. She'd never felt the least interest, just the numbness. And now she felt like a traitor, to Paul and — far worse — to herself. How could she possibly be attracted to a man who treated her so poorly?

He was there; he was a buffer. That was all, absolutely all. And she wasn't only attracted to him. She was also indignant and outraged by his methods. To top it all off, she still didn't even know if she should really believe him or not, because he was a fabulous actor, slipping from accent to accent with barely a thought.

"You really are absolutely beautiful, you know."

Mandy started, choking on her beer, staring involuntarily into the heavy-lidded sparkling green eyes that were now resting on her in the most sensual fashion. She swallowed warily. "Thank you," she muttered. Then she asked, "You really are a cop?"

He chuckled softly. "Yeah, I really am."

Mandy stared out to sea again while confusion overwhelmed her. His voice . . . the huskiness in his voice. What had happened to him suddenly? The cut-and-dried manner was gone — as was the hard and passionate man who had vowed he didn't touch married women, who despised her for marrying an old man.

"Uh . . ." She cleared her throat, searching for a safe topic of conversation. "What is Julio doing with Roberto? They don't seem a bit alike."

He shrugged. "They're not. Juan is with him because they're second cousins or something. I think Roberto is merely in it for the money."

"The money?"

"Mmm. The Garcias still have family in Spain, and a number of wealthy Colombian connections. If I've gotten things right, Roberto is a mercenary. He's been hired for his expertise. That's why I don't trust him.

God, you're beautiful."

"Would you stop that!" Mandy snapped after a moment. He'd changed his tone so quickly that it had taken her time to catch up, and now she knew that she was nearly as red as the twilight.

"I can't seem to help myself," he said, swallowing the last of his beer, then crushing the can in one hand while he continued to stare at her.

She swallowed the last of her beer, compelled to return his stare, fascinated, horrified.

He took her can from her hand, brushing her fingers with his own, rising to his knees, a breath away from her.

"You hate married women. Especially me. I married old Peter Blayne for his wealth and possessions, remember?" she told him quickly. Too quickly. Breathlessly . . .

"I know," he told her softly, his arm moving around her. His face wasn't an inch from hers. She felt the power of his chest and shoulders, saw the smoldering green fire in his eyes. "I know all that. But don't you feel it? The sea and the breeze and the night, you — and me?"

"No! No!" Mandy told him hastily. "I don't feel anything. Just that you hate me. Remember?"

He shook his head. "I don't hate you, Mandy, though I keep thinking of all the reasons why I should. I think and think of all the reasons why I should stay completely away from you. I tell myself over and over again that you're married. That I'm a cop. That you're completely off limits. But, Mandy . . . I tell you, I can't help myself. No matter what I think, I see you. I see those golden eyes of yours, that tawny lion's mane. I see your body — oh, God! Do I see your body! Naked and gold and glistening, lithe and curved —"

"Stop it!" Mandy shrieked, trying to edge away as his knuckles brushed over her cheek. She lost her balance instead and toppled over into the sand.

He was right behind her, stretching over her, bracing his weight on his hands, his palms beside her head. He seemed to cover her, his legs entangled with hers.

"Get up —" she began in panic.

"Oh, Mandy! I can't!" he vowed passionately, and she felt all the sexual quality of him, the power in his thighs, the brush of his hairy chest against her skin, the ridiculously sweet pressure of his hips on hers.

"Roberto! Roberto is watching us!" she protested.

"And I must convince him that we are

lovers," Miguel whispered softly, shifting, bringing himself halfway to her side, cupping her jaw in his hand to bring her face to his.

"Amanda, I can't bear this. Being with you, night and day. Sleeping beside you. I'd sell my soul for you. I can't care that you're a married woman, I can't think of anything. I have to have you!"

Heat like liquid fire exploded through her — right along with a raging sense of panic. He was way too much male. She didn't know what to do with him; she didn't know how to escape him. She felt lost and overwhelmed and desperate!

"Wait. Wait!"

"Hold me, Mandy. Just hold me!"

Hold him? His arms were vise clamps around her, his body an inferno of steel. She was quivering like a cornered rabbit, straining against him with all her might — futilely.

"Miguel . . ."

"Oh, Lord, I was in agony, listening to you! I envisioned the two of us in a Jacuzzi, sipping champagne, just barely touching, coming nearer and nearer, until you were mine."

He shifted, touching her. Lightly. Fingertips against her cheek, stroking her throat,

running over her collarbone, so near the neckline of her halter top. Fingertips . . . dancing dangerously over the mounds of her breasts, fascinated with the naked flesh of her midriff. Gentle, tender, erotic in their motion, in their very being. And she was powerless. Shivering and aware and powerless, and so keenly touched by the vibrant heat of his body, his weight, the rough feel of his legs.

"Champagne . . . you and me. The warm waters rushing around us. Mandy, you've got the most beautiful breasts I've ever seen."

"Miguel, don't you —"

"God, you're glorious . . . splendid. Champagne and pizza. Completely naked . . . us . . . together."

"Damn you! I'll strangle you once we're free."

"Remember when you touched me? This morning? Oh, Mandy, I felt desire in that touch. I know that Peter Blayne's an old man. I know that you're young and sensual and I can't see any reason why we shouldn't —"

"There are a million reasons!"

He smiled, totally disbelieving her. And then his fingertips were moving again. Just gently stroking her ribs . . . then moving

higher, brushing her breasts. Her nipples were hard, and he could feel it, and that was making him grin even more widely.

"I'll report you. If we live I'll report you to all your superiors. Every one of them! They'll fire you."

"You're just saying that, Mandy. I can feel you. I knew this morning that you wanted me."

"I do not!"

"I don't care about anything! Report me. I'd give my job — my life — for one night with you."

Oh, no! What had she done this morning? Threats weren't working; they didn't mean a thing to him!

"Please . . ." she whispered, but even that did nothing.

"You've cast a spell on me," he told her huskily. "I can't let you go. It's all that I can think about — you, me, tangled together, hot, sweating, straining."

"Miguel, you're a cop! I'm a married woman!"

Suddenly he was laughing, staring down at her and laughing. Then he rolled away from her and sat up, wrapping his arms around his knees and staring out at the sea once again.

"Mrs. Blayne, you're the most ridiculous

liar I've ever met," he told her with curt amusement.

"What?" Stunned, she scrambled to her feet and stared down at him, her hands on her hips. She felt relieved, furious — and bereft.

He gazed up at her, still smiling. "Amanda Blayne, you're Peter Blayne's daughter-in-law, not his wife."

"How do you know?"

"Because I managed to get through to the Coast Guard on the radio."

"What?"

"I keep telling you — I'm a cop. Sworn to protect and all that jazz. I'm sorry I haven't tried to stop a bullet for you yet, but I did get to the radio."

Her temper flared out of all proportion. She should be jumping up and down with joy that someone had been advised of the situation, but he'd just made such a fool of her! Without thought she suddenly leapt at him, pummeling his chest and shoulders.

"You bastard! You didn't bother to tell me! Instead you pulled this little act. I'll kill you! I'll wring your stupid neck!"

"Whoa!" he protested, stunned by her vehemence, falling backward into the sand at her assault. He collected himself quickly and caught her flailing fists, then rolled and

cast a knee over her hips and stretched her arms over her head, where he held them while he leaned against her, panting.

"Don't touch me! I swear, I *will* report you! How dare you?"

"Roberto is looking!"

"I don't give a damn!"

"You'd better — unless you want Roberto in this position!"

"What diff—"

"A lot, Mrs. Blayne. I'm not going to rape you, but Roberto would give his eyeteeth to do just that!"

Mandy went dead still, clenching her teeth and staring up at him, trying to regain her breath.

"You son of —"

"Hey! You lied to me! I risked my neck to let you know that I was a police officer. You lied —"

"I did not! You assumed that I was Peter's wife! You judged me without a —"

"You could have corrected me!"

"And why should I have bothered?"

"Courtesy, Mrs. Blayne. Common courtesy. Especially in this situation!"

"Courtesy! Oh —"

"Shush!"

She grated her teeth together again. He was staring down at her with an emerald

spark in his eyes. He was amused.

And she was far too aware of him all over again. His fingers, curled within hers. His thigh, cast over her hips. His warmth. Everything about him that was male, that called to something inside her despite herself. She was quivering from the effect of his touch. . . .

"Let me go, please, Miguel," she whispered.

He stared at her a moment longer, his eyes growing dark, tension suddenly lining his face. He sighed and released her, but still lay at her side.

"You asked for it, you know," he told her.

"Men!" she snapped. "They say you're all alike, and I believe it! You came at me with all kinds of insinuations and I just played along because *you* were the one who deserved it!"

He laughed again, and she was aware once more that she liked his smile, liked it very much.

"The champagne in the Jacuzzi was a killer," he told her.

She stiffened. "I was acting for the benefit of our captors, and you know it."

He shrugged. "You're just such a good little actress!"

"Oh, stop, please." And don't stay so

close, please don't stay so close! she added silently, cast into an agony of confusion. It was just the circumstances, she told herself.

She closed her eyes. "Thank God you got to the radio! When is help coming?"

"I don't know."

Her eyes flew open again, and she edged up on her elbows to frown at him. "What do you mean you don't know? You just told me —"

"I mean I don't know! I tried to tell them where we were, but I'm not positive. It only takes a day to reach Cat Cay — we were on that old scow for two nights. I think that they motored in circles, backtracking on purpose. I still think that we're somewhere near Cat Cay. But there must be hundreds of these little swamp islands around. It may take time. And this has to be handled carefully. The Coast Guard can't just zoom up. That's not the way you handle a hostage situation. You could —"

"Get shot?"

He shrugged. "That's not going to happen, Mandy." Distracted, he called her by her given name, not by the acid "Mrs. Blayne."

She looked from his profile to the ocean, picking up a handful of sand, letting it fall through her fingers.

He stood up abruptly and reached a hand down to her. "Let's walk on the beach. Our two hours are almost up."

"How can you tell?" she asked him despondently.

"Because," he said softly, "I can read the sky. And Julio has come out to take Roberto's place as watchdog."

Mandy glanced over her shoulder. It was true; Julio was sitting where Roberto had been.

She looked back to the strong hand being offered to her. She hesitated a moment longer, then took it. He pulled her to her feet, cast an arm around her and started walking idly down the beach.

Mandy went along because she felt she had little choice. It did feel good to move; it felt wonderful to be outside, rather than in that dim stuffy room. It felt good to have his arm around her. To know that he was with her, even if she still wanted to strangle him. Yet at the same time she knew that she needed him. He was her security, her buffer against fear and madness. This would end; all things ended. But for now . . . the evening sky was beautiful; the breeze was delightful. He was at her side — far better than facing Roberto's leers alone.

They walked through the surf, and the

cool water bathed her feet. If she closed her eyes she could pretend that she was just on an outing, away for the day, taken to a primitive paradise on the winged sails of the *Flash Point*.

She sniffed suddenly and managed to cast Miguel a wry smile. "I don't even know your last name."

He gazed at her, hesitated a minute, then said, "Ramiro."

"Miguel Ramiro," she said. Strangely, he hesitated once again.

"Not exactly."

"Not exactly?"

"Well, don't tell these guys. My name is Sean. Sean Michael Ramiro."

"What?" Mandy started laughing. Maybe it was hysteria. She stared at him incredulously.

"Sean Michael Ramiro?" She moved away from him, almost doubled over with laughter, so incredible did she find it all. "Now I know you're a liar!"

"I told you I was born in Dublin!" he retorted.

"You said you were Cuban —"

"I said *half*-Cuban! My father was Cuban, my mother is Irish."

She was still laughing. "What a combination!"

146

"Oh, yeah! I forgot! You're Miss DAR! Daughter of the old *Mayflower!*"

She was still laughing so hard she couldn't even take offense.

"Sean?"

"Yeah. Want to make something of it?"

"No, no!" She held out a defensive hand, but too late. He splashed over to her, gripped her hands, slid a foot behind her ankle and sent her crashing into the surf, then dropped down beside her.

"I'm sorry! I'm sorry!" she shrieked when he made a move to dunk her.

But he didn't dunk her. He touched her cheek, his weight and warmth against her again, while the cool surf raced delicately around them both. She felt the power of his arms on either side of her, saw the tension in his eyes, and she might well have been spellbound.

His head lowered. His lips brushed hers. . . . Just brushed them. And then his eyes were on hers again. Like the sea around them, reflected by the sinking sun, touched by the coming moon. They quested and they sought . . . and she must have answered.

Because his lips met hers again, with a coercive hungry pressure. His kiss filled her with that same hunger, captured her with

fascination. She tasted sea and salt and passion and heat, felt the sweep of his tongue over her teeth . . . deep into her mouth. Filling her, entering her with a spiraling heat that sent a searing wonder rippling through her. He wasn't really touching her, just his mouth. Just the tickle of that growth of beard against her flesh, the fire of his lips, the fever of his mouth . . .

"Hey! Your two hours are up! She goes back to her room!"

Startled, they broke apart at Julio's announcement, shaken from the moment.

Mandy stared at Sean Michael Ramiro in absolute horror. She didn't accept his hand, nor did she even notice Julio, standing on the beach.

She raced back toward the house, eager now for her prison, desperate to be alone.

# 7

When darkness came to her shuttered prison, it came completely.

Mandy was absolutely convinced that she would go mad. She couldn't see her own hand in front of her face. She hadn't known that she was afraid of the dark, but then, she'd never seen darkness so complete.

For hours she lay on the mattress, still soaked from the surf, shivering, then going deathly still before shivering all over again. Sometimes it seemed that her mind was blank; sometimes it was as if a cacophony of thoughts and ideas raced within it.

And always it came back to two things. The darkness. Haunting, suffocating, ebony darkness. And Miguel. No, not Miguel. Sean Michael Ramiro.

Her feelings, his touch. The strident need she was beginning to feel for him. The moral horror that she could be so vulnerable, so dependent . . .

And so hungry. To be held, touched, loved. To laugh, to play and enjoy the play.

She yearned for him now in a terrible

aching way. She thought that she could endure the darkness, if only he was next to her. Here, in this hell within paradise, he had become her salvation, and more. It seemed ridiculously complex; the emotional and the physical; the desire, the need. It seemed so incredibly basic and primitive. She simply wanted to fit against him, as nature had intended, without thought, without words.

There was no way to escape her sense of disloyalty, no way to lie in this utter darkness and not think of Paul, not think of the baby. No way to do anything other than lie there in anguish and agony, suffering the ceaseless gnawing of a fear that came not just from circumstances now, but, like desire, from instinct.

She went still when the door opened at last. The streak of light that entered was painful, as blinding as the darkness. Mandy closed her eyes against it, casting her arm over her face.

The light was quickly gone. Her whole existence suddenly centered around her other senses.

Someone was in the room.

She could feel that presence so strongly! Logic warned her that it could be Julio or Maria or Señora Garcia. A trembling within

warned that it could too easily be Roberto.

But her world now knew no logic. She didn't need to be afraid; it was Sean. She knew from the presence that filled the room; she knew from his salty scent, the sound of his breath.

He stood just within the doorway for several moments, his eyes adjusting to the darkness. Then, very slowly, he came toward the mattress. He reached it and fumbled along the edge, then smoothed his hand over the sheet.

She shifted, giving him room. He started suddenly, aware of her movement.

"You're awake?"

"I'm awake."

"My God, it's darker than a coal mine in here."

"I couldn't find the light switch," she said, trying to joke, but she had no idea what his reaction was, since she couldn't see his face.

He didn't answer as he stretched out beside her. She didn't dare touch him, but she knew his position. Hands laced behind his head, ankles crossed, feet probably dangling over the edge.

"You okay?" he whispered after a while.

"Of course. Why wouldn't I be?"

She imagined that he might have grinned. "I guess you're not afraid of the dark."

"Terrified. But what could I possibly do about it?"

"Ask for a lantern."

"Would I get one?"

"Probably." He hesitated. "I don't think Julio means to be cruel. He just doesn't know that it's as black as Hades in here. Not that it matters if you're sleeping, but you've been in here quite a while. I'll get a lantern tomorrow."

She didn't answer him. She wasn't sure what to say. She was excruciatingly glad of his presence; he was like a lantern against the darkness.

She was also excruciatingly aware of him — and the last moments they had shared. She was frightened, not of him, but of herself, and so keyed up that she would never sleep, so miserable that she longed for nothing except oblivion.

The silence seemed to grow in the darkness and become a black cloud above them, filled with the portent of wind and rain. They did not touch, though they were no more than an inch apart. Then suddenly Mandy sneezed, and that sneeze ended the silence.

"Bless you," he muttered, turning toward her. His hand brushed her arm, and suddenly she knew that he was above her, that

his dark brows were furrowed with concern, and that his handsome features had hardened into a scowl. "You're shivering like a leaf, and you feel like an ice cube!"

"Do I?" Mandy murmured.

"Yes, you do." He quickly stood, pulling at the mattress, fumbling and swearing when he stubbed his toe against it.

"Get up — can you?"

"Of course I can," she murmured, confused. "But why?"

"There's a top sheet on this thing, and you need to get under it. Take your clothes off."

"What?"

"Oh, come on! I can't see a damn thing in here. Besides, I've already seen you. Your clothes are still all wet from the beach, and you'll get pneumonia if you sleep in them. And then, should the time come when you need to move quickly, you won't be able to. Take your clothes off."

"I think I'd rather risk pneumonia!"

"Than me?"

How could a voice do so much? Reach out through the air and darkness like a velvet brush, teasing, warming.

"Umm."

"Still don't trust me?"

"Not in the least."

"Well, that's okay. I don't trust *you*, either."

"I'm not asking you to take your clothes off."

"Not yet. You'll get to it, though. Women are all alike."

She rolled off the mattress, laughing, perplexed. Somehow he had brought light and warmth into the room. And also that sense of security that was so very easy to rely on, so very easy to need — and so very dangerous. More dangerous, perhaps, than Julio and his accomplices.

"Laugh at me, will you, Mrs. Blayne?" he charged softly, and she knew that he was walking around to her. He hunched down in front of her and felt for her. She didn't know what he was looking for, but he found her breast.

"Hey! And you're asking me to take my clothes off?"

"Sorry, I thought it was your face."

"Umm. You'll get yours one day."

"Promises, promises. Off with 'em, lady."

"I don't think this is proper police procedure."

"Off!"

"Well, move, then!"

He did. Feeling like a stripper in broad daylight, Mandy shed her soggy cutoffs and

154

top, then groped with a fair amount of panic for the sheet.

It was there, in his hands, ready to be wrapped around her. She sensed that he was laughing at her.

"I've already slept with the . . . real . . . you, you know."

"Oh, shut up!"

She was still shivering, but she did feel much better; she hadn't realized how chilling her wet clothing had been. But even now, with the dry sheet wrapped around her, she was cold.

"Lie down now," he said huskily.

"What wonderful relationships you must have, Mr. Ramiro! Take off your clothes. Lie down."

He laughed softly in the darkness, and once again she felt touched by the sound, brushed by velvet.

"When it works, do it. Lie down."

Gritting her teeth, she did so, cocooning herself in the sheet. Then she tensed as he crawled over to her. He didn't keep his distance this time; he brought his chest to her back and wrapped an arm around her waist, pulling her close to absorb his heat.

She must have been as stiff and unyielding as concrete, though she made no protest, because he chuckled softly again. "Ease up.

I'm just trying to make you warm."

She didn't know that she had held her breath until she released it in a long sigh.

"I'm not the big bad wolf."

"Are you sure?"

"Positive. Why do I make you so nervous?"

"I'm not nervous."

"You are."

"Well, I have a right to be! Since I've met you, you've knocked me down, thrown me around. . . ."

"What's a lover for?" he teased. "Mandy — Mrs. Blayne — I do apologize for my rougher methods."

"And your gentler ones?" she murmured without thought.

His arm tightened slightly around her midriff. "Meaning?"

"Nothing!" she said quickly. What had caused her to say such a thing?

And even as she asked herself the question, she knew the answer. The kiss. The real one, in the salty foam of the surf, interrupted by Julio's appearance.

In the darkness she felt his every breath, knew his every movement, no matter how slight. Knew him, living and breathing beside her.

Silence spread again, total in the dark-

ness. And in that silence she thought it would be the easiest thing in the world to turn to him, to give in to temptation under cover of darkness.

She'd always known that she was young, that she would make love again one day. But one day had always meant some indeterminate future. It was something she hadn't dwelled upon, had not imagined easily. It would be awkward and difficult, and she would be nervous and afraid and, certainly, making comparisons. She had even begun to imagine how difficult it would be to remove her clothing, or watch a man disrobe, knowing his intent.

She wore no clothing now, but it was dark. And in the darkness she would not have to see a man's face. Not have to know if she brought pleasure or ennui, nor bear visible witness that she found it not thrilling in the least, but actually distasteful. . . .

But it *would* be thrilling. With him. For her. She knew from his eyes, from his laughter, from his words, from the hands that touched her so well, from the hard length of his body, taut and warm against hers.

It was easy to forget because of circumstance. Easy to imagine that the darkness could cover her, and she could hide from

truth and light and thought. Easy . . .

She would never do it; not even the darkness could take away her memories. And it wasn't just Paul; it was Paul and the baby. If one of them had made it — just one of them — she wouldn't have felt as if she had been stripped of everything. Everything that mattered. She wouldn't have been so afraid of emotion, of reaching out. But she had learned that pleasure brought pain.

She hadn't known that she was crying; her tears were as silent as the night. Then suddenly she felt a thumb against her cheek, wiping away the moisture there.

"How long?" he asked her very softly.

And she knew exactly what he meant. "Three years ago."

"What happened?"

She had to breathe very deeply before she could whisper out her answer. "A drunk driver," she said flatly. "The baby was killed instantly. Paul lingered a few hours."

"And the driver?"

"He died, too. There wasn't even anybody left to hate."

He didn't say anything else to her; he just ran his fingers gently, idly against her cheek, then over her hair. And he stayed there, beside her, his warmth all around her.

And in time she slept.

She awoke to find his glittering green eyes upon her.

The absolute darkness was gone; hazy light filtered in, like a gray fog. She could see him now, and herself, too well.

In the night she had turned to him. Turned and twisted and left half of her sheet behind. Their legs were completely entangled, her left one beneath his, her right one thrown across his thigh. She'd made a pillow of his arm — which he couldn't possibly move without tearing out a handful of her hair. Thus his patient and amused stare as she opened her eyes wider and wider with the realization of her position.

"Oh! Get off me, you —"

"Hey, you're the one on top of me, Mrs. Blayne."

And of course she was. Clenching her teeth and emitting a soft oath, Mandy moved her legs away from his and wrenched furiously at the sheet. It wouldn't give, not until he laughed and shifted his weight. Groaning, she wrapped it around herself and stared disgustedly at the ceiling, drawing another soft chuckle from him.

"Can't you go somewhere, do something — get out of here? You're never around

when I —" She broke off abruptly.

Naturally he pounced on her words, leaning on one elbow to watch her closely. "When you what?"

"I have no idea. I was just talking."

"You were not. You were about to say 'when I need you!' "

"I do not need you." She paused, lowering her lashes. "You're just better than some of the alternatives around here."

"Wow! What an endorsement!"

"Will you please go do whatever it is you do when you're not around?"

"Ah, jealousy becomes you."

Mandy sighed with exaggerated patience. "I'm not jealous." Then she turned suddenly, holding the sheet tightly to her breasts, surprised that it really did seem nice to wake up and find him there, smiling at her — even if she had been definitely disturbed at first.

"I'm curious," she murmured, remembering what she had intended to say. "Here I am, entirely harmless, and they keep me under lock and key. And there you are — at least two hundred pounds of you — and they let you run around. Why?"

"Because I'm madly in love with you. I'm allowed to be here to keep a lid on you. I'm a kindred spirit, a refugee, too, or so they be-

lieve. I'm one of them — a gardener — pulled into the bedroom. And you, Mrs. Blayne, are the farthest thing from harmless that I've ever come across."

"What?"

"You half killed me the other night."

"*I* half killed *you?*"

"Umm. Scratching, flailing, slapping — you're about as harmless as a basketful of vipers."

"Oh, really? Funny, you don't look much worse for wear!"

"But I am. You might well have cost me months of normal sexual activity."

"What?" she shrieked, astounded at his accusation.

"You must have learned your kicks from Bruce Lee. Honestly, I felt mortally wounded. My mother would never forgive you. She's expecting grandchildren one of these days."

She saw the grin he couldn't keep hidden then. "Oh, will you please get out of here? Go join your fellow refugees!"

The humor instantly fled from his eyes. "A refugee, Mrs. Blayne," he said, "is one who seeks refuge. I was born in Dublin, but both my parents were American citizens. Therefore I never had any need to seek refuge."

He rolled away from her and rose, leaving her feeling a strange remorse; she had been teasing him, and she wasn't sure what she had said to make him draw away from her with such disgust.

His back was to her, his hands on his hips. "It isn't a dirty word, you know," he said.

"What?"

"Refugee, Mrs. Blayne. Little Miss Mayflower Princess. This country was established because people sought a better life. The Irish have come, the English, Italians, Germans and so on forever. That's part of the reason we're so unique, Mrs. Blayne. What do I do out there? I talk with them — in Spanish. I try to watch which way the wind is blowing, I try to read people. For your safety, Mrs. Blayne. If you had bothered to learn some Spanish —"

"Why should I have?" she snapped, simply because she needed some defense; he was definitely attacking. "It's an English-speaking country!"

He swung around then, and to her surprise he was suddenly on his knees on the mattress, green fire in his eyes and radiating enough tension to make her shiver. "Yes, Mrs. Blayne, yes! It's definitely an English-speaking country. And you're right — those who seek its shelter should learn its lan-

guage! But what kind of an isolationist are you? Nine out of ten Europeans learn at least two languages. They have to. They have to be able to talk to their neighbors. Haven't you ever wanted to learn for the simple joy of learning. Relating? Are you so smug, so satisfied with what you are, that you feel no need to give?"

"What the hell is this?" Mandy retorted. "A soapbox? I took another language, Mr. Ramiro — it just happens to have been German, not Spanish. And I'm not a linguistics whiz. I'm ever so sorry. And if you think that I'm a bigot, I'm sorry about that, too, but it's certainly your prerogative." Mandy was gaining steam as she continued her argument. Gripping the sheet, she rose to her knees to face him, as angry as he was. "You'd better face a few facts, Mr. Ramiro! We had a lot of real criminals dumped on us! As a police officer, you should know that! And I don't care if a murderer is German, French, English, Japanese or all-American mongrel — he shouldn't be walking the streets!"

"So what are you saying? The Cubans are all murderers?"

"I didn't say that and you damn well know it!"

His hands suddenly clamped down on her

bare shoulders; she felt their leashed force and the blaze of emotion that seemed to leap from him to her. And then, just when she was certain that he would either shake her or scream at her again or both, he released her with an oath of disgust and scrambled back to his feet.

He strode straight toward the door without a backward look, opened it and slammed it behind himself.

"Oh, you stupid son of a bitch!" Mandy muttered after him. But then she realized that tears were stinging her eyes, and she didn't know why.

She hurried up, stumbling to grasp her clothing, racing for the bathroom. Brackish water, a little yellowed from rusting pipes, spewed from the spigot. She closed her eyes to ignore the color and splashed her face. Why did they keep getting into all this? Why didn't he understand . . . ? And why the hell was she worrying about him when she was still a kidnap victim?

She sighed and realized that she wasn't really frightened. Not anymore. Julio seemed more like a misguided child than a menace. Except that he did know how to use a gun.

But she didn't believe that he would really hurt her. The only person she was afraid of — bone deep! — was Roberto, but she

didn't have to worry about Roberto, because Julio seemed determined that no harm would come to her.

"This is insane!" she whispered aloud.

She had faith that this would end, and it was strange what that feeling did for her morale. Strange, but even her arguments with Sean made her feel stronger — impatient, but optimistic.

"Pain in the . . ."

Her cutoffs and top were still damp, but since she had no other choice, she took a brackish and slightly yellow shower, then donned them again. When she had finished, she noticed that a delicious aroma was reaching her from beyond the door of her prison.

Sean had simply walked out. Why shouldn't she do the same?

She stalked over to the door and wrenched at the knob. It didn't give; since Sean had left, someone had come to bolt the door.

"Probably did it himself!" she muttered.

"Hey!" She slammed a fist against the wood. To her surprise, the door opened. Julio was standing there, clean shaven, attractively dressed in a clean cotton shirt and jeans.

He looked just like a nice kid — except

that he was still carrying the gun tucked into his boy-next-door blue jeans.

"Good morning, Señora Blayne. We expect to hear something from your husband by tonight."

He smiled at her as if Western Union was simply sending the money to get her out of a rather sorry jam.

"Great," she muttered.

"Coffee?"

"Please," she accepted, with just a trace of irony. He indicated that she should precede him into the kitchen. His mother was there, smiling at Mandy with her usual sympathetic apology as soon as she saw her. Eggs and bacon were cooking in a skillet, and two kinds of coffee were brewing: the thick sweet Cuban blend and what was — according to the nearby can — Maxwell House.

Julio noticed the direction of her gaze. "Mama brewed it specially just for you."

Marvelous, she thought. Cater to your kidnap victim. Except that that wasn't really true, and she knew it. Señora Garcia was very upset that Mandy had been taken; she had made both kinds of coffee in a sincere effort to do anything in her power for Mandy.

She went up to accept the cup the woman offered her, telling her thank you. Señora

Garcia smiled, and Mandy glanced out the kitchen window to the beach beyond.

Maria, Roberto and Sean — Miguel! She had to remember that, no matter how mad she got! — were all sitting around, paper plates discarded, laughing and chatting while they drank coffee.

Maria, it seemed, was growing quite fond of Sean. She kept placing her red polished fingertips on his bare bronzed arms as she spoke to him, her dark eyes beautiful with laughter.

And Sean . . . well, he was laughing back.

Oh, nuts to you! Mandy decided belligerently.

*"Señora, por favor . . ."*

She turned around. Señora Garcia had pulled out a chair for her at the table, where she had set down a plate filled with bacon and eggs. Mandy thanked her again and sat down.

Julio was sipping his coffee by her side. She picked up her fork because she was hungry, but after a few minutes she turned to her captor and spoke to him. "You know, don't you, that what you're doing is very wrong?"

He gazed at her sharply. Then he lifted his hands and let them fall. "My father is getting old, and he is very ill. Too many years in

a dank prison. He will not live long. Using any means that I can manage, I will see to it that he knows freedom before he dies."

"But —"

"Señora Blayne," he interrupted very softly, "I was three years old when Batista was overthrown. He was certainly not a prize, but we went from one dictator to another. In the States the exiles pray for another revolution. In Cuba, those who have not been indoctrinated into the new regime work for the next revolution. When I was a child gunfire raged, people bled, and people died. The needs create the means, don't they? Spying is fine — when it is for your country. A spy must be hanged when he is from the other side. This is life. Violence is an ugly thing, but it can also be a way of life. Secrets, trial and error, violence, abduction. They are all means to an end. I will see my father free. It is that simple."

"Not here it isn't!" Amanda protested, frustrated. "Julio, this is a huge country! Peter Blayne doesn't run it, he just plays his part. The courts can be slow, justice slower, but they're the best shot we've got! Julio . . ."

"I cannot go back," he said flatly, rising. "If you want some time away from your room, now is it. The day is beautiful, the surf is warm. Come out to the beach."

She rose along with him, ready to take her plate to the counter. Señora Garcia took it from her hands, smiling.

Mandy stepped outside with Julio. The others fell silent as they passed by. Mandy caught Sean's eyes on her, but they were filled with the sun's reflection, and she couldn't read their expression.

She gazed at him just as blandly, then walked on toward the surf with Julio.

"What happens," she asked softly, "if Peter Blayne doesn't respond to you? I'm telling you right now, he doesn't have the power to walk up to a federal penitentiary and demand that your father be released."

Julio stared at her. "He'd best find that power."

"You'd kill me?"

He sat down on the sand, letting the water rush over his bare toes. Mandy did the same. "I would have to send him a piece of you next."

"A . . . piece of me?"

"A finger, Mrs. Blayne."

She thought that she would keel over into the water. It wouldn't happen; the Coast Guard were on their way. Sean . . .

Sean was laughing away with the charmingly voluptuous Maria up at the house.

She lowered her head, thinking that no

matter what he thought of her, Sean would never allow her to be . . . dismembered.

"I would not wish to harm you," Julio added.

"Thanks," Mandy breathed bitterly. She turned around, looking back to the house. Sean, with his guarded gaze, was still watching her.

And so was Roberto, in that fashion that sent horrible chills down her spine. There was something about his grim look that was like a rabid dog's. She felt that she could almost hear his teeth gnashing, as if he would devour her like a shark.

Shivering, she looked back to the water. To the sea. It stretched out endlessly, as if they were alone in the world. With nothing better to do and a yearning to move, Mandy stood and started walking out into the waves.

"Where are you going?" Julio demanded sharply.

She turned and stared back at him, laughing with real humor. "Where could I go, Señor Garcia? I'm going to swim, nothing more. I certainly don't expect to swim back to Miami, if that's what you're afraid of."

He had the grace to laugh sheepishly in return, and Mandy kept walking until the

water came to her chest, then she began to swim.

The sharks were still fresh in her mind, so she didn't venture too far, but it felt so good to be moving. She swam against the current; she swam with the current. She floated on her back and felt the sun on her face.

When she got back to the beach, Julio was gone. He was sitting with the others nearer the house. They had switched from coffee to beer to cool them against the heat of the sun.

Mandy lay back in the sand for a while, resting, then headed for the water once again. She knew the physical exertion would help her to sleep, to keep from thinking.

When she came out again, she faltered. The others had gone into the house; only Roberto waited for her.

Roberto, who liked to keep his gun out, smoothing it with his fingers while he stared at her. He stroked that gun like . . . like a man would stroke a woman.

Mandy kept her distance from him, tossing her hair back, squeezing the water from it. She realized from the direction of his eyes that the soaked shirt was tight and see-through against her breasts.

Sucking in her breath, she crossed her arms over her chest and strode past him,

heading for the house. He didn't follow her — except with his eyes.

In the house she discovered that Maria was loudly playing a portable radio. The girl was sitting in the parlor, idly dangling one long leg over the arm of the sofa, listening to the music. She looked Mandy up and down and smirked at her. Mandy ignored her, aware that she was damp and that her hair looked like a mop. What did it matter?

In an annoying way, though, something did matter. Mandy was still itching to slap Maria. She didn't like having that scornful laughter directed her way, nor did she like the way the girl watched Sean. Exactly what Maria wanted was written all over her lovely face, expressed soundlessly in her sensual pouting lips.

Poor kid, the teenage years were rough. Poor kid hell!

Mandy returned Maria's stare with a shrug, then looked around the kitchen. Lunch was on the table. Julio and Sean were eating; Maria had apparently already finished.

Señora Garcia laid out a plate for her. It was fish, deliciously spiced. Mandy sat and ate; Sean and Julio both glanced at her, then resumed their conversation.

She grew irritated again that Sean Ramiro

— policeman *extraordinaire* — still did nothing. Then she noticed that even while he was eating, Julio carried his gun, one hand in his lap, ready to make a grab for it.

When Julio finished eating he went up to his mother, encircling her waist with his arms to say something. Sean leaned across the table to her. "Want to go back outside?"

She would never understand what possessed her to snap back at him, but she did. "No, thanks. We bigots like to be alone!"

He sat back, lashes shielding his eyes, his mouth tightened in a grim line.

Mandy stood up and waltzed past Maria and her radio, surprised to hear a voice with a beautiful Bahamian accent announce that it was almost four o'clock.

Swimming had done one thing for her; it had caused time to pass. But, like an idiot, she had resigned herself to a locked room when she might have known freedom.

With a sigh she sank down on her mattress, then realized with a bit of a start that there was a kerosene lantern on the floor, and a book of matches.

Sean had kept his word.

With shaking fingers she lit the lantern. It occurred to her that she could probably light a fire and burn down the entire place. It also occurred to her that they might let

her burn to death, and she wasn't desperate enough — yet — to risk that.

She frowned suddenly as a little pool of light fell around her. There was a book beside the lantern. She picked it up and read the title; it was on Caribbean fish. It might not be compelling, but it was certainly better than nothing. It had probably been the only thing that Sean could find in the place.

Smiling slightly, she began to leaf through it. Then she began to yawn, and to her amazement she found that she was drifting off. She blew out the lantern and let sleep come.

Later, probably much later, because it had become dark, she awakened with a start. Puzzled, she rose up on her elbows, keenly attuned to the darkness, frightened to the core, but not sure why.

And then she knew. There was no sound, no movement — but she knew. Someone was in the room.

And it wasn't Sean.

Someone was in the room and moving swiftly. She opened her mouth to scream, but a hand came down over it. A heavy sinewy weight fell against her, and she heard a terse whisper in Spanish.

Madness catapulted through her. She

couldn't scream, so she tried to bite. She tried to kick and flail and fight, but that wiry arm remained around her, firm and unrelenting.

She could feel his breath. She could see again that image of gnashing teeth, of brutal hunger.

She tried everything, but she couldn't dislodge the hand over her mouth nor the weight bearing down on her.

She heard the sudden tearing of fabric and realized that his free hand was on her halter top. She felt his palm on her flesh, hot, urgent.

That was when she managed to twist her mouth free at last in a spurt of desperate energy. She gasped for breath, then screamed as loud as she could, and long.

His open palm crashed against her cheek, and the world seemed to spin. But it didn't matter, not at all. Because the door had burst open, bringing help.

She needed no light, no sound, no movement. She recognized the presence filling the doorway, filling the room.

Sean.

## 8

One moment Roberto was above her; the next he was not.

Light streamed surreally into the room from the parlor beyond. Gasping for breath, Mandy clutched the torn halter top to her, scrambling to her feet.

The still ebony night was immediately shattered. She was suddenly surrounded by shadows and shouts, and between those bursts of staccato noise she heard the heavy sounds of fists landing against flesh.

There was a loud crash. Roberto and Sean had gone flying through the doorway together to land on the parlor floor, both grim, both bloodied — both still at it. Shaken, Mandy followed them. Julio was yelling; Maria was screaming; and Señora Garcia was watching the proceedings, white-faced.

Just then a gun went off. Mandy screamed again, but no one heard her that time. Sean and Roberto had both ceased fighting at that shot, twisting to stare at Julio.

Mandy didn't understand what followed. Everyone was speaking in Spanish. Roberto

was obviously swearing vehemently and trying to make some point. Every bit as vehemently, Sean was arguing his side. Señora Garcia tried to say something, and Maria started up again, staring at Mandy, then spitting in her direction.

Julio shouted out a command, which everyone ignored, so he shot another bullet into the ceiling — which finally brought the silence he desired.

With everyone quiet once again he started to talk to Roberto, and then to Sean. Finally he paused to stare at Mandy who was standing, wide-eyed and ashen, in the doorway. He cocked his head with interest, then shrugged and spoke to the two men again. Roberto protested; Julio swore.

And then, whatever the argument had been, it was decided. Sean and Roberto both stood and walked grimly out the front door. Señora Garcia crossed herself and stepped into the second bedroom, slamming the door. Julio followed the two men outside.

"What is going on!" Mandy finally screamed, clenching her fists at her side.

Maria, elegantly decked out in a long gauzy nightgown that nicely displayed her attributes, gave Mandy another of her scornful looks and spoke disdainfully. "You

— you are the problem! You will get him killed!"

"What?" Mandy demanded, startled and alarmed.

"It is all your fault."

She'd had it with Maria, and no one else was around. Mandy strode to her in a sudden fury and grabbed a handful of dark glistening hair. "You tell me this instant what is going on!"

"Oww! Let go!" Maria screeched, trying to free her hair. "Julio says they are welcome to fight it out over you! And Roberto is a killer, you stupid *puta!* You will get Miguel killed!"

"Julio is not going to let them kill one another!" Mandy snapped.

"Roberto will break Miguel's neck! And all because of you!"

"He tried to rape me, you stupid little witch!"

"You should have enjoyed him —"

"Enjoyed? Rape? If you like him so much, sweetie, you're welcome to him! Now get out of my way!"

Mandy shoved Maria aside, wondering just how much of a killer Roberto was. Any man could look tough with a gun, and that seemed to be the source of Roberto's strength. She tried to assure herself that he

was nothing but hot air, and that Sean could take care of himself.

But she was frightened. Very frightened. If something did happen to him, she wouldn't be able to live with herself.

If she lived at all, she thought grimly, because she would fight Roberto herself until she had no breath left in her body.

Mandy swung open the front door. The natural coolness of the ocean breeze touched her cheeks soothingly, but she felt no ease as she paused and stared into the star-studded night. She could see the three of them down near the surf.

Julio's gun was in his hand; Sean and Roberto were wrestling on the sand, coming together, drawing apart, falling to roll on the beach together.

Mandy ran down to where Julio stood. He was watching the action with no apparent emotion.

"Why are you letting them do this!" she screamed at him. "You can make them stop."

"I cannot. No one can."

"You've got the gun —"

"Miguel says that you are his, only his. Roberto says that you are no virgin to be returned untouched. If you've had one lover, he should have rights, too."

"You didn't kidnap me for that vulture's amusement, Julio! Come on, think! You're in charge of this thing, aren't you? Julio, you're wrong in what you're doing, but you're a man with morals and ideals. You —"

"I am not in this alone now! If Roberto loses, he loses!"

"And if he doesn't? Julio! I can't believe this of you!" She paused, swallowing, because there was a set expression on his handsome face. "Julio! I am a person, not the spoils of war! And you know that!"

"Roberto cannot shoot Miguel. They are evenly matched, no weapons. That is fair — and it's all that I can do."

"Fair . . ." Mandy paused in horror, because beyond Julio, the two men were on their feet once again, carefully circling each other.

Mandy caught her breath. There was a scratch on Sean's shoulder, and a smear of blood at the right corner of his mouth, but he looked all right otherwise. The shimmering fury of the fight was in his narrowed eyes; he appeared more than ready to keep up the battle.

Roberto was the one looking the worse for wear. He was wiry and strong, but he simply didn't have Sean's powerful shoulders or arms. Roberto had already accrued one

black eye — which was puffing and turning an ugly green color right now — and his jaw was swollen, too. But he still had a look of blood lust about him, as if he was playing right now. As if he would win when he was ready.

Sean suddenly ducked his head and made a lunge for Roberto, throwing him to the ground. They rolled together, then split apart. Roberto didn't look so self-assured this time, but he smiled slowly at his opponent and reached into his pocket, drawing out a switchblade.

"Look out!" Mandy screamed.

Sean saw the blade. It made a rushing sound as Roberto brought it slicing through the night, and Sean ducked. Roberto struck nothing but air. The pattern was repeated. Sean was a second ahead of it every time.

Mandy spun on Julio. "You told me he had no weapons! You said that it would be fair. You said —"

"I cannot intercede! Don't you understand? He must beat Roberto, or Roberto will not respect him."

Mandy didn't think that Roberto would ever respect anyone. No matter how this ended, he would try to stab Sean — or anyone — in the back whenever it suited his purpose.

She started walking across the sand, but Julio caught her shoulders. "What are you doing?"

"Roberto has a knife. Miguel will have me!"

"Get back here! Do you want to wind up cut?"

"I'd rather be cut," Mandy retorted vehemently, "than handed over like a trophy!"

"No!" Julio said, but she wrenched herself away from him, ignoring his gun as if it didn't exist. She didn't believe that he would shoot her.

Sean saw her coming. "Get out of here, Mandy!"

Roberto laughed, thinking to take advantage of the distraction. He lunged; Sean escaped in the nick of time. Mandy instinctively reached down for a handful of sand to throw in Roberto's eyes.

She did throw the sand, but it didn't matter. In that split second Sean had kicked Roberto's wrist, sending the switchblade flying out into the night.

Then Sean was flying, too. He threw himself against Roberto, sending the man down on his back, with Sean on top of him. He rolled Roberto over, wrenched the man's arm behind his back, then straddled him.

Mandy gasped with relief and sank onto

the sand herself. She watched as Julio walked over to the two men and spoke to them, clipping out orders in a soft but furious rush of Spanish.

Mandy's fingers dug into the sand. She realized suddenly that she was touching something metallic. Her eyes fell to her fingers, and she saw that she had the knife. Her fingers curled completely around it. While the men were occupied with one another she slipped it into the pocket of her cutoffs.

Sean got back to his feet then; Julio was still talking to Roberto in scathing tones as Sean walked over to Mandy. He threaded his fingers through his hair, grinning at her, and reached down to help her to her feet.

She accepted his assistance, staring at him. "Are you — are you okay?"

His grin deepened and he shrugged. "Yeah, Ma, you should see the other guy."

She lowered her head, smiling, then allowed him to pull her to her feet. He slipped an arm around her, and they returned to the house together.

Maria was waiting in the kitchen. When she saw Sean, she gave a little cry of ecstasy and raced toward him, ignoring Mandy. Maria leaned on his free shoulder, kissing the cut there between bursts of excited concern.

Amanda eyed her with tolerant patience, raising a brow to Sean and moving away.

He set Maria away from him, speaking softly but firmly. She touched his shoulder again. "I will take care of it —"

"There is no need, Maria. It is nothing. I . . ." He paused, pulling Mandy back to his side. "We are going to bed."

He started walking, leading Mandy with him. She glanced back to see Maria standing there, and despite everything she felt sorry for the girl.

She and Sean seemed to share an opinion of Maria: that she was still a child, a child trying to play in a grown-up's world, no matter how lovely her face or figure.

I could be jealous, Mandy thought, and it was a disturbing idea. It was . . . the circumstances, she told herself. But it was more, and she knew it. Their time together had been limited, but it had also been very intense. She felt that she knew him better than people she had known for years and years. He angered her; he intrigued her. He absolutely fascinated her.

The other bedroom door opened before they reached their own. Señora Garcia, still ashen, came out. She spoke softly to Sean, and he replied in kind. She smiled at last, nodded, then returned to the bedroom she

apparently shared with Maria.

Mandy glanced back once again. Julio and Roberto still had not come in. Maria remained where she had been, though, watching them. Watching them just as tragically as Scarlett O'Hara had watched Ashley Wilkes walk into a bedroom with his Melanie.

Then she couldn't see Maria, because Sean prodded her into the bedroom. He lit the lantern before shutting the door.

Mandy stood still, feeling a little rueful, a little shy — and more than a little confused.

Sean placed the lantern by the bed, then noticed her standing there. He frowned curiously. "What's with you?"

"Thank you."

"For what?"

"You saved my life."

He shrugged, casting himself back on the mattress, locking his fingers behind his head, then gazing at her with an amused grin. "I didn't save your life. He had no intention of killing you."

"But I'd have rather died," she said softly. "And — and he might have killed you."

"I should hope not!" Sean snorted.

She walked over to the mattress and sank down beside him on her knees, then lightly ran a finger over the red scratch on his

185

shoulder. "Shouldn't you clean it?"

He gritted his teeth and caught her hand. "It's no big deal. Just leave it alone."

She snatched her hand away, reddening. But he didn't notice; he was suddenly sitting up, playing with her torn shirt, trying to find a way to make it stay completely where it belonged.

"It's all right. Just leave it!" she snapped.

He drew his hand away, scowling. "If you walk around like that tomorrow we'll be in trouble all over again. In fact, if you hadn't flounced around today, all this might not have happened!"

"What are you talking about?" Mandy demanded furiously.

"You — in the water! Making that stupid outfit look like something from a centerfold."

"It's not *my* stupid outfit! Nobody warned me to dress for a kidnapping. And Maria didn't exactly give me the best stuff she had!"

"You could have stayed out of the water!"

"Oh, yeah? I'd like to see you locked up for hours and hours on end without going completely mad!"

He didn't have a ready answer for that one. He closed his eyes and lay back down, sighing. "I am going mad, I think," he mum-

bled. He kept talking in a flat monotone. "If I'd stayed locked up with you, I would be mad. And I wouldn't know anything."

Mandy hesitated a second. "What do you know?"

"Not too much," he admitted. "Juan was supposed to be back by now, but he isn't."

"Is Julio worried?"

"Not yet. He will be by tomorrow night, though. But if we're lucky, by tomorrow night we may be able to spot the Coast Guard."

Mandy moistened her lips. "What happens if Juan never makes it back? What will Julio do then?"

"Nothing," he told her.

"Nothing?"

"Stop worrying, will you? Things will break soon."

She didn't answer.

"For God's sake, lie down, will you please? Get some rest. If things do move, you'll want to be alert."

She lay down beside him, not touching him, but all too aware that he was there. He didn't speak.

"He threatened to chop off one of my fingers," Mandy murmured at last. "Julio did. To send to Peter."

There was a soft sigh from beside her.

"That was a threat, nothing more."

"It sounded real."

"What good is a threat if it doesn't sound real?" He sat up, leaning over to blow out the lantern.

"But —"

"Mandy, quit it! Trust me. Everything is going to work out all right. Please, go to sleep."

He flopped back down on the mattress, and the ebony darkness surrounded them once again.

There had been exasperation in his voice, and the harsh sound of his temper rising. Cast once again into a vortex of confusion, Mandy lay still and concentrated on each breath she took.

It wasn't fair; he was blaming her for things that were beyond her control. She'd tried to thank him for risking his life, but even that had annoyed him.

"I didn't ask to be here!" she snapped suddenly, whirling to face him, though she couldn't see him at all.

"I didn't say you did."

"You have an attitude about this whole thing! In fact, you're one great mass of attitudes! I have to thank you, because I couldn't have dealt with that weasel myself. But it's not my fault he's such scum, and it's not my fault I've been given such

ridiculous clothes to wear."

"I —"

"You just shut up for a minute! Don't you dare blame me for anything! I didn't make you come along — that was your choice."

Silence followed her last emphatic words. He didn't move, and she wondered what his reaction would be to her sudden show of temper.

"Sean?"

He chuckled softly, and the sound touched her like a caress in the night. "Are you quite through?" he asked.

"Quite!"

"Good. I'm not blaming you for anything — except for the sleep I'm missing right now."

"Sorry," she said stiffly.

"Lie down."

"You're at it again."

"I'm not." She couldn't see his grin, but she could feel it. "I didn't tell you to take your clothes off, I just said to lie down."

"You —"

"You —" His movement was swift, startling, as he gently shushed her with a hand over her mouth. "*Querida,* go to sleep!"

Meekly she sank back onto the mattress, his touch, his voice, reducing her to quivers.

*Querida . . .*

He'd said it so softly. *Querida* . . . darling, loved one . . . sweetheart. It wasn't just the word; it was the way he had said it, in Spanish, as if there wasn't an English word that would do justice to his meaning.

He curled up beside her, his back to her. She tried breathing again, deeply, counting each breath. She was no longer irritated, or even hurt, but she was still confused, both by him and by her own feelings. And also by the yearnings she felt in the darkness.

She tried to sleep, but she felt as if she was in the center of a maelstrom. It was of her own making, but it was there nevertheless. She heard the beat of her heart, each breath she took. And each breath that he took. She imagined that despite the space he had left between them she could hear the beat of his heart.

She couldn't sleep; she couldn't even keep her eyes closed. She felt a restless energy that defied the night, and if she closed her eyes too long, she thought of Roberto. She remembered waking up, not being able to see, yet knowing he was the one above her. She remembered feeling his hands, knew again the horror of failing in her fight against him. . . .

She took a deep breath, then exhaled. Sean wanted to sleep, but maybe she could

sit with the lantern on the other side of the room. Maybe he wouldn't mind.

Sean. She felt awareness ripple through her again, and she couldn't begin to understand herself. She should have been thinking of the million reasons why she didn't want anything to do with him. She should have been burying herself in guilt — even in pain. But none of that mattered, not tonight.

She didn't even really want the light; she wanted *him,* awake. Whispering to her, talking to her, reassuring her. She wanted to run her fingers over the sunbrowned sleekness of his chest, press soft kisses against his skin, taste the salt of the sea on his flesh. . . .

It was dark, but she knew that she burned crimson. How could she be thinking this way? Feeling this way?

She sat up abruptly, determined to reach carefully across him for the lantern and matches. She would take the light to a corner of the room and read her book. That might distract her from the thoughts that were playing such havoc with her mind.

But when she groped her way over him the rounded curve of her breast fell against his arm, and her bare midriff collided with his naked chest. The short crisp hairs there seemed to tease her mercilessly, just as the

contact of their bodies, hot despite the coolness of the night, seemed to create a kinetic energy so startling that she drew in her breath.

He caught her arm, holding her where she lay. "Mrs. Blayne, just what are you doing?"

"I was . . . just . . . I was —"

"Mrs. Blayne, please don't touch me unless you mean it."

He said it jokingly, lightly, but she knew that he wasn't teasing.

"I won't . . ." she began, but the words froze on her lips. "Don't touch me unless you mean it," he had said. And she had meant it with all her heart and soul and being . . . this night.

The midnight blackness left no room for reason or thought, for a past or for a future. All she knew was that she wanted him. Wanted to touch him. To be touched. To go wherever touching might lead them.

She leaned over him, pressing her lips against the hollow of his shoulder, holding them there for a fervent moment, then pushing the tip of her tongue between them, tasting his flesh, closing her eyes at the sleek salt sensation, savoring the elusive liquid quivering that burst and streaked through her like dancing stars. Savoring his gasp, the catch of his breath, the shudder that racked him.

"Hey!" He clutched her shoulders harshly, wrenching her high above him. Even in the night she could see the glitter of his eyes. His muscles were taut, his whisper harsh.

"I said —" he swallowed sharply and continued through clenched teeth "— not to touch me unless —"

"I mean it," she interrupted him abruptly, her voice as harsh as his. She didn't want to talk about it; she didn't want to be warned. She wanted to be held. She wanted to make love. To feel the world spiraling around her, to arch and writhe and roll in sensual splendor and temptation.

Still he only held her.

She tried to whisper to him, but sound eluded her.

And then it didn't really matter, because he lowered her against him, slowly, until their bodies touched completely, her length on his, legs tangling, her breasts hard against his chest, their mouths not an inch apart.

Then touching.

Perhaps he was still distrustful; perhaps he had a reason to be so. He held her shoulders when he first kissed her, just touching her lips, then pulling away. Then he touched them once again, curiously, questioningly.

193

He tasted them next, his tongue an exotic paintbrush that swirled across them like sable. He traced the shape of her mouth, then pressed his lips against her shoulder.

And then it was as if he gave up all thought of reason. Of sanity. Of the past. Of the future.

His arms wrapped strongly around her; his lips were hard against hers, almost bruising in their sudden passion. His tongue made an intimate invasion, demanding total entrance, total surrender, bending the night magic of her body solely to his will, throwing her heart to the four winds of chance.

He held her in his arms and rolled with her, sweeping her beneath him, and the magic continued. His body against hers felt incredibly good, right, as if they had been made not just as man and woman, but as this man meant specifically for this woman, this woman meant just for this man. His body seemed to meld to hers, a fusion of heat, of fire. Like flint to stone they sparked, drew away, then sparked again . . . and ignited. It was a blaze she never wanted to put out. . . .

He drove his fingers through her hair, holding her still to meet his kiss. He cupped and massaged her skull, cherished the rich-

ness of her hair. She stroked his nape and then his back, skimming lightly over his spine with her nails. And she thrilled to the pressure of his hips against hers, his desire evident.

He broke the kiss, easing away from her, longing with all his heart to see her. To see the color of her hair. To watch her as he touched her, stripped her . . . slowly, relishing each new bit of golden flesh revealed to his gaze.

Rolling closer to her, he ran his fingers over her cheek, then kissed her again with slow fascination and let his hands roam, exploring the roundness of her breast, soft and yet firm, the nipples taut beneath the thin cotton material. Just thinking of them, he felt an inner combustion. Now. He had to have her now. . . .

But he forced himself to stay under control. He stroked her naked ribs before seeking out the tie of the halter top, gently undoing it, letting the material fall aside. Urgency claimed him again, hot and strident, as her naked breasts fell freely into his hands, taunted his palms. He lowered his head to her, drawing a pattern with his tongue in the deep valley between her breasts, then feeling the splendor of imagination obliterated in the magic of truth as

he savored her with his lips, the gentle tender grazing of his teeth.

He felt dizzy with desire. He moved his hands against her, fingers slipping beneath the waistband of her cutoffs, dipping low upon her abdomen, then nearly yanking at the snap and zipper. She issued a soft little cry, and he kissed her to silence her, the motion of his hands edging the cutoffs lower and lower.

And then it was he who cried out, an oath of impatience, and he moved away from her, grasping the tattered hems of the cutoffs, easing them down the wickedly lovely length of her legs.

He wanted the light. He wanted to see her: the glorious fan of sunlight and wheaten hair; the shimmering desire in her eyes; her features taut with passion. The rise of her breasts; the dip of her belly. Her back; the curves of her buttocks. He wanted to see all of her.

He started to move off the mattress, and she realized his intent. Crying out softly, she rose to meet him, grasping his shoulders, burying her head against his neck and seductively pressing her breasts against him.

"No! Please."

"I was just going to light the lamp."

"No. No light. Let it be darkness. Let it be magic."

He should refuse. He should tell her that there could be magic in the light. He should not allow her to make love in the darkness.

Done in the darkness, in the ebony night, it would not be real. It would not exist in the morning's light.

"Please, Sean. Please."

Her whisper, her breath against his flesh, stirred the blaze of his near-desperate passion once again. He couldn't refuse her anything.

Kneeling, they moved together. Kneeling, he felt the exquisite femininity of her body, touched so thoroughly by his own. He kissed her, explored her and forced her back at last, pressing her down upon her stomach.

He couldn't see her; he had to know her. He pressed his mouth against the small of her back, against her spine. Lust burned raw inside of him. It was torture; it was delicious.

All along her spine he kissed her, moving his hands down over her buttocks, down her legs, knowing their shape. Down to her feet, and even there he played, kissing her toes, stroking the soles of her feet, massaging them. She arched; she moaned softly; she

made little inarticulate sounds. Dear God, he wanted to see her! He smiled a little grimly, even a little maliciously, for the movements of her body cried to his, though she choked back her cries of arousal, of readiness.

He had no intention of being had so easily.

When his fingers left her feet they stroked, slowly, excruciatingly slowly, to her inner thighs, urging them apart, finding she had no strength for denial.

He rolled her over. She was as pliable as a kitten, as passionate as a tigress as she reached for him, whispering incoherently for him to stop, to come to her.

"Not yet," he whispered against her lips. He waited there, above her, as his fingers played between her legs, as she gasped and arched against him, holding him, pushing him away, trying to touch him in turn.

Her nails scratched lightly over his chest, explored his back, tried to dip beneath the waistband of his cutoffs and met with frustration. She tugged at the button and the zipper with trembling fingers and found frustration again. They would not give for her. And again for him it was agony . . . and it was ecstasy.

He kissed her, his tongue delving deeply

into her mouth. And then he whispered of the wonder of her body, and what it was doing, whispered with his lips just half an inch from her mouth until she thought she would go mad.

"Sean!"

"What?"

"Take — take your clothes off."

"Aha! I told you that you would get to it eventually. All women are alike!"

"Sean . . ."

"Mandy, I'd strip for you anytime. In private, of course."

She half giggled, half sobbed.

And he thought that if he waited any longer he would explode, and they would have to pick up the pieces of what had once been a man. In seconds he had obliged her, tossing his cutoffs somewhere into the magical black arena surrounding them, returning to her with the full strength of his desire evident.

She touched him, and his impatience soared. He held her face with his hands, spread her thighs with his knees, kissed her deeply and entered her deeply.

The black magic of the night swirled around them. At first the tempo of their loving was slow, then frenetic. Kisses, caresses and the spiraling maelstrom of desire

set them apart from the world. This was passion, born in the darkness, bred by fear and sensation, gratitude and natural hunger. And something more. . . .

He had to be mad. He was lost within her. Lost in the welcoming embrace of her body, shuddering with sensation, volatile, ecstatic, as he had never been before. Touching her inside and out, knowing her, caressing her, reaching the pinnacle together, holding each other, drifting.

It was passion only, he told himself.

Strange. When he touched her damp brow, when she curled against him, when the curve of her breast so comfortably touched his chest and her slender leg was cast so trustingly over his . . .

It was passion.

Yet it felt ridiculously as if he were falling in love.

# 9

When Sean awoke, it was barely dawn with just the palest filtering of pink light entering the room. He could make out Mandy's huddled form, curled so trustingly against him, lips slightly parted as she breathed, her lashes falling against her cheeks, her hair falling over her shoulders — and his own.

He eased away from her and carefully pulled the covers to her shoulders. He wanted to hold her, to glory in her all over again, but the shield of darkness was gone, and he knew innately that she had been his only because of that darkness.

Sean rose silently and donned his cutoffs. He needed to be alone. He crept quietly from the room, closing the door tightly behind him.

Julio, on a mat outside the door, was awake, watching him, the ever-present Magnum at his side.

"I'm just going down to the beach," Sean said.

Julio nodded and lay back down on the mat. Sean continued on out the kitchen

door. No one was really awake yet. No one but him.

He was glad. There was no time here like the breaking of the dawn. No time when the heavens appeared more magenta, no time when the coming sun kissed the sand more gently. A breeze stirred the trees and the rippling water.

He walked over the soft dunes and neared the water, listening to the soft rush of the tide, gazing at the glittering droplets caught and dazzled by the coming sun. Again the irony of it all struck him. Here, in this incredible Eden, they were prisoners. It should have been a place of freedom. No crime should touch this shore, only laughter and tenderness and . . . passion.

They should have made love beneath the stars, not on a shabby mattress inside a primitive cabin in the dark. This was a place of exquisite loveliness; it should have remained unsoiled.

Sean sat down and wrapped his arms around his knees.

So many things in his life had been beautiful, he thought.

Havana had been beautiful. Once upon a time it had been a fantastic city, a playground for the rich and famous. There had been dancing and music, beautiful women,

poets and musicians, artisans and scholars. The warm Caribbean breezes had touched the patios of homes and nightclubs; the palms had swayed; the air had been touched by perfume.

Once upon a time . . .

He had been only six the last time he had seen Havana, but as long as he lived he would never forget that night.

Revolution had been brewing for a long time. The old men at the cafés had talked about it; the young men had shouted about it. Batista had been a dictator, and it was very true that the poor had suffered beneath him. Yes, revolution had been brewing. His father simply had not seen it clearly enough.

As a six-year-old Sean had adored both his parents. They'd met in New York City, where his mother had been a model and his father had been selling superior Havana cigars. They had fiery tempers, but totally different cultural backgrounds. Love had always been the tie that bound the two of them. It had been imperative that they learn about each other's cultures to appreciate and understand each other. Consequently, Sean had been born in Dublin, beneath the benign eyes of his maternal grandparents.

And consequently they had been in Havana on the night the gunfire began.

He could remember it all so clearly. December, but a hot night. His father had been downstairs on the patio, talking with a few cronies. His mother had been in the kitchen, humming, fixing rum punches for their company. Sean had been sitting at the kitchen table, laboriously practicing his handwriting.

And then it had started, a rat-tat-tatting somewhere down the street, so soft that they had ignored it at first. But then there had been screams, and his father, such a handsome man with his flashing dark eyes and lean whipcord physique, had come dashing up the stairs.

He'd shouted that they must go, that they must get to the airport. Sean could remember his mother bursting into tears when it became clear that his father was not going to join them.

"You're an American, too! You're an American citizen! This is not your —"

"I am an American, but I am also Cuban. Siobhan, go, now, for my son's sake! I will meet you in the States. I will meet you!"

And so they ran. His father's friend, Xavier, got them through the streets. Streets littered here and there with bodies. With soldiers, with revolutionaries. With the injured, with the dying. Streets that seemed

alive with screaming.

At one point, they'd been stopped — by a looter, of all things on such a night. His mother had been held while he, a child, had struggled ineffectually. That had been when he decided he would never be helpless again.

With the pure fury of a child he had escaped the man holding him and bitten the man attacking his mother, giving Xavier the chance to wrest the gun from the man. Xavier had killed him, and their mad dash for freedom had continued.

They'd reached the embassy — and they'd gotten out.

But he'd never seen his father again, nor Xavier. They'd settled in Miami, where his mother had spent the next ten years of her life waiting for news of his father. When it came, it was bad. He had been shot that night. He had died with the revolution.

Adjusting to life in Miami had been hard. Sean spoke Spanish fluently, but his English had an Irish accent, and all the kids had made fun of him. Nobody had cared much what you sounded like in New York, because New York had been full of all kinds of people. But not Miami — not then.

Cubans began entering the city in droves, escaping to freedom. The federal govern-

ment helped them, which led to resentment. Sean's life became ever harder. No one could understand a Cuban boy named Sean who had an Irish mother.

Somewhere along the line — the third grade? — he'd created a new world for himself. He started telling his schoolmates that Ramiro was Castilian, that his mother had married his father in Madrid.

Then his mother found out about the story. She'd gone as white as paste and started to cry in a way that tore his insides all to pieces. "Sean! How could you? How could you deny your father?"

That had been the last time he had ever done so. He had gone to his mother, and they had cried together. When he went to bed that night all he could think about was his father, his laughter, his temper, his total devotion to his wife — and to his son. His love for the world at large and for his own heritage.

From that moment on he was proud of what he was. Irish, Cuban — and American. American all the way.

And naturally, as time passed, things evened out. In high school half his classmates were various forms of Anglo, half were various forms of Latino. He played football with a natural ability, and by his ju-

nior year that made him incredibly popular.

He went to college in Nebraska on a football scholarship. He liked Nebraska, but not as much as home. And though he earned a law degree, he didn't want to practice. He wanted to be a cop. He'd wanted to be one ever since that night in Havana, when he had learned that law and order were precious commodities.

Then, when he'd first come home, he'd fallen in love. Her name was Sandra Johnson, and she had been beautiful. Blond and blue-eyed and blue-blooded all the way. They'd met at a nightclub and fallen in love to a John Denver tune, slow dancing beneath the colored lights. All he'd really known about her was that she worked in her family's business as a receptionist. That seemed to be all he needed to know at the time. They met every night. They made love on what seemed like every beach in the state.

She was passionate, lovely, and everything he had ever desired.

But on a cool September night, when he was twenty-four and thought that he owned the world, he had received a blow that nearly destroyed him.

She met him that night, tremendously nervous, teary-eyed, anxious and excited.

She blurted out instantly that she was pregnant, then awaited his reaction.

He was thrilled. A home and a family. He was ready for them both. A child, his father's grandchild, to hold and love and nurture — and to whom to give the world, just as his parents had given it to him. America, with all its merging fascinating cultures.

He'd held her tenderly, and they'd planned their life. They would look into the nice new town houses on Miller Road, and they would be married in St. Theresa's. His pay wasn't great, but it was sufficient.

Sandra had been starry-eyed then, as happy as a lark. They had to meet each other's parents, of course. Sean knew that his mother would love Sandra. And by this time in his life he could see no reason why the Johnsons wouldn't like him.

He arrived at their house neatly suited. He was somewhat stunned by the mansion on the water, but he hadn't come from poverty. His mother had done well modeling, and his father's investments had all been in the U.S. His mom had a wonderful old home in Miami Shores. And if anyone was "class," it was Siobhan Ramiro.

But not to the Johnsons.

When the maid led him into the elegant receiving room Sandra was nowhere in

sight. Only her mother and father were there, greeting him politely but informing him that Sandra was gone.

Where? he had demanded, confused.

And then it had all come out. They were terribly sorry, but didn't he understand that they were "the" Lockwood Johnsons; they couldn't possibly allow their daughter to marry a — a refugee.

Lockwood Johnson went on to say coolly that the baby had already been aborted.

Well, he — a cop — had gotten arrested that night. His temper — Irish, Cuban or all-American — had soared to a point where he had seen nothing but red, and he'd charged Lockwood Johnson with all the fury he had learned on the football field.

Johnson had probably expected something along those lines. He'd whistled, and four bodyguards had come rushing in. Even then, it had taken them fifteen minutes to wrestle him down.

He could still remember Mrs. Johnson murmuring something about the behavior of "riffraff," but all he really knew was that he had woken up in a jail cell.

All he could think at the time was that the Johnsons were the ones who deserved to be in jail. They'd murdered his child; they'd taken a piece of his heart.

Logically, he had known that they represented an extreme. His friends, his best friends, his co-workers, all came in mixed nationalities. Half the Cuban girls he knew had married Anglo men, and vice versa. Of course there were still cultural differences. Some people resented those who spoke Spanish; some thought it was good to know two languages. Things didn't change that quickly. But people were people, and friendships formed where they would, as did love — when it was allowed.

He had decided then that he wouldn't fall in love again. Especially not with a blonde.

So what the hell was he doing now? It was ridiculous; it was impossible. He should be staying as far away as he could from Mrs. Amanda — Anglo — Blayne.

He closed his eyes tightly then opened them to the lightening sky. He realized that he was clenching his fists so tightly that his nails were cutting into his palms.

He wasn't in love, he told himself dully. This whole thing was nothing more than circumstance. He had known her only a few days, and she'd turned to him only because she was frightened and lonely. She'd turned to him in the dark, hiding.

He straightened his shoulders. God! If they could just get off of this damned island!

He tried to bring himself under control, but anger filled him. He reminded himself that under no circumstances could he risk her life, yet he was ready to run headfirst into Roberto, just to end it all. Last night had been ecstasy; this morning was hell.

"Sean?"

He turned around and saw her standing there. All blonde and all beautiful. Thin and lithe and curved, and yet suddenly so Anglo that he wanted to scream. Her face was so perfect: tawny eyes alive above the high Anglo cheekbones. He couldn't read her expression; she seemed a little pale beneath her tan. She carried two cups of coffee and pressed one toward him.

He accepted, and found himself staring at her legs. Long legs, slimly muscled. He thought about the way they had wrapped around him, and he felt dizzy once again.

Good God, he wanted her. With all the heat and tempest and passion inside him, he wanted her. Right here, on the beach. He wanted Julio and Roberto and even Mama Garcia and Maria to drop dead, to fall into a hole. He wanted her naked beneath him on the white sand, far away from society. Far from a nightmare that he had forgotten, far from a place where an unborn child could be killed because of his heritage.

She laughed softly, just a little bit nervously. "Aren't you going to ask me to sit down?"

"No. Thanks for the coffee. Go away. What are you doing out here, anyway?" He scowled, staring back toward the water. He felt her stiffen and knew it was for the best. He didn't have any difficulty being friends with beautiful Anglos, or with dating them, or with going to bed with them, for that matter.

Just falling in love with them.

"I just walked out with the coffee. No one stopped me."

"Well, walk somewhere else."

She told him exactly what he should do with himself and turned on her heel.

Where the hell was the damned FBI? he wondered. One lousy little kidnapping and they hadn't appeared yet! They had a lot of nerve calling the cops yokels!

She walked away, not back to the house, but down the beach. He felt as if part of him had frozen over.

He turned slightly. Roberto was outside now, sitting near the door, training his damn Magnum on Amanda.

Sean looked back in her direction. She had finished her coffee and thrown herself into the surf.

For a long while he just sat there, watching her swim. Then she stood, wringing her hair out. Her ribs were bare, gleaming with water. The torn halter she had somehow mended was clinging to her breasts like a second skin. The cutoffs were doing little better at her hips.

Sean twisted slightly to see Roberto watching her, leering. Sean stood and marched down the beach. With no thought whatsoever, his temper soaring toward red again, he strode through the shallows to reach her, then grasped her shoulders, shaking her.

"Let me go, you animal!" she snapped. Her beautiful tawny eyes were red-rimmed. From the salt water? Or had she been crying?

He started to soften.

"I mean it! Get your filthy hands off me!"

He released her. Just like that.

"You liked my filthy hands well enough last night," he sneered.

"That was last night," she said coolly.

"Good. Because if you keep on the way you're going, it's not going to be my filthy hands on you — it will be Roberto's. And if you think I'll battle it out for you again, lady, you'd better think again."

He turned around and walked away from her.

By the time he reached the house Señora Garcia and Maria were outside. Maria had on a cute-little-nothing bikini. Accomplice to a kidnapping or not, Maria knew how to dress. She headed down to the water.

And at that moment Sean felt like speaking Spanish. He noticed that Amanda had stretched out facedown on the sand, a good distance away from them all. He strode back into the surf. Maria was just a kid, but right now he felt like nothing so much as playing kids' games in the water with her.

It was the longest day Mandy had ever experienced in her life.

When she awoke she was glad of the solitude he had given her. Though she was bundled in the covers, she felt her nudity acutely. Her nudity, and her body. Muscles that had been unused for a long time were delightfully sore. She felt guilt and she felt shame, yet she felt like a cat at the same time, wonderfully stroked and petted and loved.

Tears came to her eyes because it had been so good. Because he had been so tender and gentle and so wonderfully savage at just the right moment. Because she couldn't remember lovemaking being such

214

a vivid experience, and because that made her feel guilty all over again, because she had loved her husband so much.

Yet even then, amid the guilt and shame, she had been all too aware of the forbidden knowledge that he had the power to ease the past, if not erase it. He was so powerful and fascinating that she savored the thought of him, just as her body savored the memory of his. His scent was still with her, as were the memories of his arms, of the way he felt inside her.

They were captives on an island, forced together, she reminded herself. It was a nightmare, and please God, it would end, and they would go their separate ways, back to the lives they had led before this one. And yet . . .

She had to see him. To talk to him. To admit that she was afraid of the light, but that she wasn't denying anything. She needed to touch him again, to know that his arms were still there — for now, at least. She needed to tell him how much she cared about him, how much she appreciated him, how much . . . she was fascinated by him.

It was almost like falling in love.

And so she had dressed, only to find her halter still ripped. She had stepped out of the room holding the shirt in place. Señora

Garcia had clucked disapprovingly, then given her a needle and thread, and she had mended the halter. Then Señora Garcia had given her coffee, and she had hurried out to the beach, anxious to see Sean again.

She had received only the most horrible slap in the face, and it had hurt so badly that she had found herself awash with pain and confusion. The only way to rid herself of them had been to dive into the water.

Then he had touched her again, and she had felt such waves of shimmering heat, of anger, wash over her that she had been stunned all over again.

What had she done but make love with him?

She spent the morning lying in the sun; he spent it playing with Maria. Damn him. Cradle robber. What the hell did she care? She had been an idiot, and that was that.

So why in God's name was it tearing her to pieces? She should be worrying about her physical well-being. Juan wasn't back yet. When was Julio going to start snipping off her fingers?

A feminine voice started to chide her in Spanish. Mandy rolled over to find Señora Garcia standing beside her with a plate of food. She shook her head; she wasn't hungry.

Señora Garcia sighed, unhappily plumped her full figure down on the sand and pressed the plate into Mandy's hands.

Mandy ate resignedly. Lunch was a thin steak with rice and black beans, deliciously cooked. She ate everything on the plate, while Señora Garcia smiled at her.

At one point the older woman disappeared, then returned with a Coca-Cola. Mandy thanked her again and enjoyed the soda. The next time Señora Garcia left her, she didn't return.

Bored, and increasingly anxious and upset despite her determination not to be, Mandy took off for the water again. She swam and swam — and suddenly bumped into another body. Hands righted her, and she found herself staring into Roberto's dark eyes.

He laughed and gave her a mocking sneer. She kicked away from him swimming strenuously in the opposite direction, only to collide with another body.

Sean.

He pulled her back against his chest, but he didn't look at her. Instead he stared over her head at Roberto, who shrugged, then swam away.

Still Sean didn't release her shoulders. The water was cool, but she could feel his

body heat like an inferno. She could feel his body, every part of it, pressed against her.

She was furious; she wanted to jerk away from him. At the same time she felt as if all his heat was seeping into her, turning her muscles to liquid. Making her wish ridiculously that they were longtime friends and lovers. That they could laugh like guilty children, that under the cover of water they could shed their cutoffs and fit together. . . .

Roberto swam toward Maria. Señora Garcia had gone back into the house. Only Julio was on the shore, leaning against the house.

It might have been a scene from a resort brochure — except for the Magnum that Julio was holding.

Mandy wanted to break the silence, to tell Sean that she hated him, that she wanted him to get away from her — now! But his whisper touched her ear, soft, silky, sensual. So raspy and exciting that her mind might have been swept completely clear of all thought, except for . . . except for that all-encompassing excitement. It raced through her; it took control of her.

"Don't move," he implored raggedly. "Don't move at all."

His arms tightened around her as he started backing into deeper water. She was

weightless; her feet didn't touch the sand. She just drifted along with him, his arms around her keeping her hips level with his.

And then they were in deeper water. So cool, when they were so hot. She didn't move; she didn't try to speak. His hands moved slightly, cupping her breasts, his thumbs grazing her nipples. A sound caught in her throat as he pressed his lips against her neck.

Then he moved so deftly that she was filled all over again with a quaking desire that was so physical it overrode even the sensation of the sun. She felt his hand near her midriff, and then his fingers were sweeping beneath the waistband of her cut-offs before sliding the zipper down. The pressure of his palm against her abdomen made her breath come too quickly, made her heart race. She thought that she was mad, then she felt that she had reached the clouds, because his mind held the same thought as hers. That simple touch, body to body, had brought this. The need . . . the desire . . . despite all else . . . It seemed somehow illicit, and therefore all the more fascinating. She should have been shocked; she should have hated him; she should have turned him away — she should have been screaming bloody murder.

And instead she couldn't wait to feel him inside her.

Her cutoffs fell, but he caught them. Beneath the water she was nude. He wrapped one arm around her waist and let his free hand play over her buttocks.

Then, swiftly, he lifted her until her legs locked around his hips.

She couldn't stare into his eyes, so she rested her head against his shoulder. She stifled the cry that rose to her lips when he thrust into her, pressing her teeth lightly into his flesh.

"Look at me!" he warned her harshly. "Laugh, as if we're talking."

"I — I can't!" she gasped.

He was filling her. She burned; she ached; she needed more.

"Mandy . . . do it. Oh, Mandy."

He jerked, forcing her head back, forcing her to lace her fingers behind his neck and stare into his eyes. His smile was so wicked that once again it was as if the fact that they could get caught made every motion more thrilling. The friction of the water, the wonder of him, the pulsing of tension rose in her swiftly. Wonderfully. Suddenly she knew that she was going to burst, and that she would scream with the joy of it all.

But she didn't. He caught her lips in a

kiss, and her animal cry of awe and shuddering satiation was caught between them. He held her tight, moving hard against her one last time, a part of her. She went lax, incapable of movement in the aftermath. Thank God he held her. Thank God that he groaned softly, crushing her against him. She couldn't have stood; she might well have drowned in reality, rather than just drowning in his arms.

The water rippled around them and actually began to grow cold.

"You've got to get these back on," he told her huskily.

"I can't move."

"You have to."

"You got them off, you get them back on."

She was so drowsy; his answering chuckle was so husky. She wanted to forget everything. She wanted to remain against his shoulder and fall asleep.

"All right," he said agreeably.

And then he let her go and dove beneath the water. But what he did to her there had nothing to do with getting her pants back on, and everything to do with getting her excited again. She started to protest, swallowed water, then wrenched the cutoffs back from him and struggled back into them.

When she finished, he was still laughing. "Not fair!" she cried.

Suddenly he wasn't laughing anymore. He pulled her close to him, against his heart. His whisper touched her ear. "I'm sorry. Do you forgive me?"

"I guess I just did."

"No, that was sex, not forgiveness. Do you forgive me?"

She couldn't say anything. She didn't know if she did or didn't; she just knew that she didn't want him to let her go.

"Damn it, Julio is waving that stinking gun of his around. Come on. We've got to go in. Night must be coming."

It was. And with the night came a horrendous argument between Julio and Roberto.

Mandy didn't understand any of it; it was all in Spanish. She was in the kitchen when it began, eating a sausage sandwich for dinner. Señora Garcia decided that Mandy shouldn't be a part of it. She hurried Mandy into her room, made her wait, then returned with shampoo and soap. Mandy knew that though her suggestion that Mandy might want a shower seemed casual, the older woman was very upset.

It also frightened her that Sean had seemed upset by the argument. He hadn't protested at all when Señora Garcia led

Mandy out. He had remained at the table, listening tensely.

Mandy ambled restlessly around the room for a while as the argument went on. Finally she decided that she would take a shower; it would kill time.

When she came back into the bedroom Sean was there, lying under the blanket on the mattress, eyes open, staring up at the ceiling. He turned to her quickly, though, and flashed her a smile in the lantern light.

"What — ?" she began.

But he didn't let her finish. He sprang up and she saw that he was naked. He walked quickly to her, then began unwinding the towel from her body. And then he began to kiss her shoulders, breasts, ribs.

She caught his shoulders. "Sean, wait. What — what was that all about? What's going on?"

"Later," he murmured.

His hands were on her hips, his lips pressed to her belly. His breath was against her flesh, and her flesh was responding.

She dug her fingers into his hair. "Sean . . ."

He nudged her legs farther apart, and his mouth rubbed over her until she thought she would fall.

She forgot the question she had asked.

She forgot everything. She gasped and hung on to his hair, because she had to remain standing.

She came near to weeping, so vital was the sensation. She twisted and whimpered and gave herself gloriously to him. And only then did he stand to collect her weak form, carry her to the mattress and find his own reward.

The wonderful heat of the night wrapped itself around Mandy so completely that the island might in truth have been their own. Yet finally, when they had lain quietly together for some time, Sean turned to her, smoothing back her still-damp hair.

"We have to do something — tomorrow morning."

Her heart pitched and thudded; reality cut her like a knife. "Why? What happened?"

"Juan hasn't returned. Roberto thinks that he's been caught. He wants to take the skiff out tomorrow and go back."

In the darkness Mandy frowned. "I don't understand."

Sean hesitated for a long time.

"He wants to take one of your fingers with him. He called Julio a coward with no convictions and told him that his father will die in prison."

"Oh, God!" Mandy gasped.

Sean's fingers grabbed painfully at her hair. "You are to do nothing! Do you understand? Stay in here when you find me gone. Don't move, and I mean it. I won't be able to follow through with my plan if I have to worry about you, too. I mean it! Now go to sleep."

"Go to sleep?"

"Yes!"

She would never sleep. And that night she didn't.

# 10

Sean didn't sleep, either; he lay awake, forming his plan.

There were certain things he had learned, and certain things that he had been taught. Individual heroics were seldom a part of police work. Shoot-outs were not day-to-day occurrences; not even the narcotics department ran around with their guns constantly blazing.

The basics of the job were to do your damnedest to see that the victim wasn't hurt in a hostage situation. If this had been a normal kidnapping, if Amanda had been stashed somewhere in the city without a resident cop, he and his partner and the team set up to investigate would have worked with the FBI, since kidnapping was a federal offense. As it was, he hadn't done any of the normal things. No paperwork in triplicate. No hours in his cubicle on the fifth floor. No arguments with the FBI.

But then, this situation was one in a million. He'd gotten to swim in the surf with a beautiful blond bombshell. What a lark.

He'd even made love to her. God, wouldn't the guys at the station be green with envy?

Yeah, oh, yeah. Except that, like some green idiot, he'd gone and gotten involved. It couldn't last; it couldn't be. He and Miss DAR just weren't cut out to make a go of things.

But face it, he had a chip on his shoulder. And she didn't deserve his anger. So until she was taken away from him, for more reasons than one, she was his, and they would touch one hair on her head only over his dead body.

No joke there, he warned himself. So far he'd played the lackey because every fool knew what one bullet from a .357 Magnum could do to the human body. If one entered his body, there wouldn't be a prayer in hell that he could ever do anything for her again. But now . . .

Damn the FBI! They should have been here by now.

Divide and conquer — the saying was as old as time, but as true. He had to surprise one of them, get the gun and, if necessary, shoot the other.

Despite it all, he didn't hate Julio Garcia. Julio was just a dreamer, out of sync with the times, believing that he could change the world. This wasn't the way to do it, but Julio

was no desperado. Sean just didn't know how far he would go.

Still, Julio would be the one he had to disarm. It would be risky, but it had to be done. Roberto was a hard-core criminal. He would slice off Mandy's finger without a second thought. Given half an opportunity, he would have raped her until she was half-dead — with no thought whatsoever.

Sean didn't think that Señora Garcia would interfere. She seemed to know that her son was diving straight for jail. She would just wait stoically for him.

And Maria? Maria was the long shot. Given a chance, she might well be dangerous. But then, she wouldn't want any of her precious beauty destroyed, either.

"Sean?"

Mandy whispered his name softly with the coming of morning, touching his arm, well aware that he was awake.

He shook her hand off. The last thing he wanted now was her touch. He couldn't waver; he couldn't think of her. He touched a finger to her lips in the darkness. "No words, no movement, no sound! Do you hear me?"

"Hey, it's my finger they're after!"

"Shut up. I mean it! Do you want to get me killed?" he asked angrily.

He thought he saw her eyes flash, even in the darkness. "No! I'd rather kill you myself!"

He chuckled softly, squeezed her hand and groped for his cutoffs. Then he stood quickly before she could say anything else and headed for the door.

As he'd expected, both Julio and Roberto were sleeping on mats outside the door. Roberto stirred slightly, gazing at Sean with wary contempt. Then Julio roused himself, so Roberto went back to sleep.

It was curious that Julio followed Sean so quickly, but it was to his advantage, and Sean was glad. He didn't look back, just hunched his shoulders instinctively and walked out the kitchen door and toward the beach. He paused just before the surf.

"You're upset, my friend?" Julio inquired from behind.

Sean shrugged, needing to get him to come closer.

"She won't be hurt, not really. She'll survive. What is one little finger, eh? They must know that I mean business."

Sean kept looking out to sea. "One little finger? Julio, I ask you, what is one little finger to you? And think about this — what if they catch you? So far you haven't hurt her. Perhaps she'll testify in your

defense. She likes you."

Julio made an ugly sound. "The Americana testify for me? No, I do not think so. Her husband will not let an innocent man go free. Why should she bother with a guilty one?"

"Don't maim her, Julio."

"What? Maim?" Julio asked with annoyance, moving closer. "Will I touch her eyes? Her hair? Her legs? The things you cherish? I will leave plenty to love. It will one day be a brand of her courage for her."

"She'll probably die out here!" Sean replied bitterly. "Your dirty knives will give her tetanus. She'll bleed to death."

"Men have survived far worse things."

Julio was there — right where Sean wanted him. He never got a chance to say anything more. Sean smashed his elbow into Julio's ribs with such force that the man doubled over, unable to do more than gasp for breath.

Sean couldn't afford to show him any mercy. He brought his knee up into Julio's chin, sending him keeling over backward.

The Magnum fell into the sand without a shot being fired, nothing but harmless metal.

Sean scooped it up and tucked it into his pants, then reached down to Julio. "Sorry,

*amigo,* but you're not touching her finger."

Julio, his mouth bloodied, still unable to stand without clutching his middle, grasped Sean's hand and stared at him heatedly. "Roberto was right!" he gasped. "I should have killed you at the very beginning."

"I think you've got a few broken ribs," Sean said flatly.

"I will scream. I will shout that Roberto should kill her."

"You don't want her dead, and you know it. Nor do you want to face a murder charge. Besides, I don't think you could shout that loud right now."

Julio winced, and Sean knew that his ribs were hurting him. "Let's go," he said. "To the door. You will call to Roberto to come outside. You will not sound alarmed, or I will put a bullet through your eyes. Got it?"

Morosely, Julio let himself be dragged back to the door of the shack.

"Do it!" Sean demanded, shaking him.

"All right! All right!" He hesitated just a second longer, then called, "Roberto! Roberto! *Ven aquí!*"

They waited, Sean using Julio as his shield. He listened, and he heard footsteps. The door opened, and though Julio had not sounded alarmed, Roberto was wary. He looked around the corner of the door — and

instantly took a shot at Sean.

Sean ducked his head without a second to spare. He fired a quick shot back; he had no other choice.

He winced as he heard Roberto scream. That was followed by another scream, then another. Maria was up, along with Señora Garcia, and everyone was screaming.

Sean shoved Julio ahead of him once again and entered the cabin, searching for Roberto.

The man was on the ground, slumped against the wall, a trail of blood trickling down the wood. Sean saw that only his arm had been hit, but blood was spouting everywhere.

Roberto was keening with pain. Maria was standing by the back door, arms up, shaking and screaming hysterically. Señora Garcia just stood there, whitefaced.

Sean inclined his head toward the wounded man. "Tend to him," he said briefly, then he carefully reached over Roberto to retrieve the other gun.

He barely noticed when Maria disappeared back into her room. He ordered Julio to sit beside his wounded friend.

"You've killed him," Julio said reproachfully.

"I have not. He'll live."

"What are you?" Julio demanded, narrowing his eyes. "You're no gardener."

Sean sighed. "I'm Lieutenant Ramiro, Homicide Division."

"Eh, Roberto, his name was real at least, eh?" Julio tried to joke to the still-suffering man. Señora Garcia was bending over him by then, trying to do something with the wound.

"Drop it — *cop!*"

His eyes shot immediately to Maria, who was holding a small Smith & Wesson with a pearl handle. He trained the Magnum on her in return. "Sweetie, you're not going to use that. Drop it."

Maria smiled and raised the muzzle just above his head, letting off a shot that splintered wood.

"Don't bet on that, lieutenant," she said calmly, adding a very explicit threat in Spanish.

He was just about to call her bluff and fire back when the other bedroom door suddenly flew open, and there was Amanda Blayne, in all her blond glory and rage. To Sean's astonishment she was wielding a switchblade, which she instantly pressed into the small of Maria's back.

"You drop it, brat. I've just about had it with you!"

As meekly as a lamb, Maria dropped her gun.

"Get it!" Sean warned Amanda, and she instantly did so. "You two — Julio, Maria — into the bedroom. *Señora,* can you help Roberto?"

Señora Garcia looked imploringly at Sean. "He needs treatment. He needs medicine," she begged in Spanish.

"I'm sorry. He should have thought of that before he shot at me."

When they had all been hustled into the bedroom that he had shared with Mandy — Mrs. Blayne, he had to start thinking of her that way again — he stood in the doorway and formally placed them all under arrest, reciting their rights. Although, if this was the Bahamas, they would have to go through it all over again, since he didn't have any jurisdiction here. Still, he wanted to play it safe.

Just as he was locking and bolting the door, Amanda started speaking excitedly. "Sean! The boat — Julio's boat — it's returning!"

Sean raced back to her and stared out the window. He turned to look at her. "I thought I told you to stay in the bedroom and not make a sound?"

Her huge tawny eyes met his. "You needed me!"

"I had the situation under control."

"Hmph!" Amanda sniffed indelicately. "She wanted to shoot . . . a certain part of your anatomy off! I rather thought you might miss it."

"I thought you didn't understand Spanish?"

"I've picked up a few words here and there."

"All the good ones, huh?"

"Sean, the boat!"

"Ah, yes."

"Well?"

He shrugged. "It could be Juan. Or it could be Juan and the Bahamian authorities and the FBI." He stared at her thoughtfully for a minute. "One way or the other, Mrs. Blayne, you'll be able to go home. Aren't you glad?"

"Of course. Aren't you?"

"Absolutely. I've got tons of paperwork waiting for me." He watched her speculatively a second longer, then stared back out the window. "As I said, it could be Juan. Or it could be Juan and the authorities. We have to find out. I'm going out. He won't be surprised to see me on the beach. You stay here. If anyone puts their face out that door — though the bolt should hold — shoot. Don't ask questions — shoot. Got it?"

"Sean —"

"Got it?"

"Oh, yes, sir! Yes, sir, Lieutenant Ramiro!"

"Damn WASP!" he muttered, pulling open the kitchen door.

"Excuse me, lieutenant!"

"What?" he asked, pausing. He felt empty. Already a gulf was opening up between them.

"I'm Catholic."

He frowned, shaking his head in confusion. "Good for you, Mrs. Blayne. What in hell does that have to do with anything?"

She smiled bitterly. "You just called me a WASP. It stands for white Anglo-Saxon Protestant. You'll have to think of something else to call me."

"Oh, Lord!" he groaned softly and slipped through the door.

He sat on the beach and watched as the boat moved closer. He sat stiffly, the gun concealed in his lap, feeling a niggling apprehension. Actually, it had gone easily. Far better than he had ever expected. No one was dead. And among the ones who were not dead were himself and the victim, Mrs. Amanda Blayne. They hadn't even been scratched.

But he was worried now that this might just be Juan, or Juan with a few reinforcements. He felt excitement and anxiety —

and, strangely, that same overwhelming emptiness.

He'd wanted it to be over, right? Sure, right. It had been a kidnapping; a woman had been in danger. The fantasy had never been real. Never. It had all occurred in the midst of a nightmare.

But now it was over, and he felt empty.

He kept his eyes trained on the boat. It was about to anchor, and he saw Juan on the deck.

And then — moving so quickly he almost missed him — he saw another man. A tall black man in a uniform.

He stood up without thinking, hailing the boat, rushing down to the shoreline. "Hey! It's all right! Come on in!"

The figure stopped trying to disappear and stood, then brought a megaphone to his mouth. "Lieutenant Ramiro?"

"Yeah, yeah! Come on in!"

"Where is Mrs. Blayne?"

"Inside! She's — she's fine!"

The old boat was suddenly teeming with people. Juan was cuffed and disappeared with someone. The dinghy was lowered, and five men boarded it. Two Bahamian officials, a man in a three-piece suit — and an older, dignified looking man with a sad gaunt face and salt-and-pepper hair. Sean

recognized him from his pictures. Senator Peter Blayne.

Sean just stood there as the dinghy came in. He was barely aware that Amanda came out of the house, that she stood slightly behind him. He wasn't aware of anything but the breeze and the sand beneath his bare feet.

"Mandy! Mandy!" The older man didn't wait for the dinghy to reach the shore. He stepped out while it was still in shallow water, soaking his shoes and his pant legs. "Mandy!"

In seconds she was racing down to meet him, and then she was in his arms. It was almost painfully apparent that they meant the world to each other.

Sean suddenly found it difficult to breathe. The older man was speaking, barely coherently, saying how frightened he had been, and what a fool, and how he'd never, never risk her again.

Sean had been as irritated as hell when Blayne had turned up his nose at police protection, but as he watched the scene and the man's agony he felt as if he should insist that this mess wasn't Blayne's fault at all. And, as it happened, if he'd accepted protection, the Miami PD wouldn't have been at the dock when Amanda Blayne was

taken by the kidnappers.

Blayne wouldn't want any assurances from him, though; Sean knew that. The older man was staring at his daughter-in-law as if he could devour her, and Mandy was lightly trying to tell him that it hadn't been so bad, that she was fine, that he certainly wasn't at fault, that she was so glad to see him.

Then Sean couldn't give the tender scene his undivided attention anymore; one of the men in the three-piece suits was approaching him.

"Ramiro? Farkel, FBI. What's the situation here?"

What was it about cops and the FBI? Farkel had only introduced himself, but Sean disliked him already. He was a thin reedy sort of man, with a narrow nose, brown eyes, brown hair and a colorless complexion. When he smiled it looked more like a grimace.

Sean indicated the shack. "Two men, two women. They're in the back left bedroom. One has a gunshot wound to his shoulder, he probably needs medical attention as soon as possible."

The FBI man frowned. "You had a gun battle here? You were probably out of line, Lieutenant. You should have waited for us

to come in. You could have caused injury to a civilian."

Sean curled his lip stiffly. "Sorry, Farkel. You see, they were going to start hacking off her fingers this morning, and it just didn't sound real nice to me."

"A finger would have been better than her life," Farkel said stiffly.

"They're in the back, Mr. Farkel. And I believe they're your responsibility now. Hey, go gentle on the old lady. She wasn't too happy about having anything to do with this."

The FBI agent walked past him; his associate — a younger blond man — glanced apologetically at Sean, who grinned in return. Some of the federal guys were okay. In fact, he was willing to bet that this one shared his opinion of Farkel.

"Damn yokel cops," Farkel was muttering. "They all think they're TV heroes."

"What's his first name?" Sean asked the young guy curiously. The man chuckled. "Fred. His name is Fred Farkel."

"He looks like a Fred Farkel," Sean muttered.

The blonde extended a hand. "Bill Duffy, Lieutenant. Sorry, he's my superior, but I'll try to be the liaison on the case in the future."

Sean nodded. Then the two Bahamian policemen walked up and introduced themselves, questioning him about the situation, too. They didn't seem to be any fonder of Fred Farkel than anyone else, and Sean had a feeling the man had made a few attempts to usurp their authority as well.

It didn't matter; it was all over for him now. All over but the paperwork.

The taller Bahamian, a guy named Matt Haines, told Sean quietly that a cutter would be coming in to take them back to Miami. Sean thanked him, then he and Bill Duffy went inside to deal with the fugitives in the house.

He was able to glance back at Mandy at last. For a moment her eyes met his. And for just a moment he thought that he saw something in them. Something warm. Something caring. Something that went beyond circumstances.

Then it disappeared. Her father-in-law's arm was around her shoulder, and he was suddenly pulling her enthusiastically forward, determined to reach Sean.

The senator's hand was extended, his smile deep and warm and real, and Sean thought in that moment that he knew why the man was elected over and over again.

"Lieutenant Ramiro! If I had a hundred

241

lifetimes, I could never thank you enough!"

Sean returned his handshake, trying to keep his eyes off Mandy. "Senator, my pleasure. I mean, I didn't do anything out of the ordinary. I mean —"

She was turning bright, bright red. He didn't seem to be able to say anything that came out right.

"Didn't do anything out of the ordinary!" Peter Blayne exclaimed. "Why, son, you were seen! Jumping off that dock, trying to board a moving motorboat. Sir, I call that above and beyond the call of duty. You're too modest."

"Oh, yes, he's modest! Terribly modest!" Mandy said — and she felt the same confusion she knew he was feeling, because they both knew, even if Peter didn't, that neither of them had been modest at all.

And this was her father-in-law! Paul's father! Oh, God, if he found out, what would he think?

She stiffened miserably. There were so many things that she wanted to say to Sean; but none of them could be said. Not here. Not now.

She stared into his eyes and felt as if her insides congealed as he stared back.

His eyes were bright, as green as emeralds, as hard as diamonds. She must have

been insane to think that there had ever been anything gentle about him. Or tender. He wasn't the man she had known, not the man with whom she had made love. With whom she had lain, afraid, in the night. With whom she had triumphed in the end.

His stare reduced the warmth of the Caribbean day to winter's chill. He was once again the stranger who had ordered her away from him on the beach, the man who had loved her — then hated her.

She lifted her chin, feeling her eyes well with tears, willing herself not to shed them. She didn't know what went on inside this man, and she decided then that she didn't want to know, that she didn't give a damn.

Circumstances . . . were over. Peter was standing beside her. She must consider the past few days a dream, a fantasy, a nightmare.

She extended her hand to Sean then, as cool as the waves that washed the beach. "Lieutenant, I want to thank you, too."

With a wry smile he took her hand. He remembered how it had felt on his body. It seemed so slim and soft and elegant — and now so remote. "No problem, Mrs. Blayne," he drawled. "Anytime."

"Oh, you'll be seeing more of us!" Peter Blayne assured him. "I'll see to it!"

Sean smiled. That was life as a cop. People you arrested wanted to kill you. People you got out of a jam wanted to be your friend for life. Peter Blayne would forget his promise. People always did.

"Sure," he said agreeably.

"Sean — Lieutenant, what will happen now?" Mandy asked him stiffly.

Sean shrugged. "The feds will press a number of charges. I assume they'll want you to testify in court." He gave her a slightly malicious grin, then laughed. "Fred Farkel will answer all your questions now. It's his ball game, as they say."

Mandy nodded. A silence fell over the three of them that seemed to puzzle Peter Blayne. It didn't matter. Two cutters had appeared on the horizon.

Matt Haines came out of the house and walked toward them. "Lieutenant, Mrs. Blayne, we'll have to invite you for a brief stay in Nassau. I hope you won't mind. We just have to clear up a few things and arrange our extradition procedures. It will just be for tonight. I'm sorry. I know you're anxious to get home."

Then everyone was on the beach — Julio, in handcuffs, Roberto, Maria, Señora Garcia, the FBI men and the Bahamians. Julio stopped in front of Mandy and Peter.

"Señor Blayne, I never wished to hurt her. But now perhaps you will understand. I wish for my father's freedom, just as you wished for hers."

Peter Blayne smiled sadly. "Julio, I told you I was doing my best. Your father will be out in a matter of weeks. But now *you* will go to prison."

"That does not matter, if my father is free."

"C'mon, Garcia," Farkel said roughly.

They passed by. Mandy was glad to see that they would not be on the same boat. She felt sorry for Señora Garcia; she even felt sorry for Julio. But she didn't ever want to see Roberto again, not as long as she lived.

She had to sit next to Sean in the dinghy that took them out to the cutter. She had to feel his bare leg, feathered with the short dark hairs, next to her own. To feel his breath, inhale his scent.

She didn't look at him; she stared straight ahead.

The cutter provided some relief; she was given a small cabin where she could bathe, and a soft terry robe that was totally decent and comfortable.

Mandy showered forever, loathe to leave the clean water. And loathe to reappear on

deck, although she knew that Peter was waiting anxiously for her. Naturally Peter would quiz her. And naturally Sean would be there. And . . . oh, God!

Eventually she went out on deck. To her vast surprise and relief Sean was nowhere in sight.

She was given a delicious rum drink and an equally good meal, and Peter sat next to her, as if he never wanted to leave her side. He told her that her parents had been wired about her safety, that he'd had a student feed her cat. He chattered like a magpie, totally out of character. Then he asked her at last, "Oh, Amanda! Are you really all right? My dear, you're all I have left!"

Guilt churned in her stomach. "I'm fine, Peter, honest."

"But how —"

She took a deep breath. "Sean — Lieutenant Ramiro — pretended to be your gardener."

"My gardener?"

She grimaced and lowered her lashes, staring at her drink. "His Spanish is perfect. He's, uh, half Cuban. He convinced them that he was your downtrodden gardener, and my . . . my lover, and that he could convince me to be a well-behaved hostage. Julio really isn't a murderer, although I think his

246

associate — Roberto — might have been. Thanks to the lieutenant I, well, I was as safe as possible the entire time. And Señora Garcia really shouldn't be punished, Peter, if there's a way around it. She was against what happened, and she was good to me."

He patted her hand. "We'll see, dear. We'll see what can be done. I'm sure you'll be able to speak in her defense at the trial."

She nodded, and then she wondered where Sean was.

Peter's thoughts must have been running along the same lines. "Where is that young man?" he wondered aloud. "What an interesting fellow. I'd quite enjoy getting to know him. He seems fascinating, don't you think?"

"Uh . . . fascinating," Mandy agreed, swallowing.

She didn't see him again, though, not on the boat. They docked in Nassau harbor and were given rooms in a hotel at the end of Market Street. Mandy had barely entered her own before Peter returned to her with a suitcase of her clothing, packed for her as soon as he'd received permission to come with the authorities to take her home.

She barely had time to dress before she was taken to the Bahamian police station. The authorities were charming, though.

They asked her a million questions, which she answered to the best of her abilities.

Then she was free — or she thought she was. The FBI man, Farkel, was there, warning her that once she returned to the States she would be called upon once again.

She had a pounding headache by then, and Farkel felt like the last straw. She thought she was about to explode and then he was interrupted by Sean.

He, too, had changed. He was wearing a lightweight three-piece gray suit, austere, but very handsome on him. He stepped out from one of the little cubicles and spoke not to her, but to Farkel. "Fred, lighten up, will you? You'd think that Mrs. Blayne was the criminal. She's had enough for today, don't you think?"

Farkel stiffened. "I was just —"

"Every dog has his day, Farkel. You'll get yours. She's free for tonight. Our plane leaves in the morning, and once she's on U.S. soil you get to give her the whole third degree."

"And tonight?" Mandy heard herself whisper.

Peter answered for her. "Tonight we're going out on the town! That nice young Bahamian officer suggested Paradise Island for

dinner, a show, even gambling." He chuckled, encircling Mandy's shoulder, pulling her close to him. "Mandy, I think we owe Lieutenant Ramiro the best dinner we can find. You, me, the lieutenant — and Paradise Island."

No, paradise is lost! Mandy thought a little frantically. But what could she do? Her father-in-law was on one side of her; the man with whom she had betrayed his deceased son was on the other.

Sean bowed whimsically, watching her in a strange way. He didn't want to go, she thought. No, he wanted to, and he didn't want to. Again she wondered if he hated her . . . or cared about her?

"A night on the town sounds good, senator," he told Peter. "Mrs. Blayne?" He offered her his arm.

Farkel snorted derisively and turned away. "Damned if they don't all think they're Sonny Crockett these days."

"Damn!" Sean snapped his fingers. "I just wish I could afford his wardrobe, Farkel."

"Your suit's not so bad."

"Thanks — your partner lent it to me."

"Gentlemen . . ." Peter began, distressed.

But he needn't have bothered. Sean didn't wait for Mandy to take his arm; he

took hers. And the cool Bahamian breeze touched her heated face as they moved out into the night. . . .

# 11

Mandy didn't know why Sean had decided to come to dinner with them. The place was lovely, the food was wonderful, but he seemed stiff and uncomfortable. She wondered if she looked as rigid as he did.

Only Peter seemed to be having a good time. He delighted in the story that the kidnappers had assumed that Mandy was his wife, telling Sean, "Good Lord! What flattery, that I should have such a child bride!"

Then he and Sean went on to discuss the situation with the elder Garcia.

Mandy concentrated on her shrimp cocktail. It was amazing. Last night she had been in absolute terror, wondering how Sean would ever stand up to two guns. Staring at her fingers, she shivered. She glanced up and found Sean's eyes on her. He smiled. She looked down again quickly, hoping that Peter hadn't caught the exchange.

"Oh, Mandy! I forgot to tell you! The team from Colorado called the school. You've been invited to be a part of the new dig."

"Really? How wonderful," she murmured.

"Dig?" Sean inquired.

"Yes," Peter said proudly. "Mandy is a paleontologist."

Sean arched one dark brow. "Dinosaurs?"

Despite herself, she grinned. "Their bones, actually, lieutenant."

"She teaches at the state college these days, but this sounds like the perfect time for a leave of absence. You could still manage some skiing out in Colorado."

"Yes, I suppose I could."

Skiing. She loved to ski. But at the moment the prospect meant nothing to her. She closed her eyes briefly. The dig, though, the dig would be good. The painstaking exploration, the wonder of discovery. The piecing together of ancient puzzles. It would be far away and remote, and she could forget all about Julio and Roberto — and Sean Ramiro.

Their main course came, pompano, broiled and garnished and savory, but Mandy couldn't taste it. She could only feel Sean's eyes on her from across the table. She wanted to scream. She wanted to demand to know what he was trying to do to her, here, in front of Paul's father.

"Do you have a family, lieutenant?" Peter asked Sean.

Sean grinned, swallowed a piece of fish,

then replied. "Well, sir, everyone has some kind of family. But am I married? No. No children. My father is deceased, my mother lives in Miami Shores, and I've got no brothers or sisters."

"Divorced?" Peter asked him, and Mandy was stunned. Peter was never this rude.

"No, sir. I've never been married."

"Never came close?"

"Oh, yeah. I came close. Once."

Peter's curiosity was quelled by the tone of that reply. No further questions in that direction would be answered.

They bypassed dessert and ordered liqueurs. Mandy found herself feeling amazed. Last night she had been wearing old dirty clothing and sleeping in a hovel. Tonight she was surrounded by opulence: plush velvet, twinkling chandeliers, marble and silver. How quickly the world could change.

As quickly as Sean Ramiro.

They left the restaurant and went into the casino. Peter chose a roulette table; Sean sat down to play blackjack. Nervous and wishing that the evening would end, Mandy restlessly decided to play the slots.

Her little buzzer went off instantly to announce a two hundred dollar jackpot, and two hundred silver coins came

spilling out into the catch tray.

She just stared at the coins, then started. Sean wasn't playing blackjack anymore. He was leaning casually against her machine, staring at her mockingly, lashes low over his eyes, looking sensual and handsome despite his negligent stance.

He touched a trailing lock of her hair. "Everything you touch turns to gold, huh?"

She jerked away from his touch. "Silver dollars, Mr. Ramiro. And my hair is dirty blond."

"Oh, I don't think anything about you touches . . . dirt."

"I work in the dirt. I dig up bones, remember?"

"I wonder why that never cropped up in casual conversation."

"We've never had a casual conversation."

"That's right. We were always pretty intense, weren't we? Need some help with your money?"

"No thanks. I'll just play it back!"

He moved closer to her, his dark head bending. "Mind if I watch."

"Yes, I do. What are you trying to do to me?"

"What are you talking about?"

"Peter is here!"

He arched a cynical brow at her. "Peter is

here?" he repeated. "And now that Peter is here you have to pretend that you don't know me? Funny, I don't see the senator as a snob."

"He's not — I'm not. Just go away, will you, please? Look, it's over. I never understood you, you never understood me. You've got a chip on your shoulder the size of a cement block. And I've got a few —"

"Prejudices?"

"No! Damn you. Problems of my own!"

"And what are they, Mrs. Blayne?"

How dare he? she wondered furiously. Confusion joined the tempest in her heart, and she was afraid that she would burst into tears right there.

She didn't. She just inhaled deeply and spoke with a voice as sharp as a razor. "No one, Ramiro, will ever need to tell me that life can be rough. I don't care what's happened to you, there is nothing — *nothing* in life like losing a child!"

She turned around in a whirl, leaving her coins in the machine, fleeing the room.

Peter would be upset, of course. He would wonder what had sent her flying out. But she couldn't even care about Peter just then; she had to leave.

Mandy had no problem getting a taxi to take her back over the bridge to Nassau and

her hotel. Once she got there she knew she had to leave a message for Peter. She did so, then started forlornly for the elevator. She didn't know why she felt so lost, so miserable. It was as if the past and the present had collided to bring her agony just when she should have been eternally grateful that she had been rescued and given a future.

She should have sensed that something was wrong the moment she entered the room, but she didn't. She didn't even bother to turn on the light; moonlight was drifting in through the parted curtains anyway. She just closed and bolted the door, tossed her handbag on the dresser and fell back on the plush double bed.

It was then that she heard the rustle of movement and saw the silhouette moving in the darkness.

She tensed and opened her mouth to scream, but a hand clamped tightly over it.

"Shut up. It's just me."

"Just you!" Furiously she twisted away from him, sitting up, wishing she could see him clearly enough to belt him a good one. "You scared me half to death! What are you doing in here? I'm getting so sick of your strong-arm tactics."

"Take your clothes off, Mandy."

"What?"

"Take your clothes off. It seems to be the only way we can communicate."

"Get out of here! I'll call the co —"

"Cops? Honey, you've got one already."

"Sean . . ."

"Mandy?"

His fingers slid into the hair at her nape, his palm cradling her skull. He held her there while he came ever closer, his lips meeting hers at last, hesitating for just a breath, then coming alive. For an instant, she clenched her teeth against him, but the warm pressure of his tongue dissolved her resistance, and with a little sigh she fell into his arms.

Circumstances changed. People did not. And darkness had come again.

In seconds he was stretched out beside her. They were both fully clothed, but she felt as if she was touching him, all of him.

But it was not passion that goaded him, not that night. He brushed her cheek, and she felt his eyes, emerald flames that defied the darkness.

"I'm sorry, Mandy."

She couldn't answer him. She shrugged.

"I can't forget what happened."

"No one has asked you to forget."

"Mandy . . ."

"You're strange, Sean. I thought I was,

but you're stranger. We make love at night, and in the morning you behave as if I'm a bee with a particularly annoying buzz. One second you're as charming as a prince, and then the next —"

"I had a few raw deals. I took it out on you."

"I can't help the color of my hair, or who my ancestors were."

"Wait a minute! Wait a minute! Get off my case. You were the one who didn't want to touch me with a ten-foot pole the second other people appeared on the scene!"

"You don't — oh, never mind. You just —"

"Mandy!"

"What?"

"Did you smell this bed? Did you touch it? Feel it. So soft, so fresh."

She didn't know why she obeyed the command, but she did, inhaling deeply. And it was true, of course. The bedding smelled wonderful.

"It's so clean," she murmured.

He ran his knuckles tenderly over her hair. "And you're so clean."

"I beg your pardon. I was always clean."

"Well, I wasn't so great."

"Really? For shame, Lieutenant Ramiro." She couldn't stop herself from grinning in the darkness. "I'd never thought your confi-

dence could be so low. I always thought you were at least okay."

"I was . . . okay?"

"Oh, definitely."

"Hmm. Well . . ."

"Well?"

"I'm great now. Want to try me? Clean as a whistle. I even shaved, and you didn't even notice."

"Oh, but I did. I think. You looked so great in that suit."

"Aha! I told you I was great!"

"Bragging will get you nowhere."

"Okay. Take your clothes off. We'll go back to brute force."

"Sean . . ."

He stopped her words with a kiss that seemed the most natural thing in the world. It always seemed to be like that; the taunts and the bitterness, but then somehow the laughter, and the irresistible urge to touch.

She would probably never know which was real, the laughter or the pain. But in the darkness, even darkness kissed by moonlight, it didn't seem to matter. When she was with him she always felt as if she had a driving thirst, as if his touch was water that cascaded over her, a fountain that sparkled and rippled, soothing and delighting, sweeping her away to new heights.

His hands moved over her, frustrated by her dress. He groaned softly. "Take your clothes off."

"Is that the only line you know?" she whispered.

"It's a damn good one," he assured her. And she laughed, laughed until his fingers rode along her bare legs to her bikini panties and teased her flesh through the silky fabric. Then her breath caught and she could laugh no more, and she was suddenly thinking that surely this would be the last time that she had to drink in all of him; the bronze flesh and muscle and sinew; the dark hair that dusted his legs and chest; the powerful line of his profile. . . .

"You take *your* clothes off," she told him huskily. "On second thought . . ."

She started working on the tiny pearl buttons of his vest. He took a deep breath, watching her, watching the tiny frown that furrowed her brow. He held his breath as she undid the vest and then his shirt, and then he expelled it with a heady groan as she brought her mouth against him, delicately touching him with the tip of her tongue. Then she grew bolder, grazing his skin with gentle teeth that sent streams of lavalike desire rippling through his body. She moved sinuously against him, her hands moving

over his back, his chest, then to his shoulders to shove the annoying material from the form she was so eager to know.

There was nothing like this, she thought. Nothing like feeling his reactions to her kiss, her touch. He trembled beneath her, yet he was taut, and with each ragged breath he took she felt bolder, more feminine, more vibrantly aroused herself. He was right: he was clean; he was great; the fresh masculine scent of his body was an aphrodisiac in itself, and she wondered at the beauty of him as her head reeled. She slipped her fingers along the waistband of his pants, teasing his belly, finding his belt buckle and leisurely working it free.

Too leisurely, perhaps. His groan resounded like thunder, and he set her aside, destroying her illusion of power. He left her to feverishly shed the remainder of his clothing, then lay back beside her.

"What's this?" he whispered huskily.

"My dress."

"Get rid of it!"

She giggled breathlessly. "I thought you were going to do a striptease and then dance."

"I intend to dance, all right." He swore softly in Spanish, having a miserable time with the tiny hook at her nape. He paused,

shrugged and snapped it, and she didn't care in the least. She was suddenly as anxious as he was to feel their bodies together.

As soon as her clothes were gone she stepped back to him, remembering their first time. She knelt down and let her hair fall over his feet as she massaged them, then dusted them with kisses. Her body was liquid as she moved against him, using the tip of her tongue at the backs of his knees and all along his thighs.

He held his breath again, as taut as wire. She waited, drawing out the moment, her hair spilling over him.

And then she took him with her touch, with her kiss.

She heard his words, sweet and reverent, in English and in Spanish, and they all meant the same thing. His fingers were tempered steel when they closed around her arms as he drew her to him, moving swiftly, stunning her with the electric force of his entry. The moment was so fulfilling that she cried out softly, only to have her words stolen once again by a kiss.

They moved together in the moonlight, until finally she lay panting in sweet splendor. She was so tired, so spent, yet each new touch awakened her anew, until she moaned softly, curling into his chest

with the sweetest sigh.

He held her there for what seemed like forever.

She didn't know when the change came, only that he suddenly stiffened and then rose before padding naked to the window to stare out at the Bahamian night.

She was too drowsy to rouse herself, and she wondered bitterly why he had decided to do so at such a time.

"What's the matter?" she asked softly.

He whipped around, like a lethal predator, and moved back to the bed, perching at the foot of it.

"What are we going to do now?" he asked her harshly.

"Sleep," she responded.

"That's not what I mean, and you know it."

"Sean, don't . . ." She lifted an imploring hand to him, but he ignored it.

"I asked you a question."

"Sean, I'm so tired."

"Then wake up. What are we going to do?"

"We're — we're going to fly back to the U.S. in the morning!" she snapped at last. "I have to go back to work. I assume that you do, too."

"And?"

"And what?"

"What about us?"

She held her breath, wondering what he was so upset about. Was he afraid that she would think she had some kind of hold on him? What was it with him? She didn't understand him, and when he was like this he actually frightened her.

She cared too much. Way too much. And she had promised herself that she wouldn't risk caring that much ever again. Her career, her love of the past, would be her life. Nice safe dinosaurs that had been extinct for years and years and years. . . .

"You don't have a thing in the world to worry about, lieutenant," she whispered wearily. "I have no intention of becoming involved with you. You're as free as a lark."

"Oh?" he said coldly.

Chills raced along her spine; she wanted to touch him and erase the tension from his face. But she had already reached out to him, and he had ignored her.

"So," he murmured, "it all came true in a way, didn't it? I might as well have been your gardener, dragged in when the odd occasion warranted it, huh?"

She was instantly furious with him — and with herself, for always falling prey to him so easily. "You stupid bastard!"

"Yeah, you're kind of right there, too, aren't you?"

He prowled over to the window once again. "I've got just one more question for you, Mrs. Blayne."

"Do ask, lieutenant."

"I'm curious as to what precautions you've been taking."

"Precautions?" Mandy echoed hollowly.

He turned so suddenly that she thought he was about to take the drapes with him. "I'll be blunt, Mrs. Blayne. I'm talking about birth control."

"Don't you dare stand there and yell at me! I wasn't planning on having an affair! I was kidnapped! I usually don't worry about birth control when maniacs are abducting me! There's an old saying that it takes two to tango, and I'm here to tell you that it's true!"

"That's irrelevant."

"The hell it is!"

"It's irrelevant," he repeated, bending over her so that his arms surrounded her like a cage. "Because any precautions I might have taken would have been evident. So we know that wasn't the case."

She felt that she really did hate him at that moment. He stood over her like some superior god, the epitome of masculine force,

beautiful still, and more hateful for it.

She stiffened her spine, as heedless of her nudity as he was of his. "You have no problems whatsoever, lieutenant. I will never again have a child. Does that satisfy you?"

For an instant she thought that he was going to hurt her, he looked so fierce. He didn't. He pushed himself away from the bed in a fury, muttering something she didn't understand. She shivered because without his warmth the night had grown cold.

She closed her eyes tightly. "Sean," she said miserably, "get out of here. Please, go!"

Once more he came back to her. He took a strand of her hair, curling it around in his fingers. She'd never seen him quite like this, and it was all she could do to keep from tearing away from him, to keep from screaming out.

"Not again, Mrs. Blayne," he said softly. "Not again. Here's another expression for you — those who play sometimes pay. And if you're given a price, my love, you will pay it."

"What — ?"

"You can expect to see me again. Quite frequently. For the next few months, at least."

A new wave of trembling swept over her,

along with a rush of conflicting emotions. She understood him now; at least, she thought she did. She'd assumed at first that he had no desire to be saddled with a child from their affair; now she knew it was the opposite. And with that knowledge she experienced a blank and cold dread, terrifying, horrible. It was if she had gone back in time, gone back to the time when the young highway patrolman had stood on her doorstep, telling her that not only her husband but her infant had been killed in the collision, the baby mercifully quickly. . . .

But for her there had been no mercy. There had been her breasts, filled with milk for a tiny life that could never draw from them again. There had been the emptiness in her arms, the rage, the despair. . . .

"Get out of here," she repeated dully.

He reached for her cheek, but she pushed his hand away. "I'll be around, Mandy."

"No," she pleaded.

And then she knew that he had misunderstood her entirely, because he swore again, then said, "What is it, Amanda? You couldn't handle a child named Ramiro? Too ethnic for your ears?"

She pressed her palms over her eyes tightly. "Yes! Yes! That's it! I'm planning to move to Boca Raton, too. Away from

Miami. Haven't you heard that saying? 'Will the last American out please re-member to bring the flag?' Please! Get out of here."

But he didn't. Not then. He straddled her and pulled her hands away from her face, then stared into her eyes with a gaze that burned into her soul. "No!" he thundered harshly. "You can't run away. Not this time!"

And then, miraculously, he released her.

She closed her eyes. She heard him dress swiftly, and then she heard him leave even more swiftly.

For at least an hour after that she didn't move. Not a muscle. She just lay there, trying to breathe.

And praying that she wasn't pregnant.

In the morning she felt awful.

The flight back took less than an hour. Pe-ter's car met them, and they reached her home in another thirty minutes.

Peter was worried and solicitous. She could only be grateful that Sean hadn't been on their plane. He must have altered his ar-rangements.

Peter had arranged for the police and the FBI to come to her; she spent the afternoon with a pleasant blond man and a sergeant

from the Miami PD. Things weren't really difficult; all she had to do was repeat what had happened over and over again. It was a cut-and-dried situation, but the culprits still had to be prosecuted.

A twinge of conscience touched her, and Mandy remembered to tell them that in her opinion Mrs. Garcia had been an unhappy bystander. She hesitated, then even spoke up for Julio, saying that she didn't believe he was malicious, just misguided. She was told that if she would say so at the trial, she might lessen their sentences.

"But kidnapping is a federal offense, Mrs. Blayne. No one can walk away from it," the FBI man told her.

"I know." She paused, shivering. "And Roberto should be locked up, with the key thrown away." She lowered her lashes. She had told them, of course, that he had attempted to rape her. She told them, too, about Sean's fight to save her from him.

She hadn't mentioned what had happened after that, though.

They left her, and she was alone with Peter. He wanted to stay with her; he wanted her to drink warm milk and go to bed and get better, since her shadowed eyes and pale cheeks had convinced him that she was sick.

He was supposed to be in Washington, and she knew it. With a dozen assurances she finally got him to go home, convincing him that she was determined to get a good night's sleep and go back to work in the morning. "All I want is Koala," she told Peter lightly.

Koala was her cat, so named not because he was cute, but because he was so ugly. He'd come to her door one day and moved in without giving her much choice.

Peter hugged her, then turned to leave at last, a haggard-looking man. She loved him so much. "Peter."

"Yes?"

"Promise me that you'll get a good night's sleep, okay?"

He grimaced. "Promise."

She thought that now her day was over. She thought that she could sink into a warm bath and try to think about the new dig. She wanted to do everything she could to create distance between herself and Sean, the things he had said to her — and the horrible things she had said to him.

But she couldn't forget him; all she could do was miss him.

She couldn't even get comfortable. She ran her bath, but before she could step into the water, the phone rang.

It was her mother, sobbing over the phone, and once again Mandy was cast into the depths of guilt, aware that any decent daughter would have called her own parents by then. She talked to her mother for half an hour, then to her father for another twenty minutes.

They both wanted to fly in immediately, but her father was just recovering from by-pass surgery, and Mandy didn't think he should be traveling yet. She managed to per-suade them to wait a few weeks, telling them that she was absolutely fine and planning on a trip to Colorado anyway. She talked about the dig with forced enthusiasm, and at last they seemed to believe that it would be all right to wait to see her until the end of the month.

Hanging up from her parents brought no relief. The phone rang again instantly, and this time it was a reporter. She spoke po-litely to him, but then the doorbell rang. An-other reporter. She spoke politely to him, too.

But when a third reporter reached her over the phone she was ready to scream. She had a pounding headache; all she wanted to do was hide.

She got through the third interview, then hurried through her small house, pulling all

the drapes shut. She finally got into the freshly filled bathtub, where she strenuously ignored the phone every time it rang.

She sat in the tub for a long time, feeling the heat ease some of her tension away. Again she tried to think about work, to plan for the trip.

The water began to cool, and suddenly she jumped out of it as if she had been scalded. It had suddenly reminded her . . . of Sean. Of a day in the surf when she had surfaced to face Roberto, when she had backed away from him, when Sean had been there — and their minds had functioned as one.

She grabbed a towel and wrapped it around herself, shaking. She closed her eyes.

She couldn't stop thinking about him. Everything, every little thing, was a reminder.

After a few seconds she groped blindly in the medicine chest for one of the tranquilizers the doctor had given her just after the accident. She swallowed it quickly.

She paused for a minute, breathing deeply. Then she walked into the living room and resolutely did the one thing that would convince her that she had been right not to try. That it was better, much better, to have him hate her than . . . than anything else.

She picked up the picture on the mantle. The picture of a happy family. Herself, Paul and the baby.

As she stared the tears welled in her eyes, and the immediate past dimmed slowly away.

# 12

Sean was back in his cubicle on the fifth floor, sipping his coffee and reviewing his file on the McKinley murder case, when Harvey Anderson sauntered in, leaning against the divider, the daily paper in one hand, his Styrofoam cup of coffee in the other.

There was such a grin on his face that Sean sat back, crossing his arms over his chest and arching a wary brow.

"Whew!" Harvey whistled. "Nice, man, nice! Damned if you don't get all the luck."

"All right, Harvey, what luck? So far the situation looks like hell to me. I'm gone for a week, and what did you guys do? You let the paperwork on my desk grow like the stinking yellow pages."

"Hey . . . !" Harvey lifted his shoulders innocently. "We missed you — what can I say?"

"Thanks. Thanks a lot."

The grin left Harvey's face. He indicated the top file on Sean's desk. "We just got the report back from ballistics. The murder weapon was a Smith & Wesson, fifteen

shots. One bullet fired, the one that killed him."

"The same gun found in the house?"

Harvey nodded. "Looks like the wife to me, beyond doubt."

"We can't use 'looks like' with the D.A.'s office, Harvey. You know that. I think it was his wife, too. We're going to need a motive — especially since she's still claiming that it was a break-in. And we can't get anyone except her stepchildren to say that there might have been trouble in the marriage. Let's work on it from that angle."

"His money was motive enough," Harvey snorted.

"Yeah, well . . ."

"Viable proof in court, yeah, yeah. We'll get it. I've got a hunch on this one." He grinned once again, "They can't all be neat and clean and wrapped up in a bundle for the feds, with glowing praise and the word 'hero' in all the papers."

Sean's eyes narrowed. "Okay, Harvey, out with it."

"Out with what?" His face was all innocence beneath his shaggy brown hair. "What's with you? When did you stop reading the paper?"

"I overslept. Hand it over."

"Man, you get all the luck. A week in the

Bahamas and the blonde to boot."

"The paper, Harvey!"

Sean snatched it from him. It was true. His name and the word 'hero' were splattered all over the front page — along with a picture of Amanda Blayne in her doorway.

It shouldn't have been a flattering picture; it was a grainy black-and-white snapshot, and she was in the process of trying to close the door. Even so, she looked beautiful. Distressed, her hair tumbling about her face. Even in black-and-white, you could almost see the color, feel it . . . smell its fragrance.

Sean glanced over the article and gritted his teeth. The article was mainly about him; she couldn't have commended him more highly.

"Damn her," he muttered, the world suddenly turning a shade of red. What was she trying to do? Buy him off?

He slammed the paper down on the desk.

"Hey! What's with you?" Harvey protested. "If she were gushing all over me, I'd be halfway to heaven. And the big boys down at city hall are thrilled. What with so much corruption going on in the police force these days, they're thrilled to have gotten some favorable publicity for a change."

Sean just shook his head. "If the PR is

good for the department, great. I just don't like being all over the paper, that's all."

Harvey didn't leave. He sat down on the edge of Sean's desk. "What was she like, huh?"

"Polite," Sean said curtly. Then he softened. Harvey wasn't actually his partner; Todd Bridges was. But homicide worked in teams, usually on several cases at a time, and the three of them, along with Harvey's partner, Jill Santini, had worked together many times.

They were friends, and Harvey's tone had been more curious than anything else.

"She's a . . . nice lady. Lots of spunk, lots of spirit. Hey, you can be the liaison between the PD and the FBI. You'll probably get to meet her that way."

"Naw, Sean. You're the man on this one."

"We're a team, right? You take it."

"Really?"

"Really."

"Wow!"

Harvey walked away, leaving his newspaper behind. Sean stared at it for a moment longer, threw it down, then picked it back up. He drummed his fingers on his desk, then picked up the phone and dialed information. He glanced at his watch. It was just after seven.

The hell with it. He dialed her number.

A soft, sleepy, too-sultry voice said, "Hello?"

"What the hell did you think you were doing?"

"I beg your pardon? Oh — Sean."

"Yeah, Sean."

"I don't know what you're talking about."

"Don't you get the paper?"

"I don't read it until I'm awake. Why?" she asked, suddenly defensive. "What did I do? Insult you?"

"No, no, you were glowing."

"Then what's your problem?"

"Too glowing, Mrs. Blayne. It isn't going to change the way I feel about anything."

She was silent, then she laughed bitterly. "Actually, I don't begin to understand how you do feel about anything. If anything I said offended you, I'm sorry. It wasn't intended. Excuse me. If you're done yelling, I have a class in an hour."

She didn't give him a chance to say anything else. She hung up.

He was left staring at the phone.

Harvey came back into his cubicle, his jacket slung over his shoulder. "Ready?"

"For what?"

The other man sighed. "You called me last night — at midnight, I might add — to

say you wanted to go over to forensics first thing this morning."

"Oh, yeah. Give me just a second, will you?"

Harvey nodded and disappeared.

Sean stared at the phone again. He picked it up, not at all sure what he really intended to do.

"Hello?" She sounded more alert this time.

"Want to go to a party Friday night?"

"Sean?" she inquired skeptically.

"Yeah, it's me."

"And you're calling to see if I want to go to a party?"

"Yeah, well, it might be a little dull. It's just a . . . ethnic sort of thing. You're, uh, welcome to invite Peter, too."

"He's out of the state," she answered, and then dead silence came over the wire. "I don't believe you," she said at last.

"Will you come?"

"I . . ."

"Please."

"You're crazy."

"Probably."

"I . . ."

"I'll pick you up at seven."

He hung up quickly. He didn't want to give her a chance to refuse him.

"Sean?" Harvey called. Todd was standing there, too, now.

Sean grabbed his jacket, grinning as he joined them. He hadn't slept a wink all night, but suddenly he felt as if he could work three shifts straight.

Todd commented dismally on the weather as they went down in the elevator.

Sean cut him off. "You all coming to the annual bash this Friday?"

"Wouldn't miss it," Todd said, perking up.

Sean grinned. "Good. Harvey, you'll get to meet her after all."

"The blonde? She's coming?"

"Uh, yeah, I think so."

Harvey grinned suddenly, rolling his eyes. "I think there's a whole lot more to this story than the papers know!"

"And it's going to stay that way," Sean declared warningly.

"Sure. Sure it will," Harvey vowed solemnly.

Harvey stared speculatively at Sean's back as they walked out to the parking lot. Sean had sounded serious, and Harvey was surprised.

He and Sean had gone through the academy together. He'd been around when . . . well, he'd been with Sean's lawyer when

they pulled a few strings to get Sean out of jail. It just . . . didn't seem possible.

He wondered who was in for the worse time, the beautiful blonde, or Sean Ramiro.

Amanda was still partially in shock when she reached the campus. In shock because he had called her, yelling, when she had given him every compliment she could, though she had been ready to scream at the mere mention of his name. And in shock because he had called her back and asked her to a party — just like that.

And also because she hadn't said no.

After a few minutes she roused herself somewhat from her stupor; it was wonderful to be back. There was a giant coffee cake waiting in her office, along with a score of her students and half the faculty. Everybody wanted to hug her, to tell her how grateful they were that she was fine, and how happy they were to see her back.

It was nice to feel so loved, but in time the furor died down.

She had an introductory class that morning, and a second, more advanced class after that. Teaching was fun. She loved it as much as she loved the subject, and it was good to be back at work. It was so . . . normal.

But when her classes were over her mind returned to Sean — and to her own idiocy. Why in God's name hadn't she just told him that he was crazy, that he was absolutely insane, and that no, she wouldn't go anywhere with him? She didn't want to get involved with anyone, and especially a man who was like Dr. Jekyll and Mr. Hyde!

She had barely sat down behind the desk in her office when Valerie Gonzales, one of the associate professors, came by. "How about lunch?" the other woman asked.

"I'm not really hungry," Mandy told her ruefully.

Valerie wrinkled her nose. "I'm not, either, but Ed Taylor came in with a decaying alligator that he's determined to preserve, and the smell of formaldehyde is driving me nuts. Let's get out of here."

Mandy leaned back and grinned. "All you want is the inside scoop."

"That's right. Are you going to give it to me?"

"No."

Valerie shrugged. "I'll buy you a Mai Tai. That ought to do it."

"Think so, huh?"

They went to one of the nearby malls, where one of the restaurants specialized in appetizers. They ordered two apiece.

Amanda refused the Mai Thi that Valerie had been sure would make her open up, but she decided that a glass of Burgundy was just what she needed.

And though she certainly didn't open up, she found herself admitting that she was going out that Friday with the "way-out cop," as Valerie referred to Sean. Mandy decided that she needed a little advice, and that Valerie might be able to help her. "Val, all he said was that it's some ethnic thing. What do you think I should wear? Is there some kind of Cuban holiday coming up?"

Valerie sipped her beer and pondered the question. "Not that I know of, so go for something casual. If they're celebrating, they might roast a pig."

"So . . . ?"

"Well, you roast them whole, in a pit in the ground. It's an all-day event. By night it's ready to eat."

"Can you teach me some Spanish? I think I'm going to feel like a fish out of water."

Valerie laughed. "I know you know some Spanish. I swear all the time and you always know what I'm saying."

"Yeah, well, I don't think that's party conversation."

"Okay." Valerie hesitated. *"Buenas noches."*

"Good evening? Good night?"

"Yeah, both. *Como está usted?* How are you? *Bien, gracias* — fine, thank you. Umm . . . *dónde está el baño?* That one is very important to every woman."

"Why?"

"It means, where is the bathroom." She chuckled softly. "Then there's *te amo.*"

"Which means?"

"I love you."

"Valerie!"

"Aren't you in love with him? Just a little bit?"

"No. I'm not in love with anyone."

"Then it's just sex."

"Of course it's not just sex."

"Wow! Then you have made love, huh?"

"Valerie, stuff some more food into your mouth, will you, please?"

"Sure, but I can't teach you much Spanish that way!"

Friday seemed to roll around very slowly. Mandy fluctuated between longing to see him so badly that she hurt and dreading it so thoroughly that she almost called to cancel.

He didn't call her. She even began to wonder whether he had been serious. He hadn't asked for her address, but then, she was certain he could get it easily enough.

At some point she realized that although he might be crazy, she was the one suffering a terrible illness. She didn't want an involvement, yet she was involved. And that made her dilemma all the worse. She knew that she shouldn't see him. Seeing him would only bring more arguments, more disaster. She still couldn't tell whether he liked her or hated her — or if he was using her.

But none of it mattered. She had to see him. And not even the memory of her tragic past could intrude on that basic desire.

The week was a slow one on campus, too. They were almost at spring break. She made her arrangements to leave for the dig in Colorado on the Monday when the vacation began. She wouldn't really be able to get too involved in the work — she wouldn't have the time — but it would be fascinating just to be a part of it.

As much as she was looking forward with dread and fascination to seeing Sean again, she was glad that she could hop aboard a plane and leave — run away — the Monday after.

Friday night did come, as things inevitably did. He had said seven; at five she was in the shower, shampooing her hair, taking a long luxurious bath. She couldn't help reminding herself that he had usually seen her

at her grubbiest, and she wanted to be perfect — as perfect as she could be.

If he was really coming for her . . .

She had never experienced anything in her life like the emotions and physical agitation that came to her unbidden that night, growing worse and worse as seven o'clock approached. She was anxious and scared and nervous — and her fingers shook so badly that her first application of mascara was applied to her cheeks rather than her eyelashes. Her stomach felt as if fifty jugglers were tossing eight balls apiece inside it. Her palms were damp; her body felt on fire. And to her eternal shame, she seemed incapable of remembering what he looked like dressed, recalling instead every nuance of his naked body. She was trying to pour herself a glass of wine when the doorbell rang.

She dropped the glass and stupidly watched it shatter all over the tile floor. She swept it up in a mad rush, raced to the door — then stopped herself, smoothing back her hair before throwing open the door.

At her first sight of him all the nervous heat and energy and anticipation churned through her anew. He was tan and clean shaven, his hair still damp from the shower. He was wearing a light suit, tailored to fit his physique, enhancing the breadth of his

shoulders and the trimness of his waistline. The most noticeable thing about him, as always, was his eyes. So green, so shocking, against the strong planes of his face. The look of character in them gave him his rugged appeal, raised him above such an undistinguished word as "handsome."

Then she realized with dismay that he was in a suit — and she was in jeans. "Oh," she said softly.

"Does that mean come in?" he asked.

"Yes, yes, of course. Come in." She backed away from the door awkwardly. He followed her. For several seconds he stared at nothing but her, then he looked around her house.

There wasn't much on the first floor, just a living room that led to the kitchen on the left, the sun porch in the rear and the staircase to the right. It was pretty, though, he thought. The carpeting was deep cream, the furniture French provincial. The screen that separated the dining area from the rest of the room was Oriental.

"Nice," he said. He meant "rich."

She shrugged. "Thank you. Uh, would you like a drink? I think I need to change."

He acted as if he was just noticing her clothing. Then he frowned. "Where did you think I was taking you?"

"A friend of mine suggested . . . never mind. Why don't you help yourself. The kitchen is all yours. I'll be right down."

She fled up the stairs, tripping on the last one, and hoped he hadn't noticed. She changed into a kelly green cocktail dress, almost ripping it in her haste to reclothe herself. It seemed very illicit, suddenly, just to be in the same house with him, half-clad. Especially half-clad, and trembling, and thinking that she would just as easily, just as gladly, crawl into a bed, onto a floor — anywhere — with him as she ever had.

Unwilling to consider such thoughts for long, she raced hurriedly and breathlessly back down the stairs.

He was sipping wine and had poured a glass for her. He handed it to her, watching her. She thanked him, then they fell silent.

"How, was, uh, getting back to work?" she asked at last.

"Fine. How about you?"

"Fine."

Silence again.

"I've got great students," she offered.

He nodded. Eventually he said, "We should get going."

"Yes."

She was somewhat surprised to discover that his car was a lemon-yellow Ferrari. He

smiled at her look, leaning over her shoulder as he opened the door to whisper tauntingly, "No, I'm not on the take. My father was a cigar king once upon a time, and he left a trust fund, which I managed to invest rather decently."

"Did I say anything?"

"Your eyes did."

She didn't even know where they were going; he drove in silence. When they got onto the Dolphin Expressway, and then onto I-95, she finally asked him.

"Miami Shores," he said simply then lapsed back into silence again.

She decided to break it. "I've been taking a few Spanish lessons."

His eyes met hers briefly in the mirror. "Oh? Why?"

"I thought I should be able to say a few things tonight."

He smiled. "That's nice."

There was something about that smile she didn't like.

He flicked on the radio. Mandy gave up, closed her eyes and leaned back in the seat. It was better than watching his hands on the steering wheel and remembering other places where they had been.

Eventually they turned off the highway and drove through a series of side streets

until they pulled into a circular drive fronting a beautiful old Deco residence. Mandy wanted to ask him whose house it was, but he didn't give her a chance. He helped her out, then hurried to the door so quickly that she nearly tripped as she followed him.

He didn't ring the bell; he just walked in. And then Mandy understood that smile.

It was a party all right. It was even ethnic. Half the people there were dressed in green, and on a beautiful rich oak bar at the back of the living room was a massive glass keg of green beer.

"St. Patrick's Day!" she gasped.

"It is the seventeenth," Sean murmured.

"You rat!" It was all she could think of.

"Sean! You made it! Come in, dear, and introduce me to Mrs. Blayne!"

She didn't need to be introduced to his mother; Mrs. Ramiro had apparently given her son the emerald green of her eyes. She was a tiny creature, no more than five-two, slim and graceful, with marvelous silver hair and a smile that could melt a glacier.

Mrs. Ramiro was charming. She had a soft brogue and an equally soft voice, and she was entirely entrancing. "I'm Siobhan, Mrs. Blayne. You come with me!" She winked and tucked Mandy's arm into her

own. Then she walked her guest around, introducing her to various people — who seemed to come in all nationalities. Spanish was spoken by some of them, but it was always broken off politely when Mandy appeared, and she was impressed with the sincere interest shown by those who met her.

At last Mrs. Ramiro brought her to the bar, where she was given a green beer.

"You look shell-shocked, child. What's the matter?" Siobhan asked her.

Mandy found herself being perfectly honest. "I thought I was going to have roast pig," she admitted finally, and Siobhan laughed. "I spent all week practicing my Spanish."

"Well, I daresay you'll get to use it. A number of my guests are Cuban and Colombian."

"On St. Patrick's Day," Mandy murmured.

"Oh, everyone's Irish on St. Patrick's Day." Siobhan laughed. "Aren't you, just a smidgen?"

Over the rim of her glass, Mandy saw Sean coming toward them, and she said very clearly for his benefit, "Oh, honestly, I don't know, Siobhan. As far as I know I'm just an American mongrel. No one ever seemed to

be able to trace my family."

Siobhan laughed softly again. "I'll warrant there's some Irish in you somewhere!"

Sean smiled down at his mother, helping himself to the green beer. "Maybe there is, Mother. I tried to call her WASP once, and she told me that she was Catholic. Could mean a good Irish priest was nestled in the family somewhere."

"You called her what? Sean!"

"Dreadful of me, wasn't it?"

"Certainly. I don't know how you stood him for all that time, Amanda!" Siobhan shook her head. "I must get back to my other guests. Please, Amanda, have a wonderful time. I'm so glad to meet you. And I promise," she added, her eyes sparkling, "we'll roast you a pig next time!"

Mandy was left to face Sean again. She sipped her beer, staring steadily at him. "You really are a rat."

"Why?"

"You knew what I assumed."

"I'm sorry about the lack of a pig. Well, actually, we do have a pig. Cabbage and bacon."

"Umm."

He set his beer down on the bar and swept hers from her hand, then looped his arms around her and brought her against him.

She stiffened, but he seemed not to notice. "There's music out on the patio. People are dancing. Dance with me, Mandy."

She didn't really have a chance to refuse. He simply led her out to the back, where a trio was playing and people were indeed dancing beneath soft colored lights.

The music was slow, and she found herself in his arms. Dancing with him came as easily as making love.

"Why did you come with me tonight?" he asked her at length.

Her face was against his shoulder; her hand was clasped in his. She could feel all the rhythms of his body, and the softness of his dark hair brushing her forehead as he bent his head.

"I — I don't know."

"Are you glad you did?"

"I don't know."

"Do you hate me?"

"I . . . no."

"You smell great."

"Thank you."

"You feel great."

"Thank you."

"Do you know what I'm thinking?"

"Do I want to know?"

"I don't know." He waited a moment, then continued. "I was thinking that I wish a

leprechaun would suddenly whisk all these people away so I could ravish you this very second."

She wondered how just his words could affect her so deeply, but they could. She was glad that she was clinging to him; she needed the balance.

She closed her eyes before she spoke. "I didn't mean what I said, you know," she told him, then hesitated. "About Latins. You know. The, uh, last American remembering the flag."

His arms tightened around her as they swayed.

"You'd marry a Ramiro?"

"That wasn't the question. You never mentioned marriage."

"I suppose I didn't. But if I had — hypothetically, of course — what would your hypothetical answer have been?"

"I — I don't think that I —"

His interruption was a whisper that swept her ear like velvet. "But you can handle an affair?"

She didn't answer him.

"You'll sleep with me, but that's it, huh?"

Suddenly she wasn't leaning on his shoulder any longer; she was being held away from him, and his eyes were searching hers.

And she was desperately wondering why she was here. Dr. Jekyll always turned into Mr. Hyde.

He started to say something, but before he could a slim dark-haired young man tapped his shoulder apologetically, smiled with rueful fascination at Mandy, then cleared his throat as he remembered his mission. "Sean, we've got an emergency call. And you promised to introduce me."

"Harvey Anderson, Amanda Blayne. What's the call?" he inquired, annoyed.

"Mrs. McKinley's being treated at Jackson. Suicide attempt. Sorry, Mrs. Blayne. They want us. Pronto."

Sean's shoulders fell as he stared at Amanda. She knew that he was really aggravated, he had wanted the discussion to go further.

So had she. He never understood her, and it was largely her fault. Still, maybe this was for the best.

"I've got to go," he said. "Mom will see that you get home. I'm sorry."

"It's all right."

"I'll call you."

She nodded, knowing that he wouldn't reach her. She was going to change her flight and leave for Colorado in the morning.

He looked as if he was going to say some-

thing else, as if he longed to. As if he longed to touch her one more time.

But he didn't. He just closed his eyes briefly, shook his head and left her.

And perhaps it *was* for the best. Because although Mandy insisted again and again that she could call a cab, Siobhan Ramiro was determined to drive her home. She kept up a pleasant stream of chatter from the north of the city to the south and, surprisingly enough, agreed to come in for coffee before driving home.

Mandy soon discovered why.

As Siobhan sipped her coffee she dropped all pretense of casual interest and stared at Mandy with her clear green eyes. "I think my son is in love with you."

Mandy couldn't pull her eyes away from that green stare. Nor could she give anything but a bitter, honest answer. "Sometimes I think he hates me."

Siobhan lowered her eyes, smiling slightly. "No, he just doesn't always handle himself very well. You see . . ." She hesitated briefly, then shrugged and continued. "I came here to tell you something. I hope I can trust you. I'm not supposed to know this. A friend of his told me about it, because I was beside myself, worrying about him. There was a spell a few years ago when he had a different

woman every week. He almost seemed to —
to delight in starting an affair. And ending
it. And they were all . . . blond."

Siobhan sat back in her chair with a sigh.
"He grew out of it quickly, though he never
became really involved again. Cruelty really
isn't a part of his nature. I should have
known all along. You see, there was this particular girl . . . well, he'd been madly in love
with her. He wanted to marry her. He was
going to meet her parents, she was going to
come and meet me. All of a sudden it was
off. I found out later that she had been pregnant — and that her parents had forced her
into an overseas boarding school after a
quick abortion."

"Why?" Mandy gasped, stunned by the
story.

Siobban smiled with a trace of her son's
bitterness. "They were very rich. And totally bigoted. The name Ramiro just didn't
fit in with their idea of their daughter's future."

"Oh," Mandy said weakly.

Siobhan rose. "Well, that's it. I — I hope
I've helped. I noticed the sparks flying at the
bar tonight, and knowing him, well, I
thought maybe you deserved an explanation."

Mandy bit her lip, rising to escort her vis-

itor to the door. "Siobhan," she said impulsively, "It *has* helped. And I hope you believe that I would never feel that way. Sean . . . Sean thinks that I do, though. I've got a few problems that he doesn't understand."

"I know," Siobhan said softly. "I know about your husband and your child. And I'm so sorry. But you've got a long life ahead of you. Neither of them would have wished you to spend it in misery."

"I'm afraid," Mandy told her.

"To care again? We all are."

"Siobhan," Mandy said again impulsively, "I'm going away for a while. To work."

"And more than that, to think?"

"Yes."

"Well, whatever you decide, I wish you the best."

"Thank you."

Siobhan kissed her cheek, smiled encouragingly, then hurried down the walk to her car.

Mandy watched the taillights until they disappeared in the night, then thoughtfully closed her door.

# 13

The dig was a recent one; the site had only been discovered about a year before. A camper had found a piece of bone sticking out of the ground in a field near the mountains. Curious, he had asked another friend to look at it, and luckily, the professionals had been called in before anything could be destroyed.

Mandy's time had just about expired, and she wasn't sure if she was sad — or grateful. There was a yearning in her to go home. She had desperately wanted to get away to think, but she hadn't really thought at all. By day she had chiseled and wrapped and plastered; by night she had lain alone and wished that she was not alone. What frightened her was that, though Sean hadn't actually said so, she knew that he wanted a wholehearted commitment, and she cringed like a child from that thought.

But then, she had thought she couldn't possibly make love with him, and that had occurred easily, beautifully. Maybe all things would follow suit. Maybe all she had

to do was take the plunge.

As the afternoon fell she was sitting in her little spot in front of the phalanges of a Tyrannosaurus rex, carefully dusting the last of the sand from them with a sable brush so that they could be prepared for removal.

There was gigantic oak behind her, and a pile of rocks before her, so although the site was filled with workers, she was virtually alone. The find had been magnificent: a dozen of these particular beasts, and then any number of other creatures they had fed upon. She was glad to be alone, yet when she did try to think she panicked and wished that she was in the middle of a crowd.

A shadow suddenly fell across her work. Instinctively she looked up.

She was so surprised that the breath was swept cleanly from her.

Sean was standing there, in a standard three-piece suit. Tall and dark and handsome, a stray lock of hair falling over his forehead, his eyes as green as the spring fields. He stood there silently, then smiled slowly.

"Hello, Mandy."

She eased back at last, just staring for several moments. She lowered her head, thinking that this wasn't exactly how she

had wanted to see him. She was in overalls and a dusty lab coat, and half the dirt that had been on the bones was smudging her face.

She shook her head, frowning, before she managed to speak. "What — what are you doing here?"

"I have a paper that needs your signature."

She frowned again. She'd heard from the FBI sporadically throughout the week, and no one had mentioned anything that required her signature.

"You're here on business?"

He hesitated a second too long. "Yes."

She smiled, looking back to the bones, delighted to see him, but wishing she'd had just a little more time.

He reached into his coat pocket for an envelope, then crouched down across from her. "This is it. You said you wanted to testify for Señora Garcia. This is a document compiled from your conversations with the FBI and the Miami PD. I need to get it back to the D.A.'s office. They've set a trial date for late September."

"Oh," Mandy murmured.

She read the document over. It had been accurately compiled and said exactly what she thought. She started to scrawl her name

on it. "Is Señora Garcia in jail?"

"No. She's out on bond." He hesitated, then shrugged. "Julio's father is out, too. Peter had been pulling strings for him."

"What about Julio?"

Sean shook his head. "He's in jail. It's probably for the best. He'll definitely get time, and this will count toward it."

Mandy nodded. "Roberto?" she asked.

Sean's mouth twitched grimly. "I don't know what the courts will decide. But he's been connected to everything — drugs, robberies, murder. If they manage the case correctly, he'll end up with a dozen life sentences."

She lowered her head, shivering a bit. She still couldn't help but feel that Roberto deserved whatever he got.

"I, uh, got a telegram from Peter."

She raised her head quickly, frowning. "You did? Why?"

He smiled and reached into his pocket again, then passed her the paper. There were only two words on it, other than the address and the signature: MARRY HER.

Her hand started to shake; she clasped it with the other one and pursed her lips. Finally she said, "I guess he knew something was going on."

"So it seems."

"And you were wrong. He doesn't mind."

"I'm sure he minds." He paused, then asked, "Do you mind what I do?"

She stared at him, then shrugged. "Police work isn't the safest profession."

"But I'm in homicide. I deal with people who are dead — and harmless."

"But the people who made them dead aren't harmless."

He sighed softly. "Mandy, narcotics is a little scary. Not homicide. The last time I pulled a gun before I was on those docks — except on a shooting range — was four years ago. You watch too many cop shows."

She grinned. "Actually, I don't watch any."

"Oh."

"Aren't you forgetting something?"

"What?"

She tilted her head back, determined that, no matter what followed, she would not be punished for anyone else's sins. "I'm a blonde. Daughter of the American Revolution all the way. Rich bitch."

"Yeah, I know. I'm willing to overlook that."

"Are you? And what made you decide that I might not be a bigot?"

He lowered his head. Lowered his head, and lifted his shoulders and hands a little

helplessly. "Mandy —"

"Oh!" she cried suddenly.

"What?"

"You're on his hip!"

"What?"

"Move back! Move back quickly. You're on my bone!"

"Oh." Red-faced, Sean scrambled to his feet, quickly moving away. Mandy hurried back to the slightly protruding bone, checking it quickly for damage.

She sighed with relief.

"Er, uh, what is he?"

"Tyrannosaurus rex," she answered absently.

"The big bad guy? The one in all the Japanese horror films?"

"Uh-huh. Except that he wasn't really so bad. See, look."

She stood, skirting the area to show him the complete layout of the skeleton. "Look at his arms — there. See how tiny they were in comparison to his bulk? He couldn't really grab and rip and tear. He could barely get things to his mouth. We think now that he was a scavenger — a carnivore, but one who went in *after* the kill had already been made."

She glanced up and blushed, surprised by the softness in his eyes as he stared at her.

"You like your work, don't you?"

"Yes, very much."

"I like it, too. You could teach — me."

She didn't know what to say. As the breeze lifted her hair and wafted it around her face, she knew she should say something but, at that moment, she couldn't.

And then the moment was gone, because Dr. Theo Winter, who was in charge, came around the oak tree with a group of workers behind him, ready to start the plastering process. Mandy introduced Sean, but Dr. Winter was understandably unimpressed with anything but the cache of bones. All he wanted was for Sean to get off the site.

It was a good thing Dr. Winter hadn't seen Sean standing on the protruding skeleton, she thought wryly.

"I guess I'd better go," he told her, surprising her. She wasn't sure whether she was relieved or disappointed.

One of the assistants was asking a question, and she knew she had no right to be standing there talking while everyone else was working. But she didn't seem to be able to move any more than she could talk.

Sean solved that dilemma. He saluted her with a rueful grin, then walked away. She simply stood there, feeling the breeze in her hair, watching him leave.

Why hadn't he asked her to dinner or something? she wondered over and over again as the day wore on. But it wasn't a question that took much pondering on her part. It was going to be all or nothing. They weren't going to date. They weren't going to go for dinner or cocktails, or to the movies, or for a picnic in the park.

They were either going to get married or not — and only if she did marry him would she get to go to dinner and the movies and for walks on the beach. Maybe after the way they had begun it would be impossible to date.

She was beginning to understand him now; maybe he even understood her. She didn't think he was insensitive to her reasons for holding back; he just felt that they could be overcome — and should be.

Mandy thought she might hear from him the next day, but she didn't. He didn't contact her hotel, and he didn't appear on the site. She wondered if he had returned to Miami already and was startled to find herself annoyed at the thought. So much for hot pursuit!

On her last night there was a dinner party for her, which she made it through by rote. She realized that she had actually been doing all of her living by rote — until she met Sean.

There were a million good reasons why she should marry him, two that were extremely important. One, she loved him. Two, if the test she had bought at the drugstore worked, she was expecting his child.

The only thing that stood against her was the panic she felt at the prospect of loving so deeply again.

And the problem, which Sean didn't understand, was that it wasn't just an emotional reaction. It was physical. Her hands would sweat, her heart would beat too loudly. Confusion overwhelmed her at the thought.

Thought . . . Once upon a time she had assumed that she would simply never have another child, because the horror of loss was so deep. Of course, if not for circumstances, she would have been responsible enough never to let such a thing happen.

And now . . . now she knew that nothing would keep her from having this child.

Her thoughts would not leave her alone, not even for an instant. Not even while she said her goodbyes, lingered over breakfast to thank everyone — and nearly missed her plane because she seemed so incapable of doing anything right. She groaned while she raced through the airport terminal and decided that she was either going to marry

Sean — he *was* serious, wasn't he? — or move to an isolated village in Alaska.

She settled into the sparsely populated first-class section of her plane and picked up a magazine. She had been staring at the picture of an elegant dining-room set for several seconds before she realized that it looked odd because it was upside down. She sighed, then froze.

Because Sean was on the plane, blocking those trying to board behind him, staring down at her in dismay.

"You're in first class?"

"What?"

"Oh, damn!"

He moved on by to let the others pass. Mandy just stared at the seat ahead of her. In a few minutes the passengers were all boarded and belted. The stewardess made her speech on safety, and then they were airborne.

At last Mandy kicked off her shoes and curled her feet beneath her, determined to get comfortable for the duration of the trip, despite the fact that her heart refused to slow its frantic beat. She didn't know if she wanted to laugh or cry. He really meant to force the issue.

The stewardess offered her champagne; she took it, intending to sip it. Instead, she

swallowed the contents with a toss of her head.

The stewardess, of course, came right back, thinly concealing a shocked expression — and offered her more champagne.

"There's really nothing to be afraid of," the attractive young blonde told her. "Honestly. Captain Hodges has been flying for twenty years. He's wonderful. You won't feel a bump the entire way."

Mandy shook her head, smiling. "I'm not afraid of flying. I love to fly."

"Oh." Confused, the woman smiled, then quickly walked away.

Mandy stared out the window. They were already high above the clouds. It seemed that they were standing still above a sea of pure white cotton. If only she could concentrate. If only she could think about anything besides the fact that Sean was on the plane.

Her stomach lurched. What was the matter with her? He really did care. He had to care, or he would never have gone so far.

She took a deep breath, shivering. Did she really want to spend the rest of her life alone? Life was full of risks, and, yes, loving was a risk. But what was life except for a lonely expanse of years without the loving?

And now that Sean had touched her life, it seem absurdly bleak without him.

But could she love again? Worry about him, day after day? Pray that he came home each night? And what about children? Could she hold a child again, always knowing how quickly that life could be snuffed out?

"Move your feet."

Mandy started at the sound of his voice, then gasped, spilled her champagne and stared up at him guiltily.

"C'mon, move your feet!"

She did so, and he slid in beside her.

"What are doing up here? You're supposed to be in economy class!" she demanded.

"I bribed the stewardess."

"Stewardesses don't take bribes."

"Everyone takes bribes."

As if on cue, the stewardess walked by, watching them with a curiously knowing eye.

"What did you tell her?" Mandy asked suddenly.

He shrugged.

"Sean?"

"Nothing major." He smiled. "I just said that you were a deranged criminal whom I was trailing from Miami. I said I didn't want to put cuffs on you and frighten the other passengers —I just wanted to keep an eye on

you." He smiled pleasantly, reached for a magazine, and gazed idly around the first-class cabin. "Nice."

"Sean, you didn't —"

"I did."

"I'll kill you!" Mandy snapped angrily just as the stewardess walked by again. The woman's eyes, cornflower blue and already big, seemed to grow as wide as saucers.

"Now, now, calm down, Mrs. Blayne," he said in a professional soothing voice. He winked at the stewardess, giving her a thumbs-up sign of assurance.

"Sean Ramiro —"

"Maybe you can plea bargain, Mrs. Blayne. Just stay calm, and I'll be at your side."

"I'm not a criminal!"

"Tsk, tsk, Mrs. Blayne. I'm afraid the State believes that lacing your great-uncle's coffee with that arsenic was a criminal offense."

The stewardess, barely a row ahead of them, stiffened and swallowed, and almost poured champagne on a businessman's lap.

"Sean, I *will* kill you!"

"Please, Mrs. Blayne. I really don't want to have to use the handcuffs."

"Oh, Lord!" Mandy groaned, sinking back into her seat and giving up. "There's

definitely Irish blood in you — I've never heard so much blarney in my life!"

"Behave," he said wickedly, "and I'll get us more champagne. I do like this," he observed casually. "First class. It's a pity the department is so cheap."

"You really got the department to send you out to Denver?"

"Of course. I had to talk to you about the trial."

Mandy groaned again and turned to face the window. She didn't see the clouds anymore; only the reflection of his face. And for all his dry humor, she thought she saw pain mirrored there.

Her heart began to beat faster. It was the strangest thing, the most awful emotion. There he was, and there it was, all the laughter, all the love. All she had to do was reach for it, but she was unable to, taking two steps backward for every step forward.

She closed her eyes, then jumped when she heard him call the stewardess back.

"Could we get some more champagne, please?" He lowered his voice to a whisper. "I can control her much more easily if I keep her a bit sloshed, you know?"

"Oh, yes, of course!"

"Ohh!" Mandy groaned. "Couldn't you

just have paid the difference for a first-class ticket?"

He started to answer her, then paused, thanking the stewardess gravely as she poured Mandy more champagne and offered a glass to Sean.

"Cheers!" he said, clinking his glass against hers.

She pursed her lips stubbornly, refusing to respond.

"Come on, where's the Mandy I used to know?"

A twitch tugged at her lips. "Damned if I know. Last I heard, you were taking a criminal back to Miami."

He started to smile wryly at her, but the stewardess returned with their lunch trays. And then, to Mandy's surprise, he didn't pay any attention to her at all. He was watching the stewardess.

The pretty woman seemed exceptionally nervous, which Mandy thought was Sean's fault, since he had convinced her that Mandy was a criminal.

The stewardess almost dropped the trays, but recovered her poise. Sean continued to watch her as she moved down the aisle, then sat back in his seat, perplexed.

"What's wrong?"

"Hmm?"

"What's wrong?"

She didn't like the way he looked. She really did love to fly, but suddenly she thought of all sorts of disasters. Someone had forgotten a little pin or something, and their jumbo jet was about to fall apart in midair.

Except that the flight wasn't even bumpy. It was so incredibly smooth that it felt as if they were standing still.

She gripped his arm tensely. "Sean," she whispered, "do you think there's something wrong with the plane?"

He stared at her. "The plane? Something wrong?" He shook his head. "I've never felt a smoother flight."

"Then what — ?"

"Are you going to eat that steak?"

"What?"

"Eat, will you?"

He didn't pay any attention to his own food. He ate it, but he was giving all his attention to the stewardess.

The woman still seemed a little shaky when she returned. She had poise, though. She smiled; she chattered. It was just that her manner was slightly different, and not only with the two of them.

Mandy tried to quiz Sean again as soon as the trays were removed, but he interrupted

her first word, murmuring, "Excuse me for a minute, please."

"Sean!"

But he was already gone. He disappeared into the little kitchen area — right behind the stewardess. And he seemed to stay there a long, long time.

When he emerged, he returned to his seat beside her like a sleepwalker, totally remote.

"Sean . . ."

"I don't believe it," he murmured distractedly.

"You don't believe what?"

"Shh. You didn't finish your champagne. Drink it."

*Drink it.* As if she would need it.

"Sean!" She slammed a fist against his shoulder.

"Shh!"

"You said there wasn't anything wrong with the plane."

"There isn't. I swear it."

The stewardess came hurriedly toward them once again, then bent to speak softly in Sean's ear. "We need you now, lieutenant."

He nodded and stood, ready to follow her again. She paused suddenly, looking back at Mandy with dismay.

"Will she be all right?"

"What? Oh, yes, of course. As long as you

don't have any arsenic on board!"

They disappeared together toward the cockpit. Mandy was ready to scream.

It seemed an eternity before he returned, though it was only about twenty minutes.

"Sean, what the hell is going on?"

"Hey!" someone complained loudly from behind them. "I take this flight constantly. What's going on? They should have announced landing by now. And we should be over land — not water!"

"Damn you, Sean Ramiro!" Mandy whispered, alarmed. "What's going on?"

He turned to her at last. "I didn't want to alarm you —"

"You didn't want to alarm me?"

"Shh! There's nothing wrong with the plane. Honest. In fact, there's really nothing wrong at all. We're just taking a little side trip."

"Side trip?"

"Er, yes."

Just then the pilot came over the loudspeaker. He sounded marvelously, wonderfully calm. He started by explaining that obviously their seasoned passengers would realize that they were not flying their usual route. He assured them that nothing was wrong. It was just that they had a "gentleman" aboard who was insisting that they

fly on to José Marti airport — in Havana.

Mandy gasped and stared at Sean. "We're being hijacked to Cuba!"

"Yes, I know," he said uncomfortably. "I tried to talk him out of it."

The pilot then turned the microphone over to the "gentleman" in question, who told the passengers in broken English that he didn't want to hurt anybody, certainly not Captain Hodges, but that he had been away from his homeland now for eight years and was determined to go back.

"I don't believe this!" Mandy breathed. She stared at Sean again. "Can't you do something?"

"I'm afraid not. He's got a Bowie knife at the captain's back and a hand grenade to boot."

"How'd he ever get on the plane?"

"How the hell should I know?"

Their conversation ended at that point, because the stewardess began calmly putting them through a crash-landing procedure just in case they had difficulty landing. There was no panic on the plane, possibly because the pilot came on again, assuring them that they had been cleared to land at José Marti.

"I really don't believe this!" Mandy whispered nervously as she prepared for landing.

"I am sorry, Mandy. Really."

"You're sorry?"

"Yeah. I'm trying to convince you that we're a great people, and all you get to meet are the kidnappers and the hijackers."

She gripped his hand tightly. "That's not true. I got to meet one really great cop."

The plane jolted as the landing gear came down.

"Hey, you're admitting it at last. I told you I was really great."

The wheels touched the ground and the brakes came on with a little screech. Mandy prayed that the runway was long enough for the jet.

It was.

In seconds the plane came to a complete stop. And then, seconds later, it began filling with the Cuban military.

Mandy quickly lost Sean. The stewardess came back for him, desperate for a translator.

It seemed to Mandy that she sat there by herself forever. Nothing happened to her; nothing happened to anyone, but it seemed like absolute chaos. There were just too many people on the plane, and at some point, the air conditioning went out.

The heat was sweltering, and just when

she thought she couldn't take it anymore an announcement was made that buses would be coming to take the passengers to the terminal, where they were welcome to exchange their money and buy food and souvenirs.

Mandy craned her neck to find Sean, but she couldn't see him. Unhappily, she started to leave along with the others.

She was stopped at the steps by a trim officer with a Clark Gable mustache. She couldn't understand him, and he couldn't understand her. All she could tell was that he was insisting she stay behind, and a case of the jitters assailed her again. Why her? Oh, God! Maybe *they* thought she was a murderess, too!

But she merely found herself escorted back to the center of the plane, where Sean was in earnest conversation with several more mustachioed officers. The talking went on and on, with everyone gesticulating.

Finally the man who looked to be the ranking officer shrugged, and the others laughed, then stared at her, smirking.

Sean turned to her then and gripped her arm. "Quick!" he whispered into her ear. "Let's go. There will be a car at the foot of the steps. Get right into it, and act as if you love me to death!"

"What?"

"Shh! Just do it!"

"I —"

"Mandy! Please!"

He didn't give her any choice. He shoved her down the aisle, then hurried her down the stairs.

The car was there, just as he had said, a black stretch limo. She climbed into the back with Sean, and was surprised when the official with the Clark Gable mustache followed.

At last they reached an impressive building with emblems all over beautiful wrought-iron gates. She managed to whisper to Sean, "Where the hell are we, and what the hell is going on?"

"The Swiss embassy," he whispered back. "The pilot is around here somewhere, too. He has to make special arrangements for fuel to get home."

The car stopped. The Cuban official was greeted by a tall blond man, but though this might have been the Swiss embassy, they were still speaking Spanish, and she was lost.

"Sean, I don't care about the pilot. What are *we* doing here?"

"They're, uh, trying to keep me here," he said.

"What?"

He took both her hands earnestly. "Just help me, Mandy. Go along with me. They know who I am."

"Who are you?"

"Oh, it all goes way back. You wouldn't want me to be stuck here forever, would you?"

She gazed at him warily. "Go on."

"Marry me. If I marry an American citizen —"

"You are an American citizen."

"Ah, but I told you, they know me! My father was involved in some things that —"

"Uh-uh! This guy is acting like your long-lost friend."

"Actually, he is. I was in school with him until the night I fled the country."

"I thought you were born in Ireland."

"I was. It's a long story." He put his hands on her shoulders and pulled her anxiously to him. "Well? They've given me a chance. The Swiss will give us a license and a minister. Mandy! Come on! You've got to get me out of this one."

She stared at him for a long, long time. At the sun above them, at the flowers, at the sky, at the beautiful mountains in the distance.

This wasn't how she had expected things to go at all. The other passengers were busy

buying trinkets as mementos of their incredible day, while she was here with Sean, listening to the most outrageous cock-and-bull story she had ever heard in her life.

She lowered her head, smiling slowly, and just a little painfully. After all these years, he had come back to his Cuban heritage, and it was his Irish blarney that was showing!

Her past flashed before her eyes. And she knew that although it would always be there, the time had come to gently close the door on it.

"If I don't do this, they'll keep you here, huh?"

"They could put me in prison."

"Oh."

"Well?"

"I don't suppose I could let that happen to you, could I?"

"It would be terribly mean, considering all I've done for you."

She was silent. He gazed at his watch impatiently. "Mandy! We have to do this before they make the fuel arrangements!"

She shrugged. "Then let's do it."

The Swiss were charming. Papers were secured, and they were ushered into a little chapel that adjoined the building. The ceremony was in French, and amazingly quick,

because everyone was rushing.

Mandy smiled through it all, wondering how Sean had ever convinced the Cuban military authorities to let him get away with this nonsense.

But when her "I do" was followed by a very passionate kiss, she assumed it would be something they could talk about for ages.

They were whisked very quickly back to the airport. The fuel had been secured, and all the passengers had reboarded with the rum, cigars, and so forth.

They were in the air before Sean turned to her sheepishly at last. "I have a confession to make. I asked Captain Rotello for special permission to marry you. I lied, though I really did go to school with him. And he did know about my father. Our dads had been friends."

"Oh," Mandy said simply.

"Well, do you hate me?"

She looked at him regally, a superior smile playing on her lips. She saw the tension and passion in his wonderful green eyes.

"Actually, no, I have a confession to make myself."

"Oh, really?"

"I knew you were lying all along. I may not speak Spanish, but I'm not a fool."

"Oh," he said blankly.

"I did intend to learn the language, of course. Completely. I mean, I'll be damned if I'll have you and our son talking about me when I don't understand a single word you're saying!"

"Our son?"

"Or daughter."

"We're — we're having one?"

"In December. Maybe November."

He swallowed then, a little stiffly. "You married me . . . because you're pregnant?"

"I swear I'll hit you! I married you because I love you! Not because of your ridiculous story, and not because I'm pregnant. Come to think of it, you did threaten me about that! But —"

He smiled, his arm coming around her as he interrupted her. "You love me, huh?"

"Yes, and you know it."

"Yeah, well, it just sounds real nice to hear the words now and then. You'd better start practicing, because I'd like to hear them more frequently from now on."

"Hey, what's good for the goose —"

"I love you, Mrs. Ramiro. Desperately. Passionately. I love you, I love you, I love you —"

Unfortunately, the stewardess made an appearance just then.

"She loves me! She married me!" Sean told the woman.

But I thought she was — you just married a murderess?"

"Oh, well, that —"

"Lieutenant Ramiro, what a line you gave me! Get back where you're supposed to be — in economy!"

But she wasn't serious. After all, it had been a most unusual flight. She merely arranged for more champagne.

Mandy laughed with him while they sipped champagne, then sobered slightly. "Is this real?"

"It's real."

"Sean . . . I may need help sometimes."

"We all need help sometimes."

"I do love you. So much. I guess I did, even on the island. I wanted to be rescued, but I didn't want to go back. Not to a life without you."

"Mandy . . ."

His champagne glass clinked down on his tray. His arms swept around her, his fingers curling into her hair. And when his lips touched hers she was hungry for him, so hungry that it was easy to become swept up in his embrace and to forget that they were on a populated plane.

He broke away from her, groaning softly,

excitingly, against her cheek. "Mrs. Ramiro, watch your hands."

"No one can see me."

"Well, they might see me! Oh, God, I can't wait till we get off this plane. Your place or mine?"

"Mine. I think we should sell *yours.*"

"I think we should sell yours." He smiled. "Oh, hell! I don't care where we go — as long as we get there!"

It took them another two hours to get anywhere; in the end he went to her house, because it was closer to the airport. And though Mandy would have thought that such a feat was impossible, he managed to disrobe them both while climbing the stairs, strewing fabric down the length of the steps, then landing them on her bed in what was surely record time.

She was so happy. So amazed that she was his wife, that they were making love on the evening of their marriage. That they were both totally, completely committed.

It was fast; it was feverish — it had to be at first.

But the night stretched before them. Time for her to warn him that she owned one of the ugliest cats in the world, time for him to warn her that his partners could be a

pain in the neck. Time to discuss things that hurt; time to talk about the past, and time to put it to rest.

And then time to make love all over again.

"*Te amo*," Mandy told him carefully, practicing the Spanish she had learned.

He smiled, tenderness blazing in his eyes, and she murmured the strange words again, "*Te amo* — here," she said, meeting his eyes, then kissing his chest. "And *te amo* — here."

With each repetition she moved against him, finding more and more deliciously erogenous zones.

"And *te amo* — here."

He gripped her hair, breathless, ablaze. He groaned, and at last swept her beneath him, pausing just an instant to whisper, "Mrs. Ramiro. I have never, never heard Spanish more eloquently spoken."

"*Querido!*" she whispered, and contentedly locked her arms about him.

He found life in her arms. And he gave her a new life, all she would ever ask in the world.

"*Querida!* My love, my love."

He kissed her abdomen and smiled as she arched to him.

She knew that she could love again.

Love a child, love a husband.

Even if he was rather manipulating and

most certainly strange — and, oh, passionate! — and . . .

"Sean . . ."

She simply couldn't ponder it any longer. It was the . . . circumstances.

# Epilogue

Sean hesitated momentarily after he opened the door, wondering what Mandy's reaction would be to the visitor he was bringing home.

"Amanda?"

He stepped into the entryway of the big old frame house they had bought and stared through the living room to the office. As he had expected, she was at her desk, her reading glasses at the tip of her nose as she pored over term papers.

Katie — a toddling and mischievous two now — was playing sedately with her locking plastic blocks, probably trying to recreate a dinosaur like the one her mother had made her the night before, Sean thought wryly.

"Mandy?" he called again.

She looked up, saw him, threw her glasses down and scooped Katie into her arms before coming to meet him excitedly, her words rushing out.

"Sean, believe it or not, I had the best time in the world today! I went into the market on Flagler because they have the

best ham in the world. I have to admit I always resented going there before, because everyone spoke Spanish, but mine has gotten so good, and I got into this wonderful conversation with the clerk and I started to teach her English! I — oh!"

Her spiel came to an abrupt halt when she saw that her husband was not alone, and she stared at her visitor in dead surprise.

Sean slipped an arm around her. "Julio stepped into my office just when I was getting off for the day. He was just paroled, and he was anxious to see you."

"Oh," Mandy murmured.

Julio Garcia, gaunt-looking in a too-big suit, smiled hesitantly and offered his hand.

She took it, balancing her daughter in her other arm.

"I had to come," he told her softly. "The government has released me. But that is nothing. I must ask you to forgive me. I must hope that you understand and can believe that I did not ever wish to harm you. That — that I know now how wrong I was." His eyes were totally in earnest.

Mandy smiled at last, feeling the assurance of her husband's arm around her shoulders. "I forgive you, Julio. How . . . how are your parents?"

He gave her a smile that seemed to light

up the room. "They are well. Even my father is well. The United States gave him a doctor who is good. And Mama, Mama is Mama."

Mandy nodded, then asked curiously, "And Maria?"

Julio laughed. "Mama married Maria off to a man with a will like iron. She is like you — one babe in her arms, one to come."

Mandy didn't ask about Juan or Roberto. Sean had assured her at the trial that Roberto faced so many charges that even if he lived to be an old, old man, he would probably never leave prison again.

Juan, too, would not come up for parole. He had been involved in a narcotics case before the kidnapping, and the judge hadn't shown him one bit of leniency.

"I am very happy for you, Mrs. Ramiro," Julio said. "Congratulations. Your daughter is beautiful."

Mandy discovered that she was able to laugh proudly. "Yes, she is. Thank you."

Katie was staring at Julio with her knuckles shoved into her mouth, but she really was beautiful. She had Sean's green eyes and a headful of ebony curls.

"You wish a son now, yes?" Julio asked.

It was Sean, lightly massaging his wife's nape, who answered. "Not necessarily. I'm

awfully fond of girls. A son, a daughter, it doesn't matter. Mandy and I were both only children, and we both wished that we'd had a brother or a sister, so . . ."

He shrugged, and Mandy flushed, because though they'd both been quite happy about it, this baby was as completely unplanned as Katie had been.

"Well . . ." Julio cleared his throat and shifted his weight from foot to foot. "I must go now, I did not wish to impose. I just wanted you to know that I appreciate how you told them at the trial that you did not think I was cruel, but needed help. And that I wished so much for your forgiveness. I have a good job already, too. I am a mechanic. One day I will own my own garage."

"I'm sure you will," Mandy said softly.

"Goodbye, then, *señora*. I wish you and your husband and your lovely family all the best."

Sean walked him to the door. Mandy watched them, hugging Katie to her.

When Sean returned she was still smiling, so he arched one of his dark brows curiously. "Okay, out with it. What are you thinking?"

She laughed, managing to hug him and Katie at the same time. "I was just thinking that I really do forgive him with all my heart.

Without him, I'd have never met this weird cop who stuck by me through thick and thin — and then married me, to boot."

"Hey, duty called. And you were such a marvelous blond bombshell."

"Yeah?"

"Yeah."

He grinned, then kissed her warmly and deeply until Kate let out an outraged squawk that Mommy and Daddy were crushing her.

They laughed together again, and their eyes touched, full of promises.

J
HADDAD   Haddad, Charles.

Calliope Day falls in
love?